A LONG DAY to DENVER

by
William Gritzbaugh

Dedicated to my wife, Deb.
Paraphrasing William Tecumseh Sherman:
"(S)he stood by me when I was crazy."

Table of Contents

Prologue

(Continued)

Table of Contents (cont.)

Prologue

A hazed-dulled sun was setting beyond a thick and ancient deciduous forest that marked the end of a vast Pioneer Corn Company field. The forest of oaks, maples, sycamores and a dozen other types, in turn, ended a mile beyond at the muddy bank of the Ohio River. At the near end of the field, a neighborhood of ticky-tack frame homes had been constructed in recent years, the classic encroachment of an expanding post-war population upon agricultural land that had been in sustained cultivation for nearly 150 years. The campus of West High School had a block-long fronting on the field but was otherwise surrounded by the neighborhood.

This field of half-mile-long rows, each containing a thousand stalks, had recently been detasseled, a process where the pollen-laden tassel is yanked by hand from the top of each six-foot plant by teenagers trudging on foot and making less than a dollar an hour. Remarkably, the child-laborers do a half-dozen rows in a typical workday, in hothouse heat, and under the watchful eyes of foremen who fire those who can't do the job with the necessary efficiency.

If the tassels aren't removed, the corn variety will self-pollinate, but with that natural process interrupted, cross-fertilization from genetically different corn plants sown nearby takes place. The result is a hybrid that might provide greater yield per acre, disease or drought resistance, or other attributes the grower wants.

In the throes of their youth, some people, young men mostly, seem compelled to pursue a metaphorical pollination of their souls in fields far beyond and vastly different from those they were born into. One could speculate that Providence has, for His own reasons, detasseled their minds in order that they, like the corn plants, seek fertilization from other fields and, in the process, attain a level of human experience unavailable to those not similarly compelled. So, a young man's perplexing eagerness to cast his fate to the wind may just be a manifestation of the Almighty tending His fields.

The corn plant, as best we know, feels nothing.

PART 1

Chapter 1
Reunion, 1971

Ohio River Valley August afternoons can be marvels of wet-blanket heat and humidity. This had been one of those and only now, at sunset, was the hint of a cooling breeze felt on the faces of the twenty or so young men who stood, sat or sprawled on the packed earth of the athletic field behind the high school gymnasium. Their vehicles, an assortment of GM and Ford models, were parked on the grass under a huge oak tree that had been allowed to grow, shade and now encroach upon the quarter-mile track that encircled the field. Two Harley-Davidson motorcycles, one a newer FL Electra Glide, the other a war surplus WLA Flathead, rounded out the all-American collection. A gangly black dog, tied to a bumper with a length of clothesline rope, slept with its head resting against the Glide's rear tire.

Assorted six packs and cases of beer were strewn under a section of bleachers where they'd been shoved hours earlier for protection from the sun as coolers and ice would have required some degree of preplanning. A four-foot paper "Welcome Class of '66" sign lay on the ground, the text nearly obscured by dirty footprints. Dozens of empty bottles and cans recently filled with Falls City, Sterling, Strohs and other brands lay scattered around.

The men, each in a phase of intoxication ranging from mellow to pronounced, periodically rose to search out another container of their favorite beer (brand loyalty being nearly as rabid as that displayed for automobiles) or, as often, to empty their bladders into a shallow railroad tie-lined depression in the ground used for decades by players, cheerleaders and marching band members as a repository for school books and other personal effects while they practiced on the adjoining athletic field. The ground around was bone-dry but "the pit" had gotten muddy.

A single arc light near the tree-lined street provided partial illumination for the gathering as the last daylight began to fade, and a battery-powered radio was tuned to WJPS AM. "Cherish" by `The Association` crackled through the speaker.

"You ready?" asked one of the men to a friend sitting Indian-style next to him.

"Fuckin' A," replied the friend…"Falls City". Stifling a burp, fist to his mouth, he glanced over at his companion. "Well, is it my imagination or are you starting to loosen up? I'm worried about you, buddy."

"I'm fine," the man responded, awkwardly standing up and brushing the ground debris from the seat of his thread-bare Levis. "You remember that hot drive across Kansas? Must have fried my brain."

He walked the few steps to the beer repository, scanned the cases and packs, then said over his shoulder, "The Fall City's 'het roi'. You got to drink something else for the first time in your life."

"Fuck it. I'm done drinking."

"Yeah, right."

A brief pause and then, "What's left?"

The man moved some cardboard debris aside. "Couple Strohs, some Sterling, beaucoup (he pronounced it, 'boo koo') Pabst and Schlitz."

"Crap," his friend said, disgust in his voice. "OK, I'll take a Sterling."

The man pulled a bottle from the case and faked a throw, causing his friend to shield his head with an arm.

"Don't throw it, asshole. Roll it."

The stubby wide-mouth bottle skidded barely within reach and the man fell onto his side as he grabbed for it. He rose unsteadily to his feet and likewise brushed the dirt and sawdust mixture from his arm and pants leg, then sat back down and fell onto his back. He lay quietly for several moments, his left hand between his head and the dirt, his right balancing the beer on his stomach.

"Whoa, I'm getting liquored," he muttered.

In a while, with some effort, he sat up, pulled off and discarded the cap from the Sterling. Blowing off the foam with a puff, he tilted the bottle to his mouth and drank off half the liquid, twisted himself back into a cross-legged position and rested his beer-clenching hands on his ankles.

"You look like the beer Buddha," Andrew Starkey observed, opening his own Sterling. He took a sip, sloshed the liquid around in his mouth, then spit it out to his front.

He took another sip and swallowed it, grimacing as it went down his throat. Though most any beer was good enough when cold, a luke-warm beer of any label was merely better than nothing.

"Say," he asked his friend, Jack Mortenson, "your old man still drive for Falls City?"

"Roger that, 25 years," responded Jack. "Log book's got over a million miles."

Andrew shook his head. "Man, 25 years. Boggles the mind. I can't imagine doing anything that long, let alone pushing an 18-wheeler around these Hoosier highways."

The young man thought a minute and added, "At least hauling beer's doing a service for mankind. Your old man is going to Heaven for sure."

Jack Mortenson nodded, then tilted the Sterling bottle again, emptied it and sent it skidding in the dirt. "Yeah, if the old man don't get in, I don't want to go, either. To Heaven, that is. He's been good to mom, and put up with a bunch of shit from me, as you well know." This time he burped loudly, drawing praise from a man relieving himself at the pit.

"Like that time we ran from the sheriff all night?" asked Andrew Starkey.

"Fuckin' A."

"Amazing what we'd do for a few beers back then," Andrew observed. He rolled his head around, wincing as he did so. "Damn neck is stiff as a board."

"Bet Sally Mason would rub it for you," Jack commented, a tease in his voice.

Andrew shrugged, "Where'd she go, by the way?"

Jack shook his head. "No idea. Took one look at this bunch and left with that bitch college friend of hers--what's her name?"

"Bethany."

"Yeah."

"Oh, well."

"Damn, Stark. She was really wanting to hang around with you. Hasn't seen you in, what, three years, then you started drinking with the old crew. She was pissed."

Andrew turned to the side and spit. He changed the subject from his former girlfriend. "Your old man was lucky. You were a saint compared to some of these shit birds."

Jack shrugged. "Maybe." Speaking of his father again a moment later, "You know, I don't see how he keeps it up. Only break he takes is Panama City for two weeks every summer, then starts his work cycle again. Just leans over the wheel of whatever Kenworth they hook up to the trailer and heads off down the road." He pantomimed his father's posture over the steering wheel and bounced on the ground. "And you know, driving is just part of it. He does a lot of unloading, too. You ought to see his shoulders and arms. Like Steve fucking Reeves. Maybe that's why we didn't push him too far, you know, Karen and me. He could have torn us limb from limb."

Andrew chuckled in agreement. "Not a man I'd want to irritate."

He'd put his hand inside his shirt and was absentmindedly picking at his chest. He pulled out his hand and flicked away something that he had between his fingers.

"Crabs?" asked Jack, eyebrows rising.

"Nah, splinter off a telephone pole."

"Splinter? How in hell…"

Just then someone yelled to them. "Stark! Jack!" Rich Enlow waved as he walked from his car.

"Hey, Rich. Where'd you go?"

"Shannon's class went to the Steak & Shake. They didn't reserve a nice dirt pile like this for their post-picnic party," Rich joked. "Two beers in the parking lot and I was out of there." He paused near the two and said, "Now, don't try to sneak off. I gotta talk to Newall for a few minutes."

"We'll be here."

As Rich strode away, Jack said, "So, did you and Rich get all caught up? I heard you guys yucking it up at the picnic."

"Yeah. Hadn't seen him since AIT down at Ft. Polk." Andrew finished the last of his beer and began peeling the label. "I think he had a tough time overseas…1st Division down in the Mekong Delta."

Jack nodded. "He and I got back home just in time for last year's picnic. Wish you could have been here." He was quiet for a moment, recalling the event. "When Rich found out you were still in 'Nam, he got really pissed off. Never seen him like that. Guess you guys didn't keep in touch much."

"Nah. Not after AIT."

As Jack came up to one knee, preparing to hit the beer repository, he paused and said, "You…uh, know what? I never told Enlow or the other guys this, but I'm drunk enough to tell you. When we used to fly into Bien Hoa, we sometimes had to load caskets. I hated it. I couldn't help myself, but I'd look at the tags, the names. I was afraid I'd see Starkey or Enlow or Murphy. After a few trips, I just didn't look anymore."

Andrew Starkey seemed not to have heard. "Speaking of Panama City," he began, "you know what I just thought of?"

"Knowing you, any number of things." Jack was glad to change the subject and wondered to himself why he mentioned Bien Hoa.

"That Florida place your family used to go to. That time I went along-- summer after sophomore year."

"Fuckin' A," recalled Jack, "our first road trip."

He remembered them well, his family's annual pilgrimages from southern Indiana down to Florida's panhandle; the endless, serpentine drive through Kentucky, Tennessee, Alabama and finally into Panama City. One summer, Andrew Starkey had been invited along; the three kids, Jack, his twin sister, Karen, and Starkey shoulder to shoulder in the back seat of his dad's Ford Galaxy 500. "Summer after sophomore year it was."

"Yep."

"You know, Karen had a huge crush on you after that trip," said Jack.

"Yeah," Andrew was indeed beginning to loosen up, but it had taken an afternoon and part of an evening of beer drinking to do it. "I could tell when she showed me her tits."

Jack shifted his one-knee position and looked over at this friend. "Now when and why would she show you her tits? You lying sack of shit."

"They were beautiful."

Jack's forehead crinkled in irritation. "You know, in some cultures the brother is supposed to kill the son of a bitch that dishonors his sister."

This caused Starkey to laugh out loud. "Now, hold on damn it. I never dishonored her. I just admired her tits. Go get us another beer and I'll tell the story."

When Jack returned with their beers, Andrew explained. "Remember that little beach house we stayed in? Our room had its own bathroom 'cause it had the two beds. You were taking a crap and had the fan on, loud as hell. I was lying on the bed waiting for you to get done, you know, just lying there looking at the ceiling. So, Karen comes strolling in and had her bikini top off, fooling around with that hook thing in back. Walked straight by me and tried to turn the knob on the bathroom door. You hollered, 'Get away from the door, Starkey.' Remember it like yesterday. That's when she notices me on the bed."

"I remember hollering at you. You never said anything about Karen."

"Oh? Well, anyway she lets out this little squeal and crosses her arms over her chest. I already had a full view, so I put my hand over my eyes. She says, 'I thought you were at the beach!' Then she runs out. Later on, she gave me a hard time for not clearing my throat or something. I told her, 'It all happened so fast, what the heck could I do?' and, 'Oh, by the way, you have magnificent breasts'."

"That's pretty bold for, what, a sixteen-year-old? What did she say to that?"

"Just pinched my cheek and smiled. Told me I was the first non-family male who had seen her 'boobies'. Now, Jack, I took that to mean that you'd seen them at some point."

"Yeah, when we used to play in a plastic wading pool in the backyard. Does that count?"

"I knew it," said Andrew. "You should be ashamed."

"Jeez, Starkey."

Andrew socked his friend on the shoulder. "Hey, you know, my folks are packing up now. Listed the house and moving to Ft. Myers."

"Think I'd heard that. Don't know who told me. They're really out of here, huh?"

"Yep. Won't have much reason to come back here anymore. Just you bunch of drunks is all I'll have left in this sorry-ass town."

"Well, you could do a lot worse than us drunks. Any one of these guys would saw his balls off for you. I would have until I learned you fondled my sister."

Andrew laughed again at Jack's extrapolation. "*Admired,* buddy. Besides, didn't I hear you already sawed your balls off for Enlow last year?"

"Oh yeah, I forgot. Hurt like hell, too." At this, they both laughed uproariously.

"Speaking of sisters," said Jack, collecting himself. "What's Kim going to do with you in Denver and your folks in Florida?"

"She moved in with her boyfriend up at IU. Soon as mom found out about that they put the house up for sale. No reason to delay retirement anymore. Their baby girl jumped out of the nest."

"Karen lived with Ned before they got married. No big deal," observed Jack.

Starkey nodded his agreement, then returned to his memories of their trip to Florida.

"Man, I can still feel that sunburn on the tops of my feet from walking on the beach. Blistered my back to. My pale Hoosier ass just can't handle that sun." He thought again about his parents' upcoming move. "I don't know what they see in it."

Jack added, "Got fried every time I went down there"-- remembering being slathered by his mother with various remedies for the annual burns. The smell of Noxzema skin cream made him nauseous to this day. "We haven't gone down to Florida with them for several years now, with me in the Air Force and Karen getting married. I think they enjoy it more without having to drag us along. At least Dad does. You know, private time with the old lady."

"Probably chases her around with a double handful of Noxzema," chuckled Andrew Starkey.

Jack grimaced at that image then looked skyward expecting to see a canopy of stars. He raised a hand to shield his eyes from the glare of the arc light, but realized the pall of dust and pollen in the air was impenetrable.

"So," he asked, "how'd you handle that sun in 'Nam?"

Starkey wiped the condensed moisture from the newly opened bottle and rubbed his wet hand over his face. Again, seeming not to have heard the question, he asked, "Say, remember those Florida babes on the beach? Man, were they tough..."

Jack responded carefully, a concerned eyebrow rising, "Uh, you bet, man. Bikini paradise." He looked over at his friend. "Now, uh, Stark, you're starting to worry me. After all these years, you finally get yourself moved out to Colorado and now you're talking like you've got the hots for a beach somewhere. Remember Jeff Thompson saying you had a 'grass is greener' disorder?"

"Yep, I remember. That time up on Mount Yale."

Jack nodded. "Man, that hike was a ball buster. Remember the thunder in that valley?"

"Never forget it," Andrew answered, then, "Don't worry. I'm not moving to Florida."

Jack felt he just had to ask, "So, uh, you've, um, gotten over your Rocky Mountain dream girl, Nancy, right?"

Starkey knew it was coming but he was stung, nonetheless, by the mention of her name. He hid it well and lied, "Yep. I've moved on. She's engaged to some guy she met at school in Greeley." He hocked and spit noisily to his left. "I've got a few women I hang around with. Just met a new one that lives out east of Denver, right near my buddy"...he stopped in mid-sentence. Then, "I pretty much work six days a week, so...well."

Jack interrupted, sensing his friend's sudden ill-at-ease. "So then, when you can't see this new one, you have some fallback positions to work with?"

"Sure. I hit the bars when I can," Andrew said. Then with a chuckle, "Trust me, the bars are much better in Denver than in New Vernon, Indiana."

Now they became quiet for a time and, glassy-eyed, surveyed the scene around them. The men were gathered in several groups of three or four, a few moving from group to group. Empty bottles and cans clinked and tinked as stumbling feet kicked them together or when lobbed towards the pit. The frequent "spish" of a container being opened made it clear the celebration wasn't winding down.

All their attention was drawn to a scuffle that had broken out at the edge of the pit. Two men had stood side by side on the ties emptying their bladders when one man's stream had splashed on the other.

"Chuck, you drunk fucker!" yelled the offended man, delivering a reflexive backhand blow to the perpetrator's chest. Chuck, jeans dropping to his ankles, retreated backwards several constricted steps. Still holding his member, he extended his free arm to catch himself as he crashed heavily to the ground. The impact knocked free the bottle he held and it skidded away, spewing foam onto the dirt. Dazed, the large man lay on his side for a moment, then bicycled his tangled feet in an attempt to rise. Giving up, he sputtered a curse and let his head fall to the dirt with a soft thud.

Guffawing friends gathered around the fallen man.

"Damn, Caleb," someone exclaimed. "You cold-cocked Fat Chuck!"

"Hey, I hit his fat chest, not his head. Son of a bitch pissed on me."

A man took Chuck's extended hand and began dragging him away from the pit and toward where the men had been clustered. Suddenly, a strong golden stream arched from Fat Chuck, leaving a wet parallel trail as he was pulled along. The dragger, startled, dropped Chuck's hand and watched as the flow continued for nearly a minute; plenty of time for the spectacle to draw even more onlookers who howled with glee and encouragement for their unconscious comrade.

"Go Fat Chuck!" a voice hollered. "Hey, Jack. Chuck's recycling your Falls City. Grab some empties and fill 'em up."

"That is fucking amazing," said Caleb. "Passed out and pissing like a racehorse."

Sean Murphy, being careful to avoid the stream, paced off its distance. "Three feet, eight inches!" he bellowed officiously. "A new West High, reclined-piss distance record!"

Jim Baxter swaggered towards the prone figure and began kicking him hard in the butt. "Wake up, Elliot!" he shouted. Hands pulled him back roughly and swung him towards the pit where, stumbling in, he slid to the bottom in the mud, only just keeping his feet.

"I'm going to kill you assholes!" he yelled, and scrambled from the pit, but not before running in place for several steps.

"Leave the poor bastard alone, Baxter," said Rich Enlow. "Tomorrow, when he sobers up, you can tell him where the bruises on his ass came from."

Baxter shouted back as he scraped the foul paste from the bottoms of his polished Weejun loafers on a bleacher seat, "He's the silly-ass drunk that has to explain how he ended up in the dirt with his pants down."

Starkey asked, "Hey, didn't he ride here on one of those Harleys?"

"Yeah, we rode over together," said Rick Adams. "Don't believe the boy will be riding home with me tonight."

"Man, he ain't riding in my car," Sean Murphy said. "Hey, there any more Strohs?"

Fat Chuck eventually trickled to a finish and the men decided to put an end to his humiliation. The care he was now given displayed his friends' affection for him and that they wouldn't tolerate his abuse. Sean found a stick that he used to lift the elastic band of Chuck's sopping underpants from behind his scrotum and let it snap down on his muddy belly. Then he and Starkey hoisted his jeans up and over his large butt. He'd worn no belt. Once it was confirmed he was still breathing and somewhat comfortable, they left him lying in the dirt and ambled back to the positions they'd occupied before his performance began.

The mingling of the men generated new conversation. "Jack, just because your old man works for Falls City don't mean you can't drink anything else. That shit will kill you sooner or later," said Sean Murphy, who had just dragged Fat Chuck into history. Then he looked to Andrew Starkey. "Hey, Stark. You bring any of that Coors beer back from Colorado?"

"Nah. You know, I didn't even think of it on the way out of town. Guess I was too focused on that 20-hour drive. I'll bring some next trip."

"Oh real fuckin' nice," Murphy responded with mock disgust. "Bet you've got your pussy-ass, Colorado Kool-Aid locked up in the trunk and won't share it with your buddies. Well, I won't be taking you to my secret fiddler place then." He was referring to the local delicacy of deep-fat fried, juvenile catfish. The best fiddlers were served in Negro joints down along the Ohio River southwest of town.

"Hey," Starkey protested, "I'm not holding out on you. I just plain wasn't thinking about beer when I headed out on I-70. I'll make it up to you next time."

"So, Stark, what's it like out there, in Denver? You working, going to school, what?" asked Rick Adams from out of the shadows beside the bleachers. He had reclaimed his seat on a case of long-neck empties.

"Working for Ma Bell, now. I'm a telephone installer, putting in phones for Hippies."

"Hippies?" asked Sean Murphy incredulously. "They let Hippies in Denver? Don't those cowboys round 'em up and lynch 'em?"

Andrew shook his head. "Nah, the town's overrun with the bastards. There's this area, Capitol Hill, I work in a couple days every week. Has all these huge old mansions built by rich miners back in the 1890s. Now they've all been converted into rooming houses and every room has a Hippy renting it, and every fucking Hippy has to have a phone."

"A fucking phone," corrected Adams.

"Right", said Starkey. He looked down at his beer for a moment. "Base pay's OK, and there's tons of overtime. It's rare I don't work six days a week. Plenty of dough for my apartment, car payment, the occasional female and beaucoup Coors."

"Then you got job security from those fucking Hippies," said Adams.

"You got me there, old buddy. But I hate to owe anything to those motherfuckers."

Starky answered with a hostility that surprised those around him.

"Tell us how you really feel," laughed Caleb.

Andrew looked around at the group, offered a faint smile and continued, "But, it's a great job. I work outside most of the time and the weather's usually pretty good. But, this is no shit, I've been 25 feet up some telephone pole in 50-degree sunshine, then a breeze will come up and the next thing you know I'm coming down off that pole in a blizzard. "Shirt-sleeve sunshine to snowstorm in a half hour."

His commentary had, for a time, made him the center of attention and Starkey wished for an opportunity to extract himself from that position.

"Got a great bunch of guys on my crew, nearly all drunken ex-GIs, like you morons," he continued. "You know, they're all married, but still want to go out partying all the time."

"So," offered Adams, "you got buds to drink beer with. That's crucial to maintaining sound mental health. The occasional fat, ugly female can also be useful."

Starkey laughed, "Hey, who said fat?" Then with an inflection that he was winding down this discussion, "And I'm thinking about taking a few classes at the community college. Need to get the brain oiled for when I decide to go back to school for real. Don't tell me Baxter and Thompson are still the only ones who've finished degrees?"

"That's a fact," confirmed Jim Baxter of the muddy loafers.

"Hey now," said Jack. "I got two years. I'm a card-carrying

sophomore at ISUE. Got some elective credits from my Air Force training."

Other voices submitted they'd done a year, a few semesters, some credits. Some had gotten good jobs at Whirlpool, Bucyrus Erie and other local employers with their high school diplomas, military service or family connections and had no intention of furthering their educations.

"But man, you just ain't going nowhere without that sheepskin," said Baxter, parroting a public service commercial running on TV at the time. It showed Abraham Lincoln speaking with a seedy job counselor, explaining how he, Lincoln, was self-educated, despite his lack of a diploma. Baxter's "sheepskin" comment was the counselor's punch line as Lincoln looked down forlornly. As the commercial ends, the counselor says, "Hey, Lincoln? You got a chauffeur's license?"

For his part, Baxter was quite proud to be one of only two members of their extended group of high school friends to earn a degree. He and Jeff Thompson were also the only ones who'd maintained college deferments, protecting them from the draft in the calamitous era they'd all graduated into. The new lottery had sealed their immunities.

The rest had found themselves in uniform. A few had been drafted, and as those names got around, others scrambled to join the local Guard and Reserve units. Some enlisted as the draft breathed down their necks. Most all those drafted or enlisting ended up in or near Vietnam, except Caleb Rollins who the Army sent to Germany. Richard Enlow, Rick Adams and Brian Brinson had served with Army infantry divisions, and Sean Murphy in the same capacity with the Marines. Sean carried shrapnel from a rocket-propelled grenade in his lower back. Brian Brinson had been in-country only five months before stepping on a mine and losing his left leg at the knee. Fat Chuck had been an Army cook assigned to an officers' club in Saigon. Jack Mortenson had been a crewman on huge Air Force jet transports and, from his base in California, flew in and out of Vietnam, Thailand and the Philippines. Their names and a dozen others, including Andrew Starkey's, were on an honor roll in the school's hallway acknowledging the military service of recent graduates.

Today's "All-School" Reunion picnic was the first time in several years they'd all been together again, a fact adding a degree of intensity to the festivities. Andrew Starkey had driven straight through from his new life in Denver, a distance of over a thousand miles, most of it on I-70. Unknown to his friends, he carried a crushing, emotional burden along with him. He'd almost skipped the event, but realized the long drive across the plains would itself be worth the trip. Nothing in his 23 years of life provided him with a greater sense of serenity and optimism than that particular highway and the vast horizons it offered.

"Hey, Baxter?" yelled a voice. "What's that all over your shiny shoes, smart-ass college boy?"

"Eat me."

"So Stark, when you moving back to Hoosierland, Goddamit?" asked Bryan Brinson from his perch on a cinderblock. It just ain't the same here without you. You can't stay out there forever, can you?"

"Day at a time, man. Day at a time. Life's been good out there." Then silently, to himself, *At least it was.*

Chapter 2
"Stark"

Andrew Starkey's friends called him "Stark" most of the time, the clipped version a term of endearment. But, if he'd made someone angry or the object of his rowdy, off-color sense of humor, the more formal "Starkey" would be invoked.

He was six feet tall and fair skinned with a full head of auburn-tinged blonde hair that grew a bit over the tops of his ears and an inch past his collar. Grey-green eyes retained most of their youthful sparkle, though lines of fatigue beneath them, out of place on such a young face, spoke of weariness as much emotional as physical.

His frame should have carried 180 pounds, but he hovered twenty pounds below that weight. Living conditions during a year-long Army tour in Vietnam had generated numerous bouts of dysentery and each bout took weeks to fully recover from. But then another canteen of water drawn from a muddy mountain stream would bring on another attack. He would drop in the prescribed iodine tablets and wait the prescribed time, only to see them an hour later sitting undissolved in the bottom of the canteen. Sweating under the weight of his weapon, ammunition vest, pack, smoke and fragmentation grenades, the choice was heat exhaustion or critter water. Eating the same food as his indigenous soldier comrades brought similar distress. Other pills successfully protected him from malaria.

Only recently had the scabbed sores on his hands and arms, the result of abrasion from jungle plants, healed over. Where the tops of his jungle boots were once tied and the leeches feasted, he'd have eruptions of blisters that itched so badly they'd awaken him at night. He knew there were parasites beneath his skin, but nothing he found in the drug stores would improve the condition. He assumed that to seek medical attention would be expensive and pointless. Once, he bought a gallon of chlorine bleach, filled a plastic bucket with a bleach-water solution and soaked his feet and ankles until the fumes forced him to terminate the ordeal. The itching and sleep disturbance continued.

After discharge and a few weeks readjusting to his civilian surroundings, Andrew began work on the loading dock at a large warehouse, the job arranged by his father through a business acquaintance. His father wanted to bring him into the family wholesale business but sensed his son was far from ready to settle into such a demanding arrangement. He remembered his own return from England in 1945. *Maybe in a year or two, but not now*, he thought.

The work was easy and, since he was living at home, the pay adequate. Several of the men on the dock were Cuban refugees and kept him in stitches nearly the entire shift. They hated Fidel Castro with a furor that was pathological in intensity. The foreman, Esteban, befriended the gaunt newcomer when he learned of his recent military service. "Hey, AnnNew," he often asked. "How many 'Com-mu-neests' you keel?" To Esteban, a communist was a communist, whether in Cuba or Southeast Asia. At first Andrew would just shake his head and call Esteban "loco". But eventually, he learned that any answer greater that zero would delight the man. One day Andrew answered, "I think five thousand." Esteban howled and hugged him lustily. "I keel tweny-tu," he said. "Bay of Peeegs." Andrew gave him a bigger number every time he was asked. Esteban always repeated the same number with a grin. "Tweny-tu," he'd say.

Andrew would ask Esteban about Cuba, the weather, the beaches, how to say words in Spanish. The man would become wistful as he described the region around Cabo Lucrecia where he worked as a Constable and lived peacefully with his wife and children until the "Revolucion" destroyed that life. His family was now here in Indiana, resettled from Miami following his release from a Cuban jail.

Estaban's friendliness towards Andrew, however, did not extend to the other white and black young men working on the dock whose interest in Cuban culture and Spanish words was more adolescent. "All you want," he'd sputter in exasperation, "Esteban, how you say, 'deeek'? Esteban, how you say, 'poosey'?"

~ * ~

Andrew had reconnected easily with his old school friends, several of whom had left the military in the year previous to his own discharge. But girlfriends were anxious to marry those men, and they were jealous of the time they spent with Starkey. His former best girlfriend, Sally, seldom returned to town, preferring the excitement of her new Ivy League life. Moreover, she'd become part of the entourage of a famous anti-war activist who traveled from city to city organizing protests.

Fix-up dates were often disasters as his aloofness and distance were interpreted as snobbery. He found himself withdrawing more and more, worrying his parents as he stared blankly at the TV screen in the living room of their comfortable home.

One day, he announced that he was moving to Denver. His parents and friends knew that trying to talk him out of it (where will you live, how will you support yourself?) would be pointless. So, as he made his preparations, he was unencumbered by such badgering. To himself he thought, *Nancy's gone, but I can still have the Rocky Mountains.*

Indeed, dreams of Colorado had helped him retain his youthful optimism these last hard years. He would look up Nancy's brother Ron and, hopefully, Danny, his Army friend who lived in a small town on the state's eastern plains. Danny had been badly wounded and Starkey hoped to find out how he had fared. A week later, he packed his Pontiac LeMans with most of what he owned, rose before dawn and headed west on his beloved I-70. When he reached the Mile High City, he negotiated a weekly rate at a Colfax Avenue motel then drove out to the Federal Center to find the VA job counselor's office. His VA contact scribbled a name on a piece of paper and sent him to an interview at a warehouse on Santa Fe Drive. He started work the next day. The wage was only $2 an hour but to Starkey it meant he was a tax paying citizen of Denver, Colorado. Now all he needed was a place to live. At first he thought of calling Ron, but reconsidered when he imagined his lost love's brother as a roommate. *Too much chance to run into Nancy,* he thought. *She's engaged and I've got to move on.*

He found a rough "efficiency" apartment for $60 a month in a converted dwelling on Logan Street. It was somewhat clean with a kitchen off the main living/bedroom, and had a front window that looked down on the dusty, root-bound yard and busy street. A common bath shared by three other apartments was down the hall.

The telephone company was backed up on installation work and it took three weeks to get a man out to connect him. He showed up one Saturday morning with a box under his arm containing Andrew's red dial phone.

"Your 'Hot Line'," the friendly installer joked.

"I wish," said Andrew. "I'm just learning my way around. Seem to be a lot of babes in town."

"Man, this town's got beaucoup puss…I mean 'babes'," the man corrected himself.

Andrew chuckled at the man's off-color reference. A thought occurred to him.

"Say, is the phone company hiring?" he asked, not really expecting a positive response.

"You a vet?" the installer asked as he confirmed dial tone and that the phone number assigned was working.

"Uh, yeah. Army."

"'Nam?"

Andrew nodded, a bit uncomfortably.

"Me, too." He extended his hand to shake with Andrew. "Welcome home," he said, then continued. "Ma Bell hires lots of vets now, or maybe if your old man works for the company. Head down to the 'Personnel Office', 15th and Curtis. Got to warn you though. They'll work your ass off."

"Pay more than $2 an hour?" Andrew asked with a smile.

"You shitting me?" laughed the man.

~ * ~

He did as he was told and, after a seemingly interminable interview process, was hired and put to work. The training was all OJT with the first two weeks spent doing "disconnects"--in other words, going to the homes and apartments of people who couldn't pay their bill and taking the phone away. The first few times he expected that people would scream and yell or otherwise try to fend him off. To his relief, Andrew had no difficulty with those who were losing their means to communicate. Nevertheless, he felt badly performing such an uncharitable function and tried to take some of the sting from the process. "I'm sorry, ma'am. I bet your check clears this afternoon and I'll be back tomorrow to hook it up again. Do you want me to save this one or bring you a new one?" He made a point to smile at the wide-eyed kids who didn't understand why the man in the green truck came to take their phone away.

Then it was off to train for two weeks with "Linsey's Lancers." Jack Linsey was a Mountain Bell old timer and taught all the new hires how to climb telephone poles with "hooks," the sharp metal, boot-mounted gaffs. The new men honed their skills in this exhausting work by climbing tall poles that ran along the Union Pacific tracks outside Brighton. In no time, they'd learned just enough to be very dangerous to themselves. Unlike the climbing style of loggers who threw their belt strap skyward and climbed towards it, a telephone company climber used only his heavily gloved hands and his "hooks," letting the sharp teeth sink into the pole with each step until reaching the height where the work was to be done. While climbing, both ends of the heavy strap dangled from one of two D-rings on the main belt. At the pole top, the climber would lean in, throw the strap around the pole, snap it on to the other D-ring, then lean away from the pole and begin his tasks.

"Remember," Jack Linsey would warn them, "that pole is not your buddy. Keep your body away from it or you'll gaff-out and take the express train to the dirt." He looked up at Starkey who was reaching, precariously, far out on a cross arm. "I hear you were a paratrooper," he yelled up to his student. "Well, you ain't got no reserve if you gaff out. You hear me boy?"

~ * ~

Once he'd completed his pole climbing training, he was assigned to a crew of installers. The crew's foreman was a wild man named Bob who, like the proverbial whorehouse madam, had a tough exterior but a heart of gold. Fellow crew members took Starkey under their collective wings when they confirmed that he, like them, was a Vietnam vet and didn't take himself at all seriously.

His OJT continued for a few weeks as he rode with an experienced installer, meaning someone with a few months on the job. In no time, he was assigned his own truck and put out on his own to sink or swim.

The job kept him at work, usually outside, fifty to sixty hours a week. He lived on sandwiches thrown together in the early morning as he prepared for another long day driving his truck from one installation job to the next. He climbed twenty-foot poles with his "hooks," crawled beneath suburban houses, punched connections in the basements of apartment buildings, stapled "quad" wire to, and drilled holes through, the ornate oak trim of turn-of-the-century mansions, all to connect one more private phone line for an impatient customer. He'd finish his scheduled jobs for the day and Dispatch would send him on newly received service requests. As he drove his truck through the snowy streets to the garage at 7PM he'd catch up to his buddies' trucks at stop lights, also on the way back in. They'd shake their heads and wave, knowing they'd see each other again soon enough at 7:30AM.

Weekends consisted only of Sunday. Saturdays were always a work day with a make-up day off scheduled mid-week. But foreman Bob would always try to catch the men before they left the garage the evening before that day off. "Starkey, you're working tomorrow," he'd yell, as the truck backed into its parking slot. If a man was able to avoid Bob and get out of the garage before being noticed, he'd be called at home. If the crewman didn't answer his home phone, Bob might show up at his door. There was far too much work to allow a day off.

Starkey developed strong and raucous friendships with several of his equally overextended crewmembers. They were all young and married, and their wives nagged them to start families. Andrew was a favorite among the wives due to his man-boyishly handsome face, and the deference he showed in his manners and compliments to even the most homely of them. Saturday nights often had a pack of three to five couples and Andrew, the odd man out, bar-hopping along East Colfax. Once, while sitting at a table overflowing with empty beer glasses, he felt the hand of a friend's wife on his thigh. He squeezed the hand affectionately and moved it away. He decided he should back off on hanging with the couples.

Unattached women often viewed him differently. He had a few clubs he'd frequent, sometimes alone, sometimes with a Mountain Bell buddy or maybe Ron, the brother of Nancy. By the time he'd finished his third or fourth beer, he could ask women to dance. The handsome face his friends' wives perceived looked haggard to these women. Sometimes they noticed the crusted areas on his hands and wondered what disease he might have. Still, he was able to connect with some females, usually those older than he. They were far more prone to talk with a man before writing him off, and Andrew was a delight to talk to, if he'd had enough to drink.

It never ceased to amaze him how many women worked for the phone company, and how many of those were in the clubs on a given night. Eventually, he connected with a lady who grew to feel great affection for the enigmatic young man. The physical intimacy he shared with her was of a playful and unselfish nature that delighted and surprised her, given the usual "one-night stands" she'd become used to. Ironically, she repaid his attentions in motherly fashion by feeding him home cooked meals, massaging his aching body and talking with him. He seemed to need to talk a lot.

Judy was ten years his senior and worked as a secretary downtown in the Mountain Bell corporate offices. She was divorced and shared custody of a daughter with her career Air Force ex-husband. They met one Saturday night at a club she frequented with several of her phone company girlfriends. Andrew had asked one of her friends to dance and had been turned down rudely. Judy thought he was cute. So, after a trip to the lady's room, she walked up to him at the bar and asked him to dance. They spent the rest of the evening together, dancing and talking. As they sat together, she took his hand and noticed the scabbed, rough areas. She asked him what might have caused the problem. When he answered, "Southeast Asia," she just stared at him for several seconds.

"Sweetie, how long have you been back?"

"Seven months."

As they left together, the girlfriend who had snubbed Andrew earlier in the evening said to Judy, "If I'd had just one more vodka tonic, I'd be screwing him tonight instead of you." Judy patted her on the head and winked at the others. "You girls have fun. I've got to go help my friend with his erection…!"

~ * ~

Over the next few months they spent many days and nights together. She showed him hiking trails in the mountain parks outside

Denver and took him on drives up to Central City and Estes Park. Her favorite times with him were the weekends when her "ex" would pick up their daughter and take her to his home in Colorado Springs. Andrew would come for dinner, spend the night, then they'd spend the morning in bed with the Sunday paper. Around noon, they'd drive up to Evergreen to a bar called "Little Bear" and dance to a rowdy polka band. Then they'd rush back to her house to be there when Jodi was dropped off at six.

She adored Andrew. She also knew the relationship would never result in marriage. The age disparity was too great, plus she really wasn't in any hurry to marry again. She also knew instinctively that Andrew would be gone should he feel pressured for a commitment. But, he was just so much fun, and, besides, he needed her. He may not have been aware that he needed her, but what counted to her was that she knew it.

Early in their friendship, a call to her daughter's pediatrician generated a prescription for a topical ointment that greatly reduced Andrew's skin problems. He was amazed and grateful. "Sweetie, sometimes you have to trust medical science," she said.

Another service she was happy to provide would have appalled the girls down at the office. Judy would have Andrew sit on the floor facing away from her while she sat at the edge of her couch. As he leaned forward, she would squeeze into a tissue the blackheads and pimples that she found clustered in his hairline on the back of his neck. She'd do the same on his shoulders and down his back. He'd repay her with backrubs.

There were periods when he wouldn't call. Some nights he needed to roam and he'd cruise the clubs. One night he was at a club called, "Mr. Lucky`s," leaning on the bar and gazing out at the dancers. As usual, a live band was playing to a large weekend singles crowd. An attractive young woman approached and smiled at him as if he were an old friend. Her look was typical "Hippy," with long straight brown hair, flowered long-sleeved top and tight, bell-bottom jeans. The pointy toes of cowboy boots showed beneath the denim. Her slim cheeks were dimpled and her nose was narrow and turned up. Tiny ears protruded somewhat comically through her straight hair. He thought she might be drunk, or maybe crazy. She began fiddling with the buttons on his shirt and said, "I'm Connie, and I've been sent here to make all your dreams come true." Her smile was as disarming as it was disconcerting. He noticed a faint but unmistakable odor of marijuana.

Andrew looked down at her and began to speak, "Well, uh...you're very pretty, but, ho, um, I…" As he struggled for words his peripheral vision picked up a familiar demonic grin twenty feet down the bar. He looked for several seconds trying to evaluate if there might be a link between the woman and grinner. Then a flood of recognition hit him.

"Danny!" he exclaimed. He looked to the girl again and she had her hands to her face looking back towards her husband. The two men walked towards each other, almost shyly, in the smoky bar, and shook hands warmly.

"You made it! You're OK!" Andrew laughed.

"How you doing, Lieutenant?" said Danny. "Call in any Dust-Offs lately?"

Chapter 3
Testimonials

Andrew Starkey was an emotional train wreck. Now, back in his home- town for a school reunion, he had surprised himself by this ability to recount, however briefly, his recent life in Colorado. For days he'd not been able to think clearly, let alone talk about trivial, everyday things. But these friends knew him better than his own family members, a fact not unusual for men his age. In this group, he knew that any conduct too far out of character would draw attention or, worse, whispered questions among themselves, like "What's with that son of a bitch? Is he too good for us anymore?"

He had craved the companionship of old friends and the solace their familiar bantering would provide. No matter what, he could always relax with Jack, Rich, Sean and Brian. Caleb was a good but less intimate friend. It was a little tougher to be around the others. He wished Jeff Thompson could have been there. Some third-year law student advice from Jeff, who Andrew trusted with his life, might have eased his mind. But for now, he wanted to sit here in the dirt with his friends, on the periphery, a spectator to a home movie of his very recent, mostly happy adolescence. He knew that since Danny was dead, Colorado was going to be a painful place to return to. He was also just beginning to come to grips with the fact that he'd killed a man, and it wasn't war this time.

Sheriff wants me to check in on the way back, he remembered to himself. *At least he didn't tell me I couldn't leave the state. Well, that gives me a chance to see Susan.* He had a vision of her standing on the porch of her small house, the high plains wind blowing her cotton dress into tight silhouette against her body. *God, I miss her. And, I'd better check on Connie and the kid. Damn it all to hell. How could this shit have happened…?*

Abruptly, his eyes were drawn to Rich Enlow. After a stop at the pit, the strapping blond six-footer strolled towards the gym building parodying a baseball pitcher's windmill wind up using a full beer bottle as a ball. With a bellowing, "1ST INFANTRY DIVISION! IF YOU'RE GOING TO BE ONE, BE A 'BIG RED ONE'!"—and he hurled the bottle against the brick wall. The resulting explosion showered the revelers with foam and broken glass.

"Hey, watch out, asshole!" hollered Baxter, whose back had been turned. "Jesus, man!"

A prodding from Enlow drove Murphy up from his seat on the ground. "Your turn Jarhead," he taunted. "Get some!"

"Yeah? Oh, what the hell." Sean stood up unsteadily and, wiping the grime from the label of a recently opened Pabst, took a few steps toward the school. He yelled, "DEVIL DOGS, SEMPER FI!" and sent his bottle crashing against the wall. The group, sensing something, began to ease back from the building.

"What's with these guys?" asked Starkey.

"Ah, a strange ritual Enlow invented at last year's reunion," Jack explained. "We came back here to party after the picnic, just like tonight. Sharon Eisenstat and Sally Mason hung around with us till it got too loud. Anyway, Sharon was a psych major at IU and she went nuts over Enlow breaking his bottle and screaming some Vietnam shit. Thought the bitch was going to have an orgasm trying to psychoanalyze him." He shook his head at the recollection. "So, she compared it to breaking a wine glass after it's held an exceptional vintage, you know, so it can never again be tainted by a less- worthy wine. I said, "Now, Sharon, that's not very scientific, so she says she's going to call one of her old professors to get his interpretation."

"Did she?"

"Fuckin' A. Called me a couple weeks later all concerned about Rich. It was nothing like her 'wine glass' bullshit. He said, 'Post Traumatic Stress, coupled with deep-seated and unresolved hostility. The young man needs therapy'." Jack spoke the professor's interpretation in a mocking lisp. "I never told Rich. Anyway, find a bottle. It does have an odd, cathartic effect."

"A what?" asked Andrew Starkey.

Rick Adams, whose first attempt to get up from his seat had resulted in a half somersault, shouted, "I'm next, Goddamit!" Unable to find a full bottle, he grabbed an empty, yelled, "4TH INFANTRY, IVY MEN !!!" and threw his bottle. It missed the wall entirely and went up on the roof of the gym. This garnered howls from the men, most of whom were searching out bottles and lining up for their testimonials.

Jack picked up a Blatz and walked toward the wall rotating his arm to loosen it for his throw. His shout of, "MILITARY AIRLIFT COMMAND, UNITED STATES AIR FORCE!" drew wolf whistles from his assembled comrades. Then he turned and hiked the bottle between his legs football center-style. It hit the wall but dropped unbroken to the dirt.

"You sorry-ass Air Force pussy!" hollered Murphy. He chased Jack back to his seat with a soggy empty beer case, flinging it at him as he sat down with Starkey. Jack two-handed the flying case like a volley ball towards Starkey who parried it with a forearm.

"USS CONSTELLATION, YANKEE FUCKING STATION!" shrieked Will Carmody as he destroyed his half-full Falstaff. Brian Brinson, having inexplicably removed his prosthetic leg, hopped towards the wall with the last Strohs. Thundering, "AMERICAL DIVISION!", he sent it crashing.

A uniformed figure watched the rowdy gathering curiously from beyond the glow of the arc light. He had picked his way among the parked cars and cycles, taking a hurried detour around a low and vicious-sounding growl emanating from somewhere in the darkness. Deputy Thompson of the Vanderburgh County Sheriff's Department recognized many of the revelers. They had graduated at the end of his freshman year. A few had been frequent visitors to his home, friends of his brother Jeff, now in law school at Michigan and unable to make it home for this special weekend. He knew he had to do something to break up the gathering before it got too much farther out of hand.

The first call from a local homeowner had come in to Juanita in central dispatch an hour ago about a loud group of men drinking on school property. He planned on checking it out as soon as he finished his speed trap duty on Oak Hill Road. But Juanita had just radioed him again. Now the homeowner was reporting the sound of breaking glass ("You've got to send someone now! They're tearing down the school and screaming the foulest language I've ever heard! They're on motorcycles, and it may be the Hell's Angels!"). That second call had really concerned Juanita, but the deputy, having a hunch who might be involved, drove his patrol unit over with little trepidation. He was, after all, six foot two, two hundred and eighteen pounds and an All State linebacker two years ago in his own senior year.

As he watched, he remembered a similar call last year at this time but the disturbance had ended before he arrived. The investigation he'd planned on pursuing never materialized. *Doesn't take a brain surgeon to figure who last year's perpetrators were*, he decided. *They've returned to the scene of the crime.* It came together now. Deputy Thompson would have attended the reunion picnic himself had he not been on duty. His Class of '69 mates expected him to show up where they were gathering once he was off duty.

He took a quick inventory of the rowdies. The one hopping on one leg was obviously Brian Brinson and the deputy wondered why he'd removed his prosthesis. *Well,* he mused, *if they run I'll catch that one for sure.* The large prone figure he assumed must be 'Fat' Chuck

Elliot. *So, that explains at least one of the motorcycles.* He remembered the homeowner's call to dispatch and chuckled to himself, *Hell's shit-faced Angel.* He noted Rich Enlow and Caleb Rollins, and thought, *They'll be peaceful enough. Now, there's Jack Mortensen. Hmm, wonder where Starkey is?* He remembered them as his brother's best friends and virtually inseparable. *Ok, there's Evans, Newell, Murphy and that prick Baxter.* He took a deep breath, adjusted his Sam Brown belt and began a determined advance toward the revelers.

"1st AVIATION BRIGADE, YOU SONS OF BITCHES!" yelled Jerry Newall, sending his bottle into the wall.

As Jack returned from a quick check on Fat Chuck's condition he stopped, then carefully turned away from the direction he'd been facing.

"Stark!" he whispered with hoarse urgency.

"I'm not into this, man."

"No! Act casual and walk with me real slow over to the corn. There's a deputy coming up, over by the score board."

"No shit? Here I come," Starkey responded, and thought, *Now, that's really all I need.*

With feigned nonchalance, the two friends slowly angled away from the group of bottle throwers and in a few steps were shadowed by the bleachers. Out of sight of the deputy, they jogged the fifty feet to the edge of the cornfield, walked in a few paces on a carpet of corn tassels and turned to watch the unfolding drama.

The hilarity ended abruptly as the deputy ambled from the darkness into the glow of the street lamp. He stopped twenty yards away, hands clinched together on his heavy belt buckle. One by one, the men became aware of his presence, elbowing one another and clearing their throats. The deputy knew his stare-down would freeze the men in place. The last thing he wanted was to send them running all over the area. When most of them had become quiet, he continued his advance.

"Man, don't do that," whispered Jack, doing a double-take at Andrew, who was squatting on his haunches, flat footed, butt off the ground a few inches and looking down the rows toward the men. "You look like a fucking gook."

Starkey ignored him and said, "Check out Brinson." The man had crab-walked backwards to the top row of the bleachers and was performing a drunken one-legged parody of a cheerleader.

"West High Wolfhounds, OOH! AH! West High Wolfhounds, OOH! AH!", he yelled in falsetto, using his prosthetic lower leg as if it were a megaphone. He froze in mid-cheer as he noticed the deputy, dropped to a sitting position and began to reattach his prosthesis.

"Remember detassling this field?" asked Andrew under his breath. "Man, what mud. Looked like our feet were stuck in buckets of tassels when we finished a row."

"Ninety cents an hour. That's what I remember," said Jack as he craned his neck to see what was going on. "Hey, by the way, how's your old Army buddy doing, that Colorado kid you met at Ft. Knox, what's his name-- Danny? You were going to look him up when you moved out there."

Starkey looked at the ground for a few seconds, then cleared his throat and spit into the next row.

"Well...," he began, "he, uh, he died. He's dead. Happened a couple weeks ago."

Jack looked hard at Starkey. "Oh, man I'm sorry. I thought, I mean I was...how did it happen? Can you talk about it, or...?" He waited for Starkey to respond, forgetting momentarily about the deputy.

"It was bad. I was there. He was in some trouble. I didn't know how bad it was until it was too late to get him out of it." He spit again. "Anyway, he was a good friend. Now he's dead. I'm Goddamn sick about it. I'll tell you more later."

Jack put his hand on Andrew's shoulder. "I could tell you were bummed out about something. That's it, isn't it?"

"That's about it."

"Damn. Didn't he have a wife and kid?"

"Yeah."

Out on the field, the men had gathered around the deputy. Most were hanging their heads and scraping the dirt with their shoes as the deputy dutifully took names, addresses and phone numbers. All had sobered up considerably. Jack and Starkey could barely make out the voice of the deputy as it rose and fell with official commands and admonitions. After several minutes the men dispersed and began collecting garbage and debris around the area.

Starkey said, "Hell, let's go turn ourselves in. Those assholes will never forgive us if we skate on the whole deal."

"Yeah, let's go."

Together they walked from the field and back into the light.

"Yo!" Starkey shouted towards the deputy, "Where do we go to surrender?"

The deputy turned towards them and pushed his hat back on his head. "Well, Mr. Starkey and Mr. Mortenson. Nice of you to return from the corn. I had both your names down for the citation already, but now you can help your friends clean up the area."

"Oh, so who ratted us out?"

"No one ratted on you, Mr. Starkey. I noticed Mr. Mortenson was here earlier so I knew you'd be in the vicinity." Unseen by the others, he gave Starkey a wink. "Anyway, for you two who missed my instructions, you'll make this area as presentable as possible now, leave the premises, and then return at 7AM with rakes, shovels, bags, bulldozers and whatever else you need to clean up every fragment of broken glass and garbage. Sometime tomorrow afternoon, I'll re-inspect and if this place isn't safe for naked babies to crawl around on, I'll turn this list over to the district attorney for his review. Are my instructions and their implications quite clear?"

"Yes sir," they replied in unison.

"We'll be here with bells on, 7AM sharp," Jack added for emphasis.

"We appreciate your professional courtesy Deputy Thompson," said Starkey. "We realize you could have been much harder on us."

"Just make this place safe for kids by tomorrow afternoon, gentlemen. If you don't, you'll see how quickly my courtesy will evaporate. Good evening, gentlemen. I've got more important duties to perform."

The men were quick and sincere in their sendoffs, "Good evening, Officer, yes, thank you, Officer, you won't be sorry, Officer. Thanks again, Deputy Thompson, etc. etc."

As he strode away, Starkey yelled after him, "Hey, Deputy. Did you ever find your swim trunks?" The deputy turned his head slightly as if to respond, then continued straight ahead and disappeared into the darkness.

After he was gone, Brinson and Murphy began giving Starkey and Jack the business.

"It's a good thing you cocksuckers crawled out of your hidey hole," said Sean.

Starkey was picking up empties and didn't respond.

"Don't call me a cocksucker," said Jack. "I told you I'm trying to quit."

Raucous groans and catcalls rose from the men.

"Anyway," Jack continued, "that kid might have opened fire on us. No way were we going to get greased for breaking a few bottles."

"Man, I thought we were beaucoup fucked," said Rick Adams as he picked up bottle shards and threw them into an empty case. "Say, do we know that guy?"

"Yeah," said Brinson. "That's Jeff Thompson's brother."

"Oh, no shit? Man did we luck out."

"Maybe so, but I'm not taking any chances," said Sean Murphy, as he salvaged and sorted the remaining full beers. "Aw right, listen up!" he yelled. "Every swinging dick is going to be here in the morning to clean this place up. The only one excused is Fat Chuck."

"Why should I have…," began Jim Baxter.

"Shut up, Baxter," said Sean. He turned and looked around. "And, Rich? Next year, would you please not start a fucking riot with your bottle-throwing bull shit?"

"Roger that, Drill Sergeant."

"Well," said a voice, "if we leave Chuck here 'til we come back, he can help, too. He'll be waking up about the time we arrive."

As they did their part to tidy up the area, Jack and Starkey continued in hushed tones to each other.

"I heard you holler that shit at Thompson, about the swim trunks. That took guts under the circumstances."

"He needed to lighten up," said Andrew Starkey.

The men had gathered most of the large-debris items and decided that they'd do a better job with some day light.

"Let's bag this shit 'til tomorrow," said Sean. "See you dickheads in the morning."

Jack and Andrew lagged behind the others as they began to drift towards the parked cars. Fat Chuck had been roused and would be given a ride home with Will Carmody. Will spread newspapers over his back seat, then helped Chuck lay down on them. Chuck's old Flathead Harley would have to remain parked by the oak tree until tomorrow.

"Man, I'm so sorry about your friend," Jack whispered. "I just know from what you told me that you were real close, you know, from your time together in the Army. Guess he had a world-class sense of humor."

"Yeah, that he did." Starkey was distressed now and had badly fallen out of the improving state he'd been in for the last few hours. "Wasn't a hell of a lot to laugh at back then, but he sure could dig it out." He was idly twisting an empty bottle in his hands. He stopped, then pushed the dirt off the label with his thumb and stared down at it for several moments. "He was a crazy fucker and just a great guy."

"And you ended up back together in 'Nam?'" asked Jack.

"Sure did."

Jack was alarmed at his friend's state of mind. Andrew had not been himself all day. Now, Jack's attempts to get him to talk about what was bothering him were having the opposite effect he'd hoped for.

"Good old Falls City," said Andrew. He stooped down and picked up a second bottle and walked back towards the wall.

"Oh shit," said Jack, his comment causing the men to look back at Starkey. "Why didn't I shut up when I had the chance?"

As he neared the gymnasium, Starkey shouted, "DETACHMENT A-115, 5TH SPECIAL FORCES GROUP!" and splattered the empty bottle against the wall. The crashes from their own bottles a short time before hadn't seemed nearly as loud. The men yelled at him, "Knock it off, Starkey, or we'll end up in the slammer!" He walked toward them still holding one bottle, then reached down for another. He underhanded a bottle high in the air and waited for it to begin its fall back to the ground. Then with a shout of, "AIRBORNE, DANNY!" he threw the last bottle at the falling one. They collided with an explosion of glass that sent the men scrambling.

Chapter 4
Drafted

A post office at 3AM seemed an unlikely place to hold a government-sponsored gathering. But the young men who were reporting for induction were so numb with their plight that the curious use of the facility hardly occurred to them. Indeed, they'd be long gone on the buses before anyone arrived to buy stamps, send packages or check their boxes. Few of those day-to-day customers would ever know of the personal drama that unfolded only hours before in the large marble hall that seemed to them so sterile and devoid of human emotion.

The draftees, pimply faced boys for the most part, arrived dutifully on time. Many sat in cars with their fathers and mothers until the last moment. Some arrived with girlfriends or new wives hanging on them, and some of those girls sobbed pitifully.

Quite a few showed up with carloads of buddies, and these arrivals were raucous and jovial. Those carloads, though filled with beer-drinking rowdies, became quiet and sullen upon seeing the dozens of young men seated along the walls with small satchels or sacks of personal items the Draft Board had instructed them to bring along. They knew they were going to leave a childhood friend at this place and there was little to be amused about. A Yellow Cab dropped off one young man. No one else appeared to come alone.

Most of the men did their best to project a tough and ready-for-anything image, but the nervousness was evident in the wide-eyed looks, the laughter at nothing in particular, the unwillingness to finish their farewells. Presently, the parents, buddies and young women began to withdraw as uniformed and intimidating Army noncommissioned officers began to walk through the throng and announce that the "civilians" needed to say goodbye so the men could begin their transformation into soldiers.

Twenty-year-old Andrew Starkey had been delivered by his two closest friends, Jack Mortenson, who himself was on a leave from the Air Force, and Jeff Thompson, who'd driven the long trip down from Wabash College to see his friend off. Starkey's parents, reluctant to say their goodbyes early the evening before, nevertheless could sense that their son wouldn't hear of any other arrangement.

"Besides," he told them, "do you really want to drive me down to the main post office at 3AM? I'll be back in a couple months. They don't send anyone straight from Basic Training to Vietnam." Of course, he really didn't know if that was true, and had little more than his father's WWII experience to rely on. But the father's reassurances to his distraught wife that Andrew would get at least one leave before shipping out overseas were all that kept her from being there that morning.

"Well, here's another fine mess you've gotten us into." The voice came from behind the three men as they stood on the granite stairs outside the building.

"Rich!" exclaimed Starkey. The three friends turned and grabbed Rich Enlow by the shoulders and pulled him into their huddle. "I thought you were at school in Terre Haute. Shit, guess there's no reason to ask what you're doing here."

"My man," said Rich, "I'm one fucked puppy. I dropped out of school at the end of last semester. You know, had that apartment with some guys, so I just stayed up there and partied." He shook his head and rolled his eyes comically. "My folks didn't think anything of it, and I figured, you know, what the fuck. Amazing how quick the draft board found my young ass."

"Jeez," said Starkey. "Well, I don't mind saying it's good to see a familiar face. When I first looked in there I almost puked."

Each expressed that, had they known, they would have included Rich in their small going-away festivities, which consisted of driving around most of the night, visiting old haunts, with a few stops to relieve themselves along various roadways. Rich said, however, that his cousin and the cousin's girlfriend had offered to drive him down, saving his parents the agony. Their belated fury at him for being so cavalier with his college deferment had now turned to a visceral dread for his safety.

The NCOs were becoming agitated with some of the extended last kisses and tearful embraces. The new inductees now heard the very first of hundreds of shouts of "Fall In!" they'd hear over the next months and years. If ever there were words that could make a person physically ill, it was that order at this time and in this place.

"Boys, you'd better get out of here. One of these guys might take off and the Sergeants will just grab whoever's standing around," joked Starkey.

"They'd better not touch my Air Force ass," said Jack.

"Press gangs went out with the War of 1812," Jeff commented.

But, it was time to leave, so with the inevitable "keep your heads down" and quick handshakes all around, Starkey and Rich were left to their fates. As they walked away, Jack Mortenson yelled back to Starkey, "You'll get back out to Colorado before you know it."

Rich was puzzled and asked Starkey what Jack was referring to.

"Road trip. Tell you about it later. Looks like show time."

The draftees gathered around a five-stripe NCO to hear instructions. First, they'd load into the buses waiting on the street out front and proceed to the US Army's Induction facility in Louisville, a four-hour drive. In Louisville, they'd have another physical to make sure nothing had changed since the pre-induction physicals they'd had several weeks before. They would talk to counselors, take some written tests, fill out many forms and, eventually, be sworn into the Army. Well into the evening they would ride the same buses to the new-recruit Reception Station, Ft. Knox, Kentucky. "Basic Combat Training" or "BCT" would begin after several days of additional processing at the Reception Station.

Some tried to sleep as they wound through the wooded hills of south central Indiana. The motion of the buses on the old two-lane highway, however, kept rocking the bewildered men into each other. Only the most intoxicated managed to remain unconscious for more than a few minutes. One boy in particularly bad shape drooled so heavily in his stupor that the front of his shirt was soaked down to his belt.

Starkey and Rich Enlow tried and failed to doze and finally decided to catch up with each other's history since high school graduation. They had seen each other only occasionally that first summer, both working construction or farm labor as it became available. Both had gone off to college in the fall, Andrew to Indiana University and Rich to Indiana State. A second summer break had come and, again, each worked odd jobs, cruised the burger joints with dates or buddies, and returned to their respective schools for sophomore year. For different reasons, both boys had descended into palpable depression that made what their families assumed was an idyllic university lifestyle a personal agony. In Rich's case, he was homesick the first year and his grades suffered as a result.

"Why can't you get me a job at Whirlpool?" he implored his father. "Boy," the dumbfounded man answered, "you're getting the education I never got. You want to paint washing machines the rest of your life?" It had never occurred to Rich that his dad hated his working life so much. Such men seldom if ever shared with mere children their feelings about life, work and their own dreams. Stunned by his dad's warning about the work-life misery awaiting anyone without a degree, he returned for sophomore year; not as homesick this time, but still with an attitude that he wanted to be somewhere, anywhere else. He partied, cut class, drank and took road-trips with his friends. He earned three credits that semester and was not invited to enroll for the next.

Andrew Starkey's tumult, on the other hand, had grown from the age-old and even predictable consequences of young love. In his case, there were two loves, and while he might have been able to persevere against one at a time, the two together completely overwhelmed him.

His first year of college in Bloomington had been clouded by misery at separation from his new loves. In the recesses of his mind he could rationally understand the "girl" part. What he was unprepared for was the longing for a "place," a region of the country he'd known nothing about until that summer after high school graduation. As he tried to focus on his studies, he'd find himself sitting in the library stacks doodling panoramic drawings of mountain sunsets. Each drawing would include a title, of sorts, along its bottom border. The title was always the same: "NANCY."

The drawings never included the girl's face but only the mountains, a straight stretch of I-70 leading to them, and always the setting sun. This stemmed from a subliminal realization that only the mountains were a sure thing. The girl was far from certain but she personified his longings, and only writing her name at the bottom of his creations made them complete. At their sad parting the summer of the road trip they'd made a promise to write each other and Andrew did his best to keep it. Her letters were prolific, upbeat and full of excitement about her freshman college life in Greeley, her sorority sisters and trips to Denver to spend occasional weekends with her brother. Ron was now a student at the University of Denver and had a very nice apartment near that campus. She wrote that she missed Andrew and couldn't wait to see him the following summer. Andrew's letters were similarly upbeat and as the year went by, he did his best to write as he promised, sitting at his desk, staring longingly at the photographs of her with his beloved Rocky Mountains in the background. He couldn't wait for summer to come so he could see her again. He'd get to Buena Vista somehow, even if he had to hitchhike.

But in the spring, a letter arrived that crushed his dream. Nancy had been offered a chance to spend the summer in Italy, a guest of the Tuscan side of their family. She'd travel over with her mother, who would remain a few weeks, then return alone, leaving Nancy with her Spinelli cousins for the rest of the summer. She wrote that she was very sorry and disappointed as well, but that it was important to the family that she reestablish the family bond. Her sincere inquiry, "Could you meet me in Italy?", had turned his abject despair to anger. How could she have known that he wanted to see the mountains again almost as badly as he wanted to see her? He wrote back that he understood and that he hoped she had a wonderful time. They'd get together someday. He asked that she send him her address in Lucca and he'd write to her there. Nancy hadn't conveyed her own palpable sadness fearing he might beg her not to go. She had to accept such a generous invitation and couldn't let her feelings for a boy she'd only spent one wonderful week with, disrupt her extended family's joy over the impending reunion.

He spent that hot summer laboring, ironically, in the cold-storage warehouse of a dairy. Weekends were spent cruising with his friends. Nancy wrote regularly, but his letters back became a struggle. The summer passed painfully but quickly for him.

As his sophomore year began, he tried to remain upbeat. After all, there were the football games, street dances and the general excitement of seeing old friends. But as the parties ended and the fall rains began, he felt himself withdrawing into a shell. Day after day he'd walk to class among the gray limestone buildings, study in the library, walk back to the dorm, go down to the lounge to watch some TV or meet friends at the snack bar. On weekends he'd partner with someone over 21 and sneak a case of beer into his room, doling out bottles in ones and twos to the other dorm rats. Sometimes he'd buy a pint of "Dark Eyes" vodka and four cans of Seven-Up, drink half the vodka and two Seven-Ups on Friday night and repeat on Saturday. Both nights he'd be happily blasted and, stumbling around campus, pick up and make out with two or even three different girls before he'd pass out or become sick. With Monday morning, the depression would return. Letters from Nancy, back in school in Greeley, were becoming fewer. Often he didn't write back for weeks.

The emerging political polarization on campus pained him greatly and he reserved special scorn for the "Greenbaggers", so named because they carried their books over their shoulders in green canvas bags purchased at the campus bookstore. That green bag was the icon of those Leftist, proto-Hippy students who felt uniquely qualified to condemn those who didn't think or look like them. They were, of course, against the war, any war, for any reason, and those poor souls actually fighting in one were a focus of Greenbagger contempt. Students enrolled in ROTC wore their uniforms to class, and confrontations with "Baggers" were becoming a frequent occurrence.

He felt as if he were losing his mind. College is where his parents wanted him to be, but he hated it. To drop out would provide only the illusion of freedom because the draft loomed. Eventually, it dawned on him that nothing, even being drafted, could be as bad as his bleak existence. So, one day during Christmas break from IU, and unknown to his parents or friends, he visited his draft board office. He leaned on the counter in front of a thirty-ish woman who'd come out to answer his questions.

"I want to get it over with. I want to go," he told the woman. "At the end of this semester I'm dropping out. I'm not going back. Put me on the list so some other guy doesn't have to go."

For a few awkward seconds the woman just stared at him. It wasn't that she hadn't yet heard everything from previous visitors, but most of those were looking for a way out, not a way in. She was professional, took his name and draft card number, made a few notes on a clipboard and thanked him for coming in.

"Mr. Starkey, why don't you just enlist?"

Andrew had visited the local recruiters and had balked at the minimum enlistments. "Four years for the Marines and Air Force. Three for the Army. I want to serve, but the draft is only two years, right?"

"Yes, honey, just two years. But, you know, well…you know what they'll do with you, and…," she paused. "and it's not just the Army… Well, thanks for coming in." She stopped at that point.

Andrew wanted desperately for her to tell him he should start packing. Sensing that she couldn't or wouldn't do that, he left the office feeling foolish and empty.

"I'm so fucked," he mumbled to himself as he shuffled down the street to the car. The thought of returning to school for final exams that he was unprepared for and might just skip altogether, made him sick to his stomach.

"Guess I'd better prepare Mom and Dad. Tell them I'll get a job down here and wait out the draft."

At 19, he was at the bottom of a spiritual pit with no rays of light showing him a way out. Even thoughts of Colorado and Nancy could not lift the pall of despair. A few weeks later, after returning to IU and, indeed, skipping half his finals, he moved back home. He walked the streets looking for a job and found one soon enough driving a truck for a distributor of books and magazines. Each day, he hoped the mailbox would deliver his salvation; the same letter other young men his age dreaded.

With his friends away at college or, like Jack Mortenson, Sean

Murphy and several others, already in the military, he was socially isolated. "Work, eat, sleep," he said one morning to his mother as she sat with him at breakfast. "If something doesn't happen soon, I'm going to have to enlist. Otherwise, I'll go crazy."

"Andrew, just be patient. Do your job, save some money. When springtime comes, you'll have a whole new outlook. Maybe you can go out to Colorado. Don't do anything rash now that you'll be sorry for later."

When he got home that night an official-looking letter was waiting for him. His parents pretended not to notice, but left it prominently by his chair at the kitchen table. Instead of taking off his coat, he sat down, opened it carefully and began to read:

"Greeting: You are hereby ordered for induction into the Armed Forces of the United States..."

He looked up at his parents who were staring expectantly at him. His mother had a hand to her mouth and tears in her eyes.

"Well, are you happy now?" his obviously angry father snapped.

"Dad," he started, "Mom, look, I'm ready. I want to go. This...is..." he held up the letter. "I need to do this."

"That's fine, son," said his father, "but it's no longer a matter of wanting to or not. You've been drafted and you have to go." He sat down at the table, took the letter from Andrew and examined it carefully. A look of bemusement shadowed his face. "Same Goddamn wording they used in '43," he said.

His reporting date was a month away. He gave a week's notice at work, and co-workers could not fathom his ebullient demeanor. "You'd think he won the Irish fucking Sweepstakes," said a puzzled supervisor. He spent a few days cleaning his room and storing away college paraphernalia. He called Jeff Thompson up at Wabash College. Jeff promised to be there to send him off unless an earthquake occurred. Andrew said he'd hope to see him but would not hold him to such a promise. His other best friend, Jack Mortenson, was soon to be home on leave from the Air Force, hopefully in time for them to have a day or two together.

One morning he followed his father out to the driveway as he prepared to leave for work.

"Dad?"

"What's on your mind, Andrew? I can tell you're up to something."

"I want to go to Colorado to see Nancy. I might not get another chance, you know, before..."

"Before you go to Vietnam. Is that what you mean?"

"Yeah."

"Damn, boy. I wish you were back up at IU."

"Not me."

"Got someone to drive with?"

"Nah. Don't need anyone."

He put his arm around his son's neck and hugged him. "Talk to your mother. If she can do without her car for, uh, how long you going to be gone?"

"Two days out, two days there, two days back. Less than a week. That gives me a week at home before I go."

"If she can do without her car for a week, then it's OK with me. You remember how to get there?"

Andrew burst into a huge smile. "I-70. Thanks, Dad. I'll talk to Mom."

"When are you leaving?"

"In the morning?"

"God, boy. Whatever."

As his father's car backed out of the driveway, Andrew ran to the kitchen to speak to his mother about the car. "Of course, honey," she said, hugging him forlornly. He waited impatiently for her to go to the grocery, then began dialing the phone. He knew he should have called Nancy first, but didn't want to risk getting her excited and then not be able to get there after all. Now, he felt reborn again and his hands were shaking as he dialed '0' for directory assistance.

The phone jangled in the sorority house hallway for only a second before a pledge answered. As Andrew waited he could hear shouts of, "Spinelli! There's a man on the phone for you!" echo down the hall. After a minute, the pledge came back on. "I'm sorry. I think she's in class." His heart sank. Then suddenly, "No, wait. Here she comes."

Andrew heard the pledge put her hand over the mouthpiece and say, "It doesn't sound like Mark."

"Oh?" replied a voice. "Hello. This is Nancy."

"Hi. It's the Hoosier."

Their conversation started slowly and painfully. "Why haven't you written to me?" she asked. "You promised. Why…?"

"I'm sorry. I'm really sorry," he said. "I meant to. I've tried." She was silent for several seconds.

"Andrew…"

"Look, Nancy. Things have been pretty crazy. Can I come out to see you? I won't be there very long. I've got to see you."

She'd begun to cry. "Andrew…just a second." She waved to a friend who, seeing her, ran over with a box of tissues. "You know I want to see you. I've wanted to hear from you so badly. I'd kind of given up on you."

"I can be there on Thursday."

"Oh, my...Really? You're really coming?" Her face was a mess, and she'd balled up a handful of tissues. "Well, OK. Yes. Please come. We have to talk." She blew her nose.

"Where can I meet you?" he said, sensing something was not being said.

"Wait...Andrew. I have to tell you something first."

"Go ahead."

"I'm kind of going with a guy."

Her comment felt like a blow to his stomach. "I'm listening."

"I just want you to know that, uh..." She struggled to find words. "His name is Mark, and he's a real nice guy. We're not engaged or anything, but..."

"Maybe I'd better not come."

"No, I want to see you. Please don't misunderstand."

"Nancy, I don't want to drive all the way out there so you can tell me about your boyfriend."

"That's not fair," she said, so softly he could barely hear. She took a breath and said, "I don't know what to say." Neither did Andrew, so he just stared at the floor.

"Andrew, I want to see you so much. Why didn't you write to me? I haven't heard from you for so long. I thought you'd found someone else. I was just trying to go on with my life."

"Well, look," he said finally. "Let's start over. How's Ron getting along? Are your folks doing well?"

For the next fifteen minutes they talked as the old friends they were. She gave him all the news about her brother and his new life at the University of Denver. Her parents were fine. Then, the shocker...Their friends Wendy and Emery had gotten married and were expecting a baby any day.

"Oh, that is so great," he said. "She's just what that wild man needs."

As her news began to run out, she asked about his family and how school was going. Everyone and everything was fine, he told her. As the conversation had progressed, he realized the trip would be a mistake. Now, since he wouldn't see her and might not ever see her again, he decided not to tell her about being drafted. He knew the news would devastate her and she'd say things she might regret later. The call had already been too emotionally costly for him, and adding her to his conscience was just too much. He decided to end the call as quickly as he could without burning any bridges.

"Nancy, I've decided that coming out now is a bad idea."

"No, please Andrew…"

"Sweetie, let's let some time go by. I've hurt you and I never meant to."

She was crying again. "Please don't do this to me," she sobbed.

"Honey, please don't cry. You know I'm right. Let's just let some time pass. Things have a way of working out, if they're meant to be. Isn't that what your mom said?"

"Yes." She had to blow her nose again. "But what if my heart can't bear it?"

Several of her sorority sisters had gathered in a doorway nearby. Some were in tears themselves as they heard her anguish.

"Nancy, remember when I told you I loved you?"

"Of course I do. Do you think a girl ever forgets the first time she hears those words?" That brought a loud sob from one of the girls in the doorway. Nancy put her hand over the mouthpiece and stomped her foot at the gathering. They went back into the room and closed the door.

"Would you believe I feel it stronger now than I did then? It's just that life's not always a real smooth road. Sometime there are bumps along the way."

"Andrew, I don't understand. What are you trying to say? Are you in some sort of trouble? You can tell me. Please."

"No, no trouble. Look, I've got to get going. I'm glad I got to talk to you. You sound great."

"Oh, sure. I'm blubbering and blowing my nose. I sound great alright."

"Trust me. You've no idea…"

"Will you PLEASE write to me? Andrew, will you PROMISE me, one more time?"

"Nancy, you have someone else in your life. Let's wait and see how that turns out. If it doesn't work, drop me a note and tell me I'm back in the game."

"But, that's not fair to you," she sniffed.

This drew an ironic chuckle from him. "I can wait. I've got nothing but time. Besides, I don't have much choice, do I?"

"I feel so rotten. I really didn't expect to ever hear from you again."

"I just told you I feel more strongly about you than ever. That's not going to change anytime soon. Now you know."

"I don't know why," she sighed.

"You don't remember how it was?"

"Of course, I do. It was wonderful. I've never…"

"Look, I've really got to go. But…look. I'll write soon. Maybe…we can…I'll send you a note. You take care of yourself. OK?"

"Please write to me, Andrew. Are you sure, I mean, won't you…?"

"Nancy, just remember one thing. No matter what happens, there's a Hoosier that loves you."

"Goodbye…Andrew."

"Bye, Nancy."

~ * ~

As the busload of draftees rolled along, Starkey leaned his head against the window and tried to conduct an inventory of his short life. He knew why he was on this bus and was content with this turn of events. His call to Nancy, while devastating, had actually provided, in retrospect, a degree of comfort to him. He knew she still loved him, and he'd made it abundantly clear that he loved her, more than ever. Now she had to factor that into her relationship with the other guy.

Fuck him, he thought to himself. *She's a sophomore. She's not going to run off and get married. If I'm still alive next year…*

It seemed strange to think in such fatalistic terms. He had just turned twenty. Many on the bus were younger. Yet here he was thinking about his future in terms of someone with a life-threatening disease; *if I'm still alive…*

Vietnam was the one barrier that stood between him and what he wanted, and he was going to remove it and possibly be maimed or killed in the attempt. The longings for Nancy and his mountains, knowing what they had cost him, nevertheless cheered him. In his own mind, he was moving "West" now, but had to deal with this little detour. Had someone been standing by the roadside as the sad bus passed, they'd have seen, against the window glass, at least one smiling face…

Chapter 5
Roadtrip

It began with a 1966 graduation road-trip west with Jeff Thompson, Jeff's brother Rob and Jack Mortenson. They'd stayed a week with the Thompsons' aunt and uncle in Buena Vista, Colorado in the shadow of the Sawatch Range of the Rockies. Their small cabin included 100 feet of frontage on the Arkansas River. The boys were astounded by the massive mountains and were on the move constantly from an hour after their arrival in the Thompson-family '58 Chevrolet Bel Aire, the use of which was contingent upon Jeff taking his younger brother along on the trip. They fished the river every day for Rainbow and Brown trout, hiked to the summits of nearby peaks, explored the town, met and hung out with some locals and slept outside by the Arkansas each night. Though they all loved their long drive west, the high mountain country and the strenuous activities they shared, the effect on Starkey had been visceral.

The fascination built up gradually as the four boys left their Ohio River town in Indiana and traversed southern Illinois towards their first goal of St. Louis. As they crossed the Mississippi via a dilapidated nineteenth-century iron bridge, the forbidding office towers of the old river city seemed to bar the way to any further movement west. But soon they were presented with a confusing and intimidating array of highway signage and there was nowhere to pull off to consult their map. However, just before taking a wrong turn that would have sent them into the rundown bowels of the city's waterfront, Andrew spied the tri-color shield of the pathway that would take them all the way to Denver.

"Hey, there's I-70!" he yelled excitedly. "Bear right. Yeah, that's it. We're on it, baby!"

Now they were engulfed in a multi-lane race track of speeding cars and trundling semis that none of them had ever experienced before. Jeff's hands were clued, white knuckled to the steering wheel, eyes darting left and right as horns honked at the old Chevy's wide-eyed passengers.

"Shit! I'm going 60 and these assholes are all going 80!" Jeff shouted over the traffic noise.

Jack was ecstatic with the spectacle of their sudden plunge into the organized chaos of big city traffic. "Speed the fuck up then!" he yelled. "We'll get run over otherwise!"

Soon enough, the Chevy was pacing the other vehicles, and they could laugh at themselves for their initial panic.

"I guess the cops can't stop you for speeding if every son of a bitch is doing the same thing," Jack surmised.

In the back seat Rob clicked a half-dozen pictures of the recently completed Gateway Arch before it and the Mississippi riverfront disappeared behind them. The others chided him later for his flatlander reaction to something so tall.

"Man, you've got to knock it off," said Jeff. "You'll be broke from the cost of film by the time we get to Kansas City. Save your shots for when we get to Colorado."

"That's right," said Andrew Starkey, "unless we see naked women running down the highway."

"Fuckin' A," agreed Jack. "There's supposed to be thousands of naked women running in huge herds all across Kansas."

"You're shitting me," said Rob, younger by three years than these recent graduates, and comically gullible.

"No, man," said Andrew joining back in. "What's funny is when cars or trucks get too close to the herd, they turn their backs, bend over and fart in unison. The noise is deafening. Been known to blow out windshields." He tried hard to keep a straight face and continued. "In the 1870s, when the railroad first came through, they would blow trains right off the tracks."

Rob looked around red-faced as the other boys howled. "I knew you were shitting me," he said.

"Will you watch your foul mouth?" said his brother Jeff. "When you're 18 and I'm long gone you can swear all you want. What am I going to do with you?"

"Let me drive."

"No fucking way," said his brother, as his friends howled again. "You know, you bastards are not helping at all."

Soon the St. Louis megalopolis began to thin out and the highway began its nearly beeline orientation westward. Every few miles the "I-70 West" shield appeared and, for Andrew at least, became an indelible symbol of youthful freedom, optimism and a sense that life in general can only get better if he kept moving in the right direction. That direction had to be "west."

On their new I-70 pathway, Missouri melted away in five hours, though the route was marred by an obscenity of billboards. Everything was advertised ad nauseam, from restaurants, truck-stops, tourist traps, radio stations and even churches. By late afternoon, they'd passed through Kansas City and crossed the Missouri River. Entering Kansas the older boys began a search for a promising exit from their highway, looking for a grocery store. Spying a suburban Safeway, they pulled into the large parking area, got out to stretch and collected all their accumulated car trash to dispose of in the dumpster at the side of the building. They entered the store expectantly and, having become conditioned to the blistering summer heat and even hotter car, were stunned by the store's air conditioning. Within minutes, they were shivering.

Rob went off on his own, but the older boys headed straight for the coolers that lined the back wall of the store. Kansas allowed 18 year olds to drink 3.2% beer, a legacy of the "Prohibition" era, and a virtual fairyland of the suds welcomed them. They gleefully perused the vast selection of six-packs and cases.

"Oh, man. Just look at that shit," said Jack. "I've died and gone to heaven."

The three walked up and down the length of the cooler, carefully considering the stacked, ice cold packs of Coors, Hamms, Falstaff, Budweiser, Schlitz and Miller.

"Jack, they don't have Falls City," reported Starkey. "Doesn't your old man come this far?"

"No, man. Just Kentucky and Indiana. Besides, they don't make 3.2."

"Hey, let's get a case of Coors and a case of Bud," said Starkey. "Maybe two of Coors."

Jeff responded, "We'd better hold it to two cases. Otherwise, we'll have to sit on it."

"Fuckin' A", said Jack. "Besides, it's 3.2 from now on, even in Colorado. We can stop and get more anytime we want." Then he said, "Man, let's get out of here. I'm fucking freezing!"

"OK, one Coors, one Bud. Everyone agreed?" asked Starkey.

"Yep. Let's hit the trail."

"One six-pack of Hamms, OK?"

"Yeah, fine, but let's get the fuck out of here."

The lady at the checkout line was amused by the novice beer buyers and asked where they were from. She also checked their IDs carefully.

"We're flatland Hoosiers," said Jeff. "We don't get out much."

"Well, don't you boys drink all this in one sitting. Take it easy, and don't drink in your car. If I hear you've splattered yourselves all over I-70 because I'm selling you this beer, they'll have to put me in the looney bin."

"No ma'am," said Starkey. "We'll take it easy and find a nice safe place to blow down all this beer."

"Wait a minute. Where's Rob?" asked Jeff. "Oh, there he is. Ma'am, please add whatever he's got to the bill."

"Well here's a big, healthy, sensible boy. At least one of you won't be sick tonight."

Rob had laid a plastic bag full of carrots on the conveyer.

"Honey, who broke that cute nose?" she cooed.

"Football," answered Rob. "It only hurts when I sneeze."

"Well, it makes you look dignified." She turned to the others with a stern look. "Don't you older boys feed beer to this young one either. He's a sweetheart. His time for beer drinking is a ways off yet. You hear me, now?" The woman's concern was very real and heartfelt.

"Don't worry, ma'am," said Jeff. "He's my brother and I watch him real close. He won't touch a drop."

The bill was just short of $9.00. The boys each threw in a few dollars, picked up their treasure and strode happily to the exit. Once outside, they stopped and basked in the superheated air.

"Fuckin' A, I thought I was going to freeze to death in that store," said Jack.

At the car, they hurriedly rearranged pillows, magazines and snack boxes to make room for the beer cases. As they pulled out, the treasure rested comfortably, stacked between Andrew and Rob in the back seat.

"Let's get a motel room, man," said Starkey. "I need a shower bad, and then I'm going to drink this whole case of Coors."

"That OK with everybody?" answered Jeff. "I'm game for stopping but if anybody feels strongly about bagging a few more miles, speak up."

"Motel, with a pool," said Jack.

"Let's drive for several more hours," said Rob, his speech muffled by the carrots he was chewing.

"You don't get a vote," answered his brother. "What do you have in your mouth? Jeez, why don't you swallow some of it?"

As they rubber-necked the straight commercial strip for an affordable motel, the car halted at a busy intersection. A portly lady and pre-teen girl stood hand in hand waiting to cross the street at the light.

"Watch this," mumbled Rob, carrot particles flying from his mouth. With that, he opened the right rear door of the car and leaned far out towards the curb. Feigning nausea, he noisily vomited the carrot-saliva mixture into the gutter. The barfing sounds he evoked were clinically precise and well rehearsed.

The woman drew her hand to her mouth in shock, then quickly moved the same hand to cover the girl's eyes. Both then retreated several steps, watching in horror as Rob spit out a final orange blob and slammed the car door closed. He rested his head in his hand against the window jamb and moaned pitifully.

Jack and Andrew were bent over in their seats, howling hysterically, tears streaming down their faces. Jeff had seen little of the display, but heard enough to know they'd best move on as soon as possible. Seconds later the light changed and they could proceed. He drove away cautiously, hands at ten and two, fearing that to be pulled over now for any infraction would find them in big trouble. He had a vision of that lady running up to the cop and recounting the horror she'd witnessed and the trauma visited on her poor child. Lawsuits and jail time would surely follow. He watched the two females in his mirror to see what they would do, and was relieved to see them shortly cross the street behind them.

"Man, I hope she didn't get our license number and call the cops," said Jeff.

"Why?" said Rob. "There's no law against puking around here, is there?

The others we're still trying to contain themselves and were pounding Rob on the back in congratulations.

"That was the funniest God damn thing I've ever seen in my life," Jack bellowed. "Rob, you've got shotgun on any road trip I ever take. Holy shit, that was funny!"

Jeff insisted that they put several miles between the puke episode and their motel. The commercial street they followed was the old highway, running for miles parallel to the new Interstate so, as they drove, there was no let-up in the number of inns to select from. Eventually, they agreed on a $20 per night option that had a large pool surrounded by grass lawn between the office's awning-shaded parking area and the highway. They got their keys, unloaded their suitcases and hauled in all the beer, being careful to shield it from the prying eyes of the front-desk manager. In minutes, they were heading to the pool, a dozen beers wrapped in a bath towel from the room.

Why they were concerned puzzled Jack. He said, "Man, it's legal out here. You guys are so conditioned to sneaking around for a couple beers that you're becoming psycho about it. Lighten up for Christ's sake. Now, repeat after me. 'I'm 18, and it's 3.2. I'm 18, and it's 3.2'."

His words did seem to have a calming effect on them. Still they were reluctant to flaunt their new alcohol freedom and only sipped their beers with their backs turned to the main office. Jeff in particular watched to make sure Rob didn't get into it, and all agreed that maintaining the younger boy's sobriety would be inarguable.

Indeed, none of them had been big drinkers in High School. Each had watchful parents, and they were not allowed to keep late hours. There had been, however, a few camping trips, one of which involved a fast get-away and police pursuit. Instead of spending a night in sleeping bags around a campfire, Andrew Starkey and Jack Mortenson had run with a case of beer for miles through muddy fields and over fences, all the while dodging a sheriff's spot light that scanned the area in search of them. Alcohol had been a much larger problem for some of their best school friends. 'Fat Chuck' Elliot, Sean Murphy and few others were becoming notorious boozers and seemed well on the way to alcoholism.

Soon they were all in the pool. No other guests were yet around. The sun was still high in the sky, the temperature hovering above 90 degrees, though it was now past 6PM. Andrew Starkey floated on his back, sun-glassed eyes staring towards the blue sky. He held a Coors on his stomach and paddled a lazy circle with his free hand. He grinned over at Jack and said, "You know, I don't think it can get any better than this."

Jack had let two open beers float free at opposite ends of the pool. He'd sidestroke to one, take a swig, then turn and sidestroke to the other end and take a swig there. On one circuit, he spit out the beer because chlorine water had partially filled the bobbing bottle.

"What a waste," he muttered to himself.

After a half hour of floating and drying off on the warm concrete deck, Rob sat up quickly and exclaimed, "Uh oh." He rose to his feet and exclaimed, "Who's got the key? I got to go take a dump." Rob stumbled across the parking lot doubled over, holding his stomach. As he reached the door he fumbled briefly with the key and dropped it on the doormat. Instead of reaching down for it, he suddenly stood erect and reached behind himself and pushed on his backside. Then he went down for the key, found the lock and rushed inside, leaving the door ajar.

"I believe the boy's got the screamers," observed Andrew. "That'll teach him to blow down a whole sack of raw carrots."

"Well, it didn't appear he swallowed too many by the look of that pile in the gutter," laughed Jack. "Of course, we're probably all in for it with all the shit we've been eating since Indiana. Jeff, how many Slim Jims do you think you've eaten?"

"Oh, about one every ten miles. I suppose I could go off any time myself."

They soon forgot about Rob and continued to enjoy their private pool and deck.

The three swimmers eventually decided it was time to get serious about an evening meal and gathered their towels, empty cans and bottles and headed back to the room.

"Now, where's he been?" asked Jeff as he noticed his brother stroll along the walkway that fronted the dozen motel rooms. They arrived together at the door and Rob waved them in with a bowing flourish.

"Aagggg!" they all howled.

"This place smells like a pile of shit!" said Jack.

"About sums it up. Man, I'm completely cleaned out and won't go again for two weeks."

Jeff went into the bathroom and opened the small sliding window above the tub. Andrew stood at the front door, opening and closing it to serve as an exhaust fan. Jack had cranked up the ancient black and white television and clicked through the three channels over and over. All were covering a sniper shooting that had taken place at the University of Texas in Austin. They watched for several minutes, speculating among themselves what could possibly have motivated the shooter, but soon their hunger took over and they locked up the room and headed for the car.

Between drinking in their room upon arrival and having a few more at the pool, Jack and Andrew had each finished a fifth 3.2 beer. Both were happily buzzed and singing profane lyrics to songs on the car radio. Jeff had held himself to only one beer, still a bit concerned that he not ask for trouble should they be stopped. He retained visions of an "All Points Bulletin" being in place, with officers on the look-out for an older Chevy with Indiana plates. The occupants were teenage sickos who needed to be taken off the streets as soon as possible. As they left the parking lot, he headed west, away from town.

A mile down the highway they spotted and agreed upon a place advertising a $3.50 buffet; somewhat pricey but it was "all you can eat." As luck would have it, it had a bar area that served 3.2 beer. Jeff and his brother went ahead and got in the long line, while the other two decided to have one beer, the first time either had sat on a barstool in an honest to goodness bar. It had a 10-for-a-dollar jukebox, and they stood happily at the box selecting songs and taking swigs from their Budweisers. After the fourth song, they'd finished their beer, agreed it wouldn't be a great idea to have another one, and joined their friends in the dining room. They piled their plates high with fried chicken, Swiss steak, mashed potatoes and gravy and coleslaw. In turn, each finished their plate and went for refills. Within thirty minutes they were slumped in their booth seats, silent and uncomfortable.

"Hey, didn't I see a softball tournament going on at that park next door?" asked Andrew, starting to stir. "Let's walk over there and check it out."

"Yeah," said Jack, "...might be some chicks."

There was, indeed, a raucous ball game in progress with dozens of locals picnicking in the bleachers and cheering their teams. The four found a less-crowded section and sat down together. After watching a complete inning, Jack looked around in his beer-induced euphoria at the happy people, the exuberant whooping players, the warm afterglow of the setting sun on the western horizon and said, "Man, this is my kind of town. Just leave me here and pick me up on the way back."

"The way back from where?" asked Jeff. "The motel?"

"No, man. Colorado."

"Yeah, right!" said Rob. "You think someone will invite you home with them when the game's over? We'll find your skeleton lying right here when we come back."

"Fuckin' A, and I'd die a happy and contented man."

He leaned back to the bleacher bench behind him, spread his arms wide between two groups of giggling girls, rolled his head left and right and grinned devilishly at each. The girls had been watching the boys cutting up and joking among themselves. Now Jack had decided to get acquainted using his emerging road charm.

"Hey ladies," he began. "which team you pulling for?"

"Oh, we don't care," answered a cute little brunette, not a day over sixteen. "You guys aren't from around here, are you?"

"Nah," he answered. "We're Hoosiers from Indiana, on our way to Colorado to climb mountains."

Andrew, uncharacteristically quiet, was leaning forward and had his feet on the bench in front of him. Then he put his head between his knees.

"Stark, you OK?" asked Jeff. "Stark?"

"No, man," he muttered. "Sick."

"Oh, great," said Rob. "Starkey's going to barf. Actually, that would be a treat."

"Shut up, Rob, or I'll point him at you," Jeff threatened. "Come on, Starkey. Let's get you out of here."

Andrew looked up from his bent-over position and was clearly sick as a dog, his face bathed in sweat. With urgency, he lurched to his knees on the lower bench, braced himself with one hand and clamped the other over his mouth.

"Better look out below!" yelled Jeff to the fans a few rows down, directly in front of Starkey. Those people, an elderly couple and a half-dozen grade school kids, perceived the threat and sidestepped quickly left and right. Rob had pulled his Instamatic from his baggy shorts pocket, wound it up and lined up his shot.

Starkey vomited violently seconds later, Rob clicking away. After the first monumental wretch, he collected himself, hocking and spitting repeatedly. Then he vomited again, less violently this time but producing a volume of liquid equal to the first spasm. There was unmistakable foaming in the vomit that had pooled on the seats and now rained audibly to the ground below.

Jack's new friends screamed and climbed quickly to the top row. They looked back only briefly. Jack watched them leave, and muttered "shit!" under his breath.

"Oh my, look at the time," Rob said, holding up his arm and melodramatically viewing his wristwatch. "We must be on our way to the symphony."

The pandemonium in the bleachers subsided as the fans retreated far from the scene and took safer seats. The game had continued with no interruption at all. The on-deck batter had turned at the first sick sounds and gave his mates in the dugout a brief description. A few baseball-capped heads had poked up, looking above the roof to the seats, but quickly returned to their game.

Starkey was escorted by his friends down the steps, back between the sets of bleachers, and towards the restaurant's parking lot. Jeff and Rob had propped him up as he descended the steps, but once on level ground, he was given a wide berth. At the car he wiped his face with a motel towel, even wiping his tongue with the thick terrycloth.

"Man, I had those chicks lined up," moaned Jack. Actually, he was suddenly not feeling real chipper himself and didn't dwell on the lost opportunity. Andrew had regained enough composure to speak. He said, "Shit! I just puked up a $3.50 buffet, five Coors and a Budweiser. What a goddamn waste."

He was given first use of the shower back at the motel. He dressed quickly in clean shorts and T-shirt, then ran across the highway to a brightly lit drive in offering fifteen cent burgers.

"Damn," said Jeff as he marveled at Andrew's recovered appetite and watched him run across the road. "Wish we'd gone there in the first place."

In the morning, they packed and loaded quickly, the anticipation of the open road before them adding a giddiness to their preparations. Starkey seemed none the worse for wear, no doubt due to the spectacular purging of poisons his body had undergone the evening before.

Jeff said, "Rob, give me your swimming trunks. I'll put them in this bag with the rest. They'll dry in the trunk."

"They're gone. I got rid of them."

"What do you mean, 'you got rid of them.'?" Jeff asked, puzzled.

"Threw them away. When I had the screamers, some squirted out into my trunks. I couldn't hold it in."

Jack heard the exchange and said, "Hey, man. That's what soap is for. You wash it out, let 'em dry and wear 'em again. You can't throw your clothes away when they get dirty."

"It wasn't dirt, man," responded Rob. "It was shit. I'm not wearing shit clothes again."

Patiently, Jeff asked "Well, which can did you put them in. Maybe they're still there and we can dig them out."

"Can't do it. They're gone. Forget about it," said Rob, irritation rising in his voice.

"Look Rob. Those cost eight bucks. You'll need them when we get where we're going and I don't know if there are any stores in Buena Vista. Where the fuck are those trunks?"

"On the roof."

"What?"

"On the Goddamn roof," Rob repeated. He began to laugh, his face beet red.

They all turned to look at him.

"You threw your swimming trunks up on the roof?" his exasperated brother asked.

"No. I threw my shit-stained, stinking swimming trunks up on the roof."

"Is that what you were doing when we saw you walking down the walkway when we came back from the pool?" said Jack.

"Yep. I didn't want them in the room. Didn't want them in the car, either. I didn't want some poor cleaning lady finding them in the wastebasket," he said. "I looked all over for a dumpster or can outside. Couldn't find one, and I sure wasn't going to take them down to the office. So, when I got down to the end of the building, I walked back a ways and heaved them up on the roof."

The others were laughing now in amazement. Rob continued. "My throw was off, and now they're hanging over the side. I'll show you when we leave."

Sure enough, as they drove past the end of the long row of rooms, Rob pointed back at the trunks hanging half off the gutter.

"Well," said Starkey, "the janitor will be real sorry when he fishes them down with a broom handle."

"Jeez, Rob. If I'd known you were going to be this comical, I'd have started taking road trips with you long ago," said Jack. "What your mind conjures up is truly amazing."

Jeff glanced back at Andrew in the rear view mirror. "How you feeling, Stark?"

"Fine buddy. Let's make like a horse turd and hit the dusty trail."

An hour later, Jeff pulled over to pay the toll for a stretch of turnpike to Topeka, the approach to which was announced by numerous rumble strips. Past the toll gate, Jeff pulled up and Starkey ran around to the driver position. Jeff felt obligated to drive the whole distance if possible since it was his car, but it had no power steering, or power anything for that matter, and his shoulders ached from yesterday's drive.

Starkey was transformed now with the uniquely American feeling arising from the freedom of the open road and the vast, uncluttered horizon before them. The high plains vistas were beyond his previous imagination and a subtle, subliminal reordering of his personality began.

I-70 was an awesome highway and nothing in their very limited driving experiences prepared them for it. The miserable and accident-intense Highway 41 that passed through their small city was a goat path by comparison. The unheard of speed limit of 75 was also a thrill though they each agreed to hold it back for fear of overheating the car's small eight cylinder engine. They sailed along, windows open, radio blasting tunes from whatever station could be gained. These became fewer and farther between as they traversed Kansas.

The Interstate seemed to reach higher as it sliced through each successive limestone hill, as if climbing steps of a subtle, continental staircase. The countryside, as well, changed as they climbed out of the Kansas River region and passed by Salina. Lush and green initially, it turned dry and beige from horizon to horizon. Half way across Kansas they began to imagine that the Rockies would become visible at the top of the next rise; if not this one, then for sure the next.

"So Jeff," asked Jack as the Chevy got back up to speed after a rest stop, " why were you so worked up about Rob's fake barf-a-rama, and completely unconcerned when Stark really had a blow out?" He had to raise his voice to overcome the road noise.

"Oh, I guess I've been reading too much. I've been studying the Theory of Torts, Tort Law, you know, when people sue each other for things. I'm like a medical student that thinks he's got symptoms of every disease he studies."

"Actually," he continued, "what Rob did could theoretically end up in court with lawyers defending us from the charges that lady might bring against us. I know I'm paranoid. You asked, so I'm telling you what I was thinking."

Andrew said, "Say, Jeff, you're really getting into this law shit, huh?"

"I am, indeed. If I can get through Wabash, I'm going to try for law school someplace. Maybe IU."

"I may still be there when you come down," said Starkey. "No way I'll finish in four years. Makes me want to puke again just thinking about it."

"You'd better stay full-time," Jack interjected. "Otherwise, they'll draft your ass. You ought to consider the Air Force. I'm going to see the world from the window of my luxurious C-141 Starlifter."

"You're shipping out in October, right?" asked Starkey.

"October 9th to Lackland Air Force Base, San Antonio, Texas. You guys will be freezing your asses off in Indiana and I'll be in the sunny south."

"Then what will you do after they train you?" asked Rob. He was leaning up and resting his chin on his hands on the seatback. Jack's enlistment in the Air Force fascinated him.

"I'll go to loadmaster school, not for sure where. They teach you how to load and unload the cargo on the bird. How to distribute weight, how to hook up parachutes to air drop the pallets. All kinds of complicated shit. I can't wait."

"That sounds so cool," said Rob. "I'm going to do something like that when I get out of school."

"I thought you were going to be a football star," said Starkey. "Aren't you starting two-a-days when we get back?"

"Yeah," answered Rob. "Don't remind me. If I'm not in shape, Coach Collins will pound me into paste. This trip is cutting into practice and he's not amused at all that I'm not there."

"He'll get over it," said his brother. "Remember, he needs raw meat and you were one of his best Freshman players. He won't want to risk having you drop out because he's a hard-ass about a special trip out west. Hell, his starting quarterback is in Europe 'til Labor Day."

"That's 'former' starting quarterback," said Rob. "Kevin Swartz will start until Schlensker gets up to speed. I'd guess he'll start the Homecoming game, not before."

Starkey rose up in the seat and looked off in the distance. "Crap. Looks like we're losing the Interstate."

They'd just passed through Hays and were detoured back to the old road, US 40. The new highway could be seen periodically, under construction off to the north. For the next few hundred miles before picking it up again near Limon, Colorado, the road would be an agonizingly slow progression of tiny towns, each appearing on the horizon as an off-white grain elevator. Unlike the Interstate, the old road snaked around the low hills giving only hints of the vistas that had been nearly constant. The driver had to be more attentive now to watch for side-road traffic, to pass cars, to be passed and to hold the car steady in the wind blast from oncoming trucks. Conversation all but ceased due to the increased driver tension and road noise.

Jack dozed, Rob busied himself with his Instamatic and Jeff read a new Time Magazine he'd bought when they stopped for lunch in Russell. Starkey still preferred to drive and avoided the stiffness suffered by Jeff because his head was moving constantly, looking ahead, then north horizon to south horizon with every hilltop view the highway provided. Back in Indiana it was rare to see a view beyond the next wall of deciduous forest or corn.

"Hey, look you guys!" shouted Starkey. Each of them struggled to emerge from their road stupors and looked down the highway. In the distance on the right stood a large, brown, log-framed sign. In two-foot high letters, it read:

"WELCOME TO
COLORFUL COLORADO"

A few cars were pulled off the highway and tourists were snapping pictures of each other in front of it. The Chevy joined them and they piled out with their cameras. A fellow tourist took a picture of the four together, snapping each boy's camera in succession. As they explored the area around the welcome site, Starkey headed towards railroad tracks fifty yards to the north. He noticed a two-foot concrete piling that had "Kansas" stenciled on the right side and "Colorado" on the left. This discovery required one more set of pictures as they, in turn, sat on the post with a leg in each state.

In twenty minutes they were back on the highway and looking for a place to camp for the night. In expectation a site would come up soon, they stopped at a grocery in Burlington and bought hotdogs and the traditional condiments. It had been a long, hot day and the 3.2 beer was beckoning.

A few miles beyond, a private campground appeared and Starkey pulled in. A price of $8 for the night seemed like a bargain, especially since their site was shaded by a large fir tree and had a well with a pump handle close by. Though they had a canvas tarp, they decided to forego a shelter and, instead, used it as a floor for their austere camp. They bought bags of ice from the camp manager and iced down the Coors cans in their cardboard case.

With the performance of last night still fresh in his mind, not to mention a somewhat achy head, Starkey held himself to less than a six-pack. Jack and Jeff were similarly conservative. Rob, being the hungriest, volunteered to build the fire and cook while his traveling companions leaned on their sleeping bags and sipped beer. After supper they formed a large square and threw bullet passes to each other, then took turns on the pump handle, rinsing off under the icy flow. All were in their bags as the sun set, and were soon lulled to sleep by the plains wind in the grass and the whine of wheels on the highway.

They were on the road again as the sun rose. The anticipation of finally seeing the Rockies, not to mention hunger, had them rolling long before the other campers stirred. In the crystal clear air of early morning, they saw the first mass of Pikes Peak shortly before descending into the Big Sandy Creek drainage where the town of Limon lay. A truck-stop buffet fueled them for the remaining three-hour drive to Denver, and they soon celebrated their return to the new I-70. A half hour more and the entire western horizon, north to south, displayed a gray-green wall of foothills, behind which protruded high, snowy peaks.

An argument ensued. "Those are clouds," said Rob. "Man, those are mountains," countered Andrew. But the debate evaporated as the distance closed and removed any doubt that the granite, sandstone, gneiss and schist barrier was not moving with the wind. In the center, squatting as if it were the headboard of some monstrous bed, was Mt. Evans. As they neared the eastern suburbs, the mountain's position as awesome backdrop to the capitol city made the sprawling metropolis even more intimidating.

The Chevy was on an elevated portion of the Interstate and rolled past stockyards and old neighborhoods with small brick homes. A confusing highway confluence with I-25 sent them south towards the city's center. They exited on Speer Boulevard, crossed the South Platte River and a busy railroad corridor. Numerous track sidings and the clock-topped Union Station dominated the view to their left.

At a stop light, Jeff began flipping through the pages of a dog-eared copy of "On the Road" he'd been carrying in the back pocket of his Levis.

"Boys, that's Larimer Street. You've got to indulge me for a while. I've got to walk in the footsteps of Kerouac."

Their plans included a dinner-time arrival at their destination in Buena Vista. Any later and their hosts would worry. So, given that it was now mid-morning, and allowing for a four-hour drive to Buena Vista, they had plenty of time to explore the town on foot.

The Chevy pulled into the large lot in front of Union Station and the boys piled out to stretch and use the building's restroom. Scores of people filled the cavernous waiting area. Many sat on massive turn-of-the-century wooden benches with their suitcases stacked nearby. Others milled around in boredom. The public address speaker was announcing the arrival of the Denver "Zephyr" from Chicago, and friends and family members crowded the doorway to the platform to greet new arrivals.

"Man, you can't stir them with a stick," Jack commented on the large crowd.

Outside, the city streets were also crowded with a mix of office workers, shoppers and tourists enjoying the warm summer morning. Lunchtime was approaching and the sidewalks teemed with those hoping to beat the rush to restaurants and sidewalk vendors selling hotdogs or odd Mexican-sounding concoctions.

"What do you figure a 'Burr Re Too' is?" asked Rob. No one knew.

"I wouldn't eat anything that guy touched," observed Jack. "Bet he lives in that cart."

Jeff herded the group the few blocks up to Larimer Street. He looked left and right, then directed them left. As they walked, the more seedy and run-down the storefronts and bars became. The worse it got, the more Jeff seemed to revel in the surroundings.

"Jack Kerouac and Neal Cassidy probably shoot pool in this dive," he said as he looked through the window of a very dark and sinister looking tavern.

A man nursing a beer at the bar yelled out the door, "Hey Gringo, chinga su madre!"

Embarrassed, Jeff backed away from the window and caught up with the others who had continued up the street.

"What did he say?" asked Andrew.

Jeff scratched his head. "Not sure. Something about 'mother'."

"You just got called a Mexican motherfucker!" Jack cackled.

Uncharacteristically quiet and contemplative, Andrew was really enjoying the tour. He'd always loved the noise and smell of trains and, particularly, the bustle of train stations, so his first indelible impression of Denver was excellent. He knew the rails led to the mountains and he could barely contain his desire to get the Chevy rolling again. But the sidewalk crowds of mostly young people intrigued him and he tried to imagine what they did in their jobs, where they lived, what they did for fun. It just had to be a fabulous place to live.

Pretty girls seemed the rule rather than the exception and, so far, Jack hadn't made any of his infamous "corn-fed heifer" comments, or worse. When passing heavy girls in the high school hallways he'd often make a circle of his thumb and forefinger, pressed them to his lips and make the sound of a squealing sow. Though this had entertained Andrew Starkey and other friends, it had, on one occasion, started a fight with a girl's boyfriend and, on another, gotten him expelled for the day when the object of his humor reported him to the Principal. Instead, he and Andrew traded comments and observations: "Holy shit. Did you see the tits on that babe?" and "Don't look now. Ok, now. Check out the knockers on that blonde." and, "Oh shit, look at the wheels on that chick. Man, this place is unbelievable. Oooh, look at that one." They'd never seen so many mini-skirts.

But Larimer Street wasn't like that; not by a long shot. Winos and derelicts sprawled in doorways. Vomit and even blood could occasionally be seen on the sidewalk. Police cars patrolled, and officers would roust the denizens of the many barrooms. Alleys were used as bathrooms. Panhandlers pestered them as they walked along.

Shortly, the novelty of Larimer Street wore thin and, crossing the street, they backtracked. In a few blocks they returned to the bustling sidewalk crowds and pretty girls. After a half hour walk they came upon the state capitol building with its golden dome. Civic Center Plaza and the public library were nearby. Even in the center of the city, a look west down Colfax Avenue provided a view of the imposing Front Range.

"Come on, Andrew. I think you'll want to see this," said Jeff, perusing a tourist map he'd picked up at Union Station. While Jack and Rob ate hotdogs on the steps outside the library, Jeff and Andrew went inside to search out the original Albert Bierstadt oil paintings of Rocky Mountain vistas.

"Can they really look like that?" asked Andrew, incredulous at the vistas represented on the huge canvases.

"Well, if they're even close, I won't complain," answered Jeff.

When they arrived back at the car they were exhausted and grateful to flop down on the Chevy's soft seats. Andrew lifted the blanket that hid their stash of beer. "The inventory is secure," he commented, relief in his voice. "If those winos on Larimer had known this stuff was here, they'd have busted out the windows to get at it."

As the Chevy hummed across the high and vast plateau known as South Park, Jeff said, "Hey, I forgot to tell you all something. Mom says that the way to get Uncle Bill to warm up to us is to learn the proper pronunciation of the mineral he used to mine. It's called 'molybdenum'. She said if we can all say and, better yet, spell it, we'll have him in the palms of our hands." So, as they drove along, they took turns spelling and pronouncing 'molybdenum' over and over. They even practiced using it in a sentence: "So, Uncle Bill. I understand you used to mine mo-lyb-den-um. What are the various uses of mo-lyb-den-um, Uncle Bill?" Each would feign the demeanor of an awestruck child. Of course, Jack broke them up with his rendition, to wit, "So, Uncle Bill, what the fuck does one do with this fucking mo-lyb-den-um? Oh, it adds strength to steel? No fucking shit? That is truly fucking amazing."

The Chevy crossed Trout Creek Pass and as they sailed around a long sweeping curve, the majestic Collegiate Peaks Range filled the horizon from north to south. Mt. Princeton, through their windshield, shocked them with its colossal mass and the peak's gray-white brilliance above a carpet of pine forest, all contrasting with a cobalt blue sky.

At a "T" intersection, they turned north and soon passed a sign that announced "Buena Vista, Altitude 7,964 feet." The pastoral scene was marred only by a state reformatory that occupied several acres of the Arkansas River's ancient flood plain.

"Cassidy did some time there," offered Jeff. The others failed to consider that fact as thus making the ugly compound an acceptable part of the natural scenery. Jack read the directions and had Jeff turn east on a gravel road, cross the D&RG tracks and head towards the river. A half mile further they turned into the driveway of a rustic cabin with attached carport where a feast of Rainbow trout awaited them, prepared by "Uncle Bill."

Chapter 6
Reception Station

About halfway to Louisville, the busload of draftees was given a 10- minute break to stretch at a roadside park. Though the bus had a bathroom, it was small and now getting putrid from overuse.

As the two friends strolled the grassy yard Rich observed, "Don't this make you kind of feel like we're convicts working on a road gang? Got the bus driver guard and a bunch of low-lifes milling around thinking about making a run for it." Andrew chuckled at the comparison but didn't join in as he normally would have. Instead, the Colorado musings continued.

"I'm not sure what hit me, man," he said, "but I've got to get back out there as soon as I can. You just can't believe those mountains."

"Well, maybe this Army shit will give you time to plan your move. You know, save some money, check out where to live. When we get out you'll be loaded with cash and can drive out there in a new Corvette."

"You know how much we're getting paid?" asked Andrew.

"No. Do you?"

"$90 a month."

"No shit?"

"$90 a month. I think a Corvette's around $8,000. What's that work out to?"

Rich thought for a while. "About eight years, I guess. Well, maybe a Ford Pinto then."

They laughed together at the thought (neither would wish to be seen riding in, let alone owning, such a car). But neither had really given much thought to their pay, given the numerous other concerns at hand.

Back on the bus, and after several quiet minutes of watching the farmland pass by outside the window, Rich looked over at Andrew and said, "I guess we're really fucked."

"Man, let's just take it a day at a time. You never know. It might be fun."

"Oh, I know one thing for sure. It ain't gonna be fun."

Buses from many locations arrived at the Induction Center in Louisville at 8AM and the men unloaded and filed through the door of a World War II-vintage, white-frame building and into a classroom. Similar buildings appeared to fill a large area. They were ordered to take seats and sit quietly as soldiers in starched fatigues passed out dozens of forms to each man.

An imperious E-4 "Specialist" next instructed them in excruciating, monotonous, condescending detail how to fill them out. "Failure to properly fill out" this or that form, said the Specialist, could result in terrible penalties up to and including a stint in the military prison at Ft. Leavenworth. That to "properly" fill out the same forms would most likely sentence the men to a tour in Vietnam was, no doubt, an irony that had not occurred to him. Names, aliases, addresses, previous addresses, next of kin, education, job history, criminal record, etc., seemed to be needed on several similar government forms. Yet another contained a list of hundreds of subversive, anti-American groups and each man scanned the names to make sure he'd not inadvertently joined some Communist front organization while in High School.

With most of the forms behind them, they were shepherded to a medical area and given a cursory physical. Blood, urine and "turn your head and cough" tests were accomplished quickly by enlisted medics. Then the men were taken to a mess hall for their first Army meal. They ate quickly and quietly, and returned one by one to the classroom.

Rich and Starkey sat together and rolled eyes at each other as the Specialist, probably in the Army little more than a year himself and clearly without overseas duty, barked the next set of directions to the men. "A senior officer" he said would be addressing them in a few minutes, and they'd best show him the utmost courtesy and respect, "or I'll have you low-crawling around the area for the rest of the afternoon."

When the Specialist left the room, Rich said, "Man, doesn't that little prick know we can handle this shit without the threats and insults?"

Starkey answered, "Consider the source, man."

Shortly, a Captain came in to address the men. His professional bearing was the direct opposite of the Specialist. His uniform was the "greens" version of a civilian business suit, and was crisp and well-tailored. Impressive brass insignia and rows of ribbons adorned his chest, no doubt, reflective of much overseas duty. High on each shoulder was a colorful patch. The one on the left had a large letter "A" in a circle, and the one on the right was a strange multi-colored triangle containing a stylized cannon and tank tread.

He spoke to the men in a friendly, almost fatherly fashion and one could feel the tension in the classroom ease as he explained what the rest of their day here would consist of. Next on the agenda was a battery of tests, he told them. One of those would be the "AFQT" or

"Armed Forces Qualification Test". It was not long, would be graded quickly, he said, and might very well play a huge role in their upcoming military service. He admonished them to take the test seriously, no matter how easy or difficult they found it to be. That test would be followed by other psychological and aptitude tests. Again, he stressed the need for the men to be serious, give their best efforts and great benefit might accrue to those showing special abilities. "After all," he said, "the Army isn't just the infantry as I can personally attest. I'm an Armor officer and commanded a tank company in Vietnam." What he said next shocked many of them. "I was drafted just like you, back in '65. I took the very tests you'll be taking and was offered an opportunity to attend Officer Candidate School." The men listened with rapt attention. "You may be draftees, you may not want to be here," he continued, "but if you consider this day to be the first day of the rest of your lives, you will never regret seizing the opportunities that this day may very well provide you." He paused a second, then said, "OK, men?" A few feeble "OKs" came back from the men. "OK?" he said again, thundering this time! "OK!" yelled the men in unison. "OK!" he said, and smiled.

He saluted them and walked out. One young man jumped to his feet and saluted the Captain's back as he left. This generated a few snickers, but the sight of the Specialist coming back in the same door brought the room back to its somber mood.

It was mid-afternoon before the tests were done. Those finishing earliest were taken outside to "police the area," which meant walking six abreast and picking up cigarette butts, twigs or anything else that didn't appear to belong in the surrounding gravel expanse.

Starkey and Rich shuffled along with the others. Due to the stress and fatigue of this horrendous day, Rich was developing a true sense of foreboding.

"We are really fucked," he moaned. "I bet all the Sergeants we have are going to be just like that little Specialist Cocksucker."

"Hang in there, buddy," said Starkey. "Guys like that always get the shit duty dumped on them, and by Army standards, handling a bunch of dirt bags like us is shit duty. He's just taking out his frustrations on us. I bet he's as bad as it gets."

"You think that Captain was here because he fucked up?"

"No, man. He's a pro, and he's just visiting. Probably has a command down at Knox and comes up here to do a 'rah rah' speech whenever they run through another bunch like us. That can't be more than once, maybe twice, a week. I bet they got Specialist Cocksucker cleaning the bathrooms in between busloads."

Their conversation was interrupted by a shout of "Fall in on me!" from a sergeant they'd not seen before. The men were ordered back into the classroom and took their seats as the new sergeant perched himself on the corner of the desk at the front of the room.

"Gentlemen," he began, "I've got some news to break to you, so listen close. We've been informed that a few inductees from this group will be sent to our sister service, the United States Marine Corps." Some of the men were devastated at this news, and made no attempt to hide their concerns.

"Sarge, if I'd wanted to join the fucking Marine Corps I could have done that in Shelbyville. I could have had my choice of jobs. I wouldn't have let the draft take me if I thought I'd go anywhere but the Goddamn Army, for Chris sakes!" exclaimed one particularly despondent young man.

"Yeah, Sarge!" chorused a few others. "We didn't know about this Marine shit!"

"At ease!" he yelled. "You men calm down and listen to me. And don't forget you're in this man's Army until I tell you different! Now shut the fuck up and listen!"

He was standing now and red-faced. "Here's the deal. We will contribute four inductees for the Marine Corps. I am asking for volunteers gentlemen. VOLUNTEERS," he shouted. "Now, I can guarantee you this. Anyone volunteering will attend boot camp at the Marine Recruit Depot in San Diego. That's sunny San Diego, California, gentlemen, not that shit hole Parris Island down in South Carolina."

This news generated a buzz of conversation among the men, some of whom were no more concerned or intimidated by the thought of Marine Corps service than they were of the Army.

"Hey, they got better uniforms," said a voice from the back.

"Marines get more pussy," offered another, which generated raucous laughter throughout the room. The men were now talking animatedly among themselves, and the sergeant let the exchanges continue for a minute. He'd had to break this news to several groups lately and was never sure how it would be received. Casualties in Vietnam were becoming heavier by the day and the recent "Tet" offensive had been particularly hard on the Marines. This group was typical, and he felt he'd gotten them back in control.

"OK, at ease!" he yelled. "Now, listen to me." He surveyed the room, staring briefly at some of the faces as if trying to communicate with them separately. "Your nation is at war, gentlemen, and Uncle

Sam doesn't use the draft because he can't find enough typists, cooks or truck drivers. Wars are won by riflemen. Your Army 'Military Occupational Specialty' or 'MOS' will most likely be '11 Bravo,' which is Infantry. It's going to be the Infantry for most of you whether you're Army or Marines. Got it? If you wanted something special you had the opportunity to enlist for it. You didn't. You fucked up. So, here you are." He glared at the whiner from Shelbyville. "Your decision needs to be made with the knowledge that you will go to Vietnam and you will carry an M-16," he said. "Don't make your decision based on the bullshit about Marine boot camp being tougher than Army. The truth is, neither will be much fun." He paused again. "So, make your decision with the knowledge that it's Vietnam for most of you, regardless of Army or Marines."

The men had listened intently. He knew that getting the volunteers he needed would be difficult. Sometimes, the "Sunny California" aspect could deliver a few of the men to fill the quota, and sometimes boys would jump at the chance to go into the Marines for two years instead of the three or four required if they had enlisted.

"Now, as you look around, I want you to think about your own situation and just maybe say to yourself, 'Hey, I can handle the Marines OK. So why don't I just volunteer and save some poor slob from having to go when he clearly doesn't want to.' Either way, gentlemen, it's a two-year deal. TWO YEARS! DO YOU UNDERSTAND?"

"Yes, Sergeant!" they screamed back at him.

The sergeant let his words sink in a few seconds, then said, "OK, I'm going down to Room 6. Any of you that think you might want to give the Marines a try, come on down and see me. If no one volunteers, our NCO staff will select the men we need and advise those chosen accordingly. Now, everybody take a 20-minute break. Smoke 'em if you got 'em, outside."

The men stood and stretched, and most headed outside to smoke and discuss the current crisis with new and intimate friends they'd not had 12 hours before.

Rich and Starkey continued to sit for several more minutes. Rich stared at the chalkboard at the front of the room. Starkey seemed mesmerized by his Number 2 pencil.

"Let's fucking do it," said Rich.

"It's the California thing, right?" answered Starkey.

"Well, that's part of it. But, you know, I think what he was trying to say is that it's six of one, half dozen of the other. We're all going to the Infantry, so do we want the Army Infantry and its tactics or the Marines and their tactics. Do you think there's a huge difference?"

"Shit, I don't know," said Starkey. "The Marines had Iwo Jima, the Army had the Battle of the Bulge. I don't see much difference. I'm pretty sure they're not storming beaches over in 'Nam, for what that's worth."

"Here's what I think," said Rich. "The Marines are volunteers. At least that's what I thought until today. But anyway, they're mostly volunteers, and they joined up to do what they do. They're motivated. Look at these dick-heads. Who'd you rather have watching your back?"

"You talked me into it."

"No shit? Man, I didn't mean, I, uh, you can..."

"It's what you said about 'watching your back'. When I was in Colorado, I met a guy who'd been over there. Wounded real bad. He told me the most important thing that guys like us can do in 'Nam is make friends, you know, go out of your way to be dependable, to be friendly with the guys you serve with. He said that's the best way to get back in one piece. If you don't have buddies looking out for you, you're dead meat."

Rich nodded. "Makes sense to me."

"I'm not saying that Army guys don't look out for each other. I'm just agreeing with you that the Marines may be a little more motivated. Come on, let's do it. Hurry up or the line will be too long."

"Holy shit," said Rich. "Holy shit."

They tried not to attract attention and walked casually out to the water fountain. Both took a long drink and looked out the door where the others had gathered. They paused a few seconds in the doorway, turned quickly and walked towards Room 6.

As they rounded a corner, another young man ran up behind them.

"I just didn't want to be the only one," he said.

"Abandon all hope, ye who enter here," laughed Rich.

"What?" said the young man.

Starkey went in first. The sergeant took his name, made a few notes, then excused him back to the break area. As Starkey rose to leave, the Sergeant said, "Son, one of those pilgrims outside will be thanking his lucky stars that you did what you did."

"Uh, yes sir," answered Starkey.

Rich was next, and Starkey waited for him in the hallway. A few minutes later they walked together back to the classroom where the men were now filing back from their break.

Chapter 7
'Bueny'

In describing his Colorado road trip, Starkey hadn't told Rich the whole story. The part he'd left out was that he'd fallen in gut-wrenching love with a girl he'd met in Buena Vista.

After the obligatory get-acquainted with Bill and his wife Doris, the four boys took little time to get their bearings, set up their riverside campsite and explore up and down the river banks. After one day to become acclimatized to the high altitude, they were begging Uncle Bill to get them onto a mountain peak.

"Say, Uncle Bill, is there any molybdenum up on Mt. Princeton?"

So, before dawn the next morning, he drove them up the steep switchbacks of a Jeep trail on Mt. Princeton. The huge mountain towered to 14,197 feet and, with a sister peak, Mt. Yale, dominated the valley in which the little town of Buena Vista was located. Bill dropped them off at the trailhead and told them he'd be back in six hours, an amount of time the boys felt was twice what they'd need. "Well," said Bill, "if you get down early, just walk back down to the corral we passed. If I don't see you there, I'll drive on up. But, I think you'll need the time." Then he became serious, "Now, listen to me. You hear thunder, stop where you are and head back down at a good clip. I don't want to have to explain to your mothers how you got your brains fried by lightning up there. You're getting an early enough start to avoid it, but you never know what Mother Nature might whip up."

Indeed, they did need the time, arriving exhausted, sunburned, rock scrapped and exuberant only a few minutes before they heard Uncle Bill's Bronco tearing up the steep, rocky road.

"We found this metal tube at the top with a scroll and pencil inside, and we all signed it," said Rob. "Were we supposed to do that?"

"Oh, no! Now they'll send you a bill for $20 each for 'Scenery Enjoyment Tax'." Bill winked at the older boys and continued, "…best to just sneak up there, look around real quick and get the hell off."

"He's just funning you," said Jack, to Rob's obvious relief.

The view had, in fact, stunned them. From their perch above 14,000 feet, other peaks of comparable height were visible at nearly every point on the compass. They looked east to Pikes Peak, northeast to the Mosquito Range, north to Mt. Elbert, the State's highest peak, northwest to the Elk Range, southwest to Monument Pass and, in the hazy distance, the San Juans. To the south were the Sangre de Christos stretching away towards New Mexico. Starkey was so hypnotized by the astounding scene he vowed to his companions that he'd eventually climb every peak if it took him the rest of his days.

Uncle Bill drove them into town and pulled over in the shade of huge Cottonwood trees bordering the city park. He pulled out his wallet, handed Jeff a ten-dollar bill and said, "Why don't you boys splash off the grime in the creek there, and then hike up to the root beer joint on the highway and get some lunch. Can you find your way home from there?"

"Sure," they answered. "Hey, thanks for the dough."

He continued, "Now drink lots of water, eat some solid food and take it easy on the ice cream. Otherwise, you'll puke your guts out."

After he'd left them, they took off their shirts, sneakers and socks and waded up the shallow creek that ran through the park. Shirts and socks were rinsed, wrung and stretched out in the grass to dry, a process that took only minutes in the warm, dry mountain air. Refreshed and energized, they ran across the empty highway to an A&W drive-in restaurant.

Andrew noticed her as she took a tray full of root beer mugs from the service window out to a pickup truck with four teenagers squeezed into the cab. She was around five feet four, with a luxuriant head of short, dark-brown hair that blew freely in the gusty wind. With a quick flip of her fingers, the hair fell back in place. She had a slender frame and small but prominent breasts. Her skin was lightly tanned, and a radiant and mischievous smile seemed a permanent fixture on her face.

As Andrew approached with his friends, she stared at him, almost losing the mugs as she stepped awkwardly off the curb. They found seats at a picnic table with a metal umbrella protruding from its center. Rob walked over to one of the drive-in spaces to read the menu printed on a plastic sign behind the intercom. In a minute, he returned with confirmation that Uncle Bill's ten dollars was enough for two cheeseburgers, fries and a large root beer for each of them.

Jack went to the window to inquire about a water fountain. "Inside," came the reply, and they took turns going in and slurping down huge volumes of water as they'd long ago emptied their canteens.

"Man," said Andrew Starkey to Jeff, "your uncle is sure a great guy. Wish I had someone like that to visit out here. This is fucking heaven."

"Hey, watch your mouth around my baby brother," said Jeff with mock seriousness.

"Don't sweat it, Andrew. You can say whatever the fuck you want to around me. I can handle it."

Jeff winced in irritation. "Rob, just remember if you slip up, and say something like 'fuck' around Uncle Bill or Aunt Doris, that you didn't learn it from me. Got that?"

"He's got it," Andrew laughed. "Rob learned all his potty language from Jack and me."

Rob was tiring of his brother's constant oversight. "Fuckin' A. You guys and the locker room. Jeez Jeff, get over it."

"And while we're on the topic of adult behavior," Jeff continued, "make sure to put a sock in it about us drinking all that 3.2 beer."

Then Andrew asked, "Say, did you see that waitress when we walked up? Man, was she tough or what?"

"Well tell her what you think," said Jack. "She's here to take our order."

Andrew had not noticed her approach with her order pad but, to his relief, she seemed oblivious to his comment. Their order was simple enough, and she was gone in a few seconds. All of them watched her walk away. She wore white Bermuda shorts and a sleeveless black top. Her legs were long and well formed.

As they waited for their burgers, they moved a few yards away to the shade of a large Ponderosa pine and lay down in the grass. Jeff was snoring in minutes. Andrew, leaning on his elbow, watched for their order to arrive at the window and, noticing it was ready for pick-up said, "I'll be right back."

As the girl reached for the tray, Andrew was behind her and said, "Hey, can I get that for you? It looks pretty heavy."

"Well, you told your friends that I was, what did you say, 'tough'? What makes you think I can't carry this little tray?"

"Uh…where we come from 'tough' means, you know, uh, well…"

"I'm listening." She looked at him impassively. One dark eyebrow was slightly raised.

He noticed a faint odor of coconut lotion and watched a drop of perspiration run from her hairline and down the side of her face.

"It means foxy, pretty. It doesn't mean tough like muscles, mean or hard."

"Oh, well, thanks anyway, but my boss doesn't want our customers waiting on themselves." She picked up the tray and deftly raised it to her shoulder, balancing it on the palm of her right hand.

Crestfallen, Starkey walked behind her towards their table. Jack and Rob were awaiting them. Jeff continued to sleep.

She slowed and turned back to him, aware she'd hurt his feelings.

"So, where is it that they talk so weird about their women?"

"We're from Indiana--New Vernon, Indiana."

"We're Hoosiers, from Hoosierland," said Rob, as they reached the table.

"Tough Hoosiers," said the girl as she set the tray down on the table.

"Guess I'll never live that down," said Andrew. "Can we start over? What's your name? I'm Andrew, this is Jack, this is Rob, and the unconscious one is Jeff."

"I'm awake. Hi there."

"My name is Nancy, and I'm from Buena Vista. Glad to meet all of you."

She walked around and shook hands with each of them. When she got back to Andrew, she squeezed his hand hard, smiling at him in an odd way. Suddenly a Ketchup packet burst inside their grip and a stream of red liquid shot straight up between them. Both had to back up quickly to avoid the mess as it rained to the ground.

"You little weasel!" he laughed.

"What? So, now I'm a tough weasel? Well!" she huffed, and wiped the ketchup from her hand on Starkey's T-shirt.

"Now, you all enjoy your burgers and holler if you need anything. I'll be around."

She sauntered off to pick up another tray, taking a quick look back over her shoulder at Andrew.

"Jeez, what a character," said Jeff. "You're right, Stark. She's a knockout."

"Wow," Andrew sighed, watching her until she disappeared around the building. "Maybe not a knockout, but she's so wholesome and clean-cut looking she makes my teeth hurt. I'm in love, man. I'm going to lick this ketchup off very, very slowly."

"You're too easy," said Rob. "I always make 'em spit on me before I fall in love."

Jack rolled his eyes at his friend. "God, 'wholesome and clean-cut'. I may puke myself. Stark, you'd better not let Sally Mason find out that you're falling for some babe in Colorado. She'll have one of her brothers relieve you of your balls."

"Man, that's over. She's going back east to school and already strutting around like she's got a pole up her ass. Anyway, I'd give up one ball to spend some time with this one. Besides, I'd still have two left..."

"Oh, it's getting thick now," said Jeff. "Let's eat and then get going back to Uncle Bill's. We've got a two-mile walk and I'm already half dead."

As the group walked from the drive in, Andrew tried to get the girl's attention with a wave but she was busy at the window. "Nuts," he said under his breath. He was already planning to come back as soon as he could.

They'd not noticed the ominous gray clouds that had gathered between the peaks and were now tumbling into the valley. Before they'd covered half their distance they were engulfed in a downpour. They ran under the awning of a gas station to wait for a let up. Across the highway lightning hit a cottonwood tree, and a resounding boom echoed down the valley.

As they huddled there, a Ford pickup drove up, the window rolled down and they saw Nancy the waitress wave them over.

She yelled above the storm, "I can't keep you dry but I can get you where you're going quicker. Want a ride? This may go on for a while."

"Hell, I mean, heck yes," Rob shouted back as they all ran over to her truck.

"There's room for one in the front. How 'bout you tough guy? The rest pile in back. Take that blue tarp and hold it over your heads. I won't drive too fast."

Andrew climbed in the cab, thanked her for stopping and wiped the water off his face with his ketchup-stained shirt. Nancy was on her way home for a rest and an early dinner. She would return for a five-to-eight shift.

"I can't eat that grease twice in one day," she said. "So, where you all headed?"

"Bill and Doris Thompson. They got a cabin on the river, another mile down and take a left at the speed-limit sign."

"Oh, I know them. He belongs to a veterans' club my dad goes to all the time. They're very nice people. Retired aren't they?"

"Yeah, that's them," said Andrew, using his finger to skim the water from his forehead. "Aunt and uncle of my buddies in the back. Bill worked at a molybdenum mine up by Leadville."

"Well, listen to you," she said, clearly impressed. "I bet there aren't many Hoosiers that can say that word correctly."

"Yeah, but I cheated. Don't tell Bill, but we all practiced spelling it and using it in a sentence. Thought it might help get us on his good side."

"Your secret's safe with me," she said with a flash of her smile.

"So far, it's worked pretty well. He paid for lunch, but we chipped in extra for your tip."

She turned at the sign Andrew mentioned. As her wheels went from pavement to gravel road, she slowed and looked back to check on her passengers. "Gosh, I hope they don't drown."

"We're almost there," Andrew said. "The Thompsons got a nice place. The cabin isn't much but they're right on the river. Bet that cost a bundle."

"You can live in Bueny very cheaply," said Nancy. "The Chamber of Commerce is always trying to figure out ways to attract retirees. Half my customers at the A&W are retired. They're just like teenagers, wanting a place to hang out."

"Well, speaking of hanging out," Andrew said, seizing an opportunity, "do you guys hang out around town when you're not working? Do you and your friends have a place you go to, you know, to shoot the shit, I mean breeze, whatever?" Andrew hoped he hadn't offended her with his language.

"Sure," she laughed. "We have well-developed social skills. As a matter of fact," she hesitated a second, then continued, "a bunch of us will be doing something when we, my friend Louise and I, get off around eight. If you're bored, come on down to the 'Corral', that restaurant across from the gas station where I picked you up. You'll see some pickups parked there and that'll be our bunch of townees."

In another minute she pulled into the driveway of the cabin and honked the horn. "Better give them a warning that you'll be running for the door. Don't want it blown off the hinges."

The three in the back had already jumped out and were bolting for the carport.

Andrew looked at her for a few seconds and said, "Thanks again for the ride. Any chance you'd let me shake your hand again, Nancy?"

She looked at him quizzically and said, "Are you mad about the ketchup?"

"Of course not. Actually, it kind of made us blood brothers."

"Sauce siblings," she giggled.

Andrew smiled as she extended her hand. "OK," he said, "how 'bout a ketchup couple?"

Her eyes brightened as he took her hand gently in his, then shifted her hand to his left hand. He opened the truck door, softening his hold and letting his hand slide from hers as he stepped out.

"Well," she said above the rain noise. "Guess you're not so tough, are you?"

"See you tonight," he said, and ran towards the cabin.

She honked again and yelled, "Bring a swim suit!"

Jeff, Jack and Starkey rode the Chevy into town and turned into the parking lot of the Corral Restaurant. Rob had elected to stay home and fish with his uncle. Actually, he was quite shy and figured the group would be mostly older high schoolers. He had no desire to be exposed for carrot puking or crapping in his swim trunks. Besides, those trunks were hanging from a motel roof in Kansas City and they'd forgotten to get him new ones before the few stores in town closed. "No thanks, I'll take a pass, thank you, have a good time," he said.

There were four pickups at the far end of the lot, and Nancy waved at them as they turned in. Her dozen friends were equally divided between boys and girls. A few were farm-ranch kids but most were from families that owned or worked in businesses in the town. The hardware store, grain elevator, Denver & Rio Grande Railroad, Highway Department and State Reformatory were represented. They discovered that Nancy's father owned the lumberyard and employed her two brothers in the business.

"Well, I only met these yahoos this afternoon, but they seemed mentally stable," said Nancy as she began introductions. "Let's see now, the big bruiser with dimples is Jeff, I think. That right?"

"Yeah, that's me," said Jeff with a wave.

"Then the stocky one with more hair than me is Jack, short for John," she said.

"Jack is right. Not short for John, though," said Jack. "Glad to meet you all."

"And, finally, the tall strawberry person with atrocious manners is Andy-drew. They're Hoosiers from Indiana and visiting their Uncle Bill and Aunt Doris Thompson," she continued. "Say hello everybody."

Hands were shaken all around and the locals' names were shared and repeated. A tiny blonde in threadbare overalls asked Andrew Starkey, "Andy-Drew? Is that really your name?"

"It's Andrew, but I'll go by whatever Nancy wants to call me," he replied.

"Oooh, that sounds serious," she replied.

Their plan was to drive out to the hot springs on Chalk Creek, a dozen miles away. There was a commercial pool facility, but they planned to wade up the creek bed and build river rock tubs where the hot-water spring entered the creek. The Hoosiers were divided up among the pickups and left the Chevy in the lot. They exchanged glances as they split up, clearly awed at the prospect of this adventure.

Andrew tried for Nancy's truck but was aced out by another boy and girl. He could have ridden in the back but opted for shot gun seat in the little blonde's ancient GMC. Jack and Jeff disappeared into other trucks.

"So what's a Hoosier?" she asked. Her name was Wendy. She had a head of bushy blonde hair that she apparently paid little attention to. Her face was an explosion of light-brown freckles spread ear to ear and over a turned- up nose. She had a crooked smile and unsettling green eyes.

"No one knows for sure, Wendy," Andrew replied. "People from Kentucky think it means 'ignorant redneck', but people from Indiana think it means 'intelligent and handsome people from north of the Ohio River'. You don't want to know what we call people from Kentucky."

"Probably what we call Nebraskans…dumb ass sons of bitches."

Andrew guffawed at this comment and said, "Hey, you remind me of me."

Her family had a small cattle operation down near Salida, a somewhat bigger town with a large railroad yard. They grew feed grains for their cattle and sold the excess to other small ranchers. "We ain't getting rich, but we wouldn't want to live any other way," she said. "'Four H' is big around here. We go up to the Stock Show in Denver every January. Got 'Honorable Mention' on my steer two years ago. You probably ate part of him in one of those 'Big Boy' burger restaurants they have back east. He was a hunk."

"So, is that what happened to your overalls, I mean, did ranch work beat them up so bad?" he said with a smile in his voice. "I guess you could say you worked your 'butt' off."

"Hey, Hoosier, these overalls have character. I would have dressed up for you, but Nancy didn't warn me we were having uppity eastern guests tonight. And don't get excited. Those aren't panties. It's my swim suit."

"Dang!" he laughed. "Oh, remind me to tell you a 'swim suit' story about our other buddy who didn't come tonight. And, don't worry. It's not a story a lady would find inappropriate."

"Oh, you're scoring points left and right," she winked.

He tried to subtly turn the conversation to Nancy. "You all go to school together, I mean, you, Nancy, and the others?"

"Yeah, we all been friends since we was little kids. Most all of us just graduated, 'cept Henry up there, riding with Nancy, is a Junior. That boy's a piece of work."

Andrew looked ahead at Nancy's Ford. She was giving the hand signal out her window for a right turn. Soon the small convoy was on a rural blacktop that followed Chalk Creek west towards Mt. Princeton. The monstrous monolith loomed to their right and the chalk cliffs on the mountain's shoulder that gave the creek its name towered straight ahead of them.

After a few miles, Nancy pulled off the right side of the road and parked in a stand of Ponderosa Pines. The other trucks pulled in alongside and the young people piled out. The boys headed behind a patch of willows and began changing into their swimwear. The girls did the same in the cabs of the pickups. Within minutes, they were crossing the road barefoot, carrying their towels. They walked down a willow-lined path to the water. The bank had some empty jars of "Fireballs" salmon egg bait, Number-8 fish hook cards and other fishing litter, and they warned each other to watch for anything that could injure bare feet.

One by one, they stepped off the bank into the frigid water and began wading upstream. The flow was brisk, mid-calf but manageable and they waded along laughing and kicking spray at one another. The Hoosiers waded together surrounded by their new acquaintances. Jeff was engrossed in a conversation with a young man named Heath whose father worked for the railroad. Heath was giving Jeff the history of the right-of-way legal battles fought between the Santa Fe and Rio Grande railroads for the Royal Gorge route. That route followed the Arkansas River through a 1000-foot-deep chasm 60 miles to the southeast of Buena Vista. Jeff vowed to stop and see it on their way home via the suspension bridge built as a tourist attraction by the citizens of Canon City.

"So DeAnn, where in hell is this place?" asked Jack, after they'd been in the water for ten minutes. He was wading gingerly, hand-in-hand with a tall large-breasted girl with curly dark shoulder-length hair. She wore a flowered cotton halter that displayed ample cleavage.

"Honey, do you kiss your mother with that mouth? My goodness! Now, see that steam rising up over there?" as DeAnn pointed to cloud-like billows that had appeared another hundred yards ahead on the right side of the creek. "You just keep truckin' honey. We'll have you all warmed up in just a minute."

Her friend Louise spoke from a few yards behind them. "Sweetheart, your top is keeping these boys real warm already."

"LU WEEZE!" shouted DeAnn in mock disgust. "I can't help my endowments. Now you mind your business!"

"Louise," said Jack, "we Hoosiers are always attracted first by a lady's intellect. Since DeAnn is very intelligent, I haven't even noticed her fabulous knockers."

Clearly delighted at the attention, DeAnn gushed, "Now, how long you boys going to be in town? I think you're going to spice things up around here quite a bit."

Andrew remained focused on Nancy. He was taking a subliminal survey of the local boys to assess who his competition for her attention might be. With some relief, he sensed they had at most, platonic interest in her.

Hmm, he thought, *she could be a lone wolf, or has a boyfriend elsewhere. I'll just take it easy and try not to scare her off.*

Just then he noticed that the sun was touching the crest line on its descent. He said, "Hey, let's wait a second and watch the sun set."

Louise put her hands on her hips and turned towards him, a hint of good-natured condescension in her voice.

"What's the matter, Hoosier? Don't you have sunsets back in Indiana?"

"Ignore this bitch," said Wendy, snapping the back of Louise's bathing suit. "Sometimes I'm dumbstruck by mountain sunsets. Me and Nancy will watch with you, and the rest of these pilgrims can keep wadin'."

But now the golden splendor of the event had gathered all their attention, and in spite of themselves, the little group stood in rapt amazement until the last sliver of sun had disappeared behind the mountain.

A few minutes later they arrived below a small complex of buildings with high wood fencing lit by pole-mounted arc lights. Laughing children could be heard beyond the fences. The entire facility was engulfed in a slow swirling cloud of steam vapor.

Nancy held up her hand and motioned for everyone to move over to the edge of the creek's flow.

"She's checking to see if the manager's watching," said Wendy to Andrew. "Depending on who's working, sometimes they get testy when we come in without paying."

"Do they own the creek, Heath?" asked Jeff to his new friend.

Heath scratched his head. "Hard to say, but they certainly have water rights for its use. As for the hot spring, well I think they own that water until it's cold."

"Interesting legal concept," Jeff said.

A few seconds later, Nancy waved them forward and said, "spread out kiddies." Then she stood aside and waited for Andrew and Wendy to come up.

"Let's rebuild 'Old Faithful'," she said, and they followed her another 10 yards up the creek. At that point, Andrew could feel the swirling water begin to warm up considerably as the hot spring welled out of the bank. Nancy and Wendy waded into a slight depression in the creek bed and began shoving bowling ball-sized rocks into place to create a six-foot long, rectangular enclosure. Andrew watched for a second and quickly joined in their efforts. The water running around his legs was now quite warm and he couldn't wait to submerge himself completely. The girls were expert in channeling the creek water so that it diluted the spring to a tolerable temperature.

"This is amazing!" said Jack. He and DeAnn had finished constructing their own tub bordering Nancy's and were reclining up to their necks in the gloriously warm water. Jeff and the others were immersing themselves in their own baths a few yards downstream.

Jack had pulled DeAnn close and had his left arm around her. She snuggled against him and kissed him on the cheek. "Now, don't we treat our visitors right, honey?" she cooed.

"DEANN!" laughed Nancy.

Nancy lounged at the opposite end from Andrew, and Wendy sat between them. She was so small and their tub so deep that she had trouble maintaining her soaking position. The current, though greatly diminished by the rock border, still was enough to keep her in constant motion. Finally, Andrew took her ankle and pulled her, squealing, onto his lap.

"Now, what would you like for Christmas, little lady?" he joked. She glanced upstream at Nancy looking for any sign of displeasure but saw only the smile of camaraderie.

"Wow," Andrew said. "If my buddies back in Indiana could see me now. Soaking in a hot spring with two Colorado foxes. Now, if I had a Coors, I…"

"Hey, asshole," came Jack's voice from behind him. "You're already with the best Goddamn buddies you'll ever have. Screw those guys back in New Vernon."

"Honey, that mouth of yours would scorch a cat's ass," complained DeAnn.

"Oh, I almost forgot," said Nancy. She looked over her shoulder, up towards the board fences, then stood and waded over to her towel. Unrolling it part way, she produced four Coors bottles, then waded back to Wendy and handed her two bottles.

"Not 3.2. Swiped them from my brothers."

Wendy, still semi-floating on Andrew's lap, produced a bottle opener that hung on a shoestring around her neck. She opened Nancy's beer then one for Andrew. Then she opened her bottle, clinked it against his and took a long pull on the contents.

Andrew looked back over the rock barrier to Jack's pool and, finding a make-out session in progress, flung a palm full of hot water on the two. Jack looked up at Andrew, grinning, and pointed out his own Coors balanced on a rock. He grabbed it and reached back to clink beers with his friend.

"Stark, remember what you said when we were floating in that pool in Kansas City, something like, 'It can't get any better than this.'? Well, what do you say now, buddy?"

"I guess I'd have to say that I am incapable of knowing just how good it can get," Andrew responded.

Wendy balanced her beer on a rock, then took Andrew's face in her hands. She gave him a big smack on the lips and sighed, "Well, I'm going to trade places with Nancy and let you two get acquainted." As she shifted on his lap his aroused state became obvious. Andrew quickly put his hand over his crotch and dipped his face in the hot water. Wendy's blush was hidden in the gathering darkness. She pushed her feet into the granulated granite of the stream bottom and floated towards Nancy's end of the pool.

Nancy had her arm draped lazily over the rocks into the icy water of the creek channel. "Oh, you're going to make me move?" she said as Wendy pushed towards her.

Wendy grinned and said, "Suffer, bitch. I got him all warmed up for you."

"Gee, thanks," said Nancy under her breath. Then she floated slowly towards Andrew and settled against the rocks next to him. She bent her knees and pushed her feet into the gravel under Andrew's extended legs.

Wendy stood up and said, "I'm going down to give Louise a hard time. You know she bought that piece-of-shit Dodge from that Mexican in Salida? Back in a minute. Hoosier, save my seat, you hear?"

Andrew was rubbing his face furiously with his hand, trying to regain his composure. "Always room for you on any lap I own," he said as she waded downstream.

"You OK, tough guy, or is the heat getting to you?" said Nancy.

"No, no, I'm great." He nodded towards Wendy. "I really like her."

"Well, you sure made a fan out of her. She's a good judge of character so I guess I can be alone with you for a while."

He reached through the water, found her hand and squeezed it lightly. "Thanks for the vote of confidence."

He leaned back and stared for a long time at the emerging stars. He had controlled his arousal and was trying hard to focus, once again, on the magnificent surroundings and, now, the young woman at his side.

The chalk cliff shoulder of Mt. Princeton on the right and Mount Antero on the left, blocked half the starry canopy. The creek's tumbling course between the two mountains created a low and hollow background echo. To Starkey's ear, the sound was powerful and almost sinister, as if some monstrous force lay beyond the mountains and at any second could come blasting down on them. The only other sounds came from the murmuring creek and occasional laughter beyond the fence above them.

"You know, I hope you guys realize how special this is," he said. "I mean, this place is incredible."

"Hey, remember who brought you here, Hoosier. We know it's special. Just because we were all born here doesn't mean we take it for granted."

He looked at her so long she was a bit embarrassed. "You OK, really?" she said finally.

"Perfect," he said, taking one more palmful of water and splashing his face with it. "Sorry to stare, but you're very pleasant to look at."

"Come on, now. I'm blushing."

He took her chin between two fingers and turned her head left and right. "I can't decide if you're Italian or maybe Indian," he said. Her face was an oval with prominent cheekbones. Her nose was narrow with a barely discernible rise on the bridge, and her eyes were large, dark and expressive.

"I'm mostly Italian. My last name's 'Spinelli'. I don't think I've got any Indian blood, but my grandmother, Dad's mom, was kind of wild looking when she was younger."

"What was her maiden name?"

"You know, I'm not sure I ever heard. I'll have to ask my mom. If it was 'Runs with Coyotes', I'll let you know."

Andrew laughed heartily. "Just so it wasn't 'Hoosier killer'," he said.

It was her turn to laugh out loud and DeAnn said, "Nancy, what's so doggone funny?"

"Andrew asked if Grammy Anna's maiden name was 'Hoosier killer'."

"I won't even try to figure out how that got into the conversation," said DeAnn.

Andrew winked at Nancy. "So, the A&W is open later than eight. How come they let you off early?"

"Oh, the owner is a great guy and he tries to give all the girls some hours. My friends Cathy and Judy work 'til eleven when they close.

Tips are pretty good on that shift," she said, "but I like to be gone from there before the drunks come in."

She looked beyond Andrew to where Jack and DeAnn were soaking. "Psst," she said, and put her finger to her lips.

Andrew leaned forward to hear her.

"Let's move to the other end," she whispered…"don't want to disturb the lovebirds." Silently, they turned and pushed with their feet until they'd reached the far end.

"The view was better down there, but they could hear every word we said," said Nancy.

"It's so dark, the sky is the show now…and you, of course."

"Gosh, you Hoosiers are so smooth."

She asked about his family and friends in Indiana, and about his plans at the end of the summer. He told her about his sister, two years younger than Nancy, the wholesale grocery business his father owned, his mother's antique collecting. He would be a freshman at Indiana University in the fall. Nancy would be entering Colorado State College in Greeley to study elementary education and hoped to someday teach third and fourth graders. She talked about her dad's lumberyard, her homemaker mother and her two brothers. One of her brothers was home recuperating from a serious wound he'd received while serving with the Army in Vietnam. He'd been discharged on partial disability status. He made periodic visits to Fitzsimmons Hospital in Denver but was expected to recover completely.

"He was shot. It went through his lung, front to back. His squad leader saved his life. They called it a 'sucking chest wound'. The sergeant put plastic bags over the holes so the lung didn't collapse."

Andrew, his interest surprising her, barraged Nancy with questions, wanting to know all about her brother's service; what unit he was with, what his job was, what part of Vietnam he served in.

"My goodness. I sure hit one of your buttons. I can't answer any of your questions. Would you like to meet him and ask him yourself?"

"If he could stand to have me around, I'd really like that."

"Actually, I think he'd like the company. He just answers the phone in the yard office and does paperwork. I'm worried about him."

"Why?"

"Oh, he's just so quiet all the time. Doesn't want to do anything. Can't even get him to come down here," she said. "Most of his school friends are gone off to the military or college. And he really hates going in to Denver for his rehab. Says it makes him feel like he's back in the Army."

"What does he have to do when he goes to the hospital?"

"They make him try to expand his lung, you know, get him to breath in both lungs like he used to. I guess it hurts quite a bit. He's supposed to exercise at home, but he doesn't." She took a sip of her beer and looked at him intently for a second. "I'm glad you're going to college. You don't want to get involved in that war."

Andrew thought for a moment before answering. "Well, I'm not real fired up about going to college. It's just what I'm supposed to do, you know, what my folks want. I've talked to all the recruiters. Jack's going into the Air Force in October and…"

"What? You're what?" DeAnn's voice suddenly rose above the stream's gurgle.

"See, I told you they could hear us," Nancy whispered.

"Hey, what's the big fucking deal?" Jack responded. "I'm going to be a loadmaster and fly around the world."

"It's too dangerous, potty mouth, and you don't need to…ummm." Jack had kissed her again to shut her up and they settled quietly back into the water.

"Unnggghhh!" Wendy was lustily clearing her throat as a warning that she was walking back upstream. As she waded past Jack and DeAnn's pool, Jack said, "Two more Coors, bartender."

"We're cutting you off, Hoosier. Any more stimulation and you'll be floating face down back to Buena Vista."

"What did she think we were going to be doing?" chuckled Andrew. "I'm not nearly charming enough to get anywhere in 20 minutes."

"Oh, I don't know," Nancy whispered. She pressed over to him, shoulder to shoulder, and tilted her face up. The opportunity for Andrew was obvious, and he lowered his head and kissed her softly.

"I knew it," huffed Wendy with fake indignation. "Can't turn my back for a second and you're all over that poor Indiana boy."

Wendy's reappearance had been a signal that everyone else, save the two couples, was ready to head back to town. Jack and DeAnn needed a few minutes to gather themselves and reluctantly stood up to stretch and dry off.

With one kiss Nancy had put Andrew into a state of bliss that left him speechless and groggy. He stood in the middle of their cozy tub, drying his upper body with his towel. As Jack grinned over at him, all Andrew could muster was a quiet "wow" and a roll of his eyes.

Nancy was taking inventory of people and gear. "Let's go back on the road, guys," she said.

"You mean we don't have to wade back?" asked Jack.

"No. We'll just head up that path there by the fence. If the manager sees us now, no problem. It's a lot warmer walking on the road."

As they stepped out of the creek onto the path, it became apparent that the outside temperature had gone down considerably. They moved quickly up the bank, around the fenced area and across the gravel parking lot of the private pool facility. In minutes, the group was walking down the middle of the blacktop road. The surface was still warm from the day's heat, but the walk back to the trucks was unpleasant since the cool mountain air was working its way through their wet swimwear. At the trucks they decided to head for the Corral and hot chocolate or coffee.

Wendy grabbed Andrew's hand and pulled him to her old GMC. "I'm taking you back for a while, Hoosier."

Back at the Corral, and in dry clothes, they pulled two tables together and ordered hot drinks. The locals entertained their guests with stories of Buena Vista history, people who had come and gone, and a drifter who'd recently been run over by the train. Jeff and his new friend had shifted their topic to Water law and chatted amiably at the end of the table. Jack and DeAnn held hands under the table and looked at each other as they sipped their coffee. Wendy sat between Andrew and Nancy and rubbed Andrew's leg while she talked about castrating bull calves. "Rocky Mountain Oysters. Now that's good eating," she cackled as the Hoosiers groaned.

Reluctantly, Jeff rounded up his friends to head back to the cabin. Uncle Bill was taking them to a trailhead for Mt. Yale before sunrise, so they needed to make sandwiches and get some sleep. Hands were shaken and backs patted all around as they were walked to the Chevy. Andrew finally got next to Nancy. "Can I come see you at the A&W tomorrow?"

"I hope so," she said. "I work four to eight."

He wanted to kiss her again but knew better than to try in front of her friends. He said, "I'll be there as soon as I get off that mountain."

Mt. Yale was a much tougher climb than Mt. Princeton had been. The trailhead on Princeton had started at timberline, high up on the mountain's shoulder, and the vertical gain had been only 2,500 feet over a two-mile hike. This trailhead was not far above the valley floor and would require a 4,500 foot ascent in four and a half miles. Still the four boys set an aggressive pace through the pine and Aspen-lined trail as it switch-backed up the mountain's side. Their leg muscles, stiff and reluctant at first, warmed and stretched quickly.

The morning sun was hot on their backs as they hiked past

timberline at 11,500 feet. Tufts of mountain grasses and tiny blossoms grew between layers of fragmented granite. Scampering picas whistled at them as they passed and fat Marmots sunned themselves on immense slabs of rock. Snow melt gurgled out of sight in rocky channels, then emerged in pools surrounded by Columbine flowers. The hikers missed none of this spectacle but still kept their focus on the 14,000 foot peak that came closer with each labored step.

The booming downpour they'd experienced in town gave them new respect for Uncle Bill's warning to make the peak and get off as soon as possible. Each would take an occasional glance to the west to see how the clouds were acting.

At 11:00AM, they stood on the summit and took turns posing atop the rock cairn. They added their names to the scroll in the metal tube maintained by the Colorado Mountain Club, and wolfed down peanut butter sandwiches. As on Mt. Princeton, the view in any direction was jaw-dropping. Andrew renewed his vow to climb all the "fourteeners" before his days on earth were over.

He had slept fitfully, but bounced from his streamside bag in anticipation of seeing Nancy at the end of the day. The mountain climb had, for him, become merely a way to make the time fly by until he could get back to the A&W. But now, with the vista again before him, he had put thoughts of her in the back of his mind. It wouldn't last.

"Man, would you look at that fucking storm!" Jack was staring in wonder at a black, swirling cloud mass developing to their north in a box canyon. Just then a peel of thunder reached them. As the sound ricocheted from the walls of the canyon, it created a resounding boom that left the four boys stunned and speechless.

Even though the sky above was clear, large drops of rain began to fall around them, blown over from the thunderhead.

"Holy shit! We better un-ass the area, pronto."

They began jogging down the rocky trail in barely controlled panic. Footing was treacherous in the loose rock, and their feet occasionally slid from under them. Hands and backsides were bruised from sudden impacts with the ground. Well down from the peak but still in view of the canyon, they breathed easier as the storm seemed content to remain where it had formed. Before they were halfway down to the trailhead it had disappeared altogether.

The group stopped briefly to finish their canteens then resumed at a more leisurely pace. Rob was puzzled by Andrew's atypical lack of banter and odd euphoric daze. As he took a final look back towards the once ominous canyon he said, "Damn, Starkey. Is she feeding you free hamburgers or something?"

"That's not what he wants to chow down on," added Jack with a raucous laugh.

"Shut up, Jack," said Jeff, pitching a handful of trailside gravel back at him. "Rob, love is a wonderful thing, and Starkey's brain is being deluged with chemical reactions that make him obsess on his love object. It happens with many of the higher mammals. He can't help it. Just don't let him walk off a cliff."

"I'm doing just fine," said Andrew. "You bastards just can't understand how a man can be affected by a truly wholesome female."

"There you go again with that 'clean, wholesome' bullshit," said Jack. "You had nice girls back in New Vernon. Sally Mason for one. You talk like she was a low-rent sweat hog."

"It's Colorado versus Cornville," said Jeff. "A classic grass-is-greener disorder. Sally never soaked him in an alpine hot spring. Bowling alleys and miniature golf courses in New Vernon, Indiana just can't compete."

"Hey, you forget that he fell for her when she squirted ketchup on him," offered Jack. "Kind of like a dog pissing on a fire hydrant, only it's the hydrant going gaa gaa for the dog."

"Come on," said Andrew. "Let's get off this mountain before Jack's hard-on for DeAnn attracts a lightning bolt. I'm not the only one who's been distracted by one of the local lovelies."

"Hey, those tits of hers would attract ten times more lighting than my meager love muscle."

"Rob, don't listen to Jack," admonished Jeff. "Always put women up on a pedestal like Stark does. In the long run, you'll be far more successful with them."

"Not with the ones with big tits," said Jack. "They can't balance themselves on those pedestals. Fall off every time."

Uncle Bill's jeep was waiting for them when they stumbled down from the trail. He was amazed at their early appearance and had intended to set up his lawn chair and read for an hour, maybe two before he expected to see them. Just the same, the threatening sky he'd seen and heard earlier that morning to the north town had become a real concern and he was gratified they'd taken his warnings seriously.

"I can't believe you flatland boys can handle the mountains like you do. I've seen kids from the church camp tossing their cookies after a half hour on one of these trails."

"Corn detasseling," said Jack, and laughed. "We're in super-human condition."

To Andrew's discomfort, Rob continued the teasing. "Uncle Bill, Starkey kicked us all the way up and down the mountain. Can't wait to get back to his A&W car hop."

"Say," Jeff asked his uncle, "did you hear any of that thunder?"

"Sure did," he replied. "Brought to mind the big guns at Anzio."

"What's 'Anzio', Uncle Bill"? asked Rob.

"Oh, a little ruckus I was involved in during the war. Now, what's this I hear about a car hop?" A moment later he had a recollection, "Ah, the little Spinelli girl. Yeah, she is a sweetheart. Now, Andrew, her dad's a pal of mine so you treat her right. Otherwise, I'll chuck your ass off those chalk cliffs." He gave Andrew a wink.

In a half hour they were back at the cabin. Jeff and Rob were baiting hooks with "Fireballs" within minutes of their arrival. Andrew and Jack walked down stream to skip flat rocks across the river and make plans for their evening with the girls.

"Think Jeff would let us use his car? We can double," said Jack.

"Nah, you take the car. I want to take it slow with Nancy. We've still got a few days, and I don't want to blow it. Shit, you'll probably be humping DeAnn tonight."

"I don't think so. She's pretty hot but even I don't want to get carried away," said Jack. "Hate to admit it to you, but I do know where babies come from."

"Good. You don't want her to chase you to the Air Force to pay for some little baby Jack." He threw a rock thirty yards to the river's opposite bank and it shattered on a boulder. "I'll walk downtown. She's got that old Ford if we need wheels."

"OK. I got DeAnn's phone number. She's expecting me to call before supper. I'll tell her you two won't be joining us."

"Yep. Nancy's off at eight. She expects me to just show up before then. Tell DeAnn you don't know what we're doing. See if she knows something that we don't."

"Right. They may still dump us," said Jack. "You are an ugly son of a bitch. Nancy's probably come to her senses by now."

"Hey, I'm not as ugly as your sorry ass. Nancy knows quality when she sees it. She wants me to meet her brother. Guess he got fucked up in the war."

"Oh, no shit?" said Jack. "Is he back home from Vietnam?"

"Yes. Still has to go back and forth to the hospital. Got shot in the chest. I really want to talk to him. You know, find out what it's like over there, what the Army's like." He skipped another rock. "The more I think about going up to IU, the more I'd like to just forget the whole thing and enlist."

"That's why I joined the Air Force. So many guys are in the military, and those pussies in college are getting over on them. Either everybody goes or nobody goes. Just get that war over with and quit fucking around."

Just then, Rob yelled to them from the cabin. "Hey Jack! Some dame's on the phone for you."

"Be right there," Jack shouted. To Andrew, he said, "See? She can't even wait for me to call."

"Well, it is getting late," said Andrew, looking at his watch. "Four o'clock already. She wants time to line up somebody else in case you ditch her. Bet she's been driving around all day with big curlers in her hair to let the local boys know there's a new stud in town."

It was DeAnn, and she wanted to pick up Jack as soon as he could be ready. He apologized to Mrs. Thompson as she'd planned dinner for them all. "Oh, I'll eat his share," said Rob.

He signaled to Andrew. "She didn't talk to Nancy. They're not planning on us getting together. You're on your own buddy."

"Oh, shit. Guess we'll just have to make our own fun then."

"Yeah. I'm crushed as well."

"So when is she picking you up?"

"Any minute. We could give you a ride downtown."

"Nah. Mrs. Thompson would be pissed if we both left. Besides, I've got a couple hours to kill. Don't want to hang around too long before she gets off work. I'd look desperate."

After dinner, Andrew sat with his hosts and their nephews and listened to Uncle Bill talk about his former career mining molybdenum for a company called, Amax. They had a huge mine north of Leadville called "Climax." He'd worked there 40 years, with only a three-year absence during the war.

In his youth, Bill had been a bear of a man standing over six feet tall and weighing two hundred pounds. But the decades of underground mine work had reduced his physical stature considerably. Still, he was energetic and fun loving, and having the boys visit was far more of a treat for him than he was willing to let on.

He regaled them with tails of mining the "Phillipson Level," "Block Cave" mining, the "chute and grizzly" loading system, the pounding headaches caused by nitroglycerin fumes from dynamite detonations, and miners getting "rocked up" with silicosis. He, himself, had a bit of the lung disorder caused by years of breathing the toxic air of the mine.

Many of his early paychecks had been accepted in shares of "Climax" stock, of questionable worth at the time, but later becoming a comfortable nest egg for his and Doris's retirement.

At seven, Andrew excused himself. They all knew he had a date of sorts and planned on walking into town. He refused offers of rides from both Jeff and Bill. "Yeah, I'm stiff from that hike all right, but a slow walk is just what I need to loosen up. Nancy will give me a ride home. See you guys back at the river."

Bill waved at him as he walked towards the highway. "Remember, be nice. Don't want to see your hide nailed on the wall of the VFW." Andrew gave a wave back and shouted, "I'll be a perfect gentleman."

The walk into town alone was a tonic for him. The air was fresh and the sky clear in a way he had seldom seen in Indiana, except maybe for a week or two in the fall. Mt. Princeton loomed to his left and he stumbled in the loose gravel at the highway's edge as he kept glancing up and marveling at its sheer mass.

People in pickups waved at him as he walked, and one truck filled with teens stopped to offer him a ride in the back. He turned down their offer, thanking them awkwardly.

Forty-five minutes later he took a seat at the table they'd sat at after the Princeton hike. It seemed much longer ago than yesterday. He watched Nancy come and go from the window several times before she noticed him sitting there. The way her face burst into a smile removed any doubt he had that she might have tired of her Hoosier admirer. He noticed that the two other car hops were now aware of him and teasing Nancy as only girlfriends can do. Another positive sign, he thought.

She ran over quickly and told him she'd be able to leave as soon as Louise showed up. A few minutes later, she came out the back door carrying two tall iced teas and a straw for each.

"Can we walk around awhile?" she said. "I need to cool off and relax. Let's head over to the park."

They stopped at the highway while trucks passed. Then she took his hand and ran wildly across the road pulling him along, her huarache sandals slapping the pavement.

"Hey, my legs are sore as heck," he said. "Can't move too fast."

The city park in the twilight was filled with children. The setting sun was just beginning to touch a shoulder of Mt. Yale, bathing the park in an other-worldly, golden blush through the leaves of the massive Cottonwoods. Parents and older siblings socialized in clusters. Dogs romped through the throng and splashed into the creek.

"Lake Buena Vista," Nancy said with a chuckle as they walked past where a low concrete dam backed up Cottonwood Creek into a small pond.

To Andrew's surprise, she continued to hold his hand as they strolled and chatted. He told her that Jack was out with DeAnn, and that Jack suggested they join them. She looked at him coyly and said, "Well this is OK, isn't it?"

"Oh, if this were any more OK, I'd need shock therapy. This is like a dream. Look at this place, and I'm holding hands with the prettiest girl in Colorado."

She squeezed his hand and slurped the remaining iced tea from her cup. She coughed and wiped her chin with a napkin. "Darn lemon seed," she laughed.

"So, how is it you've got time for some stranger like me. I mean, you're, uh..."

"Well...," she said, hesitation in her voice, "there is a story there." She seemed in no hurry to continue, and they walked along for several minutes in an awkward silence. Several people waved and smiled at the two as they strolled around the busy park.

"I had a pretty serious boyfriend," she began. "Fred...went with him for a year. Then he went off to Boulder, you know, CU." She kicked a ball back to a group of shy six year olds.

"We wrote back and forth and got together at Christmas. I missed him so much. He was just so much fun, always joking around with everyone." They sat on a small bench near the creek. "So, this last June he comes home and he's gone 'Hippy'. I mean long hair, Hippy freak. He was a little different at Christmas, but nothing drastic. It was so neat to be with a 'college man' when we went out." She made little quote marks with her fingers when she said, "college man."

"But this summer he'd gone off the wall. All he wanted to talk about was the Vietnam War and President Johnson. Whenever we'd be with other people he'd start badgering them on politics as if he'd attained some higher level of social consciousness and they were all numbskulls. He was just so angry and irritated."

Andrew listened not knowing quite how to respond. For the moment, however, he was content to listen to her voice, and he was gratified that she'd share this part of her life with him.

"I shouldn't tell you this..." She looked around, somewhat nervously. "He was really into pot, you know, marijuana."

"Really?" Andrew said. "Where'd he get that stuff?"

"I don't know. Up at CU, I guess," she shrugged. "But he wanted me to try it. I said, 'Fred, I'm not going to do that. My God, are you crazy?' So, we'd go out and I'd sit with him in his car while he smoked it."

"How did it make him act? I mean, did his eyes spin around in his head or something…"

She giggled. "No. He'd just look out the window and say, 'Wow', over and over. Then he'd fiddle with the radio. I got bored and made him take me home."

"So, he could drive like that?"

"Yeah. Of course, in Bueny there's not a lot to run in to. He got me home OK." She shook her head. "He just got so darn weird." She stood up, suddenly, and took his hand again, pulling him out of his seat. "What finally did it for me was when he got after Ronnie, my brother. There was this big Fourth of July barbeque at the VFW. My dad and mom, Ronnie, your friends Bill and Doris, all these other people were there. Ronnie's sitting with these World War Two guys and they're just drinking beer and joking around. It was so nice to see my brother having fun…" She choked, and put her hand to her mouth. Tears had come to her eyes and she brushed them away with the back of her hand. She took a breath, sighed and continued. "He was having fun with these old guys, talking about him and his buddies eating these 1944 C-Rations. I guess it's food in a can like beef and potatoes, hash or whatever. But, the worst one was ham and lima beans. So, now it's 1965 in Vietnam and they had to eat twenty-year-old…," she tilted her head down, covered her mouth and whispered, "'Ham and Motherfuckers' because they hadn't used them up in World War Two."

Andrew guffawed at Nancy's use of such a foul word. She blushed and put her hands to her face.

"I'm so sorry, Andrew. I would never use such a word, but can you imagine those poor little lima beans generating such hatred?"

She cleared her throat as Andrew laughed. "Ahem," she said, "anyway, they were all just whopping it up about, you know, Ronnie and his buddies eating this terrible stuff. Ronnie was making these comical faces…" She reached in her pocket and retrieved the A&W napkin to wipe her nose. She took a deep breath, shrugging as she did. "Then Fred starts in with this anti-war stuff and how 'there's nothing funny about the American aggression in Vietnam, blah, blah, blah'. Everybody just looked at him. I was just mortified. He's got this stringy hair down to his shoulders, wearing these holey bell-bottom jeans-- worse than Wendy's last night--just looks like a slob, and he's lecturing these older gentlemen and my brother." She stepped ahead and turned to look at him.

"I didn't mean to spoil our walk, Hoosier."

Andrew smiled. "Don't be silly, Nancy. I want to hear this," he answered. "This is something I'm dealing with myself, you know, going off to college while so many guys my age are over there. That's why Jack joined the Air Force. He's smarter than I am but he just couldn't see going to college with all this shit going on." He took her hand again. "So tell me, what happened."

"Well, it got ugly. Some of those VFW guys are very tough. A couple of guys threatened to throw Fred over this fence. Another wanted to drag him behind a motorcycle. Ronnie tried to calm everybody down but I could tell he was in pain, breathing hard and his face beet red. My mom was all upset, trying to keep Ronnie quiet and my dad was the maddest I've ever seen him."

There was no moon yet and the canopy of Cottonwoods was making it difficult to see where they were walking. They angled towards the brightly lit highway. Andrew hoped to lighten her mood, but wanted the story to continue.

"Say, is there any chance we could drive out by the chalk cliffs in that beater of yours?"

"Beater? That truck's been babied since it was new in '58." She socked him playfully in his arm. "Sure, I'll show you the church camp."

"Church camp?"

"Yes. Right near the cliffs there's a religious camp for high school kids. They always have a bonfire and sing-alongs in the evening. We could stroll through and no one would even notice us."

Andrew didn't like the sound of this, but would follow her anywhere.

"OK," he said.

On the drive, her mood did brighten and she told him stories about Wendy, DeAnn, Louise and her other girlfriends. He laughed more than once at her description of their antics in high school.

"Won't you miss it?" she asked as they drove along. "I mean high school."

"Maybe, a little. I'll still have the friends forever. But the day-to-day grind I'll be happy to give up."

"Oh, I think you'll remember them as some of the best days of your life."

Andrew looked over at her, smiling to himself. "I went to a wedding just before coming out here," he said. "Buddy of mine got a girl in trouble. Anyway, the Best Man's toast said something like, 'May the happiest day of your past be the saddest day of your future.' That's not exact, but close. If high school was the worst, then I've got it made."

"You must have a spark of sentimentality in you to remember that toast. That's a good sign in a male. You're good raw material."

"For what?" he asked.

She parked the truck near a large horse corral that Andrew recalled passing in Bill's Jeep on the way up Mt. Princeton. They walked towards a log portal that arched over the dirt road. A sign read "Freedom Ranch." Andrew pointed off to the right. "That's the road Bill drove us up to get to the trailhead."

"You guys must be in pretty good shape to have climbed two of these monsters since you got here. Princeton almost did me in when I hiked it last summer."

They walked hand in hand down the dark roadway as it twisted its way towards a complex of cabins and other structures. They could hear voices and singing below them. At the bottom, the road opened to a large common area and a throng of teenagers was gathered around an open fire pit. They ringed the fire, arms around one another, swaying in time to the hymns they sang. The facility was set in a small basin bordered by a low hill on the east and the steep wooded slope of Mt. Princeton on the west. The road they'd walked down continued through the center of camp and provided a back exit that led down to Chalk Creek and the hot springs road. Rough-hewn cabins lined the hillside, and below, facing the common area, were staff facilities and a dining hall.

Other campers and staff strolled between buildings and around the common area. Boys could be seen through the windows of a large log structure gathered around a pool table.

"See? We can walk around like we're in the middle of a small town, anonymous and everything."

"This is a great place," he said, looking around. "Smells like barbequed chicken. That must be their mess hall."

"Gee, if I'd known you were hungry, I'd have snuck you a cheeseburger."

"No, I had supper. Just noticing the smell." He put his arm around her shoulder and hugged her to him. She rubbed her head into his arm.

They strolled to the south end of the camp and looked out on the Arkansas River valley. A three-quarter moon was just beginning to show above the horizon, and they watched until it fully emerged. Walking back they stopped at a log bench in the shadow beyond the bonfire's glow. She softly gripped the biceps of his left arm with both her hands, resting her head against them, and watched the group swaying and singing.

A young woman of the camp staff saw them and walked over. "I

know you two are hoping someone will invite you to join us at the fire."
Her smile was pleasant and infectious.

"She does, but I'm trying to lay low."

"Thank you for asking," said Nancy. "We're just enjoying the
evening here in your beautiful camp. We hope you don't mind."

"Of course not. This place is so special. Can you believe those
stars? Please stay as long as you like. At least until we have lights out,
anyway."

"Yes ma'am. We'll be long gone by then," said Andrew. They
watched her walk towards the fire. When she reached the swaying
young people she dipped between two singers, inserting herself into
their line.

Andrew hugged Nancy close to him and turned her face up with his
hand. He kissed her lightly on the lips, then on the tip of her nose and
again on the forehead.

She looked at him through the darkness and heaved a sigh.

"Now, what am I going to do with you?" she said softly.

"Take me back to your truck, Miss Hoosier-killer."

Her face became serious and she took his hands. "Umm, Andrew?"

He could tell what she was thinking. "Don't worry. I've been
warned to treat you like a lady. Something like, I think, ending up with
my hide nailed to the wall of the VFW."

"VFW? Who...?"

"Bill said he's friends with your dad."

"Oh? How did..."

"Jeff told him we'd met. Bill said you were a 'sweetheart', and to be
nice to you. How am I doing so far?"

"Come on, time to go," she said, the smile returning to her face.

When they arrived, he opened the driver's side and led her to get in
first. "I'm used to having a girl on the right side," he said.

"Chauvanist," she giggled. She turned facing him on the seat
and put her arms around his neck. She kissed him once, then again,
lingering a few seconds. She looked at him intently and kissed him
again opening her mouth slightly. He responded gently with his tongue
and hugged her to him.

His emotions flooded over him and he had to turn his head, breathe
for a time, and wait for his heart to slow down.

"Jeez, sorry," he panted. "It's not every day I get to kiss someone
like you. I don't want to pass out and find myself lying in that corral
tomorrow morning."

"I'd just put you in the back and dump you out at Bill's place," she answered, and snuggled her nose against his shoulder.

After a minute, his heart returned to near normal and he found her mouth again. They caressed each other and kissed passionately until a car drove up the road from the camp and bathed the pickup in its headlights. They slouched down below the dashboard, then slid up again as the car passed. Both were in need of catching their breath, and they leaned their heads together to rest. The large moon had emerged above the pines and it held their attention as if it were the screen at a drive-in movie.

"This may sound old-fashioned," she whispered after they'd sat together for a time, "but I need to be home by midnight. I know they don't sleep 'til I come in, and it's just something I've always done for them. Please don't be mad."

"What time is it? Oh, eleven fifteen. Mad? Are you kidding?" He kissed her hands, then up her arm. "Yes, I'm enraged and out of control."

She laughed, "Stop!" and rubbed the top of his head.

"OK. Maybe you can finish the story now."

"You mean the Fred story?"

"Yes, if you don't mind talking about it."

She sighed and began, "Well, luckily I wasn't with him that night. We'd just agreed to meet there, you know, I'd go down with my folks. But everyone knew we had been going together for a long time. Anyway, he just got in his car and left. The next day, he called me but I wasn't home. He didn't leave a message with mom. He just hung up."

"He must have been feeling bad."

"I suppose," she said. "Next, I heard he had packed up and gone back to Boulder. That was over a month ago and I haven't heard a word since."

Andrew noticed her hands were moist with perspiration.

"But, you know? I fell so out of love with him that day that I haven't missed him at all. If he called me, I think I could be polite, but I'll never go out with him again."

"We'd better get going. Want me to drive?"

"Can you handle a beast like this…three on the tree?"

"No sweat, honey. We got stick shift in Indiana. Rubber tires, too."

He handled the stick and clutch easily, having learned to drive in a Ford Falcon with a similar arrangement. When he shifted to third he pulled her over to him and she leaned her head back on his shoulder. They drove in silence until he pulled over at the Thompson's mailbox. He pushed in the headlight knob and turned off the engine.

"You'll be ten minutes early," he said. "Will I blow it if I ask to see you again tomorrow? Before you answer, it doesn't have to be like tonight. Maybe we can just walk in the park for a while. I know you have another life."

"Yes, I want to see you tomorrow. But, I don't work. How about you come over to the house. I want you to meet my brother. That is, if you still want to."

"I really do want to talk to him. What time would be good?"

"How 'bout you come for dinner, around five. He gets home at three-thirty and takes a nap. I'll warn him that a Hoosier is coming over who wants to hear about his Army days. I don't think he'll mind." She kissed him on the cheek. "And I know you'll be careful with what you ask about. He doesn't need to remember bad things."

Andrew got out and she slid to the driver's seat. He closed the door quietly and pushed down the lock button.

"You go straight home, young lady. By the way, where is home?"

"The gray two-story behind the lumber yard. Barbequed chicken. Show up hungry."

"See you at five, Nancy."

The pickup crunched down the gravel road and accelerated. He watched after her and listened as she went through the rough gears until reaching cruising speed. As he turned away she beeped her horn three times in rapid succession. "Maybe a dog in the road," he thought, then smiled as he realized she was saying goodbye once more. "Holy shit, I'm in love," he said out loud.

"Good for you, asshole."

It was Jack, sitting in the dark on the porch swing. Andrew, startled at first, gave a wave to his friend.

"Didn't think you'd beat me back. Nancy makes a point of getting in early."

"Not surprised."

"So, how'd it go for you?"

"Not bad. Not bad at all. She's going to Aspen with her mother first thing in the morning and wanted to get home at a decent hour. I couldn't take much more anyway. My tongue's about sucked out by the roots. Got terrible blue balls."

"So, she's hot stuff?"

"Well, I kept things under control. You must have had a hell of a good time."

"Man, I'm head over heels," Andrew said, slapping himself with his hands. "I've got to get a grip."

"You wouldn't be the first pilgrim to have a summer fling get out of control, buddy. But you didn't do the nasty dance or anything did you?"

Andrew laughed softly. "No way, man. Far from it. But, she's, I don't know…I, uh…"

"Come on, let's get some shuteye," said Jack. "We can do the play-by-play in the morning. My tongue's killing me."

Chapter 8
Ron

The next day, Jeff dropped Andrew off at the lumberyard a few minutes before five. There was still a buzz of activity going on with men loading trucks with two-by-fours, pre-hung doors and bundles of cedar shakes. He walked down a dirt road on the south side of the yard, then turned north on a similar, apparently unnamed, street. The grey two-story was another two hundred yards up the street. A large lawn began a full fifty yards before he reached the house. A John Deere yard tractor he assumed was used to keep it mowed was parked under a lean-to next to a detached garage. Nancy's pickup was in the garage.

A young man was sitting in the sun on a springy lawn chair reading a newspaper. He wore cut-off jeans and a white T-shirt that read "High Country Lumber and Supply."

As Andrew approached, the man put down his paper and watched him impassively for a few seconds. Then he stood and stuck out his hand.

"You must be Andrew."

"Yes sir. You've got to be Ron."

"That's me. Glad to meet you. Take it easy on the 'Sir'. I work for a living."

Andrew almost replied, "Yes sir" again but caught himself. "OK," he said.

He was Andrew's height, just shy of six feet. He had a shock of dark- brown hair, parted on the right side, and a mustache that grew just past the corners of his mouth. He was otherwise clean-shaven but a five o'clock shadow was showing. His frame could carry a more robust body, but it was evident he was severely underweight.

Ron began refolding the day's Denver Post.

"So, you're the Hoosier that wants to hear about the Army, huh?"

"Yes, if you don't mind the intrusion." He looked around at the expansive lawn. "Man, this is a beautiful yard. That's a good-looking John Deere in the shed. I'd hate to mow this with my four-and-a-half-horse Briggs & Stratton. Take me all week."

"Thirty years old but runs like a top. I can get Nancy to ride it if I just start it for her. Kind of like Tom Sawyer getting his buddies to white wash the fence."

"Ha. She's too smart to fall for that. I bet she loves riding that thing around."

"You're probably right," Ron chuckled. He could hear the affection for his sister in the young man's voice. "Sounds like you're getting to know her pretty well."

"Oh, we're just friends," Andrew said, "But, uh..."

"Why don't you drag that thing over here." Ron pointed to a lawn chair several yards away that matched his. "So, you were thinking about joining up?"

"Just thinking." Andrew hoisted the chair and put it down at an angle facing Ron. "I'm going to college next month, like Nancy. But I've talked to the recruiters, you know, Army, Navy. My folks would have a shit fit if they knew about that." He adjusted his chair again and sat down. "You must have guys like me asking you dumb questions all the time. It's just that, man, you've been there, what you've seen... God, how do I put it. You can always be proud, you were there, you measured up. You..."

"Hold on there, troop," Ron said with a bemused smile on his face. "I get the idea."

"Sorry," said Andrew. "I have a tendency to get carried away."

"I know what you're trying to say. Not unusual for a guy your age to want to do something different, something against the grain."

Ron rocked in his chair a while and Andrew waited patiently for him to continue. He'd just displayed some of his immaturity to Ron and didn't want to do so again.

"You know what I'd do?" said Ron. "I'd go to school at least one full year, then decide what to do at that time. Don't get pissed off some day and enlist. That's like getting drunk and waking up with a tattoo on your ass."

Andrew laughed out loud at the analogy. "Like don't do something rash in the heat of the moment."

"Exactly. Then, depending on what you want to do or what you want to get yourself into, there are lots of ways to go."

For the next half hour, he described for Andrew the various facets of the US Army and what his day-to-day life might be like. He told him about Armor, Artillery and the Infantry, and how these units interacted. He was also able to tell Andrew which post he'd probably end up at if he selected a certain military job.

"You pick Armor, you'll go to Knox, near Louisville, Kentucky. You pick Artillery and you'll head down to Ft. Sill in Oklahoma. Infantry can get you sent to a variety of places, some of them shitty. Polk is the worst, down in Louisiana. Gordon and Stewart are in Georgia along with Benning. Benning is not too bad. You could hit Florida one weekend, Atlanta the next."

Andrew listened intently and asked questions only when he was as sure as he could be that he'd not sound stupid or silly. He had never realized how intricate the workings of the military really were. Still he wanted to hear from this real veteran what Vietnam was like.

"Ron, tell me what you did in Vietnam, I mean, what sort of unit were you in, what did you do all day, how was it, did you go…"

Ron held up a hand. "Got it. I was with the 173rd Airborne Brigade. We were a…"

"Holy shit. You were a paratrooper?"

Ron liked this kid. "Tell you what," he said. "You need to go let Nancy know you're here. She's doing barbeque on the grill. Ask her to bring us a couple beers, and say hello to mom. Then we can talk some more."

Andrew walked up to the screen door of the kitchen and noticed that a grill on the patio was already stoked and ready for use. He saw movement inside and knocked softly.

A woman in her mid-forties, he guessed, opened the door for him and welcomed him inside. She was Nancy's height and not much heavier. Her hair was as full as her daughter's but fell to her shoulders. There was a hint of gray beginning to show. Andrew thought she was beautiful, and felt his face flush.

She smiled at him and, as had Ron before her, said, "You must be Andrew. I'm Anita, Nancy's mom. You're even more handsome than she told me. Let me go find her."

Anita yelled up the stairs to Nancy and she shortly came bounding down, taking the stairs two at a time.

"Hi, Hoosier!" she said with a huge smile. "Did you meet Ron?" She was barefoot and wore cotton shorts with a Madras print and a T-shirt like her brother's.

"Yes. We've been talking for a while already. He, uh, sent me to get a couple beers. Is that OK, Mrs. Spinelli?"

"Sweetheart, if Ron wants to drink a beer with you, you must have passed his test. Nancy, help Andrew find the beer. Oh…," she said, wiping her hands on her apron, "it's just the four of us for dinner. Nancy's dad and brother, Steve, have a shindig at the Rotary tonight."

"Bunch of drunks," said Nancy.

"No they're not young lady," said Anita, and swatted her daughter on the bottom.

"Mom!" said Nancy, and pointed to Andrew.

Anita giggled. "They'll be home late. You can meet them next time."

"I'll look forward to it," he answered, and thought, *What a relief.*

Nancy had pulled two bottles of Coors from the refrigerator. Anita said, "Honey, take him in to meet Grammy Anna."

"Oh, I forgot. Come on Andrew." She put the beers down, took his arm and whispered to him as they walked out of the kitchen. "Grammy's had a stroke and doesn't respond. Just act like she's normal. For all we know her mind is OK, but she just can't express herself."

An elderly woman Andrew guessed to be in her late seventies sat in a rocker near a window that looked out on the lumber yard. She had a needlepoint project in her lap that appeared to have been dormant for quite some time. Her face was expressionless as she stared out the window.

"Hi, Grammy. I want you to meet my friend, Andrew." Nancy put her arm around her grandmother and turned her gently towards him. "He's here visiting from Indiana."

"I'm glad to meet you, Grammy." He smiled at her and then looked at Nancy. "I can tell you two are related. You both have the same nose."

Grammy seemed to look between them, then turned back to the window.

"We'll be right outside if you need anything." Grammy stared blankly ahead. Nancy kissed her on the cheek and led Andrew back to the kitchen.

"Thanks. Hope you didn't mind."

"Of course not. She's your dad's mom, right?"

Anita answered for Nancy. "Yes. We put her by the window so she can see Chuck when he walks around over in the lumberyard." She sighed, "We keep hoping she'll come out of it. Anyway, we'll give you the family history when dinner's ready."

"Here you go," said Nancy, handing Andrew the beers. Then she cocked her head and asked her mother, "Mom, what was Grammy's maiden name?"

"Why, O'Hare. Nancy, shame on you. You know that."

"That's right. I'd forgotten. Andrew said I looked like I might have Indian blood 'cause of our family nose. See Andrew? I'm a docile Italian-Irish combination."

"That's a relief," he chuckled.

She winked at him and said, "Well, I've got to get going on the chicken. You must be starved."

"Can I help with anything?" said Andrew, trying to use his best manners.

"No sweetheart," said Anita. "We can handle it."

Back outside with Ron, he handed him a bottle. "Your mom is sure a nice lady. And I met Grammy."

Ron nodded. "Real sad. One day fine, the next day she can't say a word and just looks off into the distance. Happened while I was overseas." He took a swig of his Coors and savored it momentarily with his eyes closed. "Man that's good. All we got in 'Nam was hot Carling Black Label."

"Ron, before you tell me about the 173rd, tell me about paratrooper training. I've wanted to do that since I was in grade school."

Ron stifled a burp, his fist to his mouth. Then he gulped and belched loudly, ending with a grin of satisfaction.

"Ronnie, my God!" chorused the two females. "Yes, he must really like Andrew," whispered Anita.

He ignored them and began. "Three weeks, down at Ft. Benning. First week, they call 'Ground Week'. Lots of running and physical stuff, getting used to the harness, doing 'PLFs', 'Parachute Landing Falls'. Then you go to 'Tower Week'. You start jumping from these thirty-four foot towers and slide down cables to a berm a hundred yards away, then climb back up the tower and do it again. The big deal is getting dropped from the two-hundred-fifty-foot 'Free Tower'. They strap you into a harness attached to a deployed chute. Then they haul your ass up on a cable to the top." He took another swig of beer. "All the time the guy in the tower is talking to you on a loud speaker trying to keep you calm and focused." He stood up and extended his arms skyward as if holding the risers of a parachute. "Calm my ass," he said. "You try looking straight down two hundred and fifty feet and keep calm. No fucking way."

Andrew laughed out loud and Nancy turned from the charcoal grill to see what the two were doing.

"Mom," she whispered at the kitchen window. "Mom, look at Ronnie." Anita opened the screen door and stood looking out at the two young men. "Yes, I see him, honey. He's coming around. It's going to take him some time, but he'll be OK." She joined her daughter at the grill and put her arm around her. Nancy reached to her mother's face and wiped the tears from her cheeks.

"I'm so glad you invited Andrew over. Wish he was going to be in town longer than a week."

"Gee, Mom. Did you have to remind me?"

"Nancy, if it's meant to be, things have a way of working out. Remember, you just met him, and you know how people can change very quickly." She kissed Nancy on the forehead and went back up the steps to the kitchen.

Ron was continuing with his description. "So, anyway, the tower guy yells at you, 'What are you?!' You're supposed to yell back 'Airborne!'. Most guys just squeak out some unintelligible jibberish or blow a spit bubble. Then he yells again, 'Goddamn it! What are you?!' The second time, most guys can yell 'Airborne!' back at him. Now…," Ron put his arms back up, looks down and bugs his eyes out comically, "once he sees you're still sane, he hits the switch and hauls you up another ten, twelve feet and the chute is released. Man, you drop like a rock for, I don't know, twenty feet before that chute grabs enough air to slow you down." Ron sat back down in his lawn chair. "There's no such thing as a paratrooper diaper as far as I know, but if ever you needed one, it's right when they haul you up those last few feet and you hear that mechanism let go, ka chung…"

"Shit," said Andrew. "That sounds real hairy."

"The good thing about it is the way you feel when you hit the ground and you realize you're not dead." Ron paused, then laughed at the memory. "Usually, there are so many guys in your 'Airborne' class that you only get to do the Free Tower, maybe once or twice. For me, that was plenty. Scared me more than the actual jumps."

"So, then what?"

"Third week is 'Jump Week'. You pretty much just polish up your techniques then they haul you out to Lawson Army Airfield. You get 'chuted up' and sit on the tarmac waiting for the command to load into the bird. They have these funny looking C-119s, 'Flying Boxcars', they call them. We had them in Vietnam as gunships. Anyway, you're sitting there and some other guys load up and take off. So you sit there, and sit there, and eventually the bird comes back and taxis up in front of your group. That's when you realize, 'Hey, where'd those other guys go?'" Andrew laughed at Ron as he made faces of a terror-striken youth. "They really jumped out of that son of a bitch! Holy shit!"

Andrew was laughing uproariously. Nancy scolded them from the patio, "Ronnie, would you two hold it down and watch your language! You're going to scare Grammy."

"Yes, ma'am. Now, hold it down, Andrew." Ron chuckled and winked at Andrew as he was collecting himself.

"Almost time for dinner," she yelled again. "Why don't you two rowdies wash up and set the table."

"OK. We'll be right there. So, anyway…," Ron continued. "you load up on the bird. Two lines of guys, 'sticks' they call them. I think it was around twelve to fifteen guys each. You sit on these nylon web benches along the side of the aircraft. Nobody's saying anything. Some guys are looking real sick. Noisy as hell inside the plane."

"I'd be shitting bricks," said Andrew.

"Plane takes off, then flies around for a while. They're only going to a drop zone a few miles across the Chattahoochee River in Alabama, but they want to build up the suspense as much as possible." He took another long pull on his Coors, then turned the empty bottle upside down and let the last drops fall to the grass.

"The Jumpmaster starts looking out the door of the bird. He's got these goggles on and he's wearing like a sky-diver chute in case he falls out the door. We jump at 1,250 feet. He leans way out the door looking for the panels on the drop zone."

"Jeez."

"So, he sees the DZ coming up and shouts, 'GET READY! Everybody stamp their foot on the deck. Then, Stand up! Hook up! Check equipment! Sound off for equipment check!' What's amazing is how these guys, most of them scared shit-less, start to respond to their training. You know, in their minds they're in denial, like 'No way am I jumping out of this son of a bitch.' But they're so conditioned that they'd probably jump without a chute."

"Oh, man," said his young guest.

"Next command is, 'STAND IN THE DOOR!' Usually some hot shot officer gets the honor to be first out. Jump master is watching for the jump light to turn green. Soon as the nose of the bird passes the panel line on the ground the pilot flips the light from red to green and the Jumpmaster starts yelling, 'GO, GO, GO!' The first man is gone and everybody just starts doing the 'Airborne shuffle' towards the back of the bird and that open door." Ron grimaced and pushed on his chest. "Need a second. Sometimes this hole gets to me," he chuckled. "Come on. Let's head to the house. Nancy runs a tight ship when it comes to meal time."

The two young men washed their hands at an outside spigot and began setting plates and silver around the picnic table. Nancy had filled a shallow baking pan with chicken that sat temptingly in the center of the table. A pitcher of iced tea was set at each end. Andrew glanced in the kitchen and saw Nancy patiently spoon-feeding Grammy and chatting at the woman as if she were lucid.

"Your sister is a very special girl."

"Yeah, you could do worse," said Ron. "She really grew up on me while I was gone."

"I think we're about ready." Anita was speaking to them through the screen window. "Nancy, turn the radio on for Grammy and let's go feed the boys. They're looking gaunt."

Shortly, they were all seated together. After Nancy said "Grace," the food was passed around and the two young men ate as quickly as good manners would allow. Anita sat at the end of the table near her son and massaged his shoulder. "I saw you holding your chest. You've got to take it easy with your story-telling. Andrew will get the point without you having to jump up and down."

"I'll take it easy. The good part is over anyway. Right, Andrew?"

"Soon as you tell me about jumping out the door at 1,250 feet. And, I doubt there's much to laugh at in that description."

"Ronnie can make anything funny," said Nancy.

"How 'bout the family history?" asked Andrew. "How'd the Spinellis end up in this valley?"

Anita began a brief synopsis. "Well, my husband Chuck's dad, Charles, senior, moved out from Omaha to Denver with the Union Pacific Railroad back in the 1920s. As soon as he got settled, he sent for Grammy Anna. No sooner had she arrived and Charles lost his job. He never said much about what happened but the rumor was that he discovered some supervisors were taking, shall we say, 'unofficial' passengers from Chicago to Denver for the National Western Stock Show."

"Hookers," chuckled Ron. "So, then..."

"That's enough, honey." Anita put her arm around Ron's neck and continued. "He made the mistake of telling the perpetrators what he knew and to knock it off before they got in trouble. But the UP discovered what was going on from another source and, to avoid a scandal, they fired everybody that was involved or even knew about it. That included Grampa."

"What a screw job!" offered Andrew, innocently.

"Well put, Andrew," said Ron with a huge smile on his face.

"Ronny!" laughed Nancy.

Anita held up her hand to them and cleared her throat. "Now, Grammy was pregnant with Chuck, so Grandpa took the very first job he could find and that was assistant station agent for the Denver & Rio Grande Western Railroad down the valley in Salida."

"Well, that's not too complicated," said Andrew, his face beginning to lose its red glow of embarrassment.

"Not really. But unfortunately, Grammy wasn't too happy with Salida. Not big enough, no shopping, no theatre, you know, like they had in Omaha. He'd tell her, 'Anna, look at this magnificent valley, all this beauty at our doorstep and, if you need some excitement, we're only a long day to Denver.' He was assuming a train trip, of course. Back then you'd get on the train here, then ride south through the Royal Gorge to Pueblo, then north to Denver. Later on, when the Moffat Tunnel was completed, you could ride the train north over Tennessee Pass to Dotsero, then change to an East-bound."

"When Grampa came down here," Ron added, "you could still ride a narrow-gauge train called the 'Denver, South Park & Southern' back over Trout Creek Pass. Then it followed the South Platte River all the way to Denver. And the Midland came directly from Colorado Springs. Four different rail routes to choose from..."

"Anyhow," Anita continued, "Grammy made Grampa promise to take her to Denver several times a year. That seemed to satisfy her, and they stayed in Salida. Chuck grew up there. Then, like everyone else, he went off to the war. That was 1943. He'd never seen the ocean so he joined the Navy."

Nancy giggled at this comment. "Every time I hear that I crack up," she said.

Anita continued. "When he came back from the war he went to the University of Denver on the GI Bill and that's where he met me. We got married after Chuck's graduation."

"So, the lumberyard in Buena Vista?" said Andrew. "How'd that come about?"

Ron took over the story. "Grandpa was a sly dude. He got to know an old guy named Smoot who was the original owner of our lumberyard. Grandpa would sometimes drive a switch engine up from Salida to deliver a boxcar of lumber Smoot had on order. Wasn't Grandpa's job to drive the engine, but he'd do it just for fun. They became real good buddies. Smoot never seemed to have enough money to keep his business running, so Grandpa began making him some secured loans. Every time Smoot couldn't pay up, he'd have him sign over a little piece of the business. This went on for years. Then one time, Smoot had to relinquish enough that Grandpa had 51% ownership. Suddenly, Smoot realized he was working for Grandpa."

Anita chimed in again, clearly enjoying the story. "But Mr. Smoot didn't mind. He was getting on in years and had no one to turn the business over to, and there were certainly no cash buyers back during the Depression. Grandpa paid him a nice salary to run the yard and no one ever knew he wasn't still the owner. He passed away just before Pearl Harbor." She paused and took a drink of her iced tea. "Then, Grandpa took retirement from the Rio Grande and started running the lumber yard."

"Yeah," said Ron. "He said he'd worked in railroading for 35 years and now it was time to get serious about a career."

They all laughed at this anecdote, and Andrew thought of his own recently deceased grandfather's very similar sense of humor.

"Grandpa had planned all along to give the yard to Chuck," Anita continued. "When we were finished at DU, Grandpa brought Chuck into the business. It's provided very well for our family, I don't mind saying."

The sun was just beginning its descent behind Mt. Yale, though the actual sunset below a mountain-less horizon would not occur for another 45 minutes. Ron was showing his fatigue.

"Andrew, we've got to continue our story another day. I'm beat."

"Ronnie opens the yard at 5AM," said Nancy. "Construction crews have to drive so far to some of their jobs they need the early start."

"I wondered why you got to lounge around reading the paper so early," joked Andrew.

"I've always been an early bird. Dad and Steve come in at eight. They get to do the social, evening crap like the Chamber and Rotary. They can have it."

"Well, I'll be in town a while yet. I'll hope to hear some more before I have to head back to Hoosierland."

They all stood at once and began clearing the table. After a few round trips to the kitchen, Andrew followed Ron out into the yard to retrieve their empty bottles.

"Nancy," whispered Anita, "I'll clean up. Why don't you and Andrew go for a drive. It's such a beautiful evening."

A few minutes later, Andrew was backing the pickup out of the garage and they headed north along the highway that followed the Arkansas River. They drove in the shadow of the mountains on their left and right until emerging back into bright sunlight as the river entered a languid stretch.

A fly-fisherman caught their attention and they pulled over to admire his artistry. As he worked his way upstream they decided to park the truck and walk down to the water. Nancy was in a playful mood and talked Andrew into removing his shoes and wading with her to the other side of the river. The cold water was deeper than they expected, and both emerged laughing as the water lapped at the bottoms of their shorts. A large, grassy area remained bathed in sunlight and they walked barefoot through its expanse, then climbed on a massive granite block.

They talked about how much fun dinner had been and how pleased and amazed her mother was to see Ron regaining some of his old sense of humor.

"That's the most comedy I've seen him display since that night at the VFW," she said. "Mom said you were real good for him."

"You know," said Andrew, "you guys aren't giving him enough credit. The guy I talked to didn't seem to be in a bad way emotionally." He pulled her over and kissed her on the forehead. "You know what I think? I think he's bored and doesn't quite know what to do with himself."

"You mean he's bored with Bueny?"

"Yeah. I'm afraid he's outgrown it. I don't mean forever, but at this point in his life he needs to spread his wings. He's seen too much and done too much to just hang around town. Is he interested in going to school somewhere?"

"He's talked about it a little. He's got the GI Bill, and Disability. Money is no problem." She was lost in thought for a time. Andrew rubbed her back, content to stare out at the valley and the mountains in the distance. He wanted to make sure his brain was seizing indelible images.

"You're right," she said suddenly. "He needs to move to Denver and go to school. The hard part is getting Mom to let go. When he first came back, he was so hurt...she just took over. But now..."

"Would your dad's business suffer if he weren't there?"

"No. Steve could pick up the slack. He did it all while Ronnie was gone."

"Good." Andrew thought another minute. "OK. Here's a problem. Your mom's going to be upset when she realizes both of you will be gone. It could be real lonely for her."

"Hmm. Good point," she said. "Nuts." She pondered a few seconds, then her eyes widened.

"I know. If Ronnie has an apartment in Denver it would give me a place to go on the weekends to get away from Greeley. Mom could run up from Bueny, and I'd come down, and she could visit with both of us. She keeps busy during the week." She turned to Andrew and put her arms around him. "Oh, you are a gem. I'm really starting to like you." She pushed him over backwards on the boulder's flat surface, crossed her arms over his chest and rested her head on them.

Andrew ran his hand through the soft hair on the back of her head. "Well, I like you, too."

She raised her head and smiled at him. "I mean you could be one of those guys who doesn't talk, you know, trying to be macho." She extended her arm and flexed her slender bicep like a weightlifter. "But you're perceptive and not afraid to express your feelings. You're what girls call a 'tender heart'."

He pushed up the sleeve of his T-shirt and flexed his own well-formed bicep. "Does this look like a tender-heart muscle?"

"Nice," she whistled. "Now, don't be offended. It's a compliment."

She took his hand and started to climb down from their rocky perch. "Let's get going. It'll get dark quick when the sun goes below that ridge. We want to cross before then."

They walked back across the grassy glade and waded back into the frigid flow. In a few minutes they were climbing up the bank to the Ford.

As the pickup approached Bill's cabin, she said, "I know you haven't asked yet, but I can't see you tomorrow or the next day. Tomorrow I work the lunch shift, then mom's taking Louise and me to Denver to shop for college, you know, 'co-ed' clothes." She did her two-finger quotes again. "She's really looking forward to it, and we won't get back 'til late on Thursday."

She pulled up in front. Rob, Jeff and Jack were throwing a football in the front yard. They waved and appeared to converse about whether to go around back and give the two some privacy. Andrew removed the awkwardness by opening the truck's door.

"I understand," he said. "When, uh..." He was in abject misery.

"Would it embarrass you if I called? They're in our little phonebook."

"Yeah. Sure. I'll just wait to hear from you," he said, trying to act upbeat. He got out and pushed the door closed. "Well," he said.

"Andrew," she looked at him sympathetically and smiled, "you're very special to me. I'm going to miss you, too. OK?"

"OK," he said, pushing down the lock button. "See you soon." He watched her drive away with as much aloofness as he could muster. As he turned toward the cabin, a bullet pass sailed his way and he just got his hands around it before it hit him square in the stomach.

"OK, asshole," said Jack. "Back to the real world. Let's go catch some fish before it gets too dark."

Chapter 9
VFW

As much for his and Doris' own enjoyment as a treat for the boys, Bill drove them down to view Royal Gorge from the suspension bridge one thousand feet above the Arkansas River near Canon City. Since Doris accompanied them, the four teens squeezed into the backseat of Bill's massive Lincoln sedan. As they pulled back into the carport after a long day in the car, the phone could be heard ringing through the cabin's screen door.

Doris walked in quickly and answered it. The boys were stretching themselves after the long car ride. Jeff and Jack were trying to talk Bill into showing them where he'd found some Ute arrowheads, upstream from the cabin.

"Now, what I didn't tell you was that the spot is on the other side of the river. So, we either wade across, or we have to get the jeep."

"No more car rides," said Rob. "Let's wade."

Just then, Doris came to the door and yelled, "Andrew, there's a gentleman on the phone for you--a Mr. Ron Spinelli."

"Really? Uh, thanks. I'll be right there." Andrew wondered about the call and hoped it had something to do with Nancy canceling her trip and wanting desperately to see him.

"Hey, Ron. How's it going?" he said as Doris handed him the receiver.

"Just fine, troop. Say, since Nancy dumped on you to go shopping I thought we could continue our Army discussion this evening."

"Uh, sure, yeah. That would be great. You sure you don't mind?"

"Hell, no. Why don't you start humping up the highway and I'll pick you up, say, in about a half hour. We'll go down to the VFW and have a few beers."

After apologizing to Mrs. Thompson for missing another dinner and absorbing the good-natured kidding of everyone about going out on the town with his new 'brother-in-law', Andrew jogged up the gravel road to the highway. He crossed over and began walking north. Moments later, he saw the familiar Ford pickup barreling towards him and heard the whine of the transmission as Ron down-shifted before pulling over to the roadside.

"Hop in, troop," Ron said. "Next stop, the Veterans of Foreign Wars. You've hit rock bottom now, boy."

"I don't think so," Andrew said with sheepish grin. "But, how am I going to get a beer in there? Do they sell 3.2?"

"Naw. I'll bring a few beers outside while you wait at one of the picnic tables. No one pays much attention. Just don't yell 'fuck' or start a fire."

The pickup rolled south for a few miles, Ron talking animatedly about the odd farming history of the valley.

"Would you believe lettuce?" he asked.

"Lettuce? You mean, salad lettuce?

"Yep. World-record lettuce harvests. Right here in Bueny."

He turned east on to the Trout Creek Pass highway, crossed the D&RGW tracks, then left again at a busy crossroads fronted by gas stations and a small grocery. Moments later, they wheeled into the club's parking area and pulled in next to a line-up of a dozen or so wildly customized motorcycles. Most had some combination of high handle bars, curving chromed exhaust pipes and leather saddle bags. Oil leakage was evident in the gravel beneath most of the engines.

"Looks like Emery and his buds are here," said Ron. "Forget what I said about yelling 'fuck'. Anything goes when these guys are partying."

Ron went inside and Andrew sauntered across the club's sunburned lawn towards a fence where several tables were lined up. A row of horseshoe pits was nearby, and a noisy contest was underway between two older couples. Andrew smiled to himself as he noticed the relative sizes of the men and women. Funny, he thought, how elderly men seemed to shrink in size but their wives grew larger.

There was an eruption of laughter and whooping inside the club. Moments later, a smiling Ron kicked the screen door open and stepped outside with two long-necked Coors in each hand. As he sat down at the table with Andrew, he shook his head and said, "You can take the Jarhead out of the jungle, but you can't take the jungle out of the Jarhead."

Andrew had no idea what Ron was referring to, and elected not to ask.

"Do those motorcycles belong to VFW guys?"

"Yep," answered Ron. "Bunch of guys from the club ride around together scaring hell out of the old ladies in Salida, Aspen and Leadville. Everybody in Bueny knows they're harmless. Of course, you wouldn't want to fuck with them."

"Not me," said Andrew. "So, who are they?"

"Oh, there's a couple ex-Marines, couple of sailors and five or six Army…a mix of World War II, Korea and Vietnam guys. All of them work around the valley doing construction, railroad, the Reformatory. Emery's the leader of the pack, so to speak. He works as a Reformatory guard. Did a tour with the First Marine Division. Got shrapnel in the neck."

Andrew took a drink of his beer. "Would you tell me a little about Vietnam? I mean, not stuff that's none of my business, you know, but what I might need to know sometime."

"Sure, sure," Ron paused and took a drink, clearly pondering what to say. "Have you ever heard someone say, 'Oh, that guy's a fill-in-the-blank war veteran, but he won't talk about it?' Doesn't make any difference if it's World War II, Korea or Vietnam. Same shit. Have you ever heard someone say that, Andrew?"

"Yes. I've heard people say something like that several times."

"Well, that's a bunch of bullshit. What they should be saying is, 'That guy's a war veteran and he won't talk about it to a dumb son of a bitch like me'."

Andrew laughed uncomfortably.

"It's like this, Andrew. You're a young guy who clearly respects military service. You don't have a know-it-all attitude. I'll bet your dad was in World War II, right?"

"Yes. He was with the 101st Airborne. Landed in Normandy on D-Day. He was in the glider troops."

"Gliders, no shit?" said Ron, clearly impressed. "We had some old guys in the 173rd that had done that. They said they'd rather jump any day than ride in on one of those 'plywood coffins' they called them. Bet your old man's one tough cookie."

Andrew smiled with new awareness suddenly emerging for his father's seldom-mentioned service.

Ron took a drink of his Coors and paused to watch the couples at the horseshoe pit. The clank of the horseshoes hitting metal stakes, and the jabbering players were the only sounds to be heard on the VFW's grassy lot.

"I'm not that unusual," Ron continued. "If someone ever asks me an intelligent question about what I did in Vietnam, I'm happy to talk to them. But, you know the most common question I get?"

"Uh, where you went on R&R?"

"No." He took another drink. "People ask me if I killed anybody."

Andrew was incredulous. "You're shitting me?" he said. He could also feel the tension and resentment in Ron's voice. His affable demeanor had changed and Andrew feared he shouldn't have asked about the war.

But soon Ron continued. "So, I usually walk away like the person wasn't even there. Then they go tell their friends that I'm a 'psycho Vietnam' guy and 'He won't talk about it.' I guess it makes them feel superior or something, like they've successfully put me in the appropriate pigeon hole."

Andrew said nothing and let Ron's anger subside. It didn't take long. Both watched the horseshoe throwers finish their match and rolled eyes at each other as the woman of the winning team picked up her partner and hugged him lustily.

"I can see the headline now," said Ron. "Local man suffocated between wife's enormous tits."

Andrew laughed out loud and took a drink of his Coors. "So, what was it like to be in the 173rd?"

Ron had unbuttoned his shirt and was absent-mindedly rubbing his chest. "Well," he began, "we called ourselves, 'The Herd'."

He'd actually joined the brigade when it was headquartered in Okinawa. It had been a first-response unit organized to meet the force projection requirements of American foreign policy. The force projection target in 1965 turned out to be Vietnam, a place that neither Ron nor his buddies knew much about before they enlisted to be elite paratroopers.

But before they learned names like "Ben Hoa," "War Zone D", "Iron Triangle," "Tay Ninh Province" and a hundred other places, the,ywere a disciplined, hard-core and motivated organization that did what paratroopers love to do, and that's jump out of airplanes. At least once a week, sometimes more often, the sky around their base was filled with parachutes descending from C130s, C123s, C47s, C119s and even the occasional helicopter. Of course, there often were maneuvers to be engaged in after the platoons, companies and battalions landed on the drop zones. Such operations usually meant long marches, carrying massive amounts of equipment, setting up defensive positions, setting up ambushes--in short, activities that paratroopers loathed. They just wanted to pack up their 'chutes, head to the trucks and go back up for another jump.

Ron got in fifteen "mass tactical" jumps before the deployment to Vietnam. From then on, it was the unglamorous but more efficient helicopter that took them into battle.

"We'd do 'search and destroy', 'cordon and search', ambushes, all the nasty shit. The guys in my squad and my platoon were the greatest, craziest bunch of bastards you'd ever want to know."

Andrew perceived Ron's wistfulness as he described his paratrooper buddies. It was apparent that he missed them and, regardless of the awful day-to-day life they led, would not have left them voluntarily.

"If you end up in the military, Andrew, whether you go to Vietnam or somewhere else, always try to be a friendly and approachable dude. Try not to carry around an attitude or a chip on your shoulder. Try to surround yourself with buddies. You do that, and you'll never be sorry. And one of those buddies just might save your life."

"Uh, Ron?"

"Yeah, I know. How did I get wounded, right?"

"Well…"

"So, we were on a company-size operation in War Zone D, north of Saigon. The choppers drop you off on some high ground, you set up an HQ, then do platoon sweeps of the surrounding country trying to see what you can stir up. At night, we'd fall back into the company defensive perimeter, but on the way you drop off ambush teams to see if any VC or NVA try to follow you back in. Pretty standard stuff. Anyway, one afternoon my rifle platoon was moving along the edge of this open field, just a bunch of dried-up rice paddies. We had some thick woods on our right and the open fields on our left. So, we're humping along and we can hear these mortar tubes firing off in the distance, you know, 'ka-pow!' 'ka-pow!' which, if you think about it, is pretty lucky 'cause it gives you time to react before the rounds come in. We all yell, 'Incoming!' 'Incoming!'"

Ron had yelled loud enough to attract the attention of a few of the biker vets that had been near the club's screen front door.

"Come on out, boys," someone hollered. "Spinelli's telling fucking lies again."

Andrew's heart sank as eight burly and semi-inebriated men began dragging lawn chairs toward their picnic table. In seconds, the men surrounded them and began a good-natured needling of Ron.

"Hey, Spinelli. Who's your buddy?"

"Gentlemen, this is Andrew Starkey. He's out visiting from back in Indiana. I think my sister's in love with the boy, so don't kill him."

Andrew did his best to hide his unease at being surrounded by such a rough crew. He gave a wave and said, "Glad to meet you guys." For a brief second, he actually thought of Nancy and it brought a smile to his face…

"Glad to meet you, too, Andrew," a very hard-looking man said. He had Marine Corps theme tattoos up and down both arms. Scar tissue from a wound on his neck appeared to pull at the corner of his mouth, giving him a look of bafflement. "Ever hear of Elberfeld?" the man asked.

"You bet," answered Andrew. "Nice little town. Surrounded by corn fields. Got a real nice roller skating rink."

"My ex-wife lives there," said Emery. "Sorriest bitch that ever walked the earth. Stay away from her."

"I sure will," said Andrew, and he meant it.

"So, what happened to Fuckhead Fred?" one of the bikers asked of no one in particular.

To Andrew's relief, Ron answered. "The little cocksucker moved back to 'Hippy City'."

"Where the fuck is that?" asked the biker.

"Boulder."

"Oh, Hippy City. That's funny."

"Now, get back to the story Spinelli or we'll kill you," said Emery.

Just then, a waitress walked over struggling under the weight of a tray covered with open long-neck beers. A biker took the tray and set it on the table for her. She was showered with dollar bills by the men. Her smile seemed to indicate that she received a large tip for her trouble.

"Do it again in about fifteen minutes, Heidi," a biker said. She waved an acknowledgement.

Ron took one of the beers and a biker passed one over to Andrew.

"Wait," said Emery, the tattooed one. He stood up and lifted his beer. "To Uncle Sam's Misguided Children..."

The former Marines in the group stood and clinked their bottles together, then tilted those bottles and drank 'til they were empty. Then the bottles were flung in various directions around the grassy expanse.

"To the uninitiated, Andrew, that's 'USMC'," said Ron. "Beer-wasting assholes, every one of them."

"Uh..."

"Talk, Spinelli."

"So, like I was saying, we're all hitting the dirt. Couple seconds later the rounds start landing all over the place. They were 'Chi-com' 61-millimeter landing in mud, so unless they hit right near you, they weren't real effective. Blow a lot of mud straight back up in the air. Then they opened up with small-arms fire. You could tell they weren't a main force VC or NVA unit because most of the firing was single shots, like SKSs, old M-1 carbines and maybe AKs firing in short bursts. Don't think I ever heard a machine gun. They were firing from a tree line at the far end of the field, about 150 meters in front of us."

Ron paused and took a slow drink of his beer. Andrew was enthralled by the story, and was surprised at the rapt attention paid by the bikers.

"So, we move laterally into the tree line and start to fire and maneuver. Our guys are lobbing M-79 rounds and our two M-60s are laying down steady bursts of six down range. The lieutenant tells my squad leader to take us wide right and try to flank the bastards. So Sergeant Lewis sends my fire team ahead with a radio to take a quick look-see. We go maybe a hundred meters, angling towards the VC position, and come to the edge of a clearing. You can see everything for hundreds of meters in every direction, except the woods where the 'Charleys' are firing from. But at least we knew there was no way anyone could sneak up on us from behind." Without a pause, he says, "Man, I got to take a piss. Save my seat, Andrew." With that, Ron stood and headed towards the club's front door.

One of the bikers said, "You know, the whole world is a shit hole but he's got to go inside to piss."

"Army pussy," someone offered, then laughed at his own comment.

The beers were having their effect, and Andrew began to relax around his new acquaintances. Nonetheless, he was relieved when most of them stood and began to move around the grassy area. A few went to their bikes to inspect this or that item. Others urinated along the fence. Andrew joined them in a measured expression of camaraderie.

"Yeah, the bitch really fucked me good." It was Emery, the tattooed and scarred one, suddenly appearing at Andrew's side. He unbuttoned his bluejeans fly and began emptying his bladder. "I'm sitting in a foxhole in Quang Tri reading her 'Dear John' letter about how she's fell in love with some Elberfeld pig farmer."

Hoping to change the subject, Andrew said, "So, you're a Hoosier?"

"More or less. Grew up on a farm outside of Bloomington. I was adopted. Don't know where I was born for sure."

"How'd you end up way out here, Emery?"

"Was at a rally in Sturgis, South Dakota, last summer. Met a couple of these guys, 'Frag' and 'Hardcore'." He jerked his thumb back towards the men. "Ex-Marines like me. They said to come back with them and they could get me a job at the State Reformatory. So, here I am."

"FALL IN!"

It was Ron returning from his trip to the bathroom. He reclaimed his seat and beer bottle. Most of the crew returned to their lawn chairs but one biker was kick-starting his Harley and soon sped off in a thundering, smoky display.

"Harold's got to pick up his kid from little league practice," someone commented.

"So," began Ron, "like I was saying…"

~ * ~

Ron radioed back to his squad leader about their position at the edge of a large open area with clear fields of fire. The squad leader ordered Ron to hold that position then led the second fire team to join with the Ron's team. As they were forming up to begin the flanking maneuver, the platoon leader radioed Sergeant Lewis to hold in place and await the result of an artillery fire mission that the lieutenant would soon call in.

"If it works," said the lieutenant, "be prepared for them to take off in your direction."

Fifteen minutes later, rounds from a 105-millimeter howitzer battery at a Fire Support Base four miles away began to land behind the VC position. The lieutenant then skillfully began directing the rounds to "walk" in closer to the VC position in increments of 25 meters, until ordering "Fire for Effect". At that point, a dozen rounds began to explode thunderously right over the enemy position. The American rounds were airbursts utilizing "VT" fuses, and their effect was devastating. As predicted, the surviving members of the VC unit began to run from their ambush position towards the open area where Ron's squad awaited them.

"Those Charleys were dee dee-ing away from that artillery as fast as they could. They usually have a preplanned escape route if things go wrong for them, and it was their bad luck that their route took them right in front of my squad."

"Sin loi, motherfucker," said one of the Marines--Vietnamese for "too bad."

"So, pretty soon we see beaucoup black pajamas and straw hats and we opened up. Must have been ten or twelve of them. Some were already wounded from the shell fire." He paused as Heidi delivered another tray of beers. Some of the men helped her retrieve their empties from the grass. She was again deluged with dollar bills.

Ron took a long drink from his Coors and seemed lost in thought.

"Talk, Spinelli," said Emery.

"Oh, yeah. So…"

A five-second fusillade of automatic fire from Ron's squad decimated the retreating VC. All fell to the ground with screams and the clattering of their weapons and ammunition belts. After watching a minute for more movement, the squad leader radioed back to the lieutenant that it looked like they'd wiped out the VC not already killed by the artillery. From behind them in the woods, Ron's squad could hear the distant cheering of their platoon members as the lieutenant spread the news.

"Of course, then you got to go check out the bodies, collect their weapons, check for documents., said Ron. "So, we spread out and approach real slow. We get on top of them and start to check them out. They're all dead as shit except one guy who's so shot up it's only a matter of time. We just make sure he's unarmed and leave him alone."

The two older men from the recent horseshoe contest walked up and were greeted warmly by the biker contingent.

"Didn't mean to interrupt, Ronnie," said one. A biker hugged the man and kissed him on the top of his bald head.

"No sweat, Joe. Good to see you. Did that roofing material work out for you?"

"Sure did," said the man, laughing and wiping the top of his head with a napkin. "Thanks for the quick service."

"Anytime, buddy. So, anyway, we all forget to watch the tree line. Sure as shit, here come a couple of VC stragglers. They're both bloody messes, wounded by the artillery, you know, limping, holding each other up. One's got an AK. They see us and we see them at the same time. It was almost funny, all these guys shitting in their pants at the same time." This brought knowing chuckles from the group.

"The whole squad is getting ready to blow them away. Then one of our guys yells, 'Dung lai, chu hoi, du ma.'. Means 'Stop, surrender you motherfuckers'." Now the men laughed out loud.

"Well, that was a mistake. The Charley with the AK drops his buddy and turns to run back into the tree line. As he turns he swings the AK around, and without even looking, squeezes off a round in our direction. That's the last thing he ever does because he's hit by about twenty rounds from my squad. Trouble is, that one wild round hit me in the chest."

"God damn," someone says.

"Went clean through my right lung. Dropped me like a sack of shit. Got a sucking chest wound, bleeding like a stuck pig."

At that point, Ron was being attended to by his frantic squad leader, who ordered his men to set a defensive perimeter. Their 25-meter semi-circle now included a dozen dead or dying enemy soldiers and one of their own wounded.

Before the platoon's medic arrived, Ron's entry and exit wounds had been plugged using the plastic packaging of a replacement battery for the PRC-25 radio. A second squad of reinforcements arrived and did a sweep of the woods from where the VC had emerged. The lieutenant and the remaining squads assaulted the former VC ambush position, firing their M-16s from the waist, and confirmed that all the enemy were KIA by artillery or by Ron's squad action. The only enemy survivor was the wounded man who'd been dropped by the VC who had shot Ron. He was blindfolded and given medical care.

Ron had been unconscious since seconds after the bullet's impact. Once the medic had him stabilized, he was carried back to the platoon's position when the mortar attack first occurred. He lay in the shade surrounded by his buddies for nearly an hour before a UH-1D Medivac `Dust Off' helicopter arrived. His only recollection as he faded in and out of consciousness was of the distant thumping of the helicopter's blades as it approached. A soldier threw a smoke grenade, and the Dust Off landed in a horrendous swirl of dust and smoke. He was transferred by the crewmen to a stretcher and carried to the aircraft. Next to board were the wounded VC and a squad member assigned the double duty of escorting Ron and guarding the POW.

Two days later, Ron awoke in the surgery recovery area of the Army 24th Evacuation hospital in Long Binh. A young Army nurse roused him with a gentle squeeze of his arm.

"Specialist Spinelli? Can you hear me? Are you awake?"

His eyes focused on the First Lieutenant's bar on her collar. Then he tilted his head and looked into her face. He tried to talk but could not muster any sound. He tried again.

"Did I...get hit? Was...I hit?"

"Yes, Specialist. You certainly were 'hit'. You're going to be OK. You've been operated on, twice actually, and you're going to be fine." She was a slender, petit young woman, a year or two older than Ron, with a narrow, high cheek-boned face and light brown hair pulled into a tight ponytail. She wore a green fatigue uniform and a stethoscope was draped around her neck.

"Hurts...bad." He raised his head and tried to look at his bandaged chest. The nurse placed her hand lightly on his shoulder and said, "Now you lay still."

Ron let his head fall back on the pillow, squinting his eyes to see the nurse's face. "You're...beautiful," he said.

"Why, thank you, Specialist. I think you're beautiful, too," a girlish giggle momentarily interrupting her professional bearing. "I know it hurts." She examined a unit of blood that was hanging from a metal hook at the bedside and ran to a vein in Ron's wrist. "You try to rest. We'll try to control your pain as best we can." She raised her hand and another woman walked over. "Patty, our soldier is awake and not too comfortable."

"Well..." said the Medic, a large, jolly-looking woman in her mid-thirties. She had sergeant's stripes on her fatigues. "We'll get that taken care of. Honey, you rest and before long I'll help you write a note to your family."

Ron convalesced for three weeks in Long Binh, and then was scheduled to be flown back to the States. This news upset him greatly, and his nurse, not completely unaccustomed to such reaction, was ready to explain the situation to him.

"Why can't I stay here until I'm well, then go back to my unit?" he beseeched her. "I've got guys that are depending on me. I can't just leave them."

"Specialist Spinelli, you've been badly wounded. A bullet entered your chest, proceeded through your lung, then shattered a rib as it exited your back. You have a nasty hole back there. Your recovery time will be much longer than you realize." She put her hand on his forehead and then moved it softly down the side of his face. "You infantry soldiers are a strange bunch. Don't you want to go home?"

"Airborne Infantry," he corrected her. "Sure. I want to go home with my squad--not before."

"Ron, you've been in-country for seven months. You haven't even taken an R&R, have you? By the time you're in any shape to return to duty, all your buddies will have DEROS'd back to the States. Now, you've done your duty and it's time for you to take care of yourself."

He was able to walk onto the C141 "Starlifter" without aid and took his seat in the plane's cavernous and spartan interior. Dozens of other "walking wounded" were seated with him, and many others were loaded on stretchers. A staff of Air Force medical personnel moved quickly among the men, making sure they were secured in their positions for the long flight to Travis Air Force Base, northeast of San Francisco. As the jet lifted off from Ben Hoa Airbase, most of the ambulatory patients cheered and applauded. Ron was crying...

Chapter 10
Promises

"Andrew!" It was Doris yelling from the cabin's back door. "A young lady named Nancy is on the phone for you."

Andrew's heart nearly jumped out of his throat, but he did his best to hide that fact. "Be right there," he yelled back, reeling in his fishing line.

"Fuckin A," mocked Jack in a low voice. "My sorry, pussy-whipped young ass will be right there."

"Eat your heart out," Andrew said over his shoulder as he climbed up the river bank.

Doris handed him the phone with a wink. He put his hand over the mouthpiece and waited a second for her to walk away.

"Hi," he said.

"Hi, Hoosier. Did you miss me?"

"Don't ask."

"Oh, you've got it as bad as I do..."

She picked him up on the highway an hour later. As he threw his arms around her from the passenger seat her foot slipped from the clutch and killed the engine. Startled, she gasped, then laughed at her own clumsiness.

"OK, Hoosier. Let's get reacquainted. Now, what was your name?"

This time, Nancy drove the pickup across the Arkansas River and up a dirt road that followed an old railroad grade. In fifteen minutes, they were parked on a ridge overlooking the tiny town and a stunning mountain panorama running fifty miles north to south.

Andrew hugged her once again, so hard this time that she faked a choking sound to get relief.

"I'm sorry," he said, releasing her gently.

"My goodness. You really did miss me," she giggled.

They kissed and embraced passionately for several minutes. Then he held her quietly and focused his gaze on Mt. Princeton, across the broad valley.

"God," he sighed. "I don't think the human mind was meant to absorb so much stimulation at one time. I actually feel like I'm losing control of my sensibilities."

"Well, we can't have that. I'd better walk you around for a while."

They left the truck and walked along the Pinion-lined roadbed.

Ancient rotted railroad ties and rusted pieces of iron were evident in the eroded ditch. The midday sun was hot on their backs, and large birds soared on air currents high above them.

"That's a Bald Eagle," she said, pointing at a huge bird gliding to their right. "See its white head and tail?"

"Wow. That thing's huge," he cupped his hands around his eyes, shielding them from the sun to get a better view of the raptor. "Bet it could fly off with a rabbit or a small dog…" He paused a second, then smiled and said, "or even a skinny Italian girl."

With that, he swooped Nancy up in his arms and began carrying her like a child.

"Andrew!" she squealed. "You're going to hurt your back. I weigh a ton."

"More like 95 pounds."

She smiled at him expectantly, but he seemed lost in thought. He carried her along like that for quite a distance and, sensing his contentment, she put her arms around his neck and snuggled her face to his chest.

A shady grove of pinions was nearby and he headed for it. In the shade of a particularly large tree they sat down together and gazed out on the valley. He put his arm around her and hugged her gently to him.

"Andrew?"

"We're leaving tomorrow."

"Oh."

He looked at her then and saw that she had begun to cry.

"I'm so sorry I had to go to Denver. We could have had more time. But, my mom…"

"Hey, like I said the other day, I know you have another life."

She was beginning to sob audibly and put her hands to her face.

"This isn't fair," she said suddenly. "I don't want you to leave."

He ran his thumb along her wet cheekbone, then pulled her to him again and buried his face in her dark hair. He inhaled her fragrance for several moments, then nibbled her playfully on an earlobe.

"Nancy," he said finally, "I'm crazy about you."

Taking his face in her hands she said, "I'm crazy about you, too. Please believe me when I say that. I know we've only known each other a short time, but there's a…I don't know, a chemistry. It's like my brain was wired for you. Do you think God does things like that?"

"Maybe. All I can say is, I feel it, too. Kind of scary, huh?"

They were quiet for several minutes, content to lean together and watch the shadows of clouds move along the carpet of pine and Aspen forest at the base of Mt. Princeton.

"OK," he said finally. "We've got to figure this out. We've got today but we've got to make plans on how we can stay connected until…"

"Until we can get together again," she finished, smiling up at him. "I promise I'll write letters if you'll promise to write back."

"I promise. Maybe I can call you sometimes."

"Sure you can. It's not that expensive. And I can call you, too."

They decided to make the best of their last day together and shove as many things as they could into it. Nancy wanted, first, to drive down to Salida and stop at the Dairy Queen in hopes of catching Wendy. "If she's not there, I'll use their phone and call her. It would break her heart if she doesn't get to see you."

Sure enough, the battered GMC was parked at the DQ and Wendy was sitting on the tailgate licking a large ice cream cone. When she saw the Ford pickup she jumped off the gate and ran towards them. As Nancy and Andrew stepped from the pickup, Wendy handed Nancy her cone and jumped into Andrew's arms, wrapping her legs around him in the process.

Embarrassed, he nevertheless hugged her tightly and returned her very passionate, penetrating kiss. Aroused by her once again, he was relieved to put her back on the ground. He glanced at Nancy with a bemused grin. "Good to see you, too, Wendy."

Nancy handed the cone back and said, "He's leaving tomorrow." She took a napkin from Wendy's pocket and wiped the ice cream from around Andrew's mouth.

"Oh," said Wendy, staring up at him. "Well, shit, Hoosier." She began to cry.

"Now, come on Wendy. You've only known me a couple days. I'm not worth crying over. And besides, I'll be back to see all of you sometime. Heck, I might just move out here."

"Hoosier, you got to understand women. We all have a built-in ability to sort the good men from the not so good. You're one of the good ones, and I'm just sorry to see you go so soon." She took the napkin back and dabbed her eyes. She turned to Nancy, reached for her friend and hugged her. "I'm so sorry, honey," she said. "I've got a feeling he'll be back. Just don't you fret."

"I know he will. Now, come on. Let's take him down by the river."

The three were soon strolling the grassy expanse of a city park that ran along the Arkansas River. The river's flow here was much greater than near Bill's cabin as several tributaries, Chalk Creek among them, had added their volume in the fifteen miles between the two points.

Andrew walked in the middle, holding hands with each girl. At a picturesque bend in the river, Nancy pulled an Instamatic camera from her purse and they ran through the roll of film quickly. Though they had several pictures of all the "couples"-- Nancy and Andrew, Nancy and Wendy, Andrew and Wendy, they wanted one of the three of them together. However, no one was around to take it, and they settled for an awkward self-portrait taken from Andrew's outstretched arm.

"So, you're going to college in the fall, right?" Wendy asked.

"Yep. Indiana University. A month from now, I'll be a dorm rat in Bloomington."

"He's going to study business," offered Nancy.

"Good. Now you stay up there and don't screw around. Otherwise, you'll get drafted like my cousin, Randy. He's in Vietnam right now and my aunt and uncle are worried sick."

Andrew didn't respond and she continued, "And I hear you already talked to Ronnie. He's lucky to be alive."

"Ron's a great guy," said Andrew. "Took me to the VFW. Man, what a bunch of characters at that place. These bikers..."

"Did you meet Emery?" Wendy interrupted.

"Yes, a rough dude. A friend of yours?"

"Kind of. You know what I said about women being able to tell the good ones from the not so good? Some of us like a challenge and think we can make silk purses out of sows' ears. That boy's got a lot of rough edges I'm working on."

"Well, did you know he's a Hoosier?"

A smile came to her face. "No, I didn't. He told you that?"

"Yep. Did you know he has an ex-wife?"

Nancy interjected, "Andrew, maybe..."

He held up his hand. "Wait a minute, Nancy. Wendy needs to know that he was hurt real bad by her. She dumped him while he was in Vietnam. It doesn't hurt to know where his sensitivities might lie."

"Well, I'll tell you this," said Wendy with a sigh. "A man like that has got to have an ex-wife, maybe two, plus a lot of Vietnam baggage. It's just hard to get the son of a bitch to open up and talk about it."

"Wendy!" gasped Nancy, surprised to hear her refer to her new man friend with such a term.

"Oh, lighten up Nancy pants. 'Son of a bitch' can be a term of endearment. Right, Andrew?"

"Absolutely," he responded. "Most of my friends are sons of bitches, assholes or shit heads on any given day."

"Good grief, you two...," said Nancy with a grimace. "I thought

Jack was the one with the foul mouth. Emery isn't the only one with some rough edges to work on."

He winked at Wendy. "Ron told me that the best way to get a tough guy like Emery to talk is to ask him thoughtful questions. You ask dumb questions, you'll get dumb answers or, worse, he'll ignore you, especially about something like Vietnam. Ask him to tell you about his Marine buddies, what kind of trouble they got in together. Stuff like that. I bet he'll get going and you'll have to stick an ice cream cone in his face to shut him up."

Nancy spoke up. "Wendy, you listen to Andrew. Ronnie has really enjoyed being with Andrew, and he's told him things that Mom and Dad don't even know."

"Now, don't get me in trouble with your folks," said Andrew.

"Don't be silly, sweetie. I'm just saying that guys like Ronnie and Emery will talk to someone they think really cares and is interested in them as people."

"Well, I'll give it a try," said Wendy, fluffing her hair with her free hand. "I think he might be worth a little extra effort."

"Have you taken him down to the hot springs yet?" asked Andrew.

"You think he'd go?" Wendy replied.

"I bet he would. Of course, you might ride out on his Harley and park in the lot instead of sneaking in the back way."

They all laughed at the memory of the Chalk Creek wade-in earlier in the week.

"I'll put him in Old Faithful, sit on his lap and he'll tell me his whole life story. Right, Andrew?"

"Wendy, with you on my lap, I'd tell you anything," he replied with a laugh.

"Come on, you guys. I'm getting jealous," said Nancy. "Andrew, sweetie pie, we need to get going."

They were soon back at the pickup. Wendy gave Andrew another huge hug and tongue-winding kiss.

"You'll be back. I can tell," she said, running her hand up and down his arm. "Look Nancy. He's got an angel on his shoulder."

Andrew looked puzzled as Nancy confirmed Wendy's observation. "Look over there," she said. "The 'Angel of Shavano'."

Mt. Shavano, another fourteener, loomed to the northwest. Intersecting drainages filled with snow on the mountain's southern slope gave the appearance of an otherworldly figure with upstretched arms. Wendy cocked her head at the sound of wind in the branches of a ponderosa. "She just whispered to me that you'll come back."

Nancy started the engine, and as Andrew opened the door to climb in, he paused, then walked back to Wendy.

"Uh, one more thing about Emery. No matter how much you think you want to know, don't ask him if he killed anybody..."

~ * ~

To Andrew's great discomfort, Nancy wanted to go by the lumberyard and introduce him to her father and older brother, Steve. It wasn't as bad as he feared.

"Call me Chuck," Mr. Spinelli said with a smile and firm handshake. He was Andrew's height and very stocky. The family nose was prominent on his broad expressive face, and deep crow's feet formed near his eyes when he smiled. "I hear good things about you from Ronnie and Anita. Hell, even Bill Thompson likes you," he winked, "so I guess we can trust you with our little girl."

Steve, looking like an older version of Ron, was equally affable, though the lumberyard's booming business kept him busy during Andrew's short visit. Ron gave a wave from the back office, a phone crooked at his ear as he took notes from a customer. Andrew walked back and shook hands with him as he talked. "See you again sometime," he whispered. "Thanks for everything."

The visit lasted only a half hour and soon the pickup was back on the main drag. Nancy was headed to the A&W.

"Now, that wasn't so bad, was it?" she asked. "My dad is a great guy and, after Fred, I wanted him to see that I can pick nice boys, too."

"Well, thank you. Yes, I really liked him. And Steve seems like a good guy, too."

"I'm really lucky," she said. "No one has a better family than I do."

The drive-in was empty, and Cathy, the only carhop on duty, was filing her nails as she sat on the bench by the order window. She seemed out of place by a decade with her piled up hair and red lipstick. After a quick introduction, Nancy said, "Let's go sit at 'our' table."

"Doggone it," she said, running her hand over the table's top. "This table's a mess. I'll be right back." She ran to the kitchen and came back with a rag to wipe away the sticky root beer residue left from the day's customers. "Cathy hates to clean up. Just wants to serve and flirt with the boys."

"Just like a girl," he said, and tickled her as she scrubbed the table. Her high laughter drew Cathy's attention and Nancy clapped her hand over her mouth. "Don't tickle me, you bum," she said through her fingers.

Andrew became somber. "Nancy, I promised Mrs. Thompson I'd be back for dinner around six. We don't have a lot of time. I'm sorry."

"Well, we had the day," she sighed. "It's been fun, hasn't it?"

"You know it has."

She took his hand, lifted it to her mouth and kissed it. She looked up at him and winked.

"Can we go somewhere more private 'til I have to leave?" he said.

They parked at the end of a dusty road that overlooked the Arkansas River's rocky and constricted channel east of town. She turned off the engine and turned to him. He took her in his arms and hugged her as tightly as he could without hurting her, then pulled her on to his lap. She extended her legs out towards the driver's seat and buried her face in his chest. Andrew ran his hand through her hair, pulled her head back and kissed her. In his passion, he ran his hand down her side and cupped her bottom. Her reaction was to kiss him harder. After a few seconds, he gave her butt an affectionate squeeze then slid his hand under her T-shirt to the small of her back. He snuggled his nose in her hair and inhaled deeply, then uttered a throaty, low growl.

"You animal," she giggled.

"You are much, much woman," he said, in his best Latin-lover accent. Nancy could sense his emotional conflict, and was flooded with affection for him, knowing that his choice had been restraint. For an instant, she thought of Fred and his awkward way. *God, what did I ever see in him? Why couldn't I have waited…* She forced the thought away.

Nancy slid from his lap and sat at his side holding his hand. "So…," she said, as her heart rate returned to normal. "So…"

"So, like we were saying a while ago, we have to stay connected," he said. "I promise I'll write. I'll try to call sometimes. But…"

"But?"

"Nancy, you're it. You're all I want. I don't want to scare you, but…"

"Sweetie…"

"If it weren't for the draft, I'd move out here to be with you."

"Remember that, Andrew. If you're not in school, you'll get drafted and you'll…"

"I know," he said. "Viet fucking 'Nam."

She didn't react to his obscenity. "Sweetie, look what happened to Ronnie and Emery."

"You mean two very tough guys that I respect, that anyone with a brain would respect? Maybe that's all any guy could want from life. To be respected, to respect himself. Both those guys have that…"

"Andrew, they could have been killed."

"I...," he was quiet for a moment. "I know that, but that's part of what I'm talking about. They took the risk. I want what they have. And I want you."

He had her pull over a hundred yards up the road from the cabin. "They may be outside and I don't want to say goodbye in front of those guys."

"I understand."

Andrew got out and walked around to the driver's side. He put his hand behind her head, pulled her to him, and kissed her lightly several times. Then he kissed her on the nose, and again on the forehead. Tears were on her cheeks.

"I'll send you a copy of the pictures as soon as I get them back," she sniffed.

"You better," he said. "Otherwise, I'll forget what you look like."

"No, you won't."

"You're right," he said, tosseling her hair. "I won't..."

He heaved a sigh. "Got to go."

"Andrew?"

"I love you, Nancy."

"Oh, ...oh, you..."

"Go. Get going."

She turned the Ford around as he stood by the side of the road, then pulled up to him again. For a second, they just smiled at each other. "Would you please go?" he said finally.

She blew him a kiss, and said, "I love you, too, Andrew Starkey. You come back to me. OK?"

"I'll come back."

He watched the pickup until it disappeared in the dusty distance.

Chapter 11
Danny

"Enlow...Starkey!" The Specialist was holding a clipboard out in front of his face. "Get your asses down to Room Six and report to Sergeant Buller! Ames, Easton, Gold and Messerschmitt report to Sergeant Doherty outside in the break area! The rest of you sit tight."

A buzz of conversation erupted around the room as the six men stood up.

"Well, here we go, Stark. I hope I'm not sorry I got us into this."

"I made my own decision, buddy. Let's go."

Starkey was shaking as he walked towards the door and he hoped no one could tell. The remaining men, sensing that the Marine Corps menace had been removed, were almost giddy.

"Bet those four yahoos are going to low-crawl for Specialist Cocksucker. Must have screwed up somehow," said Rich as they walked down the hall.

"Come in, men," said Sergeant Buller. "Well," he looked at them with his hands on his hips..."they can't use you. You'll be staying in the Army. I hope you're not too disappointed." His smile seemed out of context given the shock he'd delivered to the two young men.

"Uh," said Andrew Starkey, "did we do something wrong. Did we fail a test or something?" Rich's eyes were wide, but he said nothing.

"No, nothing like that. Four other inductees were selected and are on their way to the Louisville airport at this time. Let's leave it at that. You're excused back to the classroom, gentlemen."

The two friends turned to leave, bumping into each other at the door. Andrew was shaking again and, once away from Room Six, leaned against the wall to steady himself. He looked at Rich and shook his head.

"Man, I can't fucking believe it," said Rich as they approached the class room once again. "I was psyched and ready for San Diego. What the fuck?"

They took the seats they'd left a few minutes before and the Specialist paused in his instructions as they got settled. Their reappearance had created a stir among the men.

"Listen up, Goddamnit," said the Specialist. "You will file down the hall, take a right at the end, go into Room Nineteen and fall in on the black lines facing the podium. Gentlemen, you are about to be sworn into the United States Army." While under normal circumstances this might have been a thought-provoking circumstance, the day's activities and Marine Corps shock made the swearing-in ceremony an anticlimax. It was over in a few minutes. A young lieutenant led them in the oath, the only variation among them being the insertion of their own names between "I" and "solemnly swear."

As they walked back to the classroom they heard the bus tires crunching the gravel drive outside. The engines continued to idle and the men knew they'd be on the way to Ft. Knox very soon. NCOs were giving instructions to the Specialist as they once again took their seats. In a few minutes the exhausted men had reclaimed their personal items and were lining up to load the buses.

"Enlow...Starkey. Over here." It was the Specialist summoning them aside. Enlow muttered, "Now what's that prick want?"

"Sergeant Buller asked me to talk to you," he said. His tone had changed and he was almost friendly. This made the two even more cautious. "He said you were pretty upset about not going to the Marines. Look, this is off the record and I'll deny telling you this." He actually looked around before continuing to speak. "Your test scores, how shall I say this, 'disqualified' you for transfer to the Marines." Neither said anything and he continued his attempt to explain what happened. "You're too valuable to the Army. Do you understand?"

"So if we'd scored lower...?" Starkey asked.

"If you'd scored a lot lower, you'd be on your way to San Diego. Got it? I'm only telling you this because Buller didn't want you to think you were in some kind of trouble. You're already under enough stress."

Both boys were incredulous. "Well, thanks," said Rich. "Appreciate you filling us in. If that's what we get for volunteering, I sure as fuck learned my lesson."

"Gentlemen, the Marines gave us their minimum standards and those were met by those four other inductees. Even though you volunteered, it's still our call on who goes where. You two get on the bus. Good luck." With that, he walked away, examining his clipboard once again.

They sat together in the back of the bus. Neither had the energy for conversation.

It was past 10PM when the buses pulled into the Reception Station for new inductees at Ft. Knox. The dazed and exhausted men lined up on yellow footprints painted on the blacktop as instructed by a tired NCO. Following some shouted instructions they were led to a white-frame, two-story barracks building, identical to hundreds of others around the vast Army post. They selected bunks and made them up with the sheets, blankets and pillows stacked on each. "Fire guards" were assigned to take successive one-hour shifts until Reveille at 5AM. They were to form up in front of the building, showered and shaved, at 5:30, and to be prepared for another long, stressful day. The men were quiet, if not asleep, soon after the lights were turned off at 11PM. The world they'd left at 3AM that morning was now a distant memory.

A tape-recorded Reveille played through pole-mounted speakers awoke the men, and they staggered to the latrine with their dopp kits. Most showered and shaved but a few merely splashed water on their faces. An NCO appeared at the door and shouted for them to "hurry the fuck up" and get outside in formation. Once outside, they found they'd been joined by men from Ohio, West Virginia and Kentucky. Some of these, though not many, were enlistees. The serial numbers on their newly issued "dog tags" started with "RA" meaning "Regular Army," unlike those of the draftees that began with "US."

The next several days would be a blur of activity to get the men ready for BCT and, more specifically, their service in a war-time Army. After breakfast the first day, they lined up for the traditional head shearing by civilian-contracted barbers wielding powerful clippers. As each man exited the barbershop, he was greeted by howls of laughter from the men who'd already suffered their own indignities. The men winced at the occasional shorn head that was misshapen, scarred or covered with sores.

Next, they were marched to a building where they were fitted for uniforms, boots and "low quarter" shoes. By now, they were impatient to forgo their civilian clothes in favor of the new, baggy "Fatigues," thereby finally blending in with the thousands of other troops on the vast post. Not only did they look ridiculous wearing "civies" with shaved heads, but such a get-up also marked them as the most recent and contemptible arrivals. Now that stigma was removed.

After an involuntary donation of a pint of blood, the men were lined up for the first batch of inoculations. These were performed by Army medics using pneumatic guns that shot a tiny amount of serum into the muscle. Both arms were hit repeatedly as the men walked the gauntlet of medics.

Each day followed a routine of filling out more forms, more tests, more issuance of gear, more shots. Inevitably, they'd be lined up to police the area several times daily.

Almost as a lark, Rich and Andrew tested for a chance to attend Officer Candidate School.

"We can be Lieutenants together!" said Rich.

"Do you really think that's possible?" asked a suspicious Andrew Starkey. "How can they make officers out of shitbirds like us?"

"Beats me. But I'm all for it if it means I outrank some of these asshole Specialists. Plus, I bet the money is a hell of a lot better."

Meals were the highlight of the day. The food was basic but served in large quantity. Evenings were spent smoking and joking on the wooden steps of their barracks, and discussing the latest rumors about their impending move to the Training battalion. New friendships were formed as they strolled the area, visited the small Post-Exchange store or lay on their bunks talking about home, girlfriends and cars. The specter of Vietnam was oddly absent from the talk.

The disparity in education and privilege among the men was vast. Rich Enlow and Andrew Starkey, both with some college and an intact family, were at the far end of this human spectrum. At the other was a contingent from West Virginia who was quite nearly illiterate. One afternoon, an angry and frustrated Sergeant called a formation and, through obscene threat and intimidation, was able to cull from the group nearly a dozen who belatedly admitted to an "inability to read or write." The gibberish they'd been entering on their forms for several days now had finally caught up with them. Even though many in the group wanted to go home, their pride prevented them from using illiteracy as a way out.

The same group had some serious alcoholics who produced bottles of whiskey as if by magic whenever they were in the barracks. One of these, though he needn't have, feigned homosexuality in hopes of being sent home. "I jest cain't stand seeing these boys in the shower, Sarge. Makes me want to skin it back." Some Sergeants questioned him in a room at one end of the bunk area. He broke down in sobs during the encounter. The following morning he was taken away and did not return.

~ * ~

After nearly a week of processing, the big day arrived. They were to shove every article they'd been issued into the duffle bags and march to their BCT company. A motley formation of one hundred and twenty men, sweating under their hundred-pound burdens, snaked its way among the complexes of identical wood frame buildings. With each turn in the route, their anxiety increased. A mile into their march they rounded a bend in the road and were met with a blast of screaming profanity directed at them from a wall of Smokey Bear-hatted Drill Sergeants. The nightmare had begun.

Their marching formation had looked like little more than a gaggle of raggedy, undisciplined, sloppily clothed teenagers, which in general, it was. It was all most of them could do to line up where the shrieking Drill Sergeants directed them. Assisting the Drill Sergeants were numerous Corporals who were soon to attend the rigorous academy to become Drill Sergeants themselves. Their intention to display their talents to the real Drill Sergeants made them particularly caustic. Duffle bags were dropped, picked up, dragged, dropped again as the men tried in vain to follow directions that were intentionally vague, conflicting and nonsensical. "Stand at Attention, fuckhead! Right face! No not that 'right', the Army 'right'! Are You Shitting Me? Get down, get down, get down!" Half the marchers were in the "front-leaning rest" position, the starting point of a pushup, at any one time. "Give me twenty, fuckhead!" echoed off the barracks walls as the penalty was imposed on dozens of men at once. When finished with the attempt to do the pushups, the trembling men would stand, only to be sent back down to do another twenty. "Get down, get down, get down! Get up, Get up, Get up! Get down, give me fifty, fuckhead!"

Sweating, confused, some near tears, some in tears, they were broken down by alphabet into the semblance of platoons of forty men. Privates Enlow and Starkey were separated now, the first time this slender thread of home had been broken since they arrived at the Post Office a week before.

At this point did their personal tormentor make himself known, for each platoon had its own Drill Sergeant. Sergeant King was black, wiry, five foot eight and solid muscle. Veins protruded from his arms and neck as he screamed and flailed at the men, grabbing and shoving them around the assembly area. His eyes were barely visible beneath the visor of his Smokey Bear hat.

"What the fuck you lookin' at troop!? Don't you be eyeballing me! Get down and give me twenty, no fifty! What's your name troop!? Russett? That's the stupidest Goddamn name I ever heard! Get over there 'Potato' Russett. Out-Goddamn-standing! The boy can walk in a straight line. You, troop, what's your name!? Starkey!? STAR KEY! Did your granddaddy Francis write the Star Spangled Banner, STAR KEY?"

"Uh," Andrew didn't know what to do or say.

"FRANCIS STAR KEY, the man wrote the National Anthem, STAR KEY?"

"No, Drill Sergeant. That was Francis SCOTT Key, Drill Sergeant!"

"You bullshittin' me!? Get over there next to Potato Russett! Get the fuck down and give me ten!"

A small item had caught Starkey's eye as Sergeant King berated him. Above the US ARMY tag sown above the Sergeant's left breast pocket were embroidered Jump Wings. The Drill Sergeant was a Paratrooper, just like Ron in Colorado.

I've got to do that, he thought. *I've got to find a way.*

The abuse went for two hours. The sun was hot by now, and many of the men were physically ill. They were sent in twos to a Lister bag for water only as their need seemed dire. If they lingered with the paper cups of water more than a few seconds, a screaming voice would tell them "Get back in formation, you fuckheads! Hurry, hurry, hurry! Get down, get down, get down, give me twenty, get up, get up, get the fuck up!"

Their barracks building was the ubiquitous two-story, white, wooden structure built for World War Two recruits twenty-five years before. They were formed into four squads of ten men each. Two squads would occupy the first floor, two the second. A small separate room on the second floor would house four squad leaders and a platoon guide. These leadership positions would be filled in a few days, after the Drill Sergeant had worn down the men and assessed the potential of those he'd been notified in advance to consider.

As noon approached, the men burst into the barracks and selected their bunks, top or bottom being the major variation. Fights erupted as men raced for their selection. A footlocker was provided for each. They were told to put their gear on their bunks and report back outside in ten minutes for chow. Once outside, they stood in formation at attention, then were marched towards the mess hall a squad at a time. Near the entrance was a structure suspending a fifteen-foot horizontal ladder. The bars of the ladder were to be traversed, hand over hand monkey-style, before joining the line for admittance to the hall. As no more than five recruits could line up at the mess hall door, recruits could only traverse the bars when the previous five had been summoned into the building. Then it was a scramble over the bars while the mess sergeant yelled at them from the door to "hurry up, hurry up, hurry up! Give me five nasty farm girls!" Once in the building the men took trays, a cup and silver and slid them along a stainless steel guide until reaching a server who handed them a plate of food. They stopped to fill their cups with milk or water and sat down at tables for four. They were being screamed at since leaving the chow line and ate hurriedly and in silence. "Hurry up, hurry up, hurry up! Get out, get out, get out!" The entire company of 120 men was run through the hall in forty-five minutes.

After their first preposterous meal, they ran back to the barracks to make their bunks and stow their gear in time for the Drill Sergeant's inspection. They'd been shown how to make a proper Army bunk in Reception Station but many had paid no attention. Now those men begged their new squad members to help them for fear they'd be culled out for special punishment.

Standing at attention in front of their new-made bunks, the recruits watched in terror as the Sergeant and his Corporals destroyed them, ripping off blankets and sheets, throwing pillows across the barracks, dumped out their foot lockers, threw boots, fatigues, belts, caps and helmet liners to the floor, screaming at them all the while. Men attempting to retrieve their gear were dropped for pushups, ordered to re-do their bunks, dropped again for pushups, made to run in place, then dropped for more pushups.

The pandemonium lasted an hour. "FALL IN!" Now it came time for them to form up and march to "PT" or "Physical Training." Exhausted and ill young men formed in front of their barracks. On the orders of the Corporals, they marched through the company area and across a street to an immense cindered field with wooden platforms placed around its borders. From the platforms, the Drill Sergeants led the men in exercises; time-honored ones like jumping jacks, squat thrusts, pushups, leg lifts, trunk twisters, more pushups followed by running in place, followed by more pushups. The Corporals walked among the men, screaming criticisms at them and making them start over their required number of repetitions. This went on for an hour.

They were marched back to the Company area and broken down by squads. The Drill Sergeants assisted by their caustic Corporal assistants then began their first instruction in "Dismounted Drill"--those basic elements of standing in formation, attention, at ease, parade rest, right face, left face, about face, dress right dress, saluting of officers and saluting the flag. Then they were instructed in how to march; forward march-step off with the left foot, halt, column right march, column left march, left flank march, right flank march, to the rear march. They were marched, instructed, corrected, marched, dropped for pushups, marched, corrected and marched some more for two hours.

The Cadre was fatigued and sweating after nearly five hours of non-stop instruction and hazing since the noon meal. The men were beyond exhaustion, many nearing a point of collapse. They were told to re-enter the barracks and get it presentable for another inspection before the evening meal. This time the Corporals gave the barracks only a cursory walk through, threw a few items, tore a few beds, kicked a few foot lockers over. "FALL IN!" The men once again lined up, waited for their chance at the horizontal ladder and their entrance into the mess hall. They wolfed down their food and drink. The screaming was less pronounced this time. When forced from their seats, they exited the mess hall and ran the short distance back to the barracks.

They entered and noted that, for the first time since five AM, there was something close to quiet surrounding them. The Drill Sergeants and Corporals were letting them have some time to collect and store gear, make their bunks again, and prepare uniforms, boots and head gear for the next day's training. The men also used the time to properly meet squad members and bunk mates.

Before too long, Drill Sergeant King could be heard on the first floor, screaming at First and Second Squads. "Are you shittin' me! What the fuck you doin' to my barracks! Look like you stowed your gear with a dump truck! Oh, here's one boy knows what he'd doin'. Must be ROTC. What's your name troop!? Ralston!? You make dog food, Ralston!? Out-Goddamn-standing, Ralston. Going to make you a squad leader! You! What the fuck you got on your face troop!? Shoe polish!? Put it on the boots troop!" A footlocker was turned over as he headed for the stairs to the second floor. "You better be squared away Third and Fourth Squad! I'll be up there in ten God damn seconds!" He yelled up the stairway, "One, two, three." Men ran to and fro finishing bunks, sliding foot lockers in place, brushing boots to a proper shine. "Four, five, six!" Boots were hurriedly laced, fatigue shirts buttoned, belts lined up properly with the buttons of the shirts and the fly line of their pants. "Seven, eight, nine, ten! Too late, too late, too late! Get down, get down, get down! Place looks like a pig sty! Every swinging dick give me twenty! Who the fuck made this bunk? You! What the fuck is the matter with you? Every swinging dick in Third Squad going to show you how to make a bunk. Third squad, take your bunks apart, every fuckin' blanket, every fuckin' sheet, throw 'em on the floor. Hurry, hurry, hurry! Now, everybody start with the sheet." And on it went until the unskilled bunk maker had reconstructed his bunk to a tolerable level of incompetence, aided by those nearby.

It was past 8:00PM now, and as the men finished their bunk making, they found that Sergeant King had gone. Suspicious, they looked down the stairs and into the unused squad leader room. Then they looked out the windows. No cadre could be seen. Men fell to their bunks and stared blankly. "FALL IN! Hurry, hurry, hurry!" The men rushed to the assembly area and formed up in a square of four squads. Drill Sergeant King then gave them a shouting, obscene-laced description of the upcoming training day that would begin at 5:00AM. It would be much like this first day, but without the mind-numbing shock and pandemonium. He didn't tell them this. It simply would have been impossible to duplicate what they'd just gone through.

~ * ~

The morning found the men surprisingly stoic and mentally prepared. The majority were in terrible physical shape and dreaded PT more than the hazing. They got both in boundless measure.

With their rudimentary marching skill-training of the day before, there was a hint of pride in them as they formed up for the march across the street to the PT field. When Drill Sergeant King gave them the command "FOR- WARD MARCH!" most actually started off with the correct, left foot. To their surprise, he began giving them instructions as they marched. "When I say, 'Double Time' that means you will begin a steady, controlled jog--what we call the 'Airborne Shuffle'. I will call cadence and you will fuckin' Shuffle at the pace of my cadence. DO YOU UNDERSTAND FOURTH PLATOON!?"

"YES, DRILL SERGEANT!" they screamed in response.

"I CAN'T HEAR YOU!"

"YES, DRILL SERGEANT!"

"ARE YOU READY FOURTH PLATOON?"

"YES, DRILL SERGEANT!"

"OK! HERE WE GO! ONE, TWO, THREE, FOUR HUP, ONE, TWO, THREE, FOUR HUP!

The men began a rhythmic jog/shuffle, barely more than a quick walk. Sergeant King kept up his cadence. His voice and inflection were honed to this activity, and the men could sense that he'd done this thousands of times. He shuffled them across the road and on to the PT field controlling their forward movement with commands of "Column left! March! Column right! March! Column half-right! March!"--the commands as appropriate at this shuffle as at the slower march speed. They responded as if they'd been doing it for at least two days instead of one.

"ALL RIGHT! NOW IT'S GOING TO GET COMPLICATED! YOU ARE GOING TO REPEAT AFTER ME! DO YOU UNDERSTAND?"

"YES, DRILL SERGEANT!"

"I CAN'T HEAR YOU!"

"YES, DRILL SERGEANT!"

"OUT FUCKIN' STANDING!"

He sang in time to their shuffle pace, "I WANT TO BE AN AIRBORNE RANGER!" The men yelled back the sentence.

"I WANT TO GO TO VIETNAM!"
Some laughed, but all repeated it loudly.
"I WANT TO LIVE A LIFE OF DANGER!"
"I WANT TO KILL THE CHARLIE CONG!"
He began the refrain.
"HERE WE GO, ALL THE WAY, AIRBORNE! AIRBORNE!"
"UP THE HILL, DOWN THE HILL, THROUGH THE HILL, AIRBORNE!"

The lyrics of the cadence, as rough and ironic as they were, sent chills up the spines of the young men. If any had lingering doubts about what sort of nightmare they were caught up in and why they'd been plucked so unceremoniously from their former lives, this simple cadence removed them.

"STAND UP, HOOK UP, SHUFFLE TO THE DOOR! JUMP RIGHT OUT AND COUNT TO FOUR!"
"IF MY 'CHUTE DON'T OPEN WIDE, I GOT ANOTHER ONE BY MY SIDE!"
"IF MY RESERVE DON'T OPEN ROUND, I'LL BE THE FIRST ONE ON THE GROUND!
"HERE WE GO, ALL THE WAY...!"

~ * ~

At mid-morning, the men were back in their platoon area having spent the previous three hours at PT and Dismounted Drill. Sergeant King and his Corporal cohort were introducing them to the epitome of punishment, the "Low Crawl" pit. The pit was roughly twenty-five feet long and fifteen wide. It contained two feet of saw dust that retained moisture nearly forever. The men would kneel at the front edge then fall to their chests in the soggy mess and begin pushing with hands and feet towards the far end. "Crawling" was a misnomer because the Drill Sergeant and Corporals made sure the men's chests were in contact with the wood chips at all times. It was more like a sustained chest skid that left the men completely soiled and wet from chin to boots. The process would also exhaust the most robust of the trainees. When they were allowed to leave the pit, only after several trips up and back, they'd use a broom to sweep the clinging mass of sopping wood fiber from each other.

Thankfully, it was time for the noon meal. Famished men ran to the platoon area to line up at the horizontal ladder, their entryway to food and comparative inactivity.

Andrew Starkey was, he felt, holding up reasonably well so far. His hands were blistered by the bars that first day. This would be his second

painful trip down their length today and he didn't relish it. When his
turn came, he gritted his teeth and went the distance as rapidly as
he could, dropped to the ground and came to parade rest behind the
first three arrivals. A soldier from second squad, Danny something,
stumbled behind him.

Standing in the door of the mess hall, gloating with his power over
the hungry men, was the mess sergeant. Sergeant Hanson was far and
away the most slovenly and unprofessional NCO in the Company. He
wore a filthy, unstarched white kitchen fatigue uniform, an odd cook's
cap and boots that were crusted over with food and grease from the
kitchen's floor. His moronic grin displayed a gap from a missing front
tooth. He delighted in summoning the men inside with taunts, like his
favorite, "Give me five little girls with pink panties!"

"You little darlins just hold on a minute," said the mess sergeant.
"Got to wait for some boys to git done first, then y'all gonna git your
chance."

"Look at that stupid son of a bitch." The whisper came from behind
Andrew. He cocked his head minutely to the right and whispered a
response.

"Yo?"

"Look at his crotch. Lean left."

Andrew carefully leaned over for a view of the Sergeant. The
man's fatigue pants, like those of the trainees, had a button fly. His
was partially open and a testicle protruded outside his uniform. The
pink ball of flesh was quite pronounced against the more or less white
uniform.

"Now I'm really hungry," Andrew whispered over his shoulder.
"Shhh."

"GIVE ME FIVE LITTLE LOVLIES WITH TIGHT TWATS!",
commanded Sergeant Hanson. The five men walked quickly through
the door of the hall and grabbed their trays and utensils. When
they'd picked up their food and drink, they found empty seats and
began stuffing themselves. Drill Sergeant Holly from First Platoon
was reaming out a table of men for their inability to name the BCT
Company's commanding officer. All four were counting out their
assignment of 25 pushups.

"Holliday. Captain Holliday," whispered a voice next to Andrew.
He looked to his right and noticed that Danny had taken that seat. Sure
enough, the Drill Sergeant walked over then, apparently, past their
small table. Suddenly he was at Andrew's ear screaming

"Private, who is your company commander?"

Andrew stood up and said, "Captain Holliday, Drill Sergeant!"

"Out-God-damn-standing, Private! Now, sit down."

The NCO walked back to the rear table where the cadre and officers ate and sat down, placing his Smokey Bear hat carefully on the table in front of him. The men watched him from the corners of their eyes and were relieved when he dropped his glare and picked up his fork.

"Saved my ass, man. Thanks."

"No problemo. Your turn next time."

When they'd finished and pushed their trays through the window to their fellow soldiers who were on KP for the day, they walked out of the mess hall and sprinted back to the barracks.

His name was Danny Sevilla, and he was from Flagstaff, Colorado by way of Louisville, Kentucky. If he'd had hair it would be dirty blonde with a tinge of light brown. At five foot, ten inches, he wasn't tall but stood half a head taller than most of the men in their platoon. His face had a rugged handsomeness, and acne scaring on his cheeks and neck made him look a little older than his 19 years. When asked, he had no explanation for his Spanish surname.

He was born in Limon, not far from Flagstaff, since that town had a small hospital. His father owned a dry-land wheat farm outside of town that he'd inherited from his own father before Danny was born. When the farm dropped in his lap, Danny's father talked his very reluctant wife into giving up their lower-middle-class life in Louisville and moving west. Danny was born a year after their arrival and first failed wheat crop.

Five more years went by with a continuing drought ruining any chance of a successful crop. Danny's dad scratched out a living in Limon as a part-time mechanic at the John Deere dealership. Finally, his mother had had enough and took Danny back to Louisville to live with her parents. The divorce was quick and uncontested. She remarried when Danny was eight to a man who was a grounds keeper at Churchill Downs, home of the Kentucky Derby.

When he was ten, Danny began spending the summer with his father on the farm in Flagstaff. His mother would put him on the L&N, alone, for the 10-hour trip to St. Louis. There, during his layovers he'd wander the cavernous Union Station. The next segment was via the Missouri Pacific to Kansas City, then the Kansas Pacific Railway the rest of the way to its brief stop in Limon. His father would await the train as it highballed south of Flagstaff, then race it in his old International flatbed with the goal of pulling into Limon's depot just as Danny would run around to the parking lot. These were the happiest days of Danny's life, and the anticipation of the annual June trips west made the last weeks of school particularly agonizing for him.

Inevitably, the railroad options began to fade. The summer after freshman year, the closest he could get to Flagstaff was Denver's Union Station after a circuitous trip via Chicago. The old flatbed barely made the 220-mile round trip, minor repairs being needed twice along the way.

A Greyhound bus all the way from Louisville was an affordable alternative, though Danny's mother feared for his safety given her opinion that "bus" people weren't as nice as "train" people. Plus, her son was free to roam all over the train rather than being stuck in one seat the entire trip.

Instead, he talked his mother into letting him hitchhike. After all, he was 16 now.

The first time, his mother and stepfather sat in the car on Highway 150 outside New Albany, on the Indiana side of the river, watching until he got a ride. The next year, he began hitching at the end of his block on Moser Street.

He had several interesting adventures on these trips and loved regaling his friends with the details. These stories always occurred on the trip west. On the return trip, at summer's end, he was so depressed he slept most of the way. Luckily, the Deere dealership had daily visits from 18-wheelers, and these drivers were happy to give him eastbound rides. More than once, he only needed three rides to New Albany, with each successive ride arranged by the drivers at truck stops over coffee and biscuits and gravy. One particularly caring trucker dropped him at his doorstep.

He managed to graduate from high school in the top half of his class, and was granted probationary admittance to the University of Kentucky at Lexington. He lasted a year, then dropped out, eager to enlist in the Army. A song by Sergeant Barry Sadler, "Ballad of the Green Berets," had seized his imagination and, well, he just had to get himself one of those hats.

When Andrew Starkey found out about Danny's Colorado connection, he was non-stop questions about what it was like to actually live there, what he did, where he went, had he been to the mountains, had he been to Denver, had he been to Buena Vista, and on and on. The fact that Danny had seen little of the state other than the Flagstaff area made little difference to Andrew. He remained obsessed with Colorado.

The occasional and awkward letters to and from Nancy had

become his only tenuous connection. But now Danny and his stories reinvigorated his fantasies of a Rocky Mountain future, even if the girl was not to be part of it. For his part, Danny missed his father and the farm and welcomed any chance to share his memories of the high plains and all the great times he had on the summer visits. He was amused by his new buddy's inordinate interest in all things "Colorado," but to Danny, the present was more than enough to occupy his imagination.

~ * ~

Day after day, the men marched to the rifle ranges, learning to fire from different positions and greater distances, then rapidly at targets of varying distances. They became proficient and confident as they fired hundreds of rounds from their M-14s. Eventually, each man earned a badge signifying his skill level of "Expert," "Sharpshooter" or, the lowest, "Marksman." Even a Marksman, however, could hit man-sized targets at distances as great as 350 meters.

Starkey and Danny became fast friends. Though the Colorado bond had been the catalyst for their friendship, it soon became apparent that both had irreverent and profane senses of humor. The fact that such humor was often beyond the ken of those around them, in fact, further cemented their connection. Both were assigned as squad leaders and were well liked by their respective squad members, both white and black, for their ongoing attempts to keep them from "shit" duty and punishment, often spending long periods in the low-crawl pit on their behalf. The other two squad leaders had spent time in College ROTC and were always pushing their men to compliance, if not excellence, in their barracks duties and inspections. Starkey and Danny, on the other hand, had become skilled at just getting by with the least possible effort or risk of retribution to themselves and their men.

One day, in exasperation, Sergeant King exclaimed, "Ralston, he outstanding! First squad, outstanding! STAR KEY, he just say, 'Fuck it!'."

Starkey had responded, "Roger that, Drill Sergeant!"

Danny cracked up at the remark, further infuriating Sergeant King.

"You think that's funny, Sevilla?" yelled the Sergeant. "Get down and give me a million! When you've done, get in the Goddamn low-crawl pit with STAR KEY! Goddamn, son-of-a-bitchin', wise-ass, motherfuckin' trainees!" Put your face in it, STAR KEY!"

That was not to say Sergeant King didn't get a kick out of the pair's devil-may-care attitude and willingness to take abuse. That, he kept to himself. A drill sergeant was trained in handling many personality profiles, and the Sergeant had trained men like them in each cycle.

They were the type that needed to mentally match necessity to the tasks required of them and prided themselves in separating that which was necessary from that which was bullshit. Such men did not do well in the garrison stateside Army. But in the far less-formal, but far more intense, wartime Army in Vietnam, they'd be dependable and aggressive soldiers.

~ * ~

One afternoon, after a particularly grueling march back from a firing range, the trainees were cleaning their weapons on the blacktop outside the barracks. Starkey heard his and another trainee's name being shouted by a corporal standing in front of the company headquarters. They double-timed up to the corporal who ordered them to report to the Company First Sergeant. The two men, from different squads, and not familiar with each other, had only a few seconds to worry about what trouble they might be in before arriving in front of the First Sergeant's desk. They saluted and shouted their names and that they were reporting as ordered.

"Private Starkey! Get your ass in here!" This command came from Captain Holliday's office. Starkey's eyes were glued on the First Sergeant's face. "You heard him, trainee. Get in there."

Starkey slid to a halt in front of the Captain's desk and saluted. "Sir, Private Starkey reporting as ordered, Sir!"

"Sit down, Starkey," said the Captain and pointed to a metal chair against the wall at the side of his desk. He stood and walked to the door and closed it. Starkey was sure he was in the worst trouble of his young life.

"So you want to go to Officer Candidate School. That right, Private?"

"Uh, well, I..., Sir!" sputtered Starkey. "Uh, yes sir! I took a test in Reception Station, sir!"

"Well, you did fine on the test. I've called you in to offer you the opportunity to attend Infantry OCS at Ft. Benning, Georgia. If you accept the opportunity you'll attend Infantry AIT at Ft. Polk, Louisiana. If you make it through that, you'll proceed to OCS. If you graduate, and that's a big 'If', you'll be commissioned as a Reserve 2nd Lieutenant and have an additional two-year service commitment from the date of graduation. OCS is twenty-three weeks." He watched the terrified young man in front of him for several seconds, letting the information sink in. He knew how overwhelming this turn of events was for someone like Private Starkey, a pimply faced kid whose biggest accomplishment so far in life was to flunk out of a university and get himself drafted. OCS was the chance of a lifetime for a young man to gain experience, confidence and self-esteem available in few other ways. As far as the Captain was concerned, there was no other way. Of course, OCS, particularly Infantry, was a sure-fire, express, train ticket to Vietnam combat.

"So, Private? Do you want to accept this offer?"

Andrew didn't hesitate. "Yes, sir." He'd added up the time in his head. *I'd still be out in less than three years,* he thought to himself.

"You're sure? You've not been pressured or coerced by me or anyone else, correct?"

"Yes, sir. I mean, No sir, I've not been coerced. I'd like to accept the opportunity."

"OK, Private." The Captain now presented a sheet of paper that required Starkey's signature. "This confirms your decision. Sign it and get back to your training."

"Uh, Sir?" asked Starkey.

"Yes, Private?"

"Sir, did you go to OCS?"

"Yes. Infantry, Class 15-66."

"What's it like, I mean, Sir, what's it like, Sir?"

The Captain, a tall, lean and blue-eyed Texan, leaned back in his swivel chair. "OCS is tough. It makes BCT look like kindergarten. The hazing, the abuse they heap on you is far more mental than physical." He picked up the pen Starkey had just signed with and tapped on his desk a few times before continuing.

"My advice is, learn all you can in AIT down at Ft. Polk. That will be the practical foundation for Infantry Officer training. In every situation you're in, imagine yourself as the one the others will look to who must know what to do, know how to respond, know how to lead. Always be prepared to be singled out and tested. Always assume your name will be called first. Establish yourself as the soldier that takes his job seriously." He paused a moment, smiling inwardly that he was counseling someone only a few years younger than himself. Then, he felt a need to share something personal and turned his chair towards the window. "I have to warn you, though. Being an officer means you won't have as many buddies, hardly any in fact. It can be lonely. Your job won't win you any popularity contests."

He cleared his throat, stood up suddenly and offered his hand to Starkey. "Good luck, Private," he said with finality.

Starkey jumped up and shook the Captain's hand. "Thank you, sir." He saluted, did a passable "About Face," and marched out of the office.

Once outside, he made a beeline for First Platoon to find Rich Enlow. He didn't see Rich among the others cleaning their weapons so went to the barracks door and shouted to a man in the stairwell. "Hey, is Enlow in there?"

The man strode to the top of the stairs and yelled, "Enlow! Your Fourth Platoon buddy is here to see you."

Rich bounded down the stairs, and, seeing Starkey, burst into a grin. "Hey shitbird! How you doing?"

"Fine, buddy. Say, did they call you in about OCS?"

"Yeah 'bout an hour ago. Told them no fucking way."

"Oh, shit."

"What did, uh, so did you talk to the Captain?"

Starkey was stunned. "Yeah, just now. Told him I'd go. Why the fuck did you say 'no', you son of a bitch?"

"Hey, come on. I just couldn't stand the thought of the additional time. I just want to go to 'Nam and get it over with."

"Man, I thought we'd, you know, go together."

"Well, I'm..., look, I wasn't expecting it, you know? They just sprung it on me. I didn't have time to really think about it. Sorry I didn't say something, but hey, we don't exactly have time to shoot the shit much around here."

"Oh, man."

"Well," said Rich, feeling uncomfortable and perplexed at Starkey's reaction, "I've got to get back at it. I'll see you at the PX tonight if the fuckers turn us loose."

"Shit. OK, see you around."

He walked across the formation area towards his barracks in a fog of confused depression. He knew that he and Rich wouldn't have been really together in OCS, any more than at BCT. It was just that now he felt his decision had been rash and poorly thought out. "Rich couldn't know something that I don't, could he?" he thought.

"Wake up, STAR KEY!" hollered Sergeant King. "You got time to daydream, you got time to give me fifty!"

Chapter 12
The Pass

They were three weeks from graduation. Though they were hardly "veterans," the men who had arrived little more than a month before as soft, confused and undisciplined draftees were now muscle-hardened and confident. Hundreds of hours of bayonet drills, road marches, weapons firing, grenade throwing, obstacle courses and, always, the low-crawl pit, pushups, horizontal ladder and a dozen other exercises had turned most of them into the material from which could be created reliable, disciplined soldiers, just like their fathers and grandfathers before them.

One Thursday afternoon, Sergeant King and the other Drill Sergeants announced that the Company would be getting a weekend pass. They'd be released following a formal inspection on Saturday morning and were free until late Sunday afternoon. The men roared their delight and immediately began feverish planning on where to go and how to get there.

Danny and Andrew Starkey considered their options and decided on Louisville. After all, it was the closest large town and, since Danny grew up there, he knew his way around. Of course, nearly the entire Company would end up in Louisville since most were too far from their homes in Indiana, Ohio, West Virginia and Kentucky to be able to get there and back in the short time allowed. Some would try, nonetheless.

They'd take a cab downtown, find a cheap hotel room and then start cruising the streets. Danny also had an agenda that he would only share with Andrew out of hearing of the others.

"Man, I know a whorehouse we can go to. Babes are decent looking and they're only ten bucks."

"Wow. You're shitting me. You know where a place like that is?"

"Sure. There's lots of them around if you know where to go. Sometimes the cops close them down, but they always open up somewhere else."

Andrew had never experienced a prostitute and was excited at the prospect. His sexual history to date was very limited. In fact, he'd only had sex twice, both times with Sally Mason the summer after high school graduation, shortly before the road trip to Colorado. She'd been very clinical about it, and made him feel like she was doing him a favor.

One night as they shared a milkshake, she said, "Look. I know I've been hard on you. You've been sweet to put up with me. But, this is different. We're no longer in high school and, now, well, I don't want to go off to Wellesley a virgin. You don't want to go off to IU a virgin. If we're careful, we can do it right and maybe even enjoy it."

Andrew liked Sally and had taken her to both proms. Their make-out sessions were passionate but she seemed to have the ability to turn that passion off like a light switch if his hands began moving below her waist. She did have great breasts, and allowed him unrestricted access to them at drive-in movies, their usual parking spots, or in her parents' basement. That was, in his mind, a pretty good arrangement. Besides, one of his friends had just married a pregnant girlfriend, and such a prospect terrified Andrew.

One sweltering Friday afternoon, Jack and Andrew were returning from a day of corn detassling. As he stepped from Jack's car, his mother yelled out that someone was on the phone for him. She met him in the driveway and said with a wink, "I think it's Sally," then waved a greeting to Jack. Andrew stood in the driveway a minute to beat the pollen-caked mud from his pants and shirt with his straw hat, then kicked off his muddy Keds and walked into the house.

Sally announced that her parents would be out very late at a business dinner with her father's boss and spouse.

"They'll be out past midnight, so if you can come over around seven-thirty, I think we can do it."

He looked around nervously 'til he saw his mother out in the yard talking to a neighbor. "You sure?" he said.

"Yes, they'll be gone…"

"No, I mean are you, uh, do you really want to do this?"

"Andrew, I care about you and I want us to do this together. I want…I want you to be the one. We need to do this. OK?"

"OK."

"Now, you'll bring a rubber?"

"Yep."

"See you at 7:30."

After a stop at a gas station bathroom with its condom machine, he parked his car a block from Sally's home and walked the rest of the way. *In case I have to leave out the back door,* he thought.

She came to the door wearing a bath robe and a pair of fuzzy purple slippers. Pushing the door closed behind him, she put her arms around his neck and kissed him lustily. "So glad you could come," she winked, then took his hand and led him to the basement stairs. It was dark in the basement but she'd lit a few candles for romantic effect. As they descended the stairs, she squeezed his hand and said, "Did you bring a rubber?"

He was already nervous enough. "Jeez, Sally. Yes, I brought a fucking rubber."

"Well, you don't have to be vulgar about it."

Their love nest was a cot covered by an unrolled sleeping bag that still smelled faintly of wood smoke from her two older brothers' deer-hunting trip. Somewhere she'd gotten a small bottle of champagne and had poured them each a glassful.

"Well, here's to us," she said, handing him his champagne. "We'll always be emotionally tied to one another, no matter what else we do in our lives." She clinked her glass to his and chugged her drink. Andrew sipped his champagne, set the glass down and reached for the belt of her robe.

"Aren't you going to kiss me first?"

"Yeah, sure."

After a long passionate embrace, he stood and took off his T-shirt and shorts. Facing away from her, he took off his jockeys, then sat back down on the edge of the cot. He was so nervous that he began to shake violently.

"Wait a minute," he breathed. "I've got to calm down."

Sally waited a few moments, then pulled his head to her breast and ran her fingers through his hair. "Oh, Andrew. This is going to be so special."

He had relaxed a bit and began kissing her again in his usual slow sensual way, the way that had always seemed to drive her crazy, at least until his hands got too busy. He laid her back on the cot and pulled the belt loose. Out of habit she held his wrist tightly. He whispered, "Sally?" and she released him, a nervous smile on her face. Then he opened her robe and pressed his face to her belly. He moved his lips down to where her pubic hair began and inhaled softly.

"Oh, my God," she whispered. "You'd better put on the rubber."

He entered her carefully, but she gasped. "Wait, wait. Oh, my God. OK, now, oh…"

Slowly he settled in, then let his full weight rest on her. "You OK, Sally?"

She was crying softly. "Oh, oh…sniff, my God."

"Honey, am I hurting you? Did I hurt you?"

"No, sweetie. Just for a second," she sniffed. "Now I'm OK."

He raised up on his arms, looked down at her and began his

motion. In only a short time he lost control and ejaculated with a cry of release. After convulsing for several seconds, he let his weight rest on her again. They were both bathed in sweat. In a few minutes he lifted himself off and lay at her side. He pulled her to him and stroked her long brown hair.

"Sorry, Sally. I guess I didn't last too long, huh?"

She giggled…"I don't know any better. I think it was perfect."

They lay quietly for some time and Andrew almost dozed off.

"You know, Andrew," she whispered, "I think it's a good thing we didn't start doing this any sooner." She snuggled her face into his chest. "I guess we know what all the fuss is about now, hmm?"

"Yes, but you were worth waiting for."

She was touched. "Oh, Andrew. Do you mean that? You're not mad at me for holding off all this time?"

"Of course I'm not mad. It was hard sometimes but we both know where babies come from. I'm sure not ready for that."

"Me neither. But when I am ready, I hope you'll be around." She kissed him again and smiled coyly.

"Uh, Sally? I brought two rubbers."

~ * ~

A convoy of cabs dropped the rowdy, starched, khaki-uniformed soldiers off in front of a seedy downtown hotel. The sidewalks were already filled with soldiers that had arrived earlier. Prostitutes cruised by in sedans and convertibles, and others stood on street corners hustling the scores of young men, most of whom could never have imagined paying for sex, much less wanting to in the worst way.

Black girls were nearly as numerous as the whites, and they made raucous and obscene overtures to the young white soldiers, who, back home in their Midwestern towns and cities would never have considered such a liaison. But here, the chance to go with a black girl excited many of them. On the other hand, the white girls, more than willing to go with black soldiers, made a much lower key approach to those men. This was, after all, the Old South and race trouble could always be just a heartbeat away.

Indeed, most of the girls on the streets and cruising in cars were not prostitutes in the sense of making a living that way. Rather, they were girls from small towns within, more or less, a 100-mile radius of Louisville and were just making a little easy money. They knew these boys would pay any reasonable price, would not be rough with them, would not take very much time, and would not argue about wearing condoms. What they did risk was to be slapped around by pimps who were in the "business" of prostitution and had no sense of humor about free-lancers from the "sticks" cutting in on their action.

As the soldiers lined up to register for rooms, Danny grabbed Andrew by the sleeve and pulled him aside.

"Let's go down the street. All these dumps are the same, so no reason to wait in line for this one."

Sure enough, several more past-their-prime hotels were available with rooms to spare. The boys checked in, threw their Army gym bags on the twin beds and ran back down the hall to the elevators.

Back on the street, Danny said, "Follow me," and began jogging down an alley. They turned left, ran another block, then down another alley. Emerging, they were outside a rough, workingman's bar called, "Robbie's Tavern."

"My stepdad hangs out here. Wait a minute." Danny looked carefully through the front window, then opened the door and walked in a step. Then he came back out and motioned for Andrew to follow him inside.

"Wanted to make sure he wasn't here. Don't want Mom to know I was in town and didn't stop by."

Andrew whispered, "Man, this is an over-21 place. How..."

"I know the bartender. He'll serve us."

"Hey, Bubba! Remember me?" Danny waved his arm through the smoky haze.

A huge black man stood behind the bar drying shot glasses. He peered over his bifocals at Danny.

"Well, shit and fall back." His mouth exploded in a toothy smile. "Haven't seen you in a coon's age. By the khakis, guess I know where you been. Come over here, boy!"

The man walked out from behind the bar and hugged Danny. He pulled the boy's Army "overseas" cap off and rubbed his shaved head with a beefy hand.

"Boy, those niggers still shaving 'em close!" He glanced towards Andrew. "Who's your buddy?"

"Bubba, this is my best buddy, Andrew. He's a fucking Hoosier, but not a bad guy all in all."

"Glad to meet you, Bubba," said Andrew extending his hand to shake. It seemed as if his hand disappeared into a warm catcher's mitt.

"Hope you ain't looking for Stan," Bubba said. "This ain't his night."

"Nah," said Danny. "Actually, trying to lay low. Just got an overnight pass and don't have time to visit with family. Don't say you saw me, OK?"

"Sure, sure. I get the message. Guess you two want a beer, right?"

"Well, maybe a couple, but only if you're OK with it."

"Shee-it. You wear the uniform, you can drink in any joint I own. Just don't start any fights or bother my ladies." He nodded his head towards two hard-looking women, one black, one white, who sat smoking at the far end of the bar. "I gets a cut from their action, and you two don't look like high-rollers."

"No Sir. We'll just have a couple beers. Thanks, Bubba."

Bubba walked back behind the bar and opened four long-neck Falls Citys. "Honey," he said to an emaciated waitress, "take these soldier boys around to the side there and serve 'em up."

As they began to follow the waitress, Bubba called after Danny. "Hey, how's Stan doing? He still working at the Downs? When he comes in, it's so crowded I don't get to visit with him much."

"Still driving that tractor. Seems to like it OK."

"All right, then. I won't mention I seen you."

The waitress took them to a far table, well out of sight of the front door and window. A cop would have to come in and walk back to catch them. Danny stuffed a ten-dollar bill in the woman's blouse.

"Man, this is a wild place," said Andrew. He was a bit uncomfortable but began to relax as the beer took its effect. "So, Stan's your stepdad?"

"Yeah," said Danny. "Man, isn't it great to be away from that fucking place?"

"It's been so long, I don't know if I can believe it yet," answered Andrew.

"Well, we'll blow down these beers, then get a cab to that little 'house' I was telling you about."

Andrew nodded. "I didn't know there were some many hookers in the whole world. This town is crawling with them."

"Hey, this is a nice town," Danny countered. "It's just when the troops are around on the weekends, the place goes ape shit. You got to come to the Kentucky Derby some time. You've never seen so many beautiful women in your life. The whole fucking town is spruced up and all the big wigs come in from everywhere. Governor comes in on a special train from Frankfort. Private planes flying in. It's just crazy."

"Yeah, I've always heard it's a blast over here. Kind of like Indianapolis during the '500' weekend."

Danny rolled his eyes. "Man, that's just a bunch of drunk Hoosiers watching pussy-ass race cars go around a track. The Derby is thoroughbred horses and all the classy people who live that life out on their estates, drinking Mint Juleps all day."

Andrew let his friend win the contest of which event was better. He'd been to neither the 'Derby' nor the 'Indy 500', and assumed both would bore him to tears. He decided to turn the conversation back to prostitutes.

"So, how come you want to go to this 'house', instead of just grabbing one of those girls we saw in front of the hotel? They looked pretty good to me."

"Be patient my friend. You'll like this place just fine. Besides, you want to hump one of those country girls in the backseat of a Chevy, or do it right in a bed with a girl that knows what she's doing? "

"You talked me into it," said Andrew, taking another swig of his Falls City. "By the way," he continued, "won't your mom get pissed that you didn't call or something?"

"Maybe. But there's no way she'll find out. Don't sweat it."

"No, man. She's your mom."

As excited as they were to be away from Ft. Knox, the fact was, both were exhausted. As they sat and talked, a blanket of fatigue descended on them. Danny went into the bathroom and splashed water on his face. He put quarters in a condom machine over the urinal, twisted the knob and two packs fell into his hand.

When he came out, he handed a pack to Andrew and said, "Come on. Let's get going or we'll end up crashing for the night."

They yelled their thanks to Bubba as they walked out. He was busy with customers and sent them off with a wave. "Now y'all be careful, ya hear?"

At the corner, it only took a few minutes before a cab came by. Danny hailed it and gave the driver a street intersection to take them to.

"Hope you got a gun," said the driver.

They rode for ten minutes, weaving among buildings in an industrial area. Ohio River bridges could be seen in the distance, lighted from one end to the other. L&N switch engines pushed freight cars on tracks that ran along the road.

"Y'all want out here?" said the driver as he pulled over at the intersection Danny had indicated.

"Yep," said Danny. "How much we owe you?"

"Two-fifty." Danny handed him five dollars and the boys got out. On the sidewalk, Andrew tried to pay his half of the fare, but Danny said, "Put your money away."

They walked most of one block down the dark street. Street lights lined the way, but many had been shot out. At an intersection, across the street, a noisy honky-tonk occupied one corner. A screen door with an "RC Cola" sign faced towards the center of the intersection allowing a view of many bodies moving around inside.

"Man, I hope that's not where we're going," said Andrew, looking around apprehensively.

"No. That place is a real shit hole." Danny pointed down the empty street. "We're heading for an old railroad hotel another block down."

Just then, they were startled by a loud "bang." They turned towards the noise and saw that a very large black woman had burst through the door of the honky-tonk. She strode onto the sidewalk and then proceeded towards the middle of the street. The boys thought she was coming after them and were on the verge of bolting away. Just before she reached the middle of the intersection, several people came out of the joint after her. One said, "Now, honey. You got to calm down. He didn't mean nothin'. He just didn't mean nothin'."

She turned suddenly, put her hands on her hips and yelled back at them. "Y'all can jes' kiss my big, fat, BLACK ASS!"

By then, her friends had reached her and had begun coaxing her back to the joint. "Now, Charlene, you got to calm down. If Raymond had a motherfuckin' brain, he'd be dangerous. You know that. Now come on back inside."

Danny and Andrew walked as quickly as they could, rounded the corner of a building and burst into hysterical laughter. They took a quick look back towards the honky-tonk and watched as the lady and her entourage disappeared inside.

"Jesus Christ," Danny huffed, rubbing his hand across his face. "I almost shit in my pants."

"I think I did," laughed Andrew.

The street was fronted by dilapidated brick buildings of one or two stories. All seemed abandoned. Mid-block, a dim, red, light bulb glowed over the doorway of a two-story building. Its street frontage was narrow but it extended a considerable distance back to an alley. An unlighted walkway ran its length. Above the door a sign read, "Yardmaster Arms." Danny tried the door but it was locked. A button was at the side of the door and he pushed it twice. Andrew watched the street nervously.

After a few minutes, they heard steps in a stairwell, then a peep hole opened letting the light within shine through. Then it closed again. Another minute went by until the door opened. A matronly white woman in a silk robe and high heels stood there and stared at the two boys impassively.

"Howdy, ma'am," said Danny. "Are any ladies working tonight?"

"Well, honey, I'm not sure I know what you mean."

"Uh, we'd like to visit your ladies."

"Honey," she said, "those uniforms don't fool me. You look like a couple of rookie cops."

Andrew spoke up. "We're not cops, ma'am."

"Come here, honey." Andrew walked towards her and stopped a foot away. She crooked her finger and tugged gently at his uniform shirt, then pulled out his dogtags.

"Well, now. I guess we can accommodate a couple of our fine soldiers. Come on in, boys."

Both were getting excited and elbowed each other as they followed the woman up the stairs. Her large butt jiggled beneath her robe and the boys rolled their eyes. Music played somewhere up ahead. They moved to the side to allow two men in disheveled business suits to descend the narrow stairwell. At the top, they were led down a hallway and into a large room that had a bar at the far end. A jukebox filled with 45s was playing, "Can't Buy Me Love" by the Beatles.

A half-dozen women sat smoking and chatting on a couch. Several more stood around the jukebox. They were all white, and ranged in age from late teens to early fifties. Most wore silk-like robes with high heels, but a few wore teddies. A woman behind the bar was bare-breasted.

As the boys entered, the women on the couch stood up. The women at the jukebox joined them and they lined up as if for inspection.

Danny immediately walked to the lineup and stopped half way down its length. He smiled at a small breasted, red-haired woman of about thirty. She smiled back, took him by the arm and led him to a door near the bar. Andrew was left alone with ten hookers staring at him!

Holy shit, he thought. He forced himself forward and angled towards the middle of the lineup. He glanced back and forth awkwardly. Then a few of the women began to kid him. "Come on, baby. I'll take good care of you." and "No, me, baby. She's a witch. Let me take you on."

His eyes fell on a woman with long black hair that cascaded past her shoulders and across her mostly bare chest. She'd not been one of the teasers, and smiled when he noticed her. Sensing his interest, she stepped forward and took his hand. "Come on, honey. I'm the one for you."

A dimly lit hallway was lined with closed doors, and sounds of lovemaking could be heard. Women moaned and men shouted as they climaxed. Andrew felt like he must be on another planet.

"I'm Kitty," said the woman as she opened the door to a bedroom. "So, y'all in the Army?"

"Uh, yes, ma'am. Ft. Knox. Guess it's kind of obvious, huh?"

"Oh, we get a lot of soldier boys in here."

She walked across the room to a small bathroom-style sink. A plastic basin sat on a chair nearby and she picked it up and began filling it with water.

"Honey, y'all undress now," she said, looking back over her shoulder at him.

Andrew took off his khaki shirt and hung it on a hook behind the door. He began to reach for the lock, but the woman said, "Don't do that." He took off his low quarters and socks, then his pants, T-shirt and briefs and stood naked by the bed. The woman called him over to her and, looking him up and down, smiled mischievously. "Something tells me this is your first time."

"Almost," he answered. "I've done it a couple times."

"Well, I'll try to be your best," she said.

"Here, hold this for me." She had him hold the basin of warm water beneath his scrotum, then, using a bar of Ivory soap, began washing his penis and testicles. The process had the dual effects of cleaning and stimulation. He was very erect as she dried him with a rough paper towel. Then, she inspected him for any telltale sores or discharge.

After he'd passed her inspection, she asked, "Now, honey, what kind of party do you want?"

He repeated the choice Danny had told him. "Uh, I guess, just straight."

"OK, just a straight fuck?"

"Yes ma'am, that's it."

"That's ten dollars, honey. Around-the-world is only five more. You sure?"

"Yeah. Just straight."

Andrew got the wallet out of his uniform pants, pulled out the bill and handed it to her. She walked to a side door and pushed the bill through a slot. A shuffle behind the door made it apparent they had little privacy.

She took off her robe and stepped out of her high heels. Andrew was stunned at how great her body looked. She was heavy-breasted, and her skin was very white and smooth. Stretchmarks from a pregnancy were barely visible. Her black pubic hair contrasted starkly with her white skin.

"Y'all going to wear a rubber?" she asked.

"Uh, oh, yes ma'am. Let me get it."

He took the packet from his pants pocket and walked back to her, trying to open it as he walked.

"Careful, honey. Let me do that." She took the condom pack from him and tore it open, being careful not to drip lubricant on the floor or bed. She put the foil in a waste basket, and motioned Andrew to sit on the bed. Then she held his erection and rolled the condom down its length…

"OK. Are we ready?" she winked. She lay back on the bed, opened her legs, and pulled him on top of her.

Chapter 13
Danny's Friend

As luck would have it, a cab was just dropping off a man and woman in front of the noisy honky-tonk as Andrew and Danny walked back up the street. They jumped in and Danny said, "Downtown." The driver floored his gas pedal and the boys were forced back against the rear seat.

"Yo, dude," laughed Danny. "Don't you like this part of town?"

When the cab resumed a normal speed, Andrew said, "Man, I about shit when you just went up to that babe and left me standing there. How'd you pick one out so quick?"

"I know her."

"You're shitting me. You know a hooker?"

"Hey, they're people, just like you and me. She's the sister of a buddy of mine."

Andrew was stunned. "Holy shit. Your buddy's sister is a hooker? Does he know?"

"Yeah. But you wouldn't live long if you said anything to him about it."

"Wow. How did…?"

"Pretty sad. Her old man would get drunk and beat the shit out of the whole family--her, her mom, my buddy Wayne. One day, she takes off. Gone for a couple weeks. Shows up again all dolled up in new clothes, wearing makeup, hair done."

Danny leaned forward suddenly. "Yo, pull over here," he said to the driver.

He continued when they were back on the street, "I never asked her all the details, you know, about how she got into it. First time I went into that place I saw her. Kind of embarrassing. So, she just walks up to me, big smile on her face and takes me down the hall."

"Did you…?"

"Damn right I fucked her."

"Wow, your buddy's sister?"

"It was great. I always liked her. I'd flirt with her when I was over hanging around at Wayne's house. I used to fantasize about screwing her. So, lo and behold, she turns up in a whorehouse. Tell me how it can get any better than that…"

Andrew, amazed, shook his head. "So, now I know why you didn't

168 ~ William Gritzbaugh

want to settle for one of those country girls and the back seat of a Chevy."

It was very late now, but the downtown streets yet teemed with soldiers. Most were intoxicated. Groups of them gathered in alleys, six packs or bottles in plain view. As squad cars cruised by, the soldiers would duck behind dumpsters or into doorways. Some would simply stare at the police, daring them to stop. When they did, the soldiers would tear down the alley, laughing as the over-weight officers trundled after them. MPs were also in evidence, and the men played no such games with them. Many rowdy trainees had already been rounded up and hauled back to Ft. Knox to spend the night in the stockade. Non-judicial punishment would be applied to them in the form of "Article 15 of the Uniform Code of Military Justice." Forfeiture of pay for a period was the usual penalty.

Danny and Andrew searched for, and eventually found, some of their squad members huddled at a street corner near their hotel. Andrew looked at his watch.

"Man, it's 3AM. I'm beat. Think I'll head back to the room. You coming?"

"Let's see what these guys are up to, first," Danny answered. "Want to see if anyone got hauled in by the MPs."

"Well, where have you bastards been?" a squad member named Simpson asked.

Danny gave him the demonic grin. "Had to check the oil on a couple babes with our dipsticks."

"You guys got laid? Where the hell at?" said Timmons, a boy from Columbus, Ohio.

"Danny knows every whorehouse in the free world," joked Andrew.

"Well, shit. Why didn't you take us along? The whores driving around here are ugly as dog shit plus they want twenty bucks."

"Now, come on, boys. You think any respectable whorehouse is going to open its doors to a bunch of shit heads like you? You got to keep a low profile. Otherwise, they won't let you in."

"Well, let's go now," said another.

"No way," answered Danny. "If I tell you where it is, they'll close down and move. I'll have a hell of a time finding their new location."

Timmons was sorry now that he didn't settle for one of the cruising girls. At this late hour, they were long gone. "You assholes," he muttered.

"Lighten up, Timmons. If we get another weekend pass, I'll take you down. Depends on how much time I spend in the low-crawl pit between now and then."

"Hey, let's find a place to sit down," said Andrew. "My ass is dragging."

They walked into the hotel's common area and flopped down on couches and overstuffed chairs.

"So," asked Simpson, "did you do an around-the-world, or just a fuck?" His tone was conversational, but still too loud for four-letter words.

"Shh," said Danny, looking around. "Watch the language or they'll throw us out."

Simpson, an affable West Virginian except when drunk, threw his head back and yelled, "Well, fuck them!"

Seconds later, the hotel's octogenarian black doorman, shuffled over. "Boys," he said, "y'all going to have to git on to y'all's rooms now. Can't be offending the other guests. Now, y'all stand up and git going." On top of being ancient, he was barely five feet tall and not over a hundred pounds. He was also fearless.

Nearly in unison, except for Simpson, they stood and said, "Yes Sir." Simpson was pulled to his feet by Andrew Starkey, who told him, "Now, shut up, asshole."

"Come on. Let's go up to my room," said Randall. "Second floor."

Moments later, they piled into the small room and found places to sit, lean or lay. Simpson was the last one in and dived between two men already lying on the bed. He rolled over and yelled, "So, like I was saying before I WAS SO RUDELY INTERRUPTED. DID YOU…" The two soldiers already on the bed jumped on Simpson and muffled his shouts.

"Damn, Simpson," laughed Danny, shaking his head. "I heard you. Give it a rest, man." Leaning against the wall, he slid down slowly, coming to rest in a sitting position on the bare floor. For a moment, he sat quietly, smiling to himself as the other soldiers wrestled for places on the bed, floor or chairs.

Though he needn't have, Danny feared further talk of whores might cause Andrew to mention Danny's prostitute friend. He had visions of them all going to the Yardmaster Arms and asking for "Danny's girlfriend." He knew she'd be terribly hurt that he'd betray her in such a way. Instead, he decided to distract them with a hitchhiking adventure.

"You hitched all the way to Colorado?" Randall asked, as Danny began to regale them with one of his stories.

"Several times," answered Danny. This drew comments of

admiration from the others. Most had hitched various distances, to and from work, maybe a hundred miles to see a girlfriend. Andrew Starkey had hitched home to New Vernon from IU, a distance of 150 miles, on numerous occasions. For a high school kid to hitch alone, over a thousand miles cross-country, was a gutsy feat in their minds. Even Simpson waited for him to continue.

"Two summers ago," he began, "I headed out for Flagstaff, Colorado where my dad has a farm. Takes me two rides from my house in Louisville to cross the river, then two more to where Highway 41 goes through Vincennes." Knowing Danny, the men expect the story will be entertaining. The few remaining beers are passed around and opened, sending foam sprays around the room.

"I stand by the highway for, shit, over an hour. Finally, this big black car pulls over. I grab my bag and walk towards the car. Man, it's one of those big Lincoln Continentals, you know, like the one Kennedy was riding in when he got greased. It's got those doors that open out from the center."

"Like a limo," someone comments.

"Yep," says Danny, taking a sip of beer. "So, there's this big fat guy driving, and a little blonde babe in the shotgun seat. Now, as I'm walking up, I can tell this bitch is pissed off that the guy pulled over to pick me up. I can see her jaws flapping at him. I'm thinking, he's going to take off. But instead, the bitch's window goes down and the fat guy asks where I'm going. I say, 'Colorado'. He says, 'Hop in the back, boy.' The bitch doesn't say anything. Just glares at the fat guy. I'm thinking, 'Just keep quiet and don't piss her off.'" The men nod and chuckle in agreement.

"So, he floors it, heading west on Highway 50. We go a couple miles and he turns around and says, 'Boy, my name is James Donald Addison. Call me Jimmy Don. This here is Dorrine.' I introduce myself and decide to work on the bitch. I say, 'Dorrine, you sure have beautiful blonde hair.' Actually, it looks like shit, you know, like straw all piled up."

"Like that lady you just banged for ten bucks," laughed Andrew. Danny knew this was Andrew's signal that his whore-friend secret was safe.

"Yeah, just like that," he says, winking at Andrew. "So, she starts patting her hair on the sides and on top and goes, 'Why, thank you, honey. Do you really like it?'" Danny mimics the woman's voice in a falsetto, bringing laughs from the men. "I go, 'oh, yes, ma'am. It reminds me of my friend, Janice. She was homecoming queen.' Well, the bitch just eats this shit up and I'm in like flint."

Danny describes how the big car sails across Illinois, then picks up Interstate 70 at St. Louis. All the while, Jimmy Don is regaling Danny and Dorrine with tales of his long career at Patoka Farms Popcorn Company. Jimmy Don is now the head of sales for the small, regional business and they're driving to Salina, Kansas for a popcorn growers' convention.

"Now, as he's driving along, Jimmy Don is taking pulls off this whiskey flask. About 2100, he pulls over for gas. I think we were just east of Kansas City. It's getting dark, and this boy is shit-faced. At the gas station he starts staggering around, talking to the other people getting gas. He's so fucked up, he gets in the trunk, pulls out a bottle of Wild Turkey and stands there refilling his flask while the attendant is gassing up the Lincoln."

The men are giving Danny their full attention as he pauses to take a swig of his beer. "So I kind of roll my eyes at Dorrine and she's just as worried as I am. So I say, 'Jimmy Don, you doing OK?' He looks at me with this big shit-eating grin and says, 'Well, I think I better let Dorrine drive awhile.' Now Dorrine hears this and, I shit you not, she says (in the falsetto voice), 'Oh, Jimmy Don. I cain't drive this big thang'." All the men laughed loudly.

"Well," he continued, "I can't believe she doesn't want to drive 'cause I'm thinking, 'Shit, I'd love to drive this beast.' So, Jimmy Don goes, 'Boy, you think you can handle this old gal?' I say, 'Sure, Jimmy Don. Just show me how that cruise control thing works'."

Some of the men are puzzled. "I never seen cruise control," Simpson says. "How does it work?"

Another soldier answers, "Aw, you just press a button and it holds the same speed without having to use the gas pedal. You only see it on real expensive cars."

"Simple as that," says Danny. "So anyway, Jimmy Don says to Dorrine, 'Honey, I'll let the boy drive awhile. I'll just sit in the back and rest my eyes.' So, off I go driving this fucking limo down the highway. Ole Jimmy Don keeps talking and talking, but eventually he starts to doze off. So, then Dorrine and I get to know each other a little better, you know, how she and Jimmy Don met when she was working at a truck stop in Effingham, Illinois a couple years back. How it was love at first sight. They got married two months later, and on and on. So, as we're driving along, she starts to move over closer to me. She keeps looking back at Jimmy Don but he's starting to snore. The louder he snores, the closer she moves towards me."

The men are all leaning forward as Danny's story begins to get interesting.

"So, she starts rubbing my arm, puts her hand behind my head and starts rubbing my neck. Man, I'm nervous as hell, but I'm also getting a boner. I don't know what to do."

Danny finished his beer and is handed another one. "Well, the next thing you know, she unbuttons her blouse."

"Oh, you're shitting me!" a man says. "Right in the car with her husband?"

Danny laughs, "Oh, it gets better. Just hold on."

"Holy shit," the man says.

"So, remember--I got the cruise control on and we're just sailing along, ole Jimmy Don just snoring away in the back seat. Dorrine takes my right hand and sticks it inside her blouse. She had pulled her bra up so her boobs were just loose in there."

"Oh, man. You are shitting me."

"Those boobs just felt wonderful," Danny said, smiling at the memory. "She's just grinning up at me like she's having the best time, and ole Jimmy Don is just snoring up a storm."

"Then what did she do?"

"Well, I've still got my hand in her blouse, and she leans over and starts rubbing my leg. I've got a huge boner, and I think she can tell. So, I swear, she starts rubbing my dick."

The men are comically incredulous. "You're shitting me! I can't believe that! No fucking shit?"

"Well," said Danny, "I'm thinking, 'It doesn't get any better than this'. But then she starts unzipping my pants. Man, I'm so damn hard she can't get it out, so she unbuckles my belt. When she does that my belt made a little 'jingle' sound and I'm thinking, 'Shit, Jimmy Don's going to hear'. But he keeps on snoring. Anyway, she finally gets my dick out of my pants, and I swear, she leans over and starts giving me a blow job."

"No! No fucking way! You have got to be shitting me!"

"Nah, I swear, man." Danny takes another swig. "So, here I am cruising down I-70 in a Lincoln Continental. Husband passed out in the back seat and his wife blowing me in the front. This goes on for twenty miles."

"Did you shoot in her mouth?"

"Just a minute, now. So, we're cruising along. I'm just rubbing her back and she's just tooting on my twinkie. Then, up ahead in the distance, I see some bright lights. I see a sign that says, 'Pay Toll One

Mile'. So, I whisper down to Dorrine. I say, 'Dorrine, we got to pay a toll.' She leans up and puts her finger to her lips, like 'Shhhh', and starts fishing in her purse for a dollar. I'm thinking, we'll pay the toll, get back up to speed and Dorrine can rock and roll some more. But, just then, we hit these bumpy ridges in the road that are supposed to warn you to slow down. They go 'thrruuummp, thrruuummp' as you drive over them. Well, that noise wakes up ole Jimmy Don. He starts going, 'What? What?'" Danny does an impression of a fat drunk waking from a slumber and the men are laughing hysterically.

"So, Dorrine says to Jimmy Don, (falsetto again) 'It's OK, honey. We just got to pay the toll. You go back to sleep.' Now there I am, pants unzipped with my dick out, pulling up to the toll booth. Dorrine hands me a dollar for the toll, and as I pull up at the booth, I lean over like I got a bellyache so the woman in the booth can't see my dick."

Now the men are rolling on the floor.

"That lady knew something was going on." Danny bugs out his eyes and mimics the toll employee looking into the car. "You know, I'm bent over, the lady in the shotgun seat is fumbling with her blouse, and the fat fucker in the back seat is flopping around trying to figure where he is."

Danny pauses to let his audience collect themselves. "Anyway, I drive away, steering with one hand and trying to zip up my pants and buckle my belt with the other. Dorrine's over there putting her tits back in her bra and buttoning her blouse. Ole Jimmy Don is coughing up hockers and spitting out the window. Man, what a pig."

"Well," laughed Andrew Starkey, "that must have been the end of that blow job."

"Yes, buddy. I'm afraid it was. Dorrine and me just played it cool and waited for Jimmy Don to square himself away. Sure enough, he tells me to pull over so he can drive again. I crawl in the backseat and sit real quiet 'till we get to Salina. They drop me off at a truck stop and I wave goodbye. Dorrine is just patting her hair and doesn't even look back at me. Kinda hurt my feelings."

Reynolds, the group's only college graduate, takes the opportunity to wax philosophically.

"Yes, Master Danny. But, tragedy befell many young lovers on the way west," he observed. "I know you'll hold the bittersweet memory of Dorrine in your heart, forever."

It was 6AM as Andrew and Danny walked back towards their hotel. Their pass didn't require a return until four that afternoon so they had plenty of time to sleep before catching a cab back to Ft. Knox.

"You want to get some grub, or just hit the sack?" asked Andrew.
"Grub."

They flopped on stools at a brightly lit diner, arms resting on the counter, heads down with fatigue. The waitress, a matronly white woman of fifty, looked them over, smiling to herself. They were both a mess, uniforms wrinkled and shirttails hanging half out of their pants. She put coffee in front of each.

"Biscuits and gravy," they said in unison.

As she walked away, Andrew whispered, "Man, I hope I don't get the clap from that hooker."

"You used a rubber, didn't you?"

"Yeah, but..."

"Don't worry about it. No way you can get it if you use a rubber."

The waitress brought their food. "Now, you kids better get some sleep before you report back."

"Yes, ma'am," they answered, again in unison.

The woman seemed to hover around them, as if hoping to hear what they'd been up to that kept them out all night. A customer came in and sat at the far end of the counter.

"Ma'am," said Danny, "I think that ole boy's trying to get your attention."

"Oh, he can wait," she said, refilling their cups again. Then she walked down to wait on him.

"Bet she wouldn't think too much of us if she knew what we did last night," said Andrew. He was beginning to feel remorse for having visited the prostitutes and was sure he was at risk for venereal disease, regardless of the precautions he took.

"Shit," said Danny. "I bet she's had some wild times herself."

"Doing what?" chuckled Andrew.

"Well, maybe she's an old hooker."

Andrew laughed out loud, but stifled himself and lowered his voice. "So, that's what old hookers do, become waitresses?"

"Hey," said Danny, "it's an honorable profession. Waitressing, I mean. Who do you have more respect for? A former hooker that's waiting tables, or ole Dorrine?"

Andrew had to consider that for a minute. "Well, let's see. Dorrine waitressed in a truck stop, met Jimmy Don, got married and then gives blowjobs to hitchhikers. Assuming this lady is a retired hooker, now she's a waitress. Hmm."

"You see?" said Danny. "Life just goes in a circle. Everybody's doing the best they can with whatever God sticks them in."

Andrew sipped his coffee. "So, you think that's what we're doing? Dealing with what God stuck us in?"

Danny pondered the question as he finished his biscuits and gravy. "I think with guys like us, God just throws us into the shit to see how we turn out. Sometimes I don't think He even knows what's going to happen."

"Well," responded Andrew, making a face, "that's real fucking comforting."

Danny gave Andrew his demonic grin. "But that's the neat thing about it," he said. "God has to wait on us. Kind of makes you feel powerful, doesn't it?"

"No," said Andrew. "No, it doesn't."

PART 2

Chapter 14
1970 Vietnam

As the column of soldiers left the path along the rice paddy and angled into the jungle, the younger ones released the bolts of their M-16s, chambering rounds with a metallic clang. This was a nervous habit that was at best an act of bravado, as if to say, "VC and NVA, you'd better run away. Here we come to kill you." At worst, it was foolish because the metallic clatter from so many weapons could be heard a long way off. The enemy who might await the column along the trail ahead would never make such a racket. To the veterans in the column, the noise was the same as whistling in the dark.

The soldiers were members of the "Civilian Irregular Defense Group" or "CIDG," and not members of the Vietnamese Army. Rather, they were a more loosely structured and hometown-oriented volunteer unit. The column was an average armed force of one company of ethnic Vietnamese, reinforced by a platoon of Montagnard scouts, who walked the point of the column as it snaked along. All told, there were 100 indigenous troops.

In their usual position, between the Montagnard point platoon and the rest of the CIDG column, walked two US Army Special Forces troopers. With them walked their interpreter, plus another CIDG soldier carrying their radio. The Vietnamese commander, Dai Hui Luc, was close by, sometimes ahead or behind the Americans, as he directed the column's movements.

The two Americans stood a head taller than the indigenous troops, and their faces, though tanned, stood out in stark contrast to the CIDG. They wore "Tiger' fatigues," so named for the black-stripe camouflage pattern that covered the otherwise jungle green and rugged fabric. Head covering was a modified "boony" hat with half its brim trimmed off giving it the look of a misshapened green derby.

Magazines for their CAR-15 assault weapons were held in pockets that lined the front of fabric vests, custom-sewn for that purpose by the camp's seamstress. Each man carried twelve full magazines plus one already loaded into his weapon. They wore pistol belts to which were attached canteens and smoke and fragmentation grenades. The weight of the belts was shifted to the men's shoulders by a suspender-style harness. Sheath knives with five-inch blades were affixed to the left harness strap with the handles at the low end. A small back pack, the same carried by the CIDG, held their food packets, poncho liner, hammock, mosquito and leech repellent and personal-hygiene items, the latter limited to tooth brush, paste and toilet paper.

The column had left Camp A-115 Ba Thanh in the hour before sunrise when the mist lay in the valley and the grass was flat from the weight of moisture. Though they wore rain ponchos against the monsoon drizzle, the men's jungle boots and Tiger-fatigue pant legs were soaked in the first half kilometer and would not dry completely until the operation ended a week later.

Ba Thanh sat in a valley at the confluence of two streams that ran deep and cold from the mountains along the Laotian border twenty kilometers away. One stream entered the valley from the northwest, the other from the southwest, with the combined flow forming a significant river that meandered its way east across the vast coastal plain to the South China Sea. The location was chosen because such valleys were routes that branched off the Ho Chi Minh Trail and allowed movement of enemy troops and equipment into the interior of the embattled country.

The camp itself sat on a kidney-shaped, low hilltop. Its dimensions were roughly two hundred meters long by seventy-five meters wide. Arrayed at intervals inside its external barrier of concertina wire, claymore mines and trip-wire flares were two dozen sandbagged bunkers, some of which served as living space for families of indigenous troops. Three CIDG companies (Vietnamese), three scout platoons (Montagnards), assorted family members and, lastly, the Americans were squeezed into the small camp. An over-crowding safety valve of sorts was provided by the hamlet of Dak Khe and, beyond that across the river, an unnamed Montagnard village of thatched, stilt-mounted dwellings. This allowed soldiers to live outside the camp but yet remain close enough to respond in minutes should the camp be threatened with attack.

Camp armaments included two 105 howitzers, one 4.2-inch mortar, two 81-millimeter mortars, several 60-millimeter mortars and two 106-millimeter recoilless rifles. A sand-bagged tower/strong point contained a 50-caliber machine gun. Several wood-frame, tarpaper-and-plywood buildings surrounded by sandbags dotted the interior space. The largest served as the "team" house and barracks for the indigenous cadre. Another structure was a common shower/latrine/kitchen/wash house for the indigenous troops and their American advisors. Still another served as the American team house and "Tactical Operations Center" or "TOC." A shed for two 10-kilowatt diesel generators stood adjacent to that building. The camp's dispensary, yet another squat, sand-bagged bunker, was located at the west end of camp. Nearby was a helicopter landing pad that was only for use if the camp was under attack. Otherwise, helicopters landed on a pad outside the camp's perimeter. The advisors themselves slept in bunkers dotted around the camp's interior.

Special Forces camps were located astride similar corridors from the DMZ down to the Mekong Delta. Others were placed in areas of historical communist dominance, the hope being to establish a clear government presence that would eventually usurp the communist base of civilian support.

Most such camps were manned by twelve-man Special Forces "A Teams," consisting of two officers and ten enlisted men, each of the latter an expert in weapons, intelligence, communications, engineer/demolition or medicine. The two-man teams accompanying combat operations might thus include two NCOs or one NCO and an officer. Common sense dictated that both team officers not be out of the camp at the same time.

SF advisors worked with and through their "counterparts" in the Vietnamese Special Forces, the Luc Luong Dac Biet. Both SF and LLDB depended on support from their respective command structures, and for most of the 1960s, this was the case. But as the decade turned, that support began to erode. Clandestine operations like "Phoenix," "C&C" and others that partnered SF with the CIA, were becoming targets of the American and foreign press and even Congressional investigations. These irritants, along with the general public's fatigue with the war's interminable carnage, created a movement to "Vietnamize" the conflict, remove the American advisors and turn the camps over to Vietnam's regular army.

The two SF troopers on this operation were only vaguely aware of this impending realignment. Their focus was on the job at hand, to enter a very dangerous region of their "AO" or "Area of Operations," find and kill any VC or NVA troops that were encountered and, hopefully, drive many others towards a blocking force of the camp's two other Montagnard platoons. Those platoons had left at sundown the day before, and were already in position to the north where a network of mountain trails descended into the river valley.

Once into the jungle, the column's movement slowed as the `yards checked out potential ambush sites and watched for trip wires and newly dug punji pits before waving the rest of the column forward. The two Americans would alternate positions between the two units, one going with the `yards and the other remaining with the main column. Once the way ahead was deemed clear, the units would rejoin.

The easiest pathway into the mountains was to follow the stream beds, but these were also the easiest places for the enemy to set ambushes. Narrow gullies with steep sides provided no room to maneuver and were deathtraps for those unfortunate enough to stumble into them. So, often the column would climb straight up out of them, the men clawing their way up the sides, grabbing rocks, vines, tree roots or anything else that would keep them from tumbling back down. Once the ridge top was reached, the unit would regroup, waiting as exhausted stragglers made their way up. The inexhaustible `yards continued ahead, always searching out the next area of potential danger.

When word went down the column that it was safe to stop for a meal, the men happily pulled off their packs, squatted on their haunches and pulled out their rations. For the Vietnamese and `yards, these were called "PIRs," and consisted of one large plastic bag of dehydrated rice and another of vegetables. Both had been filled with water that morning before leaving the camp's perimeter, and were ready to eat shortly thereafter.

The Americans' food was in the form of "LRRP" rations, an acronym for "Long-Range Reconnaissance Patrol," and pronounced "lurp"--a freeze-dried concoction that was similarly made edible with the addition of water, either hot or cold. The Americans, of course, preferred "hot" and accomplished this by putting a match to a small ball of plastic explosive called "C-4" and holding a canteen cup of water over the vigorous flame. In a minute or two, the water, near boiling, was poured into the ration's plastic bag. These rations, though basic, were much preferred by the soldiers who had access to them, the alternative being the boxed "C rations" that were bulky, much heavier and, for the most part, foul-tasting. For an infantry soldier to carry a week's worth of C rations was nearly impossible, and intermittent resupply by helicopter, common in American infantry units, was not available to indigenous troop operations.

Meal breaks gave the SF men a chance to radio back to the camp, advise their approximate location and provide a general situation report, or "sit rep." The Lieutenant, the Executive Officer and second in command of A-115, reached for the PRC 25 radio that sat on the ground next to the fifteen-year-old Vietnamese boy-soldier who was assigned as his "radio telephone operator," or "RTO." He freed the antenna from its folded-down position, lifted the radio onto his lap and keyed the black handset.

"Gummy Taster, Gummy Taster, this is High Plains, High Plains, over."

A few seconds later, the radio crackled softly. "High Plains, this is Gummy Taster. I hear you Lima Charlie, over."

Lieutenant Andrew Starkey keyed the handset again. "Taster, this is Plains Alpha. Got you Lima Charlie, also. We are grid Golf, I repeat Golf. Coordinates Kilo, Lima, Tango, Yankee. You copy, over?"

"Roger, Alpha. I have you grid Golf, coordinates Kilo, Lima, Tango, Yankee. How's the weather, over?"

"Sunny, 85 degrees. Beach is crowded. Bikinis in abundance, over."

Sergeant Danny Sevilla squatted nearby, heating his canteen cup over a C-4 fire ball. He rolled his eyes at Lieutenant Starkey. Tran, their interpreter, smiled at the odd American humor and returned to his half-eaten PIR.

"So, Alpha, it's not a stinking, drizzling monsoon morning where you are? How'd you end up in sunny California, over?"

Andrew keyed the handset again. "My mistake, Taster. Guess I was hallucinating. It sucks here, too."

"Roger that, Alpha," chuckled Sergeant Garnett, the A Team's senior communications specialist, from the TOC bunker back at A-115. "How's Bravo doing?"

"Oh, as usual, feeding his face. Killed a foot-long centipede an hour ago, and he just had to see how it tasted with Tabasco, over."

Suddenly, several rifle shots shattered the jungle stillness. The bullets cracked through the wet tree leaves above the two Americans. Both rolled to the ground and reached for their CAR 15s. A split-second later, the jungle erupted with bursts from automatic weapons as the indigenous soldiers responded to the enemy fire. Two CIDG grenadiers fired their M-79s wildly into the surrounding undergrowth. The rounds exploded close by sending mud and plant matter high into the air that rained back down on the men.

"Shit!" Danny exclaimed in a hoarse whisper. His dive for cover had caused his canteen cup of hot water to splash on his jungle boot. It took only a second for the super-heated liquid to reach his skin. The ball of plastic explosive continued to burn between the two Americans, adding yet another hazard.

Andrew pushed his weapon's selector switch to full automatic and, using a tree root as cover, raised up to view their surroundings. The Vietnamese operation commander, Captain Luc, was yelling for the men to cease fire. Soon the monsoon drizzle was, once again, the predominant sound. Acrid fumes from exploding grenades and rifle fire mixed with the smell of the soldiers' rations to create a noxious odor.

"Hang loose," Andrew whispered to Danny. "I'll take a look-see."

He rose to a crouch, motioned to Tran, his interpreter, to follow and began walking up the ridge. He heard Danny behind him on the radio to Sergeant Garnett back at the "A" camp.

"Gummy Taster, this is Plains Bravo. We had some contact. Plains Alpha's checking things out. We'll report back in five or ten, over."

"Uh, roger, Plains Bravo. Make it five. Out."

As Andrew and Tran picked their way among the dozens of prone men, the soldiers began to rise up, checking to see if anyone had been hit by the enemy fire. They began a low chatter among themselves, gathering their gear and replacing the empty magazines of their M-16s. As they had done hours earlier, the young ones were noisy with the reloading of their weapons, thinking it would intimidate their unseen enemy.

Thirty meters up the muddy hillside, Andrew found Dai Hui Luc and several Montagnard scouts gathered around a fallen Viet Cong soldier. He'd been hit in the chest and abdomen by at least five bullets.

"Ah, Trung Hui," said Captain Luc as Andrew joined them.

"Beaucoup VC, Dai Hui?" Andrew asked.

"No," Luc answered. "Maybe squad."

Tran was uncomfortable around the Captain due to the man's chronic tubercular cough, and stood away from the group. Dai Hui Luc spoke some English and would summon him if the need arose.

The VC was not dead but given the copious blood flow pooling beneath him, he soon would be. A Montagnard bent over him, opening and closing his fist in the dying man's face. There was no reaction in the glazed eyes.

"Weapon?" asked Andrew.

A Montagnard standing several meters away held up a Chi-com SKS carbine for the American to see.

Andrew smiled at the man. "Outstanding," he said. The scout smiled back, displaying a row of beetle nut-stained teeth. "Well, maybe the blocking force will get them. Too bad Sergeant Mai didn't set out a Claymore."

Dai Hui Luc coughed softly into his hand. "Yes. Next time, Claymore," he said.

The VC was dead now, and the Montagnards rolled him over looking for documents and gear. One pulled a tightly rolled hammock from the man's pack. It was passed around and offered to Andrew.

"No, thank you," said Andrew, in Vietnamese. "Already got one."

Dai Hui Luc pointed up the ridge trail and spoke again to Andrew. "We go."

"Good," said Andrew. "We go."

"How's your foot, twinkle toes?" said Andrew as he sat back down next to Danny.

"About burned the fucker off. Call me a Dust Off."

"You hurt bad?"

"Nah, just shitting you. What happened up ahead?"

"Dai Hui thinks it was a squad of VC humping the trail. Just stumbled into us and the first guy fired those rounds with an SKS. The `yards greased him. The rest dee dee'd. Maybe they'll run into the blocking force."

"Or tell their buddies up ahead we're coming."

"Yeah."

The soldiers repacked their gear and were moving ten minutes later. After another kilometer along the ridge line, the column began a steep descent into a valley far below. The footing was treacherous and the men had to move carefully to avoid tumbling onto those below them. At the bottom, a stream meandered through a 100-yard-wide flood plain overgrown with knee-high grass and sapling trees. The stream's depth was deceiving, and as the men tried to cross they found themselves, at first, wading up to their waists, then up to their necks. The current carried them to the far side where they grabbed handfuls of grass drooping from the bank and pulled themselves along until the slope of the stream bank allowed them to wade out.

First to cross, the Montagnard scouts fanned out in a 180-degree arc and moved to the edge of the jungle on the valley's far side. The rest of the column then exited the stream in comparative safety.

Local intelligence sources reported that the NVA had a base camp somewhere along this valley. Captain Luc and his American advisors hoped that its discovery and destruction would result in more enemy KIAs, either with this impending assault, or later at the hands of the blocking force.

Lieutenant Starkey squatted in the grass with the senior Montagnard scout, Sergeant Mai. Mai was barely five feet tall, dark-skinned and very intense. He'd been searching the edge of the jungle intently with Andrew Starkey's binoculars for several minutes. He put down the binoculars but continued to stare into the gloomy, rain-soaked undergrowth. Mai turned back to another soldier, muttered a few words to him, and sent him to report back to Dai Hui Luc.

Andrew could tell that the jungle ahead of him had been thinned out and trampled down over time by many enemy soldiers. Where those soldiers were now was no small concern. They might have moved on days ago, hours ago, or they could be laying in ambush in the jungle.

As he sniffed the air, there was no telltale smoke odor from cook fires; only an unmistakable smell of "death," he thought to himself. Something stunk real bad in there and it wasn't shit, food, unwashed bodies or anything like that.

Mai handed the binoculars back to the American and nodded towards the jungle. "We go," he said. He then duck-walked past the American and whispered orders to several men squatting in the grass and waved his arm at several others further back. The scout platoon of twenty men moved forward, all their eyes on Mai. He made a chopping motion with his arm in the direction of the jungle to their right. Immediately, the men formed a line and began a cautious advance from the river bottom into the dismal undergrowth.

Andrew followed Mai as the Sergeant nervously entered the thick jungle. He looked at Andrew and made a face to acknowledge the smell coming from the camp. Andrew heard the muffled clink and rattle of gear behind him and turned to see the CIDG troops forming up in the positions just vacated by the scouts. He made eye contact with Sergeant Sevilla, pointed towards the CIDG, and mouthed, "Watch those guys." It occurred to him that should the Montagnards make contact in this jungle edge, the others might start shooting in their direction. He could only hope that Danny and Dai Hui Luc would keep control of them.

Thirty meters into the jungle they entered the expanse of the base camp. It consisted of a trampled-down circular area roughly forty meters in diameter with a zig-zag pathway that led back to the river. Tree trunks showed rope abrasions from hammocks and other gear that had been suspended from them.

Mai directed half his scouts to the furthest upstream point in the cleared area where they set up an M-60 machine gun. One soldier put out a Claymore mine, also pointing it up the valley, and was unrolling the cord that ran from the mine to the hand detonator. The remaining men fanned out to the left and right of the machine-gun strong point. Mai sent a man back to tell the CIDG it was safe to advance, and soon the abandoned camp was filled with curious soldiers.

Items of equipment in the form of rotted uniforms, ammunition pouches, ration tins and a crushed AK-47 magazine were scattered around the area. Nothing they found could establish a timeline for the enemy's departure. Eventually, the source of the putrid smell was identified. It was indeed the death smell of two badly decomposed NVA soldiers that lay half buried several meters outside the base camp's perimeter. That hastily abandoned grave surely indicated that the NVA took off at the sound of the column's ridge top firefight, only a few hours before.

Sergeant Sevilla and a few CIDG gathered at the grave, pondering what fate had befallen the dead men. Given that the jungle insects had only partly consumed the remains, they'd been dead for no more than a week. Large chunks of flesh were missing from the legs and lower torsos of both soldiers.

"Blast wounds," Danny muttered to himself. He turned to the CIDG. "Ka-fucking-Boom," he said under his breath. The soldiers grinned at him nervously.

"Yo," Lieutenant Starkey whispered as he approached the grave.

Danny turned to him. "Probably got greased somewhere else and they dragged them back here so some GIs wouldn't get the body count," he surmised.

Andrew nodded. "Man, they're tore up bad. Maybe some gunships caught them in the open. I'll tell Dai Hui to add them to his KIAs. That's three for this operation already and it's not even 'Pok' time."

Danny rolled his eyes. "And only a thousand rounds of 5 5 6."

Andrew took a quick walk around the camp and saw that the CIDG were beginning to relax and rummage in their packs for food. Dai Hui Luc was squatting in the center of the camp with his platoon leaders and Sergeant Mai.

"Well, no element of surprise and nobody home," Andrew said, returning to Danny's position. "I'll go see what they want to do next. Bet they want to go up high again."

"That's my guess," said Danny. "If we go upstream, we'll get bushwacked sure as shit. No telling how many NVA are up the valley." He motioned towards some of the Montagnards who were guarding the jungle's edge. "Check out those guys. They're nervous as hell. We need to get the fuck out of here."

Andrew joined Dai Hui Luc's group. "Dai Hui, we go back up the mountain?" he asked.

"Yes. Beaucoup NVA up river." Dai Hui Luc wasn't afraid of a fair fight, but marching his 100 soldiers into a well-prepared ambush by a force of unknown strength was out of the question. Ordering an airstrike in the days ahead via his Special Forces counterparts made more sense.

The Dai Hui took a moment to catch his breath, then coughed into his hand while the men waited respectfully for the spasm to pass. Then, with an impatient wave of his hand, Dai Hui sent them back to their platoons.

In minutes, the soldiers were packed up again and forming to follow the Montagnard scouts up the steep slope, behind the base camp. The men at the perimeter were standing, preparing to move to the front of the column. As a scout was walking out to retrieve the Claymore mine, he suddenly shouted a warning in his native Hre' language. Several more men also shouted alarm. Then the jungle erupted with automatic weapons fire slicing through the camp from the upstream undergrowth.

Two Montagnards fell immediately. Men dived to the ground and began firing in every direction. Enemy RPG rounds screamed overhead and exploded in deafening crashes.

Dai Hui Luc lay on the ground unable to speak due to his continuing cough spasm. He waved his arm frantically to direct the men's fire, and after the initial few seconds of panic, the men began to orient their return fire as directed.

Danny and Andrew lay together near the scout perimeter. Both had emptied their twenty-round magazines in long bursts in the direction of the enemy fire. Tran and the radioman were prone next to Danny, the RTO shielding his head with the PRC-25. Andrew looked out and saw that the scout who'd placed the Claymore mine was dead, the detonator still in his hand. When Danny had reloaded a full magazine into his CAR 15, Andrew crawled toward the dead soldier. When he reached him, he took the detonator, pushed off the wire safety and squeezed the plunger repeatedly. The huge explosion of the Claymore now added to the pandemonium of rifle fire and exploding grenades. The directional mine's blast sent a screaming scythe of small ball bearings into the jungle and seemed to reduce, if not end, the enemy fire.

Dai Hui Luc, having regained some of his voice, could be heard giving orders. Seconds later, the men's fire faded away. Sporadic fire from the withdrawing enemy could be heard upstream. It was far off now, an apparent effort to hit anyone attempting to follow their retreat. Now, the jungle was quiet again, except for the pitiful moans and cries of the wounded men.

Andrew had covered his head with his arm as the Claymore detonated, and lay for a minute while the explosion's sandy debris rained down on him. Hearing that the fire had died off, he turned and low-crawled back to Danny.

Danny had crawled over to a tree and was sitting with his back resting on its base. His eyes were closed, and he was breathing heavily.

"Yo," Andrew said as he arrived next to him. Danny opened his eyes, looked at Andrew and closed his eyes again. "Man," he breathed, "that was too fucking close."

Andrew leaned on the tree trunk and reloaded his weapon. He surveyed the area and saw that the men were securing a perimeter and tending to their wounded comrades. Luc and the other leaders were moving from position to position, praising, calming and reassuring the soldiers.

"Take a look," Danny said, still somewhat breathless. He was holding up his CAR-15.

"Holy shit," Andrew exclaimed in amazement. A bullet had hit Danny's rifle just below the bolt opening. Luckily, it had ricocheted away without hitting him. The weapon was useless.

"Damn weapon saved my ass. Just raising up to fire when the round hit. Knocked me silly."

"Let me look you over. You sure that round didn't hit you someplace?"

"Nah," answered Danny. "I'd know by now. Man, my hands are still shaking."

Andrew tugged at the pant legs of Danny's tiger fatigues, then gently pushed his hand against his friend's mid-section. "No blood. Guess you're OK. You always were one lucky son of a bitch."

Danny rose up gingerly and began shaking the feeling back into his hands. Then he noticed that the bullet's impact had dislodged the weapon's full magazine. It lay undamaged on the jungle floor.

"Oh, now I get it," he joked. "They didn't want me dead. Just didn't want me shooting back."

Andrew shook his head in astonishment. "Well, let's save that magazine. I think we can get you an M-16. Looks like we've got some dead ones who won't be needing theirs."

"Save it?" Danny said. "Shit, I'm taking this one back to the 'World' with me as a souvenir."

Andrew handed Danny his CAR-15, took the damaged one and walked over to Dai Hui Luc, who was squatting with his platoon leaders, drawing in the dirt with a stick. They had suffered four dead including the two `yards killed in the NVA's initial burst of fire. Two more were wounded and would not survive unless they could be evacuated.

"Ah, Trung Hui. We need chopper."

"Yes sir," Andrew acknowledged. "I'll see what I can do." He held up the CAR-15 for the men to see. "Sergeant Danny, beaucoup lucky."

The soldiers chattered in amazement and passed the broken weapon around. A man walked over to where the casualties were gathered and retrieved an M-16. He returned to the group and handed it to Andrew. "Sergeant Danny," the man said with a smile.

"Gummy Taster, this is Plains Alpha, over."

"Roger, Alpha. Have you Lima Charlie. Go ahead."

"Taster, we had some contact. Need a Dust Off. You got a bird in the area, over?"

"How many, over?"

"Six. Two still breathing but not for long, over."

"Bravo?"

"Bravo's OK, but I'll let him tell you what happened to his CAR-15."

"Roger, Alpha. Can't wait to hear. Let me check on a bird and I'll get back to you. Do you need a 'jungle penetrator', over?"

"That's a negative, Taster. We got a clear area. Wait one." He pulled out his map and moved his finger along the grid lines of the valley. "Taster, we are in grid Hotel, repeat Hotel, coordinates Yankee, Zulu, Whiskey, Mike."

Back at the A Camp communications bunker, Sergeant Garnett found their location on the wall-mounted map of the camp's AO.

"Roger, Alpha. I know the area. Plenty of room for a Slick." Several team members had gathered in the TOC as the news of casualties was passed around the camp. "Are you still in contact, over?"

"Negative. We are green at this time."

"Roger, Alpha. I'll get that bird as soon as I can. Bunch of worried faces around here. You take care. Out."

Danny and a squad of CIDG went forward to check out the area from where the enemy fire had come. That fire, and the blast of the claymore, had littered the jungle floor with leaves and other plant debris. Twenty meters out, they came upon two dead NVA troopers. The bodies appeared to have been caught in a hurricane. Most of their uniforms had been blown off by the force of the mine, and their pith helmets, ten meters behind their bodies, were riddled and shredded. An RPG launcher lay near them and one man wore a Chi-com pistol in a leather holster.

A blood trail led them to another young NVA with gunshot wounds. His eyes were wide and his mouth was brimming over with bloody foam. His fingers still grasped the pistol grip of an AK-47. As Danny and the others knelt and watched the jungle to their front, a CIDG put his foot on the AK and pulled the boy's hand off the pistol grip.

Danny picked up the launcher, unbuckled the pistol belt from a dead man and handed them to the soldier who held the AK.

"Dai Hui," he said. The clearly delighted CIDG walked back to show the trophies to Captain Luc.

Danny motioned to a soldier standing over the dying NVA. "Het roi?" he asked. The CIDG poked the man with the muzzle of his weapon, watched for a second, then responded, "Fini, het roi."

Dragging their dead and wounded along on ponchos, the soldiers moved back to the jungle's border with the river bottom. Staying just inside the treeline, they moved downstream towards a large oxbow area that would allow the approach and landing of a helicopter.

The PRC-25 crackled. "High Plains, High Plains. This is Minuteman One Niner, over."

Andrew Starkey keyed his handset. "Minuteman One Niner. High Plains, over."

"Plains, this is One Niner," answered the helicopter pilot. "We are in-bound your location, ETA Romeo Foxtrot November. Show me something, over."

Andrew walked out into the oxbow, pulled the pin on a smoke grenade and threw it a few meters away. He could hear the beat of the UH-1 "Huey" helicopter's blades in the distance but could not yet see the aircraft in the gray monsoon mist. Purple smoke began to spew out of the canister and was soon billowing down the valley.

"One Niner, identify smoke, over."

"Wait one," came the pilot's reply. "Looking…"

Another minute passed. The helicopter's blades continued their drumming beat. Andrew Starkey was feeling like a six-foot, pale-skinned sitting duck as he knelt in the open area with the radio. The indigenous troops watched from the treeline.

Damn, I hope there's not a sniper out there, he thought as he searched the dreary sky.

The radio crackled again. "I've got purple smoke, Plains."

"That's us, One Niner. I can see you now." Andrew stood up, his CAR-15 held over his head as a reference point for the pilot's approach. Involuntarily, he gritted his teeth for a bullet impact that he thought was a real possibility.

Soldiers now dragged the casualties towards Andrew. The helicopter slowed and began its descent to the valley floor. Door gunners on either side of the Huey swung their machineguns back and forth in anticipation of having to return fire at any second.

As the aircraft landed, Andrew lowered his weapon and moved to the side. The CIDG began loading the wounded and dead men on to the bare metal floor of the aircraft. The day's captured weapons were piled next to them, except for the Chi-com pistol which Dai Hui Luc now wore. Danny's destroyed CAR-15 was thrown in at the last moment.

Andrew walked to the pilot's door and shouted above the noise of the aircraft's jet engine and spinning prop. "Thanks for helping us out, buddy," he said. The pilot was a young warrant officer and his sleeve displayed the Americal Division patch. His teeth were clamped to the plastic end of a small unlit cigar.

"Left a bunch of pissed-off VIPs cooling their heels at Minh Long." The pilot laughed above the din. "Any of our guys hit?"

Andrew held his boony hat down with a free hand to keep it from being blown away by the aircraft's down draft. "No. All indig."

"Good," the pilot answered. "That will really piss off the VIPs."

"Don't tell them. There's lots of Carling Black Label at Minh Long," said Andrew, the comment bringing a further laugh from the pilot. The fact that high-ranking US officers were left waiting while their special helicopter was used to evacuate non-American casualties was the furthest thing from his mind.

For this was not a proper "Dust Off," but rather just a utility aircraft out performing the mundane task of flying a route from one base camp to another, ferrying VIPs, average soldiers, mail and movies. However, when the need arose, those duties were put aside and the crisis of the moment became paramount. The pilots would be the first to admit that the chance for some excitement transcended the risks inherent in such diversions. It would never occur to them to ask the nationality of the casualties.

Andrew walked back to check the progress of the loaders, then stepped back up on the helicopter's skid.

"Can you take one more guy?" asked Andrew. "One of the dead guys has a brother. Want to send him back with the body if we can. Just take them all back to Ba Thanh."

"No sweat. They don't weigh much," the pilot answered.

Andrew moved away from the copter as the pilot prepared to take off. He gave a wave to one of the teenage door gunners. The boy sat on a web seat facing outward from a square notch behind the craft's open bay. An M-60 machine gun was mounted on a metal pedestal between his legs. The belt of ammunition for the gun fed from a metal box, then up and over the curved side of an empty "C" Ration can attached to the gun's flank, and into the bolt. The jury-rigged can provided just the right angle of entry to prevent the belt from jamming. A nylon seat belt and the gun's pedestal were all that kept the gunner from falling out should he be hit. An armored vest over his chest gave him a modicum of protection. His crash helmet would not stop a bullet, and nothing except goggles protected his face. He grinned at Andrew and gave him a nod, his hands remaining glued to the handles of the machine gun.

The helicopter lifted off the ground in a huge blast of wind. Soldiers squatted in the grass, shielding their heads with their arms. The pilot swung the tail boom around, dipped his nose and sped back down the river valley, his skids just above the water's flow. Both door gunners fired bursts into the high hillsides in an effort to thwart any enemy fire. Soon the craft was out of sight with only the staccato beat of its blades fading in the distance.

Dai Hui and his Sergeants were shouting now for the men to form up and move up the hillside. Luc waved a "Thank you" to Trung Hui Starkey. Had the helicopter not been available, the wounded would have had no chance to survive. Luc tried not to think of such a circumstance, but knew that such a possibility was rapidly approaching. He could only hope that his commanders would provide the same support when the Special Forces were gone.

~ * ~

The next few hours were spent in an exhausting serpentine climb to the ridgeline, 800 feet above the valley floor. The captain wanted to get his men high up on a point and set a defensive perimeter for the night. In such a position, they could not be easily attacked, and the men needed rest badly. This was only day one of a week-long operation, and the casualties suffered thus far did not bode well for their remaining time in the mountainous jungle.

Despite his tuberculosis, Dai Hui Luc was able to maintain a steady pace. He marched along with an ornate walking stick; his M-16, food, hammock and other gear carried by a soldier assigned that task. Indeed, how could his men complain if the Dai Hui, who was "beaucoup dow," could keep up?

He had seen many Americans come and go over the years since the first showed up in 1962. He marveled at how young they were becoming. Those first Special Forces men had been senior Sergeants and veterans of World War II or Korea. They were highly skilled confident professionals who clearly loved what they did. Now, the soldiers from America were often barely out of their teens with no previous combat experience. Nevertheless, he found them to be well trained, motivated and brave.

He particularly liked the two men on this operation, the Lieutenant, Starkey, and the Sergeant, Danny. They had accompanied him on other operations like this one and, though there were always firefights, the enemy had typically been local VC, and friendly casualties had been few. Today's action was against an NVA unit, albeit probably a weak and under-strength one. Nevertheless, NVA activity was not a good sign.

Dai Hui hoped that the day's battle hadn't dispirited the two men. As he listened to the soft banter between them he knew he had no reason to be concerned.

"You think there might be a whorehouse at the top of this ridge?" Danny said over his shoulder to Andrew Starkey. Lieutenant Starkey, catching his breath, leaned against a tree, took off his boony hat and wiped his face with it.

"If there is, I get the redhead."

"No way, man. She's mine. Don't want her soiled by some fucking Hoosier."

The worst part of the climb was over, and now the column was working its way along the narrow ridge top. The monsoon rain, which had abated about the time they had entered the abandoned NVA camp, had returned only briefly since then. With any luck, the men could set up their "NDP, or "night defensive position," and feed themselves before the rain returned and the utter blackness of the jungle night descended upon them.

Word came down the column that the `yards had secured a high point on the ridge a few hundred meters ahead. The worn-out soldiers soon swarmed the overgrown site. Sergeants began a survey of positions for the two machineguns, and Claymore mines were placed where the ridge trail entered and exited their location. Andrew and Danny accompanied Dai Hui Luc as he walked the perimeter and instructed the men on fields of fire and Claymore placement. Other soldiers quietly trampled and hacked at the undergrowth with machetes to clear areas for their hammocks and gear.

Returning from the inspection, Danny motioned to Andrew to follow him to a place where the `yards were setting up their night positions. They both selected spots between two trees with four-inch diameters and strung their hammocks out. When the hammocks were suspended tightly so as to keep their sagging bodies a foot off the ground, they strung nylon cord between the trees directly over their hammocks. Then they spread a poncho across the line and tied the four ends to other trees, thus creating an A-frame roof for each hammock. This simple arrangement would keep both themselves and their gear out of the rain. What it wouldn't do is shield them from mortar rounds,

RPGs or small-arms fire.

Indeed, American infantry units would never allow such a set-up, requiring instead that soldiers prepare a foxhole with grenade sump anytime the unit stopped for a prolonged period. Some units actually built sandbagged bunkers each night in anticipation of enemy ground assault or mortar attack.

Special Forces soldiers didn't follow that "SOP" or "Standard Operating Procedure," preferring instead to follow the lead of the indigenous units they worked with. Seldom did this include fox holes, not to mention steel helmets or flack vests.

Andrew was laying in his hammock, his pack, radio and CAR-15 resting on the ground underneath. A light rain had begun and, as the water ran off the edge of the poncho, he pinched the fabric, creating a channel that the water followed into the empty canteens he held up.

Danny had his recently inherited M-16 broken down and was running a cleaning patch up and down the barrel with a metal rod. He looked over and watched, smiling, as Andrew finished his refilling. Andrew shoved his canteens back in their cases on his web belt and motioned to Danny to throw him his canteens. The water drawn from a muddy stream hours before was emptied and replaced by the pure rain water.

"It doesn't get any better than this," said Andrew, topping off Danny's last canteen. "We won't get dysentery drinking this monsoon moonshine."

"Yeah, but you're going to get it again anyway from eating with the `yards yesterday. Blood pudding and monkey rolls. Boy, you just never learn."

"You ate the same shit I did."

"True, but I'm from Kentucky. My guts are chrome-plated."

"Well, I've been taking 'no shit' pills. Doc Bippus promised me I wouldn't shit as long as I keep taking them. When we're a day out from Ba Thanh, I'll quit taking them and see what happens."

Danny chuckled. "Thanks for the warning. On that day I'll warn the `yards to stay up wind from you."

Andrew's eyes suddenly widened and he swung his legs out of the hammock.

"Damn."

"Leeches?" Danny inquired.

Andrew was standing now and carefully unbuttoning his tiger-fatigue pants. "Dirty little bastards," he swore. Numerous leeches were attached to his penis and testicles. He reached down to recover his leech repellent from his pack. He squirted a small amount on the creatures and they quickly dropped off.

"Well, it's a good thing there wasn't a whorehouse up here after all," said Danny with a grin. "Can you imagine a whore's face when she wants to wash off your dick and sees a half-dozen leeches stuck on that bad boy?"

Had they not been where they were, in a jungle camp subject to attack at any moment, Andrew would have laughed out loud at Danny's description. Back at Ba Thanh, they'd have expounded about whores and leeches for another half hour to the delight of their teammates. But in this setting, humor was subdued.

"That whore would turn to waitressing real quick after that," Andrew offered. Then, "Shit, I got a couple at my boot tops. Can feel them moving."

Danny put his weapon down and reached over for Starkey's CAR-15. He dropped out its magazine, pulled open the bolt and extracted the round that had been in the chamber. Then he ran a clean patch down its length.

By now, Andrew had removed several more blood-fattened leeches that had settled where his jungle boot laces had been tied around his pant legs.

"Thanks, Sarge," he said, as Danny handed the weapon back to him. He shoved the magazine back in and chambered a round as quietly as he could.

Danny had begun eating the LRRP ration he'd not finished at lunch. It was cold and gelatinous, but he couldn't risk igniting a C-4 ball in the gathering darkness.

"That Claymore you fired blew away two NVA," he said between bites of food.

Andrew was taking slow drinks of water from his canteen and savoring the purity of the water. "Maybe the `yards greased them," he responded.

"No, man. It was the Claymore. One of us got another one with small arms."

Andrew lay back in his hammock, saying nothing.

A few minutes later, one of the CIDG soldiers walked over. "Trung Hui, lai day," he said, and gestured for the Americans to follow him. Both picked up their weapons and accompanied him to the edge of the ridge. Dai Hui Luc was squatting there with Mai and staring across the valley with his binoculars.

"Ah, Trung Hui. You see…" he pointed off to the north.

Andrew saw a point of green light on the hillside a half mile away. With Luc's binoculars he could see that it was a lantern hanging in a tree. Several men, possibly NVA, but more likely VC, could be seen moving around their own campsite. Andrew handed the binoculars to Danny.

After watching them for a minute Danny whispered, "Those boys would shit a brick if they knew we were here."

Andrew turned to Dai Hui Luc. "Bet we could hit them with an M-60. What do you think, Dai Hui?"

Luc considered this for a second. "No," he said, finally. "VC shoot back."

In spite of themselves, the little group had to cover their mouths to stifle their laughter.

"CIDG, VC all sleep," the Dai Hui said.

With that, the men returned to their positions. It was very dark now, and Andrew and Danny had to pick their way carefully to avoid stepping on sleeping soldiers. When they found their hammocks, they crawled in and covered themselves with flimsy nylon poncho liners.

Andrew reached beneath the hammock for the handset of the PRC-25. "Better call home," he said.

"Gummy Taster, High Plains, over."

"Plains, you got Taster here."

"Taster, we're socked in at point Echo. Repeat Echo. Don't lob any H&I out here, over."

Sergeant Garnett laughed softly. "Don't worry, Plains. No harassment nor interdiction tonight. Get some rest. Out."

Andrew lay quietly for a long time, unable to sleep. He could hear Danny snoring softly a few feet away. Their defensive position on the ridge was cloaked in abject soggy blackness.

The stillness was suddenly broken by an odd hissing sound that began softly, became louder, then ended abruptly with an audible thud as if something large had impacted in soft mud. Then, it was followed by another identical increasing hiss, then muffled impact.

Quiet chatter could be heard among those soldiers startled by the sounds.

Danny spoke out of the darkness. "Two mortar rounds. Both duds," he said. "Those VC knew we were here all along."

Both men knew they should lay on the ground in anticipation that the next rounds would not be duds. Neither, however, moved from the hammocks. Fatigue had eroded what common sense would dictate. Danny was soon snoring again. No more rounds were fired at them.

Andrew lay sleepless, eyes open, staring into the darkness. He wanted desperately to sleep, not only for its recuperative effects, but as much for the escape it provided. And, there was always the chance that he'd dream of Colorado, and of Nancy.

Chapter 15
Opportunities

He had finally written to her shortly after meeting Danny Sevilla in Basic Training. Danny's non-stop stories of Colorado had overwhelmed him and, reluctant as he was to risk a note back from her announcing her engagement or, worse, her marriage, he simply had to reconnect with his most intense Colorado memory. That she had written back, immediately, a ten-page epistle of shock, irritation, concern, affection and, lastly, news of her life and mutual friends had cheered him beyond words.

In fact, she had not mentioned the boyfriend, and Andrew tried hard to decipher if this meant her lack of commitment to that man, or if it meant nothing at all. He decided to try and write to her at least every other week. After all, he thought, the ball was in her court now, and he was in no position to challenge anyone for her affection. He knew he still loved her, but to dwell on his powerlessness over her actions could only drive him crazy. He would just take things a day at a time.

The appointment to "OCS"--"Officer Candidate School"--added to his emotional turmoil. His two years would, if he graduated, become closer to three. Nancy and Colorado had not occurred to him when the Captain called him in to offer the school. The only thing that had really occurred to him was that to become an Army officer might make up somehow for his abysmal performance in college. Subliminally, if not consciously, he knew his life needed a jumpstart to get back on track. A preoccupation with the Rocky Mountains and a girl had helped to put him in his current situation, and he couldn't let those same distractions govern his actions now. They would have to wait.

Following Basic Training, Rich Enlow, Andrew Starkey, Danny Sevilla and nearly the entire balance of the company were assigned to "AIT" or "Advanced Individual Training" for infantrymen at Ft. Polk, Louisiana. The alphabet once again separated Andrew from his hometown friend, Rich; however, it kept him and Danny together to their mutual delight.

Infantry training in AIT was intense, physically demanding and unabashedly "Vietnam"-oriented. Andrew did his best to heed the words of Captain Holliday when he was admonished to seize the opportunity and begin to take his training very seriously. OCS would follow AIT, and he had to prepare himself for what he assumed would be an unfathomable ordeal.

After AIT, Danny was headed to Ft. Benning, Georgia, and parachutist school. Then it would be on to Ft. Bragg, North Carolina for Special Forces training, rumored to be the roughest in the Army. So, he and Andrew, the irreverent cut-ups of BCT, became serious student trainees at Ft. Polk. Such was not the case for the majority of the trainees, most of whom displayed a cynical and fatalistic attitude, to the consternation of the cadre.

As tough as AIT was, weekends were usually free, with the men piling into cabs for the short drive to Leesville or, on occasion, taking a bus ride to New Orleans. Monday morning PT was frequently an agony of hangovers and dry heaves.

Eight weeks at Ft. Polk flew by, and soon the troops were packing their gear. Most were headed home on leave and then on to become replacements in infantry divisions in Vietnam. Rich Enlow was going to the First Infantry Division. Only a few were going on to additional training.

At the airport, the gate agent announced the impending departure of Danny's small commuter plane, headed for Columbus, Georgia. Andrew Starkey was headed home to Indiana for a four-day pass before he also would head to Ft. Benning and Infantry OCS.

"I'm going to be a paratrooper before you are, shit bird," Danny said with his trademark grin, shaking Andrew's hand. "Remember, if you ain't Airborne, you ain't shit."

"Don't rub it in, asshole. I'll figure out a way to get into jump school if it kills me."

"Well, maybe when you become a Lieutenant, tell them you want to go to the 82nd or 101st. You'll get jump school, and then you'll get killed. But, what the hell, right?"

"Right, but at least I'll be a paratrooper and they can put jump wings on my headstone," Andrew said, sardonically. He retained hopes of somehow working the system to get that cherished badge of the paratrooper.

As Danny turned to head for the gate, Andrew spoke after him. "Hey, if nothing else, I'll see you in Colorado in a couple of years. OK?"

"OK, buddy. You go get your lady back from that pussy frat boy, then come look me up in Flagstaff. If I'm not there, I'm dead." With a wave, he was gone.

~ * ~

Nothing could prepare a twenty-year-old young man for what was mordantly referred to as the "Benning School for Boys." The meat grinder of Vietnam was using up Infantry platoon leaders at an astounding rate. Not only were casualties among them high, but unlike previous wars, a one-year tour of duty forced a constant replenishment of junior officers. The OCS system thus became a factory of replacement parts for the Infantry machine.

The prescribed twenty-three weeks of training began as a mind numbing hazing ritual that sought to break down as many men as possible as soon as possible in order to arrive at a core remnant who could be molded into junior leaders of better-than-average intelligence, toughness and adaptability. As a result, the initial dropout rates were large. Young men who months before had jumped at the chance to attend, now sought a way out in droves, even though it meant immediate transfer to Infantry Divisions in Vietnam. Men actually went AWOL and then turned themselves in knowing they'd be dismissed from OCS. Replacing them in the various company-size units would be men who were sent down from other, further along, companies due to some failure in the academic portion of the training. Those who broke under the intense hazing were not offered such second chances. The hazing was particularly harsh on the draftee Candidates without college degrees. They were the youngest, roughest lot and would not have been considered for commissioning had not the Army's need been so desperate. Companies beginning with 200 men shrank to graduating classes of 120, inclusive of men who had been "recycled." "Tac" (short for "Tactical") Officers were the "Drill Sergeants" of OCS and were usually recently minted ROTC or OCS Second Lieutenants themselves. One Tac Officer was assigned to each platoon of Candidates, and their full-time job was to abuse, intimidate, threaten and humiliate their charges relentlessly, day and night, until the time when the program allowed the torment to be toned down. This was generally at the end of the first eight weeks.

At that point, a ceremony was held to herald that the Candidates had turned "Black," and were now allowed to wear black-felt tabs beneath their OCS insignia. "Black" status meant that they'd made it through the worst of the hazing and were considered viable officer material. Though the program was far from over, turning "Black" allowed the candidates the opportunity to actually visualize themselves making it through, not to mention providing status among the many other OCS companies in training. Now, as the hazing was tempered, the academic part of the program became more intense. Saturday night passes to Columbus, right outside the Post's gate, were a welcome respite.

Candidates were instructed in tactics at several levels of command, from Division down to Squad. They were taught weapons systems, the interaction among the combat arms of infantry, armor and artillery, air support by Air Force or Navy aircraft, helicopter assault, mechanized infantry assault and, of course, ground assault. Always there were classes in Infantry Hall, a building officially known as Building 4 and mockingly referred to as "Bedroom 4" due to the number of exhausted Candidates asleep at their desks. The men marched scores of miles to dozens of outdoor instructional areas, formation after formation, inspection after inspection, firing range after firing range and, on weekends, "punishment tours" (meaning marching for hours with an M-14 at Shoulder Arms) due to the accumulation of demerits for some imperfection of personal or barracks orderliness.

Vietnam was a foregone conclusion for the men, and as they marched to class day after day, they sang an eerie dirge that mimicked the '50s song "Poison Ivy." Where the original artist sang "Poison Ivy," those words were replaced by "Viet Nam," to wit, "Vee et Naaammm, Vee et Naaammm. Late at night while you're sleeping, Charlie Cong comes a creeping all around."

Yet cynicism, apparent at BCT and rampant in AIT, was not in evidence. Every man in OCS, regardless of whether draftee or enlistee, was now a true "volunteer," and none could say they hadn't known what they were getting themselves into. Those who did have second thoughts continued to drop out until the very end of the program.

In week sixteen, another milestone was reached when the Candidates turned "Blue." This was a particularly momentous time since, as Blue candidates, they had to be saluted by the Candidates from other companies that had not yet reached that level. Graduation was only weeks away, and the men needed to get used to returning salutes and, in general, carrying themselves with the extra dignity that came with being an officer in the US Army.

The war-time Army had grown so large, and its needs so desperate, opportunities for specialized training abounded. Evidence of this was presented one day as the Candidates stood in the mess hall line for the noon meal. A Candidate with a clipboard went from man to man asking what, if any, additional schools he might like to sign up for. Ranger school, Jungle school, Airborne training, Special Forces and foreign language school were the main choices. Since they'd soon receive Infantry commissions, the Army was only too happy to add to the new officers' base of experience and skill before their inevitable trips to Vietnam.

Andrew Starkey, somewhat stunned at the casual presentation

of such options, took only a second and answered, "Airborne," then watched carefully as the man made note of his selection. He hesitated another second, then said, "Special Forces." The Candidate nodded, made a second check on his clipboard and moved to the next man.

Andrew watched as most of the others shook their heads in a negative response to the offers. He shrugged, and returned to his conversation with a friend.

"Did you sign up for anything?" he asked Officer Candidate Conaway, a blonde, freckled farm boy from Iowa.

"Fuck no, man. Infantry's bad enough."

~ * ~

One afternoon, the men were summoned to the mess hall where they were greeted, quite collegially, by the Tac Officers and the unit commander, Captain Bolling. They were presented with orders for their first post-commission schooling or unit assignments. Most were going to infantry divisions in Vietnam.

Andrew had realized his dream of attending Airborne training and, assuming a successful completion, would go on to Ft. Bragg, North Carolina, and the Special Forces Officers Course. As he stared down at his orders, he couldn't believe his good fortune. "Man," he thought to himself, "all I did was talk to a guy with a clipboard."

As his beaming mother pinned the gold bars of a Second Lieutenant on his epaulets, he felt dazed. "Dad," he said, incredulity in his voice, "it's been eleven months, almost to the day, since I got on the bus at the post office. Now I'm an officer. I just can't believe it."

"Boy, it was the same in World War II and Korea. There are always kids like you just itching to stick their necks out. I just wish Nixon would get us out of that God damn war."

~ * ~

Jump School was just as Ron described it those few years ago as they sat sharing beers in the sunny backyard of the Spinelli home in Buena Vista.

For young soldiers just out of BCT, AIT and other arduous training, Airborne School was not physically demanding. What it did demand in good measure was "guts," determination and physical coordination.

Quite a few men were too awkward to be considered safe, and were cut from the class. Others who had only recently volunteered to learn to jump from airplanes at 1,250 feet found themselves balking at the 34-foot training towers. Class ranks were reduced accordingly.

Repetition of techniques honed the necessary skills. Intimidating "Black Hats," the NCO cadre of Airborne School, made sure the repetitions were constant and exact.

Whether it was in the painful exercises they did while suspended in parachute harness from the rafters of a training shed, to Parachute Landing Falls from a six-foot platform, to leaping from the 34-foot towers, to dropping from the 250 "free" tower when the paratrooper trainees floated down under a canopy for the first time, repetition turned the odd activity of jumping from an aircraft in flight into a routine endeavor.

In the third, or "Jump" week, the men were on the Lawson Field tarmac, strapped into their "T-10" parachutes, awaiting the first of five trips to the drop zone in the venerable C-119 Flying Boxcars. Every class included men who had never before been in an aircraft, commercial or military, and to jump out of "a perfectly good airplane" their very first time in the air was the source of much good-natured ribbing.

As each plane departed with a full load of paratroopers, then returned empty, the remaining "sticks" of men did their best to hide their anxiety. However, their turns soon arrived, and as they filed onto the aircraft, the enormity of what they'd trained for hit them like a prop blast.

Minutes after taking their seats on web benches, the engines roared and the plane was bouncing down the runway. Now 1,500 feet above the Alabama country side, the plane banked and began its approach to the drop zone. The noise of wind and engines was deafening as the jumpmaster shouted his instructions to the nervous men.

"Get ready! Stand up! Hook up! Check Equipment! Sound off for equipment check!" The men feverishly checked the man's parachute pack in front of them, then looked over their own reserve parachute and harness. From the front of the aircraft bay back to the man who would be first out the door, the men shouted that the equipment check was complete. None felt confident that they'd checked anything. The engines changed pitch and the big transport slowed and lost altitude.

"Stand in the door!" yelled the jump master. Each man gripped his static line with one hand, his reserve parachute with the other, and tasted bile. A forty-year-old Colonel had the honor to be first out. Wide-eyed, he stepped to the wind-blasted doorway, set one Corcoran boot on the edge, grabbed the door sill and felt a hurricane on his bloodless fingers.

The jump master watched the warning light. Now the red turned to green.

"Go! Go! Go! Go!" he yelled. The Colonel launched his body into the void.

Hearts in their mouths, yet responding as trained, the men performed the prescribed one-foot-forward shuffle towards the rear of the aircraft, sliding their static lines along the cable. The C-119 rocked as two-dozen bodies cascaded out the doors on either side.

In seconds, both sticks were out the door and into the screaming wind. The first sensation was of tremendous horizontal speed, followed by abrupt deceleration as the parachute deployed. Then, silence.

One by one, the men regained their senses and glanced skyward to check their canopies for malfunctions. Finding none and breathing rapidly, the men began looking around at the other descending paratroopers. Some tugged their risers to maneuver and avoid collisions with other men.

For a few seconds they could enjoy a view of the lush countryside and the meandering Chattahoochee River that marked the border between Georgia and Alabama. However, the ground was coming up quickly and the training took over again. Arms reached high up on the risers as the men tried to gage their direction of drift. At the last second, they pulled the risers to their chests, spilling air from canopies in a direction that would reduce the speed of impact. Knees were flexed and teeth were clenched.

Parachute landings are seldom textbook, even in the routine circumstances of a training exercise. Men crashed heavily to the ground. Most bounded back up immediately and began screaming "Airborne! Airborne!" Those suffering hard landings, or to "crash and burn," rose less quickly. Most shook off the pain and were happily screaming along with their comrades.

The Airborne School commander, a full colonel with numerous combat jumps in World War II, drove around the drop zone in his jeep and yelled for the men to pack up their chutes and run to the trucks. In a few minutes, another Box Car would be in-bound and the drop zone had to be clear.

Andrew's landing was hard but he'd not been injured. He was up pumping his fist and shouting with the others when the Colonel's jeep roared past. "Stop dancing around and get the fuck off my drop zone!" the officer yelled.

Man, I did it. I really did it, Andrew thought as he jogged to the "deuce and a half" truck with his parachute, the adrenalin continuing to pump through his veins. "I wish Danny and Ron could see me now."

The next day, they had two more jumps, then two more the following day. With five successful jumps, they were awarded the "Silver Wings" of a US Army Paratrooper. To Andrew, the simple badge was more valuable than his Lieutenant's gold bar, though OCS had been infinitely more demanding. He felt that the jump wings gave him a connection to all the GIs who had ever earned them, unlike the gold bar that only served to separate him from common soldiers. The irony was that, without the gold bar, there'd have been no jump wings, and certainly no Special Forces.

~ * ~

What had for years been called the "John F. Kennedy Special Warfare School" had recently been amended to the "US Army Institute for Military Assistance," the renaming a symptom of political correctness that was being forced on the wartime military establishment.

Andrew Starkey would attend the twelve-week Special Forces Officers Course conducted by the USIMA. The SFOC was considered a "gentleman's course" in that it contained virtually no physical nor mental hazing. They would be assessed and graded, to be sure, but the attendees were, in theory, already "professionals" in motivation, if not experience.

So, for the first time in his 14 months in the Army, he was being trained without shrieking Drill Sergeants, Tac Officers or Black Hats. As he entered the classroom with dozens of other aspiring officers, he thought, *Man, it doesn't get any better than this…*

The goal of the SFOC was to instruct US Army officers in the theory, structure, skills and utilization of the twelve-man "A Team." Such a team contained ten highly trained enlisted men, two each of whom were specialists in either light or heavy weapons, communications, intelligence, combat engineering and demolitions or medical. Each of those specialists was cross-trained to a lesser extent in each of his non-primary specialties.

Theoretically, a team could organize, train and, with the cooperation of indigenous "counterparts," lead a battalion of troops in behind-the-lines operations against Warsaw Pact invaders of Western Europe.

The concept also worked well in Vietnam with the irony that SF was training an established government's irregular troops to fight off the behind-the-lines insurgency of a communist-indoctrinated cohort of fellow citizens, called "Viet Cong." The VC were being supported by North Vietnam, China and the Soviet Union, and field operations by such SF-trained and led irregulars could be greatly complicated should they encounter North Vietnam's "NVA" regular army units. Though the quality of NVA troops could vary greatly depending on many factors, such encounters called for the more heavily armed and supported units of Vietnam's regular army or, more often, the infantry divisions of the US Army and Marine Corps.

The leadership of an A Team consisted of a Captain and a First Lieutenant, each of whom might be called upon to lead half the team should circumstances require such a split. In Vietnam, those two officers' prime focus was the political and logistical interactions and intricacies of dealing with the leadership of Vietnam's irregular military so that the SF sub-specialists could do their jobs. Similar political and logistical interactions with US military units that operated nearby, or sometimes in conjunction with the SF-supported indigenous units, were similarly important.

"We're just school teachers," said some of the old SF veterans, with wry grins. There was some truth to this since the first job after recruiting soldiers would be to train them. More often than not, the indigenous leaders were as untrained as the common soldiers, but had to be shown the utmost deference lest they become sullen and uncooperative. So, Special Forces soldiers, whether officer or NCO, had to be consummate diplomats as well as teachers. Only when the troops were trained and their leaders motivated could effective offensive operations be conducted.

SFOC student officers surveyed each of the sub-specialties incorporated into the A Team so as to gain a firm understanding of and respect for the skills of the enlisted members. Their training was divided between the class room and field exercises, and those exercises always began with a night parachute jump.

Andrew Starkey and the other students, nearly all novice paratroopers, learned that there's nothing blacker than a night jump when there's no moon, nor even enough ambient light for them to perceive the horizon. After jumping from the thundering C-130 "Blackbird," they had no idea in what or on what they'd eventually land. This was problematic, since weighted down with weapon and heavy rucksack, to land in a stream or pond just might kill them.

Some warning was, oddly enough, provided by their rucksacks. On exiting the aircraft, the rucksack was attached below their reserve parachutes. At 200 feet (or best guess) they'd release it to dangle on a long length of nylon cord since landing with the rucksack could break one or both legs. If they heard a splash instead of a thud when the rucksack hit, they had seconds to prepare by pulling the safety pin behind the T-10's quick release plate. If the water was deep, they'd strike the quick release plate that rested against their sternums and swim away from the parachute and possible entanglement in its risers and canopy; seconds weren't much, but better than nothing.

A final ten-day field exercise required the students to utilize all the classroom and field skills they'd learned and put them to use in the simulated hostile nation of "Pineland." They would parachute into Pineland (rural North Carolina), make contact with rebel commanders and assist them in organizing, training and leading citizen insurgents in military operations against their communist oppressors. The role of loyalist troops was played by paratroopers from the 82nd Airborne Division, also stationed at Ft. Bragg.

As usual, the men plummeted from the red glow of the aircraft's interior into the pitch-blackness of midnight. Eyes straining uselessly for any point of reference, Andrew and a class mate landed in a cemetery, each tumbling into different granite headstones. Amazingly uninjured, the two lieutenants wandered around for twenty minutes trying to find a way out of the large, spooky acreage. Emerging finally through a brick archway, they were greeted by a woman's shriek coming from a parked car. Carrying their parachutes in large canvas bags balanced on their shoulders, they looked like giant hunchbacks. The car started abruptly, tires spinning to gain traction in the soft mud, the driver laying on the horn in panic. As the car fish-tailed away, Andrew commented, "Hell of a place to take a girl parking."

"Check this out," said his friend with a chuckle. A condom, unused, lay on the ground near the tire tracks. "Bet that ole boy takes her to a motel next time."

Successful completion of the field exercise marked official completion of SFOC. The officers were awarded a numeral "three" prefix for their MOSs and the honor of wearing the "Green Beret." Orders were cut and Andrew Starkey was on his way to the 5th Special Forces Group, headquartered in Nha Trang, South Vietnam.

Chapter 16
In Country

At Ben Hoa Air Base, he and 250 other replacements stepped off the "World Airways" DC-8 and into an oven blast of tropical heat. After several days of processing at nearby Long Binh and another few at 5th Group HQ in Nha Trang, he was assigned to C Company in Danang.

"Sir, do you have a Sergeant Danny Sevilla with any of the teams?" he asked of the 5th Group S-1, a major who, due to previous wounds, was limited to office work.

"Sevilla? Hell yes. Light weapons. We've got the wildman up at A-230, Loc Mai. That's B Company. Friend of yours?"

"Yes sir. Met him in Basic. We're pretty good buddies."

"Well," he said, and paused, "Uh, he's actually back in the 'World' now. Went home on emergency leave. His dad died suddenly."

"Oh?" said Andrew. "Do you know if it was his real dad or stepdad?"

"I guess I don't really know. He was going to Colorado. Does that tell you anything?"

"Shit. That's his real dad. They were close. Bet he took it hard."

The major nodded. "He'll be back in-country in a week or two. I'll send a note to him in the Loc Mai pouch that you're going to C Company. The way things are going, we've got people moving all over. You just may bump into him sometime."

~ * ~

For two months he was assigned to the S-4, or supply section of the Danang headquarters. The work was boring and routine. Then came a welcome reassignment at an "A" camp assisting in the training of new CIDG recruits. He wasn't an official member of the team, but it was pretty close to the real thing. On this assignment he experienced his first combat when he accompanied the new recruits on their first patrol. An ambush by the VC wounded one boy and sent many of the recruits running wildly down a jungle trail. The soldiers that didn't panic laid down a huge volume of return fire that drove the ambushers away. For the first time in his life, Andrew experienced the bolt of fear and panic that follows the sound of guns fired in his direction, the sound of bullets impacting and ricocheting, the crack of air pressure felt on the face as those bullets passed close by. In seconds, that panic was replaced by the heightened senses that make a man choose between "fight" or "flight."

Seeing that others stood their ground, he turned towards the enemy and, wide-eyed, sought to kill those who had tried to kill him.

Back within the safety of the camp's defensive perimeter, as the young recruits shared stories and reveled in their baptism of fire, it occurred to him that he was an outsider who struggled to share their camaraderie. The other American on the operation, a senior NCO with combat experience in Korea and Vietnam, could only smile as the twenty-one-year-old lieutenant tried to share experiences with the CIDG in broken phrases of English and Vietnamese.

"Boy," he said, putting his arm around Andrew's shoulder, "your first firefight, your first combat, that's real fucking personal. More personal than anything you'll ever experience."

Andrew responded with a nod. "Man, you got that right."

But the Sergeant expounded…"You go through something like this 'Nam' shit, you should be with your own kind. Would have been better for a young officer like you to start out your career with an American unit like the 1st Division. Then, once you've got a few years under your belt, you move over to SF."

"So, you think coming straight into SF was a mistake?" Andrew asked.

"Not a mistake, just not the best choice. You'll do your two years, get your ticket punched, then be back on the street in Hometown, USA, wondering what the fuck it was all for. You'll never get a chance to serve with guys like yourself, grow up with them a little bit, take pride in being part of a STRAC unit. Hell, you might have learned to like this man's Army, make it a career. Without a base of 'Regular Army' experience, SF will just fuck up your head."

Andrew listened, not sure where the Sergeant was coming from. "How so?"

"Well, eventually it will occur to you that you're a mercenary. You're risking your life for these little bastards for money. What you get out of it in return is your business. But whatever that is, it ain't enough."

"You mean $650 a month isn't enough?" Andrew said wryly, opening a beer for the Sergeant and one for himself. He pulled the rough-cut bench away from the table and sat down. "So, what's the difference between SF and an infantry division? We're all doing this for the Vietnamese."

Sergeant Nevils took a long draw on the Carling Black Label. "If you were with the 1st Cav, the 82nd, any other bunch of ordinary GIs, you'd at least be risking your ass for your buddies, your own kind."

Andrew took his own long swig, wincing as he swallowed the

warm beer. "I guess I see what you mean."

"Damn right. You get greased out here, the dinks don't give a shit. You'll be replaced by some other OCS kid two weeks later. But if you were with your own, at least they'd miss your sorry ass. And your buddies would never forget you, no matter how long they live."

The man paused, studying his beer can. "Don't get me wrong," he continued…"An A Team can be like that, too. When SF first came to 'Nam, we showed up as a team, we fought as a team, and we went home as a team. Now, we do the 'replacement' thing with guys coming and going all the time. Just when you get to know the new guys, you're being rotated back to the States. Fucks up the whole 'A Team' concept."

"Aw, come on Sarge," Andrew said, holding up his can for a toast. "De Oppresso Libre."

"Airborne," said the Sergeant. He crashed his half-full can into Andrew's, sending foam flying.

Andrew killed his beer, walked to the Carling case and brought back two more cans. The Sergeant took the church key and punched open his beer.

"I think," he continued, "at the end of this tour I'm going to cash in. Twenty-three years is enough of this shit. I'm going to buy me a nice, dark, smelly tavern back in North Platte, Nebraska and just kick back."

"You married Sarge?"

"Was. Not now."

"There any women in North Platte?"

"Oh, a few," the sergeant answered with a grin. "Fucked 'em all at least once."

Andrew laughed out loud. "Well maybe some new ones moved in since you left."

A wistful look came over the Sergeant's face. "The last one, I still remember her. Little Italian lady. Darkest eyes, cutest little titties, best damn cook west of the 100th meridian."

That was the last thing Andrew needed to hear. Nancy's lovely smiling face flashed in his mind. "Yeah," he said, "I had a little Italian lady once."

"Well now, Lieutenant. You must not be a complete waste. Italian women are particular who they fuck."

Andrew redirected the conversation. "Maybe your Italian lady is still there in North Platte."

The sergeant swallowed, nodding his head. "She is. Writes me a note every once in a while. Italian women are more sentimental than the typical American mongrel female. They can go through a bunch of men but if they like you they keep a little torch burning for you."

Andrew liked that image. *A little torch. Yeah, maybe there's still a little torch,* he thought. "So, have you let her know you're coming back?"

"No. Come to think of it, maybe I better do that. That way, she can get rid of whoever she's with now and be ready for me when I arrive."

"Now, that's confidence," Andrew said, smiling.

"Airborne," said the sergeant.

With the end of that assignment he was sent back to his supply job in Danang. The frustration again began to build, but finally his dream was realized when he learned that the Executive Officer at A-115 Ba Thanh, had been sent back to the States due to severe intestinal illness. The next day, he was on a Huey headed into the western mountains.

The A Team commander, Captain Miller, a stocky, rusty-haired Californian, showed him around the camp, introducing him to his new team members as they were encountered at various positions. Next, he was introduced to Dai Hui Luc, the LLDB senior officer and camp commander. The Dai Hui greeted Andrew warmly and was very interested in where he came from in the United States.

"I'm from a state called, 'Indiana', Dai Hui. They call us 'Hoosiers'. Vietnam has rice paddies, Indiana has corn fields. Rice paddies are much more beautiful."

"So," Dai Hui repeated, rubbing his chin. "Hoosiers?" It sounded like "hooder." "Hoosiers same same VC?"

The Americans looked at each other and burst into laughter. This was Andrew's first experience with the Dai Hui's sense of humor.

"Yes, Dai Hui. Hoosier same same VC," said Andrew. "But we've all surrendered."

The next stop was a bunker dug into a dirt mound near the camp's concertina wire boundary. A sandbagged pathway led down to a plywood door. Inside, he found a ten-foot square expanse with firing slits cut in the walls. A bunk and rough-cut desk were in one corner. Empty ammunition boxes served as chairs and bunk-side table. "Playboy" magazine foldouts adorned the walls, and a broken mirror hung from a nail. On the desk, a Model 1911, Colt 45 pistol and holster lay coiled in their web belt.

"Keep that weapon handy," said Captain Miller with a grin, gesturing towards the pistol. "The rats in here are big as dogs."

"I'll bet," said Andrew, surveying his austere new home.

"This is your home for the time being," said Captain Miller, sympathetically. "As guys DEROS, you can move to a better houch. Everybody starts out here in the 'penthouse'."

The two men walked from the bunker back into the blazing afternoon sun. As Sergeant Garnett walked by with his CIDG counterpart, the Captain called out, "Wait one, Teddy." The Sergeant waved back and sat down on the sandbag wall of a mortar pit.

Captain Miller turned back to Andrew. "Well, get your shit unpacked and we'll see you in the Team house for chow around 1800. You'll have radio watch tonight, 0200 to 0600. I've got a new 'Jay and the Americans' tape, so you'll have some decent entertainment."

"Thanks for the tour, Sir. See you at chow."

As the Captain walked away, he stopped and turned again. "Oh, by the way, we're getting a new weapons man next week. Heard he's a buddy of yours. Sergeant Sevilla."

Andrew burst into a smile. "No shit? That's great news, sir. He's a good man."

"Figured you'd be happy. They're turning Loc Mai over to the ARVNs and splitting up the team. Soon as I heard, I put in for one of their weapons men. Sevilla's name came up."

Then the Captain had one final afterthought. "Oh," he said, "Sevilla will get Sergeant McCullough's bunker when he DEROSs. Around here, weapons men are higher on the totem pole than First Lieutenants."

Having lost his father recently, Sergeant Danny Sevilla was greeted with particular warmth and sympathy by his A-115 teammates. His reputation as a talented and gutsy SF trooper preceded him.

"The Sergeant Major said you're best light-weapons guy in C Company," said Sergeant Vites, the other weapons specialist. "Now, don't feel any pressure, OK?"

Danny responded with a grin. "I'm just a poor Kentucky boy trying to make an honest living." Looking around the team house, he said, "Say, where's that new Lieutenant dude, Starkey?"

Sergeant Garnett spoke up. "He's out with a platoon of CIDG guarding some farmers while they repair a paddy dike. Back before dark."

That Lieutenant Starkey was good friends with "the best light-weapons guy in C Company" actually garnered respect for him that otherwise might have taken months to earn. Their reunion later in the day was warm and raucous, with Danny making sport of the "stars and bars" his friend earned in a mere 23 weeks in OCS.

"How in hell can they give a guy like you Lieutenant's bars in six months when West Point takes four years?" he snickered.

"Why don't you ask President Nixon?" Andrew retorted. "With

tears in his eyes he said to me, 'Lieutenant Starkey, I'm sending you to Vietnam to prevent Sergeant Sevilla from fucking up my Army.' You don't really believe we ended up together by coincidence, do you?"

Such exchanges had, for the most part, to be conducted outside the hearing of Captain Miller. Interactions between enlisted men and officers had to retain the air of professionalism and mutual respect. Otherwise, morale and discipline could suffer. Nevertheless, their obvious affection for one another, growing as it had out of months of stateside training, was acknowledged and accepted by the Team members. Sitting in a small outpost, surrounded by enemy soldiers sworn to kill them, a bit of levity was no small luxury.

The irony of separation and unlikely reunion was not lost on them.

"See?" said Danny in his best fake redneck accent, "God done throwed us in the shit again. He must be one bored son of a gun."

Chapter 17
Vietnamization

The irritating jiggle of the land-line telephone awoke him in the bunker. He picked up the hand set, pressed the "talk" button and brought it to his ear.

"Yo."

"Sorry to drag you out so early Lieutenant. Captain Miller wants you for a team meeting. Something's up."

"Roger. Be there in a minute."

He threw his legs off the bunk and leaned forward, rubbing his face with both hands. A canteen sat on the ammo-box table. He reached for it, took a swig of the warm water, swished it around his mouth and spit it out against the sandbag wall. Then he took another and swallowed it. The remaining water he poured into the palm of his hand and rubbed that into his face and the back of his neck.

"Shit. Wonder what's up?" he thought.

Lieutenant Starkey and Sergeant Sevilla had returned from their latest combat operation the previous afternoon. Exhausted as the troops were, they held their heads up and chests out as the remaining garrison formed up to welcome them back in. A few of the younger CIDG fired their weapons in the air in long bursts as NCOs yelled at them to stop wasting ammunition.

As the column passed by the American team house, Danny and Andrew peeled away and were greeted by their A team.

"Welcome home, gentlemen," said a smiling Captain Miller. "Looks like we've got to pay you again this month."

"Sir, make sure you dock Sergeant Sevilla for his CAR-15," joked a mud-caked and haggard Lieutenant Starkey. "I've never witnessed such utter neglect of government property."

"Oh, I think we can write that off," the captain answered, throwing his arm around his young sergeant. "As a matter of fact, I'm trying to figure out a way to get you a purple heart. May be a long shot, but I'll give it a try."

"No blood, Captain," said Danny, matter-of-factly.

"Yeah, but it knocked the shit out of him, sir," Andrew interjected. "Let me know if I can sign something as a witness."

"Tell you what," offered Sergeant Garnett. "I'm going to put myself in for a purple heart if you two don't get the fuck out of the team house and shower up. You're the two ripest pieces of shit I've smelled in a long time."

"Speaking of shit," said Danny, a smile spreading on his face, "you should have seen this 'officer and gentleman' squatted over a punji pit about two clicks out. Those pills he was taking wore off and he started blowing out a week's worth of LRRPs. Looked like one of those old farm spigots that's not had any water run through it for a long time. Just brown water squirting out like…"

"Goddamn it, Sevilla! I'm trying to eat," exclaimed Sergeant Pampe from across the room. He threw his fork down on a tin plate and leaned back in his chair in disgust.

~ * ~

"Well, I can't sugarcoat this, men," said Captain Miller. "They're splitting up the team." He paused as the men looked at each other and muttered epithets. "OK, at ease," he said after a few moments.

"Half of us will go back to C Company headquarters in DaNang. The other half will stay put. The orders I received today in the pouch call for myself and Sergeants Fullerton, Garnett, Langer, Nickles and Pampe to go to DaNang. Lieutenant Starkey will remain here with Sergeants Bippus, Muehlenbein, Racster, Sevilla and Vites."

"Sir, what the fuck…?" Sergeant Garnett began.

Captain Miller held up his hand. "Hold on. There's more." The captain looked at Starkey. "The camp itself and the CIDG will be merged into the 2nd ARVN Division. Officially, they'll be referred to as 'Mountain Rangers'. The remaining SF guys will be reassigned to MACV."

Danny was incredulous. "Shit, sir. They can't do that to us. You mean we're no longer 5th Group?"

"That's what I'm being told. Fact is the 5th SF is getting kicked out of the war. The Joint Chiefs don't like the way we do business. Anybody says I said that, I'll deny it."

A week later, a CH-47 "Chinook" cargo helicopter arrived to take the departing half of the team back to C Company HQ in Danang.

"Well, Starkey," said Captain Miller, as he threw his duffle bag on to the back of a jeep for the ride down to the helicopter pad, "You're a twenty-two-year-old First Lieutenant with your first command. How's it feel?"

Andrew hadn't thought of it that way. He felt that he and the other men were being discarded and abandoned by Special Forces.

"Not too good, sir, but I'll make the best of it."

The small remaining team of American advisors did their best to help the overwhelmed Dai Hui Luc with his own painful transition from LLDB to the regular Vietnamese Army. Bureaucracy, politics and bullshit became his day-to-day grind.

Within a few weeks, however, he found respite back in field operations, for those above the Dai Hui were happy to have someone else carry the fight to the enemy. They preferred the safety and comfort of cities like Danang or Saigon. So, Luc delegated his staff work and stayed in the mountains as much as he could.

No Americans would accompany him now. Their mission, as part of "Military Assistance Command Vietnam," was ill-defined but it was not to include a direct combat role for this small American team.

"Maintain communications, maintain your intell sources, keep the heavy weapons serviceable, keep the generators humming, run the dispensary, stay out of trouble," the Americal Division Brigadier General said to a perplexed Lieutenant Starkey as he toured Ba Thanh.

"You're in the Americal AO son, and we'll take care of you. But you've got to let the Vietnamese run the show, just like you weren't here."

"Off the record," he said, "MACV wants you SF guys to DEROS out, then they'll bring in their own people. They want no Special Forces taint on their show. How's it feel to be a turd in the punch bowl, Lieutenant?"

In fact, it was very boring. Day after day the men did their best to keep busy. Sergeant Bippus kept the dispensary humming with the sick and injured of the Vietnamese and Montagnard villages. Sergeant Sevilla gave classes in some of the more obscure weapons used by and captured from the VC. Other NCOs split their time between the hard labor of rebuilding and improving the sand-bag firing positions for the mortars and artillery pieces and assisting their allies with whatever transition issues that arose.

Lieutenant Starkey made timely visits around the camp, then went to the team house to read, write home and, otherwise, kill time. But, shortly, the war caught back up to them.

Sensing weakness, the NVA ordered their VC allies to become increasingly active in an effort to gain knowledge of how the 2nd ARVN Division would operate. It didn't take long for them to see that reduced American participation greatly enhanced their freedom of movement through the area. Infiltrating through the river valleys, they knew the ARVNs would stay high on the ridges to avoid a fight. This wasn't always a sure thing, but there were very few Vietnamese commanders as gutsy as Dai Hui Luc. The percentages were with the Communists.

Mortar attacks became more common, the fire often inaccurate and ineffective. One morning, Lieutenant Starkey and Sergeant Sevilla walked out to the helicopter pad to examine the two-foot impact craters from a mortar barrage fired the night before. Digging into one of the holes with an entrenching tool in search of the round's tail assembly, Danny stirred up instead a plume of pepper gas.

As the two men scrambled away with beet red, burning faces, Danny exclaimed, "They must think we're like those anti-war assholes back in the World. Spray some tear gas and everybody heads for the coffee house to sing 'Kum Ba Ya'."

The first signs of what became a cycle of crisis for Lieutenant Starkey began with a radio call from a Montagnard operation only a few kilometers west of the camp. A soldier had been killed by a booby trap and the body needed to be retrieved. As was often the case, the dead soldier had another family member on the operation that also needed extraction. Since Ba Thanh had nearly daily visits from an American helicopter delivering people, mail and movies, Lieutenant Starkey had no trouble getting the pilot to ferry him out to the scene. Fifteen minutes later, the chopper hovered precariously over a steep hillside trail. Balancing himself with one foot on the craft's landing skid and a knee on the slippery metal floor, soldiers lifted up to him the bloody ninety-pound body of the dead soldier. He struggled mightily to wrestle the dead man into the craft without falling out himself. Covered with the dead man's blood, Andrew then reached out his arm to help the casualty's younger brother aboard. As the craft pulled away from the hillside, Andrew slumped into the web seat, then held the hand of a despondent sixteen-year-old for the sad flight back to camp.

A few days later, a distant fire fight brought Dai Hui Luc to the teamhouse. "Trung Hui," he said excitedly, "we need chopper."

"Dai Hui, you are supposed to call for your own Dust Off helicopters at Quang Ngai."

"No! They not come for two days."

"Two days? Why would…?"

Dai Hui shook his head in exasperation. "Two days!"

Andrew sorted through his options. In his mind, to call in a standard Dust Off mission with its gunship support as if it were an American unit needing help or, as had been the case until recently, a Vietnamese unit with American SF assets, would raise questions, be delayed or declined, and probably get him in big trouble. After all, a Brigadier General had just ordered him to, "Let the Vietnamese run the show."

"That ain't going to happen," he mumbled to himself.

So, once again, Andrew was on the radio, calling bases in the area to track down an Army utility helicopter in the vicinity.

"Minuteman One Six, this is Sonar Hybrid. We've got some casualties. Can't get a Dust Off soon enough. Can you assist, over?"

"No sweat, Hybrid. On the way."

On the pad, Andrew jumped into the chopper with his rifle and combat gear and carrying a PRC-25 radio. "Head due north, two clicks," he yelled over the engine and prop noise. "I'll get them to pop smoke when we're on top of them."

A few minutes later, the helicopter landed in a jungle clearing among the prone bodies of soldiers who were still firing at a hidden enemy. Andrew helped the Vietnamese load their dead and wounded into the craft and spoke briefly to the grim unit commander. As the craft lifted off, Andrew looked back at the man and felt like he was abandoning him.

Back at the camp, Starkey expressed remorse to a team member about the fuzzy mission details he'd given to the helicopter crew.

"Lieutenant, stretching the truth to get the job done is as old as the US fucking Army," said Sergeant Muehlenbein, sympathetically. "You tell them the whole story and good people die. You got a better chance to get forgiveness than to get permission."

"Yeah. But what worries me is I get a bird shot down trying to help the Vietnamese when we're supposed to let them do it themselves."

"So, Lieutenant. You're going to be on that bird, right?"

"Roger that."

"So, you'll be dead. What can they do to you then, piss on your grave?"

As these events multiplied, Andrew was becoming a nervous wreck. Not only was he ignoring his "run the show" orders, he was risking his life in the process. But it wasn't just his life. He refused to let others, even Danny, ride along. Yet, each helicopter had a pilot, co-pilot, two door gunners and, sometimes, a crew chief--additional American lives he was putting at risk in his effort to help those who had come to trust and depend on the Special Forces. Those soldiers on the ground wouldn't be interested in the inanities of "Vietnamization."

~ * ~

At 10AM one blistering morning, a frantic Vietnamese NCO ran into the teamhouse. "Trung hui! We need chopper!"

This one sounded bad. No deaths, but four wounded and the enemy hadn't broken off contact.

"Minuteman One Niner this is Sonar Hybrid, over."

"Hybrid, this is One Niner. Hey Hybrid, you same same Plains Alpha?"

"Hey, buddy. Same Same. How come you haven't gone back to the World yet, over?"

"Second tour. What can I do for you?"

"One Niner, need you to pick up some WIAs for me. Unit still in contact. Can do, over?"

The radio crackled. "Wait one." The pilot was radioing back to his base for permission to go off course. "Uh, Roger, Hybrid. We can assist."

A half-hour later, the UH-1D "Slick" landed at Ba Thanh. Andrew climbed aboard with his gear.

"Looks like you're short a door gunner," he said to the still cigar-chomping pilot. The port-side gunner was missing along with the M-60. The starboard gunner was in place, hunched over his gun.

"Bolt on the gun cracked. Left him at Minh Long scrounging for a replacement."

"Damn," said Andrew. "I can't bullshit you. This LZ may be hot."

"Strap in there and try to look like a hard ass," yelled the pilot. "VC won't know the difference…I hope."

The absent crewman's communications helmet was fastened to the web seat, and Andrew put it on as he climbed into the door-gunner position. As the chopper lifted off, he was still struggling with the safety belts. Strapped in as tightly as he could manage, he braced one boot on the machinegun pedestal and released the bolt on his CAR-15.

The hilltop LZ was barely large enough to allow the helicopter to land. The pilot orbited high above, watching for the smoke grenade thrown by those on the ground to display wind direction. Abruptly he began a dizzying cork screw descent that left Andrew facing nearly straight down. At times, the craft's motion shifted and removed the centrifical force that, along with his safety belt, kept Andrew from falling out. He gripped the CAR-15, pushed against the pedestal with his foot and asked God to please pay attention.

Numerous enemy rifle rounds hit the helicopter during its final approach, but as it sat down on the hilltop it was shielded by the steep slope. Luckily, no harm was done to its mechanisms nor the men aboard. Andrew was relieved to be on the ground, though waves of nausea clouded his mind. Spilling out from the door-gun position, he helped the soldiers load their wounded comrades aboard. After a few minutes on the ground, he gave the pilot a thumbs up and climbed back into the chopper.

"Let's un-ass the area!" Andrew shouted into the helmet mike.

The pilot lifted the craft to tree-top level, dropped its nose, and sent it screaming down the hillside, dodging and weaving among stands of jungle trees. Andrew held his rifle tightly against his shoulder preparing to fire, his free hand instinctively clutching his safety belt for fear he'd yet tumble from the sky.

Back on the pad at Ba Thanh, he unbuckled himself and staggered away from the helicopter. Sergeant Bippus and a three-quarter-ton truck were waiting to carry the wounded up to the camp's dispensary.

Breathing deeply, Andrew finally was able to approach the pilot's door. The man stepped out and, with the other door gunner, walked around inspecting the craft. Bullet holes were found on the engine cowling and along the tail boom.

"Goddamit, Plains," the warrant officer yelled, "we need gunships on a run like that."

"Yeah, I know," Andrew answered feebly, then burped a drive heave. "Owe you another one."

The pilot spoke to his gunner and shook his head in exasperation. Both looked at Lieutenant Starkey with irritation, gave a wave of dismissal and climbed back aboard.

Danny arrived in a jeep as the craft rose into the air. He slid to a stop and watched as Andrew bent at the waist and vomited violently.

It took nearly an hour for the motion sickness to subside. Danny sat with his friend outside the team house as Andrew repeatedly swigged, sloshed and spit out warm beer to try and calm his restive stomach and purge the taste of bile.

"Boy, you just never learn."

"Learn…what?"

"Let the dinks take care of themselves. You're going to get yourself killed. We're 'short', man. We're out of here in a month. Back to the 'World', baby."

Andrew leaned back against a sandbag retaining wall, his eyes closed against the bright sun, sweat streaming from his face. "Think we'll make it?" he asked.

"Yes, Lieutenant. We're going to make it. Now, swallow some of that beer instead of spitting it out. It's unfucking-American to do that."

"By the way," Danny said, as he stood and headed back into the team house, "There's some mail for you. One has a Colorado return address."

He sat on his cot in the hot, airless bunker and read Nancy's letter over and over.

"Dear Andrew,

As usual, I've not heard a word from you for quite some time. I pray you are well. Since Ronnie has received a few letters, I long ago interpreted your silence as a sign to me that our friendship has somehow changed.

Mark has asked me to marry him and, although no date has been set, I have accepted his wonderful proposal. Because of my affection for you, I wanted you to hear this from me directly rather than from Ronnie or someone else.

May God keep you safe in His arms my friend.

Love Always,

Nancy

The tears were real but they did not overwhelm him. He had actually imagined she might already be married and Ron couldn't tell him. As far as he was concerned, "No date has been set" left him in the same position he occupied when he called her before he entered the Army. To lose her slowly, inexorably, was to lose her nonetheless. It just prolonged the agony.

Chapter 18
Bad to Worse

The first round hit near a firing slit in the bunker's wall, and the concussion jarred Andrew's head against the frame of his metal bunk. More mortar and recoilless rifle rounds exploded as he struggled into his pants and boots in the dark bunker. He strapped on the 45, grabbed his CAR-15 and ran for the TOC.

Sergeant Racster, on radio watch, was yelling for him as he pushed open the door.

"Lieutenant!"

"Yo. Get on the horn to Americal Operations. Tell them we need gunships and a Dust Off to stand by. I'm going to see…"

Another explosion flashed behind him in the sandbagged trench that led to the generator shed. As he listened, the generator suddenly whined loudly, then died out.

"Shit. I'll be right back."

Starkey ran out to the narrow roadway that ran the length of the camp. Cordite was wafting through the air and smoke was billowing from the generator shed. He crouched behind a sandbag wall as more rounds hit the middle of the compound as the enemy gunners "walked" the rounds through the camp. Flames now could be seen coming from the roof of the Vietnamese team house. A door flew open and several bloody soldiers stumbled from the small building. They crawled next to the sand bag berm and lay down along its length.

Andrew listened for a few seconds, then sprinted towards the dispensary. On the way, he met Sergeant Bippus running towards the TOC.

"Lieutenant! Sevilla's been hit. He was in the mortar pit trying to fire an illumination round to light up the VC firing positions."

"Is he bad?"

"Not good, sir. Two indig in the pit with him are het roi. I've got Tran and Vo working on him."

"Any other casualties at your end?"

"Don't know."

"OK. Go on back to the dispensary. I think they may follow up with a ground attack. I've got gunships and a Dust Off on standby."

Andrew ran back to the TOC. "Rac! Tell Americal to launch the Dust Off and the gunships ASAP. Tell them we got casualties and expect a ground attack."

The incoming rounds had stopped and the compound was now swathed in an eerie choking mist of the chemicals of combustion. A nearly full moon, no doubt a precursor of the attack, added a glow to the pall that lay low to the ground. Hopefully that same moon would allow the helicopter support to be launched.

The Vietnamese had pulled four dead soldiers from their team house and laid them out under ponchos. Three wounded men were now being dragged down the roadway towards the dispensary. All the faces looked shocked and grim.

Dai Hui Luc found Andrew in the roadway and called to him. "Very bad, Trung Hui."

"Yes, Dai Hui. Will the VC attack.?"

"Maybe. CIDG are ready."

As Andrew finished a second survey of his men and their assigned fighting positions, he could hear the first faint thump of helicopter blades in the distance. Soon two Cobra gunships and a Dustoff began high-speed passes over the camp, the blades popping loudly as they did severe 180- degree turns and began to circle at 250 feet.

Sergeant Muehlenbein brought him a PRC-25. "Call sign 'Roll Tide six', Lieutenant."

Andrew keyed the handset. "Tide six, this is Sonar Hybrid. Thanks for coming. Can you see us OK, over?"

"Uh, not bad, Hybrid. You've got some fires burning. Casualties, over?"

"Got six WIAs. Take a look at our perimeter for sappers. If you see anything moving in the wire, kill it."

No answer came for several seconds. Then the gunship pilot's voice crackled, "Uh, Hybrid, no can do. Too much chance hit your people, over."

"OK, Tide six. We'll make do. Can you put the Dust Off on the ground, west end? I'll be there with lights, over."

"Uh, roger, Hybrid. We'll look for you."

Andrew ran with the radio under his arm back down to the dispensary. Danny and the other casualties lay together on bloody ponchos. Twenty feet away, an "H" formed from painted river rocks marked an emergency helicopter LZ, but it could barely be seen from the air in the moonlight. Grabbing two red lense flashlights from a box near the pad, Andrew pushed their switches on and stepped into the center of the "H". Checking the strength of each light's beam, he was thankful that he'd checked the batteries regularly.

He could hear the orbiting gunships but could not see them as they banked and turned menacingly, looking for a VC ground assault. The Dust Off was standing off, awaiting a signal to land for the casualties. Spreading his arms wide, Andrew waved the flashlights skyward.

Thirty seconds later, the thundering mass of the UH-1D filled the air directly in his face, nearly blowing him off his feet. A large red cross was painted on its nose beneath the pilots' windshield. Backing away, he shielded his face from the flying dust and dirt of the down draft.

Now he ran to the pilot's door. "Thanks, buddy. We'll get you out of here in a second."

"Anytime," a smiling Captain answered. "Give me a thumbs up when we're clear."

Soldiers were loading casualties one at a time. Danny was the last one. Andrew knelt down by his side. "Hey," he yelled, but his friend was unconscious. Blood was oozing from beneath a pressure bandage on his side that had been applied by the Vietnamese medics. In the moonlight he could see that Danny's closed eyes were beginning to swell badly. He felt in the poncho for his friend's hand. Finding it sticky with blood, he squeezed it and said, "Hang in there, buddy. You're going to make it. You're on the way."

Soldiers came for Danny, and Andrew lifted with them and ran to the helicopter. The on-board Army medic looked him over without comment, waved Andrew and the others away, and spoke though his mike to the pilot. A moment later the craft prepared for departure.

Andrew took a quick look around and jogged to the front of the aircraft. Once in front of the windshield he gave the pilot a thumbs up, then jogged away to avoid the prop blast. The helicopter lifted off in a hail of dirt and debris, did a 180-degree turn, and sped off into the night sky.

The gunships continued to orbit the camp for fifteen more minutes. After consulting with Dai Hui Luc, Andrew agreed a ground assault was unlikely. It may not have been planned at all, or the quick response of the gunships caused the VC to rethink the attack. He got on the PRC-25. "Much obliged, 'Tide six'. See you next time."

~ * ~

Days later, the five remaining team members heard that Danny was safely at the 91st Evac hospital in Chu Lai and would soon be sent on to a hospital in Japan. No further information was available.

Andrew and Sergeant Muehlenbein collected Danny's gear to ship back to Danang from where it would be forwarded to the address of Danny's mother in Kentucky.

"Hey, Lieutenant," said the sergeant, surveying the musty, empty bunker. "You can move in here now. One of the nicest houches in Ba Thanh."

"Nah. I'd have to get to know a whole new family of rats. Mine are old friends now."

Reading Nancy's letter once again that day, he heard voices heading toward his bunker.

"Trung Hui! We need chopper!"

Hours later, exhausted and laying on his bunk, the beat of helicopter blades and the contorted faces of wounded soldiers fresh in his mind, he reached to the ammo box for a sheet of USO paper and envelope. Sitting up and taking a pen, he wrote on the envelope:

To be opened in the event of my death.

On the page, he wrote:

"Dear Mom and Dad, if you are reading this, I didn't make it…"

He finished his will, read it over, folded it and put it in the envelope. Lifting the lid of his footlocker, he placed it at one end where it couldn't be missed when they came for his gear.

Never having contemplated such a document before, he felt foolish making the small requests, like using some of his $10,000 Servicemen's Group Life Insurance money to help a cousin with college, and bequeathing his .22 rifle to Jeff Thompson. Yet, he felt an odd sense of relief as he sealed the envelope. *At least,* he thought, *they'll know I cared about them…*

For several minutes he sat on the bunk trying to decide if he should write to Nancy. *No,* he elected. *What could I say? 'Dear Nancy, I'm history.'? She's got her life. I'm not getting out of here. Best thing is to just disappear.*

PART 3

Chapter 19
Denver Dream

Some weekend nights, when he was short of cash or not up to the club scene, Andrew would walk the few blocks up Logan Street to Colfax, then east several blocks to a venerable establishment called, "Argonaut Liquors." He'd pick up a six-pack and saunter slowly back to his place, taking in the sights and sounds of the Denver night, the eclectic storefronts, police shake-downs, drug sales, hookers and bus-stop denizens. Upon his return to the old house he'd unscrew the light bulb over the entryway, flop on the porch's broken-down couch, put his feet up on the brick wall and crack open a beer.

A parade of people would walk by, some singly, some in twos and threes. Most affected the appearance of the counter-culture, and their conversations, hushed though they were, generally seemed to address a search for drugs; words like 'grass', 'acid', 'weed' or 'hash' occurring most frequently.

If anyone noticed him sitting quietly in the dark they rarely acknowledged his presence, nor did he say anything to them. The neighborhood was utterly transient and not a place where neighbors would interact.

As he finished a can he'd flip it over the wall into the dusty front yard, then open another. Once most or all the beers had been discarded in this fashion, he'd go up to bed.

This night, he had just opened a fifth beer, was quite mellow and enjoying the warm night and his own company. Like ghosts, a half-dozen men appeared out of the darkness at the side of the house. Andrew had not noticed them until the largest man stumbled as he was walking up the stone steps. Once on the porch, he stared down at Andrew for a long time, apparently sizing him up. He was an Indian, Andrew guessed, probably from the reservation in Wyoming. The rest of his group stayed gathered at the foot of the stairs, seemingly to await some result. An odor of hard liquor was conspicuous.

Andrew had no fear of the man and, in fact, was buzzed enough to welcome the distraction. He met the man's gaze awhile then held out his open beer to him. The Indian walked the few steps to Andrew's outstretched arm, took the beer and took two sizable gulps. He handed the can back and Andrew finished the remaining liquid, then flipped the empty can into the yard. The Indian smiled at him in acknowledgment of the subtle comradeship and took a seat on the brick wall. This seemed to relax the remaining men and they all came up the steps to the porch.

One of them pushed through from behind his friends and began berating Andrew.

"You steal our land, you kill our people!" he shouted, and seemed intent on starting a fight. The others restrained him, and the big Indian said, "Oh, shut up," in a condescending tone.

He looked back at Andrew. "We're looking for a place to crash," he said.

Andrew jerked his thumb towards the old house's common area. "Help yourself. There are some chairs inside and I'm done with the couch. 'Course, I don't own the place. Just renting a room."

The big man nodded. "You're pretty generous for a white man. Must have some Indian blood in you."

"I'd be honored if I did."

"Bullshit," said the Indian.

Andrew was intrigued. "I'm Andrew. Who are you?"

The man answered with deep and slurred speech. "My people call me 'Hawk'." He had shoulder-length black hair and a face that was large, round and pockmarked. His nose was prominent and somewhat off-kilter.

"Glad to meet you, Hawk." Andrew reached towards him and shook his hand.

As he resettled in his seat he noticed Hawk's boots.

"So," said Andrew after a moment of contemplation, "were you 82nd or 101st?"

The man wore badly scuffed Corcoran jump boots, standard for Army paratroops. By mental deduction, he guessed Hawk to have been a draftee who volunteered for an elite unit, even if it meant Vietnam.

Hawk seemed unsettled at the question and glanced back momentarily at his nervous friends. "You're a scary guy, Andrew. You see me someplace?"

"The 'Corcorans'."

Hawk glanced down. "Oh, yeah," he chuckled, relieved. He wiped a large hand over his face. "82nd. How 'bout you?"

"Special Forces," said Andrew. "Airborne."

"Airborne, all the way," answered Hawk. "You make it to the dance?"

"5th Group, up in I Corps. You?"

"Near the DMZ, mostly. Got back to the Res' last year. Nothing's changed there."

"Welcome home, Hawk."

"Same to you."

Andrew could tell that Hawk's friends were getting very antsy. "Well," he yawned, "I'll turn the couch over to you and hit the sack."

"You gonna drink that?" asked Hawk, eyeing Andrew's last Coors.

"No man, it's yours." Andrew handed him the beer.

"I'll buy it from you." Hawk pulled a huge wad of bills from his shirt pocket. He peeled off a ten-dollar bill and offered it to Andrew.

"Man, where'd you get that dough? You must have a grand in there."

The angry Indian spoke from behind, "Hawk, let's go. Fuck that white man."

Hawk turned and stared down the complainer, then turned back to Andrew with a friendly smile on his face.

"Wolf Pup is Hunkpapa Lakota. It's in his blood to hate whites. The rest of us are Crow. We've learned to be friendly and make beaucoup wampum off our white brothers."

"Sure does look like it," said Andrew, looking past Hawk at his friends. "Keep your money, Hawk. You can buy me one sometime."

"OK. I'll be around."

"So, the dough?" Andrew asked again in a quieter voice.

"Flower Children," Hawk answered, with emphasis on the first word of the phrase.

Andrew looked confused.

"I sell 'happy grass' to the Hippies."

Andrew laughed out loud and shook his head. He lowered his voice to a whisper and said, "You sell 'weed' to Hippies?"

"All day long. They like to dress up like Indians, so they like to buy happy grass from an Indian." Hawk smiled broadly at the irony. "I charge them double."

"Damn, that's funny," Andrew said. "Keep taking their money, Hawk."

Andrew stood then and, unsteadily, walked past Hawk towards the front door. The angry Indian was being consoled by two of the others, and he glared at Andrew as he entered the house. Early next morning when Andrew came down to retrieve his empty cans and buy a Denver Post, the men were gone.

Chapter 20
Connie

"Mr. Lucky's" had gotten crowded and it was difficult to hear over the din of drink orders being yelled to the bartenders.

"We need to get a table," said Andrew.

Connie surveyed the smoky expanse, a hand shielding her eyes from the bright lights over the bar.

"There's one." She walked to it quickly to head off a couple who were moving that way from the dance floor. She threw her beaded bag on the table and sat down, giving the couple a "Cheshire Cat" grin!

The two men joined her and a waitress arrived to take their order.

"You know, if you had a phone, I'd have called you a long time ago," said Andrew.

"Two pitchers," Danny said to the waitress. As she walked away he answered, "We had a party line for a while. Bitches out there spend their time listening in on conversations. We'll get one when we can have a private line."

Connie scooted her chair so she could sit close between them, a hand on the inside of each man's thigh. She was getting quite drunk on top of being stoned. As they talked, she looked adoringly at each.

"Damn, Lieutenant," Danny said, reaching past his wife and grabbing Andrew by the shoulder. "You sure are a sight for sore eyes. Kind of skinny, though. Aren't you getting fed regular?"

"Tell you what. Stop with the 'Lieutenant' bullshit and I won't tell Connie about that time…"

"OK, OK," laughed Danny, holding up his hand.

"You tell me anyway, Andrew," purred Connie, squeezing his thigh.

Danny said, "I've already told her most of the stories, Andrew. That's why she married me."

"Connie," said Andrew, "next time we get together, I'll make a list of 'Danny' stories and you can tell me which ones you haven't heard."

"It'll be a short list," Danny said, hugging his wife's neck in the crook of his elbow and tossling her hair. "Now Andrew, tell me how you ended up with the phone company."

"Short story. Guy comes to put in my phone. I ask if Ma Bell's hiring. He said, 'Yep.' I applied and the rest is history. That's why I'm so skinny. No time to eat."

"You come out to Flagstaff, baby, and I'll fatten you up," cooed

Connie. As she spoke, she leaned towards Danny and lost her balance. Danny pushed her back to vertical.

The two pitchers were delivered. Andrew reached for his wallet. "Put your money away," said Danny.

"Thanks, money bags," said Andrew. "Now, tell me what you guys do for a living."

"Ooooh, that's real interesting," said Connie, a devilish grin on her face.

"We got the farm," Danny began, putting a finger to Connie's lips as if to silence her. She opened her mouth and took his finger inside. He pulled it out and wiped it off with a cocktail napkin, rolling his eyes at Andrew. Andrew winked back.

"Raise a little wheat. Actually, we rent the fields out and get a percentage of the harvest. Get money from the government for letting some acreage lie fallow."

"Nice work if you can get it," said Andrew with a wry grin.

"Roger that, Drill Sergeant," Danny replied. He began pulling the shirt tail out of his Levis and lifted it halfway up to his chest. A jagged scar eight- inches long and one-inch wide was evident just below his ribcage. It was the light-pink color of a somewhat recent injury.

"This got me $400 a month disability and a 'Purple Heart'."

"Damn," said Andrew. "That looks a lot better than the last time I saw you. You had a hole this big, bleeding like a stuck pig."

"Stop!" Connie exclaimed. "You two talk about something else."

"Should have warned you, Andrew. Connie sees the world through those rose-colored glasses you've heard about. Doesn't want to see, hear or feel any unpleasantness."

"No problem. So, tell me more about the farm. Can I come out sometime?"

"Come out? Hell, man, you can move out and live with us," said Danny.

"You sure can, baby," Connie offered. "We got nothing but room… nothing for miles around but wheat and wind."

"Don't forget Susan."

"Oh, yes. We do have one neighbor, Susan. She's taking care of our daughter, Janon."

"Janon? You've got a kid, then?" asked Andrew, clearly surprised. "Danny, you've been busy."

"Just turned fourteen months," Connie slurred, fishing in her purse for pictures.

As Andrew looked through the small stack of photos, he said, "Man, you've really turned into a domestic son of a gun. Gentleman farmer, heroic war veteran, now a father. Kind of chokes me up to be in your presence."

Danny was refilling their beer glasses again. "A man's got to keep busy, Andrew."

Connie stood carefully, pushing on the men's thighs as she rose. "I have to go pee."

"Connie, don't go outside. They'll hit you with another cover charge," said Danny as she walked away. She looked back and winked.

"Why would she go outside?"

"Smoke another joint," answered Danny, matter-of-factly.

"I thought I smelled weed when she first came up to me."

"Yeah, she loves the happy grass," Danny observed. "Not all bad, though. Makes her horny as a three-balled tomcat."

"Happy grass," Andrew chuckled. "That's the second time I've heard that term. Must be unique to Denver."

"Could be. Picked it up from a guy I do some business with."

Andrew smiled and looked down at his beer. "Connie's a pretty lady. You're a lucky man," he said. Then, "That weed's expensive. Bet it takes a chunk of that disability check."

"Nah. I've got a cheap source." Danny began looking towards the restrooms. "Back in a minute," he said, and walked off in that direction.

He'd only been gone a minute when Andrew felt a hand on his shoulder. It was Judy. He rose, smiling, put his arms around her and hugged her. She returned his smile, took his face in her hands and kissed him warmly.

"Wow, do I know you, Miss?" he said jokingly.

"Yes, you do. Very intimately, in fact."

"Sit down, if you can," he said. "I'm with an old Army buddy and his wife. They're quite a pair."

"Well, the way that woman was feeling you up, I couldn't tell who was with whom. When I saw him go after her, I just couldn't leave you sitting alone."

"Nice to see you, Judy. You with the usual crew?"

"Of course. No one made me a better offer."

"Sorry I haven't called for a while. Will you let me make it up to you, or is it too late?"

"No, lover. It's not too late."

"Tomorrow night?"

"Date. Dinner at six. My place."

"Great. You still drink that purple swill?"

"If you mean wine, yes I do," she giggled. "You go to Argonaut and tell Mr. Robinson you want his best eight-dollar Cabernet."

"And I'll also bring along a fine two-dollar six-pack of Coors."

Judy stood to leave. "Well, that was easy. I've got my man back." He rose with her and she kissed him again. "See you at six," she said.

"I saw that," said Connie as she and Danny returned to the table. "A little old for you, isn't she?"

"That's my friend, Judy. Great lady. Met her just after I moved to Denver."

Connie maneuvered herself back between the two men and replaced her hands on their thighs. "Now, where were we?" she said. Her head was beginning to droop and she'd lean on Danny's shoulder, then on Andrew's.

"Dragged her out of the parking lot," said Danny. "Fucking bouncer wanted another three bucks to let us back in. Then, I noticed the boy had jump wings tattooed on his arm. I said, 'Airborne' and he waved us though."

Andrew smiled. "So, Connie probably forgot to use the lady's room, right?"

"Oh, no, baby. I just squatted between a couple Volkswagens. Nice puddle for them to step around."

The men laughed out loud. "Baby, I think it's about time for us to head back to Flag," said Danny. "Andrew, you've got to come out. When can you make it?"

"Any Sunday but this one coming up. Moving into a new apartment," he answered. "Sunday's the only day of the week I'm off for sure."

Danny displayed his demonic grin again. "Well, it's better than 'Nam, right?"

Andrew suddenly realized that Danny was bombed, too. "Uh, you sure you guys can make it back tonight? You can stay at my place if you want."

"Nah, we'll make it." Danny began drawing a map on a cocktail napkin. "OK, a week from Sunday." He handed it to Andrew and said, "Come as early as you can. I'll show you around while 'Flower Child' is at church."

Connie, trying but failing to lift her head as she spoke said, "Baby, you're going to love our little farm."

They stood and headed for the exit, Andrew and Danny guiding Connie. Andrew waved at Judy as she walked to the dance floor with a man half a head shorter than herself. He wagged his finger at her as if in reprimand. She blew him a kiss.

In the parking lot, Connie insisted on showing them where she had piddled between the cars. As they approached, there was, indeed, an irate woman struggling to unlock her car without stepping in it. As Connie began to laugh hysterically, the two men ushered her quickly away.

Danny was driving a brand new Ford Pickup. Andrew, holding up Connie while Danny unlocked and started the truck, whistled as he viewed its luxurious interior and sampled the new vehicle smell.

"Wow, man. I had no idea how much money there was in wheat farming."

"You come on out to Flag and I'll show you how it's done, buddy."

Connie gathered herself and turned to Andrew, throwing her arms around his neck. She kissed him lustily, her tongue probing and winding around his. Andrew, not knowing what to do, kissed her back, his eyes open looking at Danny.

"What's mine is yours, Lieutenant," he said, grinning. "I told you that weed makes her crazy. She'll blow me all the way to Limon."

Chapter 21
Ma Bell

The alley was muddy from the previous evening's rain shower, and the truck's tires hissed through the mess until Andrew pulled over beneath the home's "drop" wire connection at the pole. He stepped from the truck and looked up at the "B-box."

"Shit," he muttered, noticing that the metal doors were ajar and wires protruded crazily from inside. His job was to run an "ADL" or "Additional Line" so the homeowner's teenage daughter would have her own private connection and phone number. He knew from experience that he'd be back to add other private lines when the girl's friends in the neighborhood found out about hers.

He went to the back of the truck and pulled the orange plastic cone from its bumper bracket and set it on the ground, then walked to the front and did the same with that cone. Opening the side doors, he pulled his "hooks" from their storage bin and began strapping them on to his old Corcoran boots. When they were snuggly attached, he strapped on his climbing belt and put on his plastic hard hat. A large spool of drop wire was pulled from the rear door and carried to the pole. He looped a length of drop wire through a clip on his belt. The clip was open-ended so that if the wire were jerked from below, it would pull free from the climber instead of pulling him down with it. Then he removed the metal caps that protected the sharp gaff tips. Lastly, he put on his gauntleted gloves, stepped up to the pole and shoved his first gaff into it.

The pole was old, bowed and heavily splintered. The sound of the gaff hitting the pole was somewhat hollow--not a good sign, and Andrew thought briefly of pulling his ladder down from its roof rack. But the second step seemed more solid.

Andrew picked the "high" side to climb, that being the side which was convex relative to the ground. The "low" side subjected the climber to the effects of gravity as he would hang below the pole's arc while he climbed. He took several steps up, held himself in place with one hand, felt for the drop wire with the other, and whipped it around to make sure he had enough slack to take him the next 10 feet to the top. After several more steps, he could grab the main phone cable that ran down the alley. Steadying himself with the cable, he brought both feet to the same level, made sure his gaffs were set in the wood and unhooked one end of the strap from the "D-ring". He leaned in, threw the strap around the pole with one hand, caught it with his free hand and snapped it on to the other D-ring. Then he leaned back, letting his weight rest against the belt.

The B-box wiring was a mess, and Andrew began sorting through the various wires by their colors. Eventually, he found his connection and pulled the end of the drop wire up to attach the metal bracket that would secure it to the pole. The metal hook that held the original drop wire was awkwardly placed on the pole's low side. To reach it, Andrew needed to step higher up on the pole. He leaned in, lifted his left foot and looked to see where best to shove it back into the wood.

Just then, his right gaff broke free as the wood cracked away. His hands were behind the pole and he tried to grip it as hard as he could. However, his weight was too much, and the main cable broke his grip as his forearms came in contact with it. Now, he was on the way to the ground, still strapped in, his chest and arms sliding down the splintery pole.

He landed hard, and collapsed into the base of the pole. For several minutes he leaned against it trying to catch his breath and assessing his injuries. He was pretty sure he'd not broken any bones, but was bleeding from numerous abrasions and puncture wounds on his chest and arms. His shirt was impaled with wood splinters of various lengths. He unhooked his belt, attempted to stand but decided to rest another minute or two.

"Well now," came a voice from behind him. "We have another stellar safety demonstration by Mr. Starkey. He's shown us all how to burn a pole. But, let's hold our applause until all the votes are in."

"Fuck you, Boss."

Supervisor Bob laughed at the profane insubordination. "Starkey, I like to keep you around to serve as a bad example." He stood over Andrew, smiling, then noticed the blood.

"Shit, boy." He started to look him over with real concern. "Can you stand up?"

"Yep. Give me a hand."

With Bob lifting him from under his arms, Andrew stood unsteadily. His hard hat had stayed in place through the fall and now he took it off and pitched it towards the truck. Bob helped him out of his climbing belt.

"Lucky you didn't gaff a leg when you hit," he said, checking to see if his crewman displayed any more obvious injuries. "We'd better get you back to the garage and check you over. Think you can drive?"

Andrew walked around for a minute and moved his arms and legs around. "Yeah, I can drive."

Back at the garage, Bob helped Andrew out of his shredded work shirt, then, using scissors from a first-aid kit, cut his T-shirt away. It was bloody and, like the work shirt, run though with wood splinters.

Bob gingerly fingered a few of the splinters protruding from Andrew's chest and arms. "Well, I don't know how else to do it," he said. "Sit down on the desk here."

"Get it done, Boss."

With that, Bob began pulling out the wood splinters with a pair of needle-nose pliers. "That hurt?" he asked, with each extraction.

"Nah," Andrew said through his gritted teeth.

This process had gone on for several minutes when Andrew asked, "How'd you just happen to drop by, Boss?"

Bob was making a small pile of bloody splinters on his desk. "Some friend of yours came by the garage just before lunch. Danny something," he answered. "Said to tell you not to show up 'til after ten on Sunday. Said you'd understand."

"Oh? Yeah, I got it. He's got a farm near Flagstaff. I'm driving out on Sunday."

Using the edge of his hand, Bob slid the bloody pile off his desk and into the wastepaper basket. Wiping his hand on his pants leg, he said, "Funny dude. Said you and him were going to poach some Antelope."

"No shit?" Andrew looked puzzled. "Wonder where that came from."

Bob shrugged. "Anyway, thought I'd let you know. Gave me an excuse to get out of the office."

"Glad you did. I'd still be sitting there in a pile if you hadn't shown up."

Bob stepped back and looked over his surgical work. Blood still oozed from some of the wounds, and he dabbed at them with a ball of gauze. "Well," he said, "I got out what I could. Some of them are so deep they'll just have to fester out."

"Yep."

With some resignation, he continued, "Ma Bell won't let me send you back to work half-naked. You go on home and take it easy." He helped Andrew drape the shredded shirt over his bare shoulders. "See you in the morning, Starkey."

Chapter 22
Flagstaff

As usual, his internal clock awakened him at 5:30AM, give or take five minutes, the result of military routine. He could hear the soft, rhythmic breathing of Judy beside him in her large bed. He sat up carefully so as not to wake her, reached for his Seiko on the bedside table and snapped its band closed around his wrist.

Her smooth bare shoulder drew his attention and, for an instant, he was tempted to touch her to see if she was close to wakefulness. *No, let her sleep,* he thought to himself. Their lovemaking hours before had exhausted both of them, yet now he wanted her again. But, the highway beckoned and he padded quietly to the bathroom to empty his bladder.

He dressed as quietly as he could in the semi-dark bedroom. As he prepared to leave, he bent over her, lifted some strands of her dark-brown hair from her face, and kissed her softly on the cheek.

"Ummm?" she purred.

"Got to get going," he whispered. "I'll call you."

"You'd better," she said softly, turning on to her side and smiling up at him. She reached out for his hand, pulled him to her and kissed him.

He stroked the side of her face. "Go back to sleep."

"OK," she murmured. "Love you."

"See you soon."

He needed to stop by his new apartment, take a shower and change clothes before heading east on I-70 for Flagstaff. Since Danny asked that he not arrive before ten, he had plenty of time. Still, he was excited to begin the two-hour trip, and hunger pangs were beginning to make him think about biscuits and gravy. Less than an hour later, he was driving into the burnt- orange glow of the Great Plains dawn.

In the minutes before sunrise, the ridgelines on either side of the highway were often dotted with antelope. When the sun had fully emerged, they were gone, following the shadows into gullies and ravines where they'd remain hidden until the sun set again behind the Front Range.

"Poach an antelope," he recalled Bob saying. "Well, there's a bunch of them out here," he said to himself.

As hungry as he was, he forced himself to pass up several options for breakfast, preferring to stop in Limon at the truck stop he and his friends chose on the road trip to Buena Vista a few short years ago.

My God, he thought. *Five years, but it seems like a century.* He counted them off. *Let's see…A year and a half at IU, just shy of three years in the Army, nine months in Denver…Shit, I'm getting old.*

As he sat down at the same table the four boys had used, he thought of Nancy and a comment she had made as they drove up the Chalk Creek road. "You must have a touch of sentimentality," she'd said.

"Yeah, I guess so," he mused, watching the long-haul trucks cruise around the large parking area. He also remembered her observation that such a quality made him "good raw material." He'd played dumb, but knew what she meant.

Even now he thought of her often, what she was doing at that moment, how she was getting along. Her picture, which had adorned his desk at IU and then his bunker wall at Ba Thanh, was now taped to the refrigerator in his new apartment. It was so worn and faded that he could barely make out her features, and was no longer sure if he would recognize her on the street.

Though Andrew made a point of not asking about her, that didn't stop her brother from updating him on his sister's latest doings when they got together for beers.

As many with new Education degrees opted, she'd begun work on a graduate degree before beginning her teaching career. She was still in Greeley, still engaged to "Mark."

Ron, in fact, had become Andrew's closest Colorado friend. Though he never verbalized it, Ron hoped that Nancy and Andrew would yet get back together. He didn't think much of her fiancée; a tweedy and, Ron thought, phony academic type who quoted Shakespeare and tried to act far older than his 25 years. The rest of the Spinelli males had similar misgivings. However, when Ron expressed his sentiments to his mother, she would shush him, saying, "Honey, she loves him. We'll all get to know him better over time."

"Mom," he'd retort, "he's just a smooth-talking 'Fred' with better personal hygiene."

"Nancy," he asked his sister, after Mark had left following a weekend visit to Buena Vista, "what do you see in that pretentious fuckhead?"

"Ronnie!"

"Well?"

"Leave me alone."

"Nancy, he's a pussy. He doesn't fit in with us, Dad, Steve and me."

"Get out of my room, Ronnie! Don't use that language with me!"

She slammed the door as he walked out of her bedroom. He heard her sobs come as he descended the stairs.

Ron kept those "Nancy" updates short, knowing that Andrew still loved his sister and was pained by her loss. Nevertheless, he knew Andrew's own failures caused her to move on.

Though Andrew had written to Ron on numerous occasions, letters to Nancy were months apart and, when one arrived, it spoke only of the hills and jungle around his Special Forces camp, the monsoon, the heat, or other weather-related issues. Sometimes he mentioned trips to Nha Trang, Chu Lai or his R&R in Sydney. They contained nothing about the future, nothing to confirm his continued affection for her except his sign off, "Love always, the Hoosier." He thought he knew why. His friend had written himself off. Andrew believed he was not coming home from Vietnam. Ron never told Nancy that, but believing it himself, he refused to give up on a possible reconciliation. The thought of a "Mark" in the family was just too painful to consider--not when a "comrade in arms" was available and, most importantly, worthy.

Finishing his coffee, Andrew took a quick look at his Seiko. "Eight-thirty. No rush." He left the Denver Post he'd purchased on the table and headed for the LeMans.

Instead of getting back on the highway, he cruised through the center of Limon. Like the truck stop, the door of every business on the short commercial strip displayed a decal that read, "Push for the Badgers" or "Pull for the Badgers," the town's high school team. He marveled at the size and number of harvesting machines in the several farm-equipment dealerships. Other businesses displayed multi-wheeled, center-pivot irrigation sprinkler monstrosities. A roar overhead drew his attention to a crop-dusting plane, the pilot's arm draped brashly along the fuselage outside the cockpit.

Back on I-70, the Pontiac climbed out of the Big Sandy drainage and approached the tiny burg of Genoa. A billboard near its one tourist attraction, a large frame building with a viewing tower, proclaimed, "See Six States."

"No way," Andrew said out loud, as he did each time he'd passed the structure over the years. "One of these days I'm going to check that out."

Thirty minutes later, he was pulling off the Interstate at the Flagstaff exit. He turned left onto a county blacktop road, drove back under the highway and pulled over at an abandoned garage. He retrieved Danny's "napkin" map from his pocket, being careful not to shred the convoluted drawing. If he couldn't find the farm there was no way to call for directions. Of course, he could always ask someone in town, if he was willing to backtrack.

The directions were clear enough and soon he was sure he was on the right road and heading in the right direction. He glanced again at his Seiko and thought, *I'd better kill some time.*

The day was clear, breezy and beautiful, and the southward view to a barely visible Pikes Peak seized his attention. He slowed down at the crest of a low hill and pulled over at a weather-beaten mailbox. A "Denver Post" box was nailed to the wooden pole below the mailbox. Both were filled with wind-blown debris, evidence that they'd not been used in a long time.

A set of cement steps were cut into the edge of the hillside and climbed ten feet to the top. He could see no structure from the car, nor when he got out to stretch, and assumed that whatever house had once been there had burned or blown away. He walked to the steps, climbed halfway up and sat down. He put his sunglasses on, tilted his face towards the sun and leaned back against the steps.

"Man," he said, the view and sun combining to sooth his soul, "it doesn't get any better than this…"

A few moments later, a sound that seemed a cross between a muffled cough and a growl interrupted his reverie. The first time he ignored it, thinking it was the wind. Then it came again, louder and closer this time. He leaned forward, took off his sunglasses and turned around. At the top of the steps sat a very large male dog. It appeared to be a German Sheppard mix, possibly with Black Lab due to its short dark fur. A wolf-like face displayed an impassive but curious expression as it stared down at him.

"Well, hi there, boy," Andrew said softly, a smile coming to his face. He lifted his hand slowly and motioned for the dog to come to him. "Come on, boy." He patted the step next to him. The dog rose slowly, seemed to think about it for a second, then walked down the steps. When he was within reach, Andrew turned his palm towards the ground and extended his loose fist carefully to the dog's nose. The animal sniffed him for a few seconds and, sensing neither threat nor fear, descended further and allowed Andrew to pet his head. Now the dog sat at Andrew's side and allowed the human to scratch his neck and behind his ears.

Andrew noticed a tag on the dog's collar and, still scratching him, lifted the tag with his free hand. He read the printing out loud. "Oscar." The dog's ears rose and fell at the sound of its name.

"You're a beautiful doggy," Andrew baby-talked, clearly enjoying the dog's sudden appearance. He let his arm drape loosely over the dog's shoulders and scratched its chest. "Sure is a nice view up here, isn't it, Oscar?"

"Damn"…the voice was feminine and came from the top of the steps. "I've got to get a better watchdog."

Given the sudden appearance of the dog, Andrew wasn't startled by yet another surprise. The dog bounded up the steps as Andrew turned to see who had spoken. A tall, lanky woman, in her late twenties, he thought, gazed down at him. Her lips were pursed in a way that betrayed incredulity at her dog's display of friendliness to a complete stranger. She had one hand on top of her head, holding down her long, sun-blonde hair as the wind gusted. The other scratched Oscar's head. A faded and threadbare cotton dress displayed a slim waist and well-shaped hips as the wind pushed it against her body. Movement of large breasts beneath the fabric showed she wore no bra.

Andrew responded, "Sorry to trespass. I should have known someone lived up there. Got distracted by your view."

"Oh, no harm done, except to my relationship with Oscar."

"That's a great dog. If he hadn't sensed I was harmless, he'd have had me for lunch." Andrew smiled, hoping to allay the concern the woman probably had. "I'll get going." He gave a wave to Oscar. "Bye, Oscar."

"Are you lost?" she asked.

"Not yet. I think I'm just about there. Danny Sevilla's place. The map he drew seems to take me over this hill, then down and around for maybe a half mile."

"So you do business with Danny?" she said, the pursed lips becoming more severe.

"Not business. We were in the Army together." Andrew sensed her curiosity was not friendly, and was ready to move on.

"So, you're old friends then," she said as a statement, not a question. "Come on up. I'll show you where you're going."

He hesitated momentarily, then walked up the steps. A few yards back from the crest, the foundation stones of the former farm house filled a depression in the ground. The hillside sloped away gradually to a nicely kept lawn surrounding a small, frame house. Like the woman's dress, the house was sun-faded beige with a roof of black asphalt shingles that appeared to have been installed recently. A Rattan couch, table and chairs were arranged on the home's small veranda. A metallic blue, late-model Mercedes 280 sedan was parked in the driveway.

"No wonder I didn't see your house," he said. "Guess you moved down the hill to block some of the wind."

"And the snow," she added, matter-of-factly.

He followed the woman towards the house, then around to the side. The ground continued to fall away for a mile to the north. A distant stream channel lined with cottonwoods ran northeast and disappeared among low hills. A group of buildings sat in a depression about halfway between the woman's house and the stream channel.

She shielded her eyes with her left hand and pointed with her right. "That's Danny's place," she said. "Looks like he's got company."

Andrew looked out and saw a two-story, white-frame farmhouse, a large barn and a few out-buildings. Fields recently prepared for the planting of winter wheat surrounded the cluster of buildings. The fallow fields Danny mentioned were off to the north towards the river. A white van was parked near the barn's open doors. As they watched, two men walked from the barn towards the van. Seconds later, another figure emerged from the barn as the first two climbed into the vehicle.

"There's Danny," the woman said. The solitary figure waved at the van as it pulled away.

She began walking down her driveway towards the road and Andrew followed behind. As they walked, the van could be seen approaching, trailing a cloud of dust. The woman folded her arms across her chest and stared hard at the two men in the van. The driver was vaguely familiar to Andrew; a large man with shoulder-length black hair. The passenger, smaller than the driver, wore round wire-rimmed glasses with nearly black lenses. He stared back at them with an odd smile on his narrow face.

As the van passed and disappeared in its dust trail, Andrew said, "That must be why Danny told me to show up after ten. Guess he had business to attend to."

The woman watched after the van until it disappeared around the hillside where Andrew's car was parked. She turned and looked thoughtfully at Andrew. "So, you really are an Army friend?" she asked.

"Yes ma'am. Met Danny in Basic Training back at Ft. Knox in '68."

She smiled for the first time. "Ma'am? Wow, do I look that old?"

"No, ma'am." Andrew was embarrassed by his own awkward response. "You look great, I mean, young. You look..."

She held up her hand. "No offense taken. So, what does Danny call you?"

He cleared his throat before speaking. "I'm Andrew Starkey. I live in Denver. Danny was wound...uh, I hadn't seen him in a long time..."

"I'm Susan," she said extending her hand to shake with him. "Would you like some iced tea, Andrew?" she said, the smile remaining on her narrow, high cheek-boned face. "Danny won't miss you for a few minutes."

"Uh, well," Andrew stuttered, "sure. I'd like that."

As she released his hand she glanced down at his arm. The abrasions from his fall were prominent. "Why, Andrew, what happened to you? That looks painful."

"One of the perils of being a telephone installer," he answered. "I burned a pole…uh, I gaffed out and slid down. Shredded my shirt with wood splinters. You ought to see my chest."

"Well," she said, taking his wrist and carefully lifting his arm, "I hope you got some good medical care."

"Only the best," he replied.

Susan was very attractive, and her touch on his arm conveyed a cordiality that had not existed only minutes before. Her hands were soft and elegantly manicured.

"My boss patched me up and gave me the rest of the day off."

"That's it?"

It had not occurred to Andrew that he should have expected anything more. "Susan," he said, "I'm lucky he didn't trade shirts with me and send me back out."

As they walked to the house, Andrew felt Oscar's wet nose nuzzle his hand. The dog held a length of knotted rope in its mouth. Andrew grabbed the free end of the rope and pulled Oscar around with it playfully. The dog dug in its forepaws and shook its large head trying to pull the rope away. The tug-of-war continued until they stepped up on the porch. At that point, the dog sat down and released the toy. Andrew threw it out into the yard and Oscar galloped after it.

"That dog is an excellent judge of character," Susan said. "Otherwise, I'd have sent you on your way."

Andrew smiled and, for a few moments, didn't respond. "You know what?" he said, finally. "An old friend made that same character comment because her girlfriend liked me. Puts a lot of pressure on a guy."

"I'd trust a dog over a girlfriend," she said, flatly.

Susan opened the kitchen door and waved Andrew inside with a flourish. "Be it ever so humble…" she said. The small kitchen was decorated with wallpaper of barnyard animals. Pots and pans hung from a metal rack over the electric stove. Recently washed dishes sat drying in a wire basket at the edge of the sink. A cotton towel hung from a hook nearby. Glass-fronted cabinets showed short stacks of dishes within. A tiny circular table with two chairs stood against the wall opposite the sink.

Something caught Andrew's eye as he surveyed the sun-bathed kitchen. "Holy shit," he said.

Susan looked at him quizzically. "I beg your pardon?"

Without comment, he walked to the corner and stared down at a rifle that leaned there. "Is this yours?" he asked, not taking his eyes from it.

"Are you kidding? That's Danny's gun. He keeps it here for some mysterious reason. I'm sure he'll tell you," she said, pulling a pitcher of iced tea from the refrigerator. She opened a cabinet and took down two tall glasses. "I guess you know about guns, too. Go ahead and pick it up if you want. I'm afraid of that thing."

Andrew hefted the rifle and ran his hands over it. With practiced motion he removed the magazine, noticing it held a half-dozen rounds. He opened the bolt, locked it in its rear position and checked that the chamber was empty. Then he tilted the bolt opening towards the window and looked down the muzzle. He smiled as he noticed the gleaming cleanliness of the barrel's interior.

"This, Susan, is an M-14, gas-operated, shoulder-fired, 7.62 millimeter, semi-automatic rifle. It's in immaculate condition. I'm not surprised it belongs to Danny."

"Whatever," she responded, sitting down at the table. She watched him with the rifle for a moment, an amused look on her face. "Did you show that much tenderness to that 'old friend'?"

Andrew blushed and leaned the rifle back in the corner. "Old friend?"

"The one whose girlfriend made the Oscar-esque character reference."

He smiled shyly. "Oh." Water had condensed on the tea glass and pooled on the bare wood of the table top. With the edge of his hand, he pushed the water from the table into the palm of his other hand, then poured it back into the glass. "Well," he said, "I sure tried." Trying to change the subject, he said. "Say, do you have a job in town? Your hands are so pretty I suspect you don't do much farm labor."

"Why, thanks for noticing. No. I mean, I don't have a 'job', per se. I'm a writer." She stood suddenly and motioned to him to follow. The next room held an over-stuffed sofa and matching chair. A Persian rug covered most of the shiny hardwood floor. In the corner, beneath a window that opened to the western view, a small desk was positioned. On the desk was a portable Corona typewriter. Bookcases stood against the wall and were filled with a set of encyclopedia, other reference books, and stacks of typewritten paper.

"No, shi..really?" Andrew said, his interest rising. "What do you write about?"

"Mostly Western romances, you know, strong cowboys and damsels in distress." She picked up a paperback that lay on the coffee table in front of the sofa. "Here's my latest," she said, handing it to Andrew.

He took the book and examined the cover. It showed a cowboy, muscular chest bursting through a torn shirt, an adoring woman cradled in one arm, and free hand holding the reigns of a stallion. A stormy horizon in the background was lined with war-painted, mounted Indians. The title was "Cheyenne Crossing."

"Wow. You weren't kidding," as he thumbed through the 200 pages, then examined the cover again. "So, you're Susan Casper?" He extended his hand. "I'm honored to meet you."

She smiled and shook his hand. "So, you've read something of mine?"

"No. Not yet, anyway. I've just never met anyone famous before."

She held up her hand in protest. "The stuff I write won't get you on 'Johnny Carson'. They're for the ladies at the check-out counter at King Soopers…you know, escape for frustrated housewives."

"But, you get paid, don't you? You make a living?"

"Barely. This stuff pays the bills while I work on a more serious novel." She pointed to the stacks of pages on the shelf. "I hope that one helps me break into the big leagues."

Andrew was truly impressed by her apparent talent. "Susan," he said, "you're an interesting lady."

She was blushing now. The stranger was beginning to interest her. He was tall, slim and attractive, though a bit gaunt; nothing that gaining some weight wouldn't fix. He looked her directly in the eyes when speaking and, so far, hadn't stared openly at her breasts. Moreover, a reference to her hands spoke of an awareness of a woman's own vanity.

She'd not expected a visitor, and had been in her robe at her typewriter before Oscar's disappearance down the old steps forced her to investigate. She'd thrown on an old dress and huarache sandals and walked quickly up the rise. When she saw Oscar sitting with the man, she was startled at first, puzzled, then angry that the dog's normally vicious bark hadn't driven away the intruder. *Maybe Oscar was lonely, too*, she thought.

"You can take that with you. After you've read it, let me know what you think. Sometimes I like to know how males relate to my writing. I'm afraid you'll find it a bit syrupy and romantic. Just remember my audience, who I'm writing for."

"Will do," he said as they returned to the small table and the iced tea. "I'd better get going soon. I didn't mean to interrupt your work." He liked this woman and was pleased that her initial hostility had faded rapidly. Still, he felt it appropriate that he not get too comfortable and risk overstaying his welcome. "Danny's probably wondering where I am."

"Tell him you were with me. He won't mind. You know, I watch their daughter sometimes when they go to Denver."

Suddenly, Andrew recalled the night he found Danny at Mister Lucky's. "Oh, you're the lady Connie mentioned. She said they had one neighbor who was watching their kid."

"That's me."

He stared at his glass for a few seconds, trying to get up his nerve. "So," he said, "uh..."

"Yes?" she said, expectantly.

"So, after I've read your book, maybe I could stop by and do a book report?"

She laughed softly. "Yes, I'd like that."

"Maybe next Saturday night?"

"You don't waste a lot of time, do you?"

"I didn't mean to be so forward. I don't have a lot of free time."

"Don't be silly. Next Saturday night would be fine. It's nice to have a man who speaks up. You begin to appreciate that when you enter the business world. Believe me, publishing is a tough business."

"Way over my head," he said. For a few seconds he pondered the logistics of his next visit. "I probably can't get here before six. Is that too late? Saturdays are a work day for me."

"No, that's perfect. But you've got to take me to a movie."

"There's a movie theater around here?"

"If you'd driven down Main Street you'd have seen it. 'The Plainsman'. That new movie, 'Easy Rider', is showing. Have you seen it?"

"Yeah, when I was in Sydney on R&R. But it's good enough to see again. Do you have a phone number, just in case?"

She scribbled the number on a scrap and handed it to him. "If you do call, and it's busy, keep trying. It's a party line and the local women are inveterate gossips."

"I'll bet," he said. "Well, I'll hit the road. Thanks for everything. I'll see you next Saturday, Susan."

She stood on the porch and watched him walk back up the hill to the steps, Oscar and he playing tug-of-war all the way. At the steps, he lifted the rope toy until the dog let go, then threw it back towards the house. As Oscar galloped after it, Andrew waved at Susan, then disappeared down the steps.

His car was dust covered, and he wished he'd closed its windows when he'd pulled over to admire the view. As he rounded the blind curve and passed Susan's new mailbox, he looked back at the house and noticed her still standing on the porch with her dog. She waved again and he honked the Pontiac's horn. A few minutes later he pulled up in front of Danny's farmhouse.

Chapter 23
The Farm

He stepped from the LeMans and looked around at the pastoral scene. A circular grassy lawn surrounded the white-frame house. Massive cottonwoods grew on either side of a root-cracked sidewalk leading to the house's porch and front door. The driveway from the road was hard-packed earth and opened into a large, flat expanse that led to the barn, fifty yards behind the house. Wooden fencing enclosed a large stock corral and bordered the driveway on the left. A "50s" vintage flatbed Ford was parked next to the fence.

Andrew glanced at his Seiko. *10:30. Right on schedule and still had time to meet a tough babe,* he thought.

"Yo!" It was Danny, emerging from the barn. Grinning ear to ear, he strode towards Andrew.

Andrew shook Danny's hand. "Man, good to see you. This place is great."

"I told you it was. So, you got my message about holding off till ten? Had some business with my partners. Didn't want you to have to cool your heels waiting for me."

"Yeah. My boss passed the word. Found me in a pile at the bottom of a phone pole. Slid down that stick, squewering myself with creosote wood spinters on the way." Andrew pulled up his shirt and displayed the many abrasions and punctures.

"Shit, buddy. Bet that hurt. Like a parachute landing in a pine tree at Ft. Bragg?"

"Now that you mention it, that's pretty close," Andrew answered, stuffing his shirt carefully back into his pants. "So, uh, 'partners'? That sounds heavy. What kind of partnership it that?"

"I'll tell you later. No secrets between brother paratroopers," Danny said with a wink.

"Can't wait. Is Connie around?"

"Nah. She'll be at church all day. She's got beaucoup cousins around here and they go ape shit after church, you know, bullshitting, showing off their babies." He motioned for Andrew to follow him up the sidewalk to the house. The wooden porch had numerous rocking chairs and a metal glider loveseat. A screen door led to the front room, which was attractively furnished with items that dated from the turn of the century through the 1930s. Wool rugs lay at angles over the hardwood floor. There was no TV in evidence. A telephone that Andrew recognized as of 1930s vintage sat on a window sill above a hot-water heater.

"This is home, buddy. My dad inherited it from his dad back in 1947. My mom and dad moved here in '48. I was born at the hospital in Limon."

"But your mom hated it and dragged your ass back to Louisville."

"Roger that. So I didn't see the place again until I was old enough to take the train by myself. Man, I love trains. They always remind me of heading west to Colorado."

"Just like me and I-70," Andrew commented. "So..."

"So, then my dad died when we were in 'Nam. I got that leave and came here to bury him and take over the farm. I met Connie at the funeral."

"Oh, no shit?"

"Yeah. Pretty bad, huh, picking up a chick at your dad's funeral?"

Andrew couldn't imagine such conflicting emotions. "Oh, I don't know. Hell, you hadn't seen a round-eye in, what, eight months?"

"Yeah."

Andrew cocked his head at a memory. "Hey, remember that time we were sitting in that diner in Louisville? You said something like 'God throws guys like us in the shit just to see what happens,' you know, like that's His entertainment. You lost your dad but you meet a fine lady at his funeral. I bet God was real entertained."

"Maybe," Danny said with a wistful smile. "Maybe you've got something there."

He stepped to a bookcase and picked up an object. "Remember this?"

It was the CAR-15 magazine that had been dislodged when the enemy bullet impacted his weapon.

"Oh, yeah," Andrew said, looking over the small metal box. "I remember it too well. That was one fucking bad day."

"Hey, we survived, buddy. Those NVA we greased aren't standing around shooting the shit in Hanoi."

Andrew shrugged and put the magazine back on the shelf. "I saw your M-14 up at Susan's house," he said.

"Susan's house? You met Susan? Man, you don't waste any time."

"That's what she said," Andrew responded, the smile returning. "I was killing time, sitting on her steps. Next thing you know I'm petting her dog. Then she shows up. We had iced tea and shot the shit for a few minutes."

"How'd you like those tits of hers?"

"Outstanding. Had to force myself not to stare. She seems like the type that wants you to respect her mind and ignore the body."

"Don't kid yourself. That body is long overdue for a workout. She's divorced from some jack-off, 'Commie' professor who teaches in Boulder."

"Oh? How'd she end up in Flagstaff?"

"Would you believe her dad is the county sheriff? Family's been in this area for a hundred years. Her place is on the old family homestead."

"So, her dad gave up farming to be a sheriff?"

"Yeah. Drought did him in. Luckily, they didn't have any debt so didn't lose their land. He lives in town. Her mom moved to California when he got elected sheriff. Divorced the boy from long distance." Danny stooped to straighten a rug and finished the rearrangement with his foot. "I never met Susan when I visited my dad," he continued, "'cause she was in California most of the time."

"So, her mom was like yours? Didn't dig the wide open spaces?"

"I guess. You know women don't want to live more than fifteen minutes from a department store."

Andrew pulled aside a curtain and looked out towards Pikes Peak. "Susan and Connie seem to like it out here," he said.

"True. Of course, Connie has me and all her relatives to entertain her. Susan has her dad and a few friends and relatives here. But, mostly she just seems to peck on that little typewriter of hers. She'll take off and go to Denver every once in a while. Stays gone for few days but always comes back."

"Probably selling one of her book deals," Andrew surmised, turning from the window. "I asked her out for next Saturday night. She's making me take her to see 'Easy Rider'".

"Holy shit, Lieutenant," Danny said, flashing his grin. "All the Army shit we went through, I guess I never realized what a civilian stud you are."

He walked into the kitchen and pulled two bottles of Coors from the small refrigerator. Rummaging in a drawer for an opener, he found one and popped open the bottles. "You know," he said, handing a beer to Andrew, "she's an 'older woman', but I guess you like those."

Andrew hadn't thought about it. "How old is old?"

"Thirty, give or take."

Andrew shrugged. "So, where'd you get the M-14? You can't just buy one at a sporting goods store, can you?"

"No way. Too easy to convert to full auto," Danny responded. "It was a gift from my partner."

"Susan said you'd tell me why you keep it at her place," Andrew commented with a nod. "Must be a 'Danny' story there."

"Yo."

"Well, if it involves a blow job, don't tell me."

Danny laughed loudly and threw his arm around Andrew's shoulder. "No, buddy," he said, collecting himself. "Much as I'd like to be on the receiving end of one of Susan's blow jobs, Connie would stake me down in a field and harvest my balls with a combine."

"That would sure keep me in line," Andrew said, joining in his friend's laughter.

Danny took a seat on the couch and Andrew pulled over a comfortable-looking antique rocker. "My partner, Hawk," Danny began, "is an Indian dude from Montana. Great guy. You've got to meet him sometime. Anyway, one day we're fucking around, down by the river. Had the 14 in the window rack. Sure as shit, we see a half dozen Antelope just below the ridge line. He decides we need to blow one away. We'd had a couple beers so I was stupid enough to say, 'Sure, buddy. Lock and load.' Well, he runs the sight up a notch, gets down on one knee and fires off a round. Fucking Antelope dropped like it was clubbed in the head. Twenty minutes later he's skinned and gutted it out in the barn. He had this skinning knife under the seat in his van and goes through that son of a bitch like a buzz saw," Danny shook his head at the recollection. "By the time he's done, I'm starting to get nervous, you know, watching up the road in case Susan's dad or his dumb-ass deputy show up to fine me for poaching."

"Did you get caught?"

"Hard to say. Hawk took the hide and most of the good meat. We buried the guts and all out in the river bottom. Coyotes dug it up that night and dragged off the evidence. The next day, the deputy comes by, acting real nonchalant, like just to say hello or some shit. Asks Connie and me if we heard any gun fire the day before and he'd appreciate it if we'd let him know if we see any out-of-county poachers. Then he goes on his way."

"Think he was on to you?"

"Maybe. But I decided right then to move the 14 out of the house, just in case. Susan said it was OK to keep it at her place in plain sight so her dad would see it if he came over. No way I can poach if I don't have my weapon, right? I told her to tell her dad, if he asks about it, that, since Janon is starting to walk, Connie doesn't want it in the house."

"Well, I bet there's a grain of truth to that," Andrew said. "So, it's a steep fine for poaching?"

"$1,000 per animal, 90 days in the stockade."

"Wow. That's a shit load of dough for some Antelope burgers."

"Steaks, my man. Antelope steaks. I'll send a couple back with you."

"The perfect crime," Andrew observed with a smile. "Your Denver buddy devouring the remaining evidence."

"Airborne!" Danny responded, clinking his beer bottle to Andrew's.

The two men were quiet for a few moments and watched two Magpies dancing on the porch railing.

"Speaking of women," Danny said, beginning to peel his beer label, "you ever connect with that old girlfriend from Buena Vista?"

Andrew didn't respond for a second, instead taking a long drink of his beer. "Nah, she's history," he said finally. "Getting married to some guy up at UNC in Greeley."

Danny took his own drink and sloshed the beer around in his mouth before swallowing. "Well," he commented, "I never met that one, but I bet Susan will make you forget her for good."

"Think so?" said Andrew, matter-of-factly.

His friend's expression of indifference was unconvincing, and Danny cursed himself for bringing up the girl. "Come on," he said, coming to his feet. "I'll take you for a tour of the estate. Pickup's behind the barn."

"Let's go."

The Ford clattered over an ancient plank bridge that crossed a weed-choked irrigation canal. Danny drove slowly around the fields pointing out things of interest.

"See that house way over there?" he said. "That's Jeff Woodward's place. This will be his wheat. I'll get a percent of the harvest, whatever that is."

At the far end of his fields, the land fell sharply down towards a trickle of water in a sandy stream bed. "That's the Republican River," Danny announced. "South Fork, to be exact. I've got a half mile of it on my land." He rolled to a stop and the two men climbed from the vehicle. Andrew followed Danny across the stream bed and onto a sandbar that held a stand of ancient cottonwood trees. Danny pointed to a Cottonwood root knob protruding from the sand. "That's where Hawk took his shot. The Pronghorn was 150 meters up towards the ridge."

"Damn good shot without setting his battle sight," Andrew observed.

"Yeah, that's what I thought."

Grass and other debris were lodged against the tree trunks two feet from the ground, and Danny began pulling off handfuls of the mass. "You don't want to be down here during a thunderstorm," he said. "Flash floods can wash away whole herds of cattle."

Andrew was really enjoying the tour, the beautiful day and the presence of one of his dearest friends. He shielded his eyes with a hand and took in the vast expanse of plains scenery.

"Man, I can sure see why you love it here," he said.

"Yeah, that I do. Can you imagine being twelve years old and having the run of this place?" Danny said, rubbing his palm over the bark of a huge cottonwood. "You know, Stark, these trees were growing when the Cheyenne and Arapaho were still around here chasing Buffalo." He made a fist and knocked on the tree trunk like it was a door. A hollow sound resonated down the silent streambed. "Don't worry Black Kettle. I'll take good care of your land," he said, as if speaking to the tree.

Andrew looked down, a bit embarrassed at his friend's uncharacteristic sentimentality. "Danny…"

"Yes, buddy, I am crazy," the demonic grin appearing. "Connie knows to bury me right here when I croak. The coyotes can have my sorry ass just like they took that Pronghorn."

They drove back to the farm house and Danny parked near the stock fence. "Let's go in the barn," he said. "I'll show you how I make the money to pay the taxes on this place."

Danny grabbed a handle on the large wooden barn door and pushed it along on the wheeled track from which it hung. A strong but not unpleasant mixture of odors wafted from the building, reminding Andrew of the farm work he'd done back in Indiana. A flood of recollections came to his mind.

"You know what? We're a thousand miles west of Indiana, but this barn smells just like fresh-cut hay and Hoosier cow shit," he said.

"Hay, cow shit, and one more thing," Danny said, walking towards several pallets covered by a canvas tarp. He pulled off the tarp and motioned for Andrew to come closer.

"What's that stuff?" Andrew looked down at rectangular-shaped burlap bundles. There were dozens of them stacked in an interlocking fashion on three pallets.

"Take a guess," Danny said, rolling his eyes.

Andrew bent over and pushed on the top of one bundle, then picked it up. He lifted it to his nose and inhaled.

"Marijuana?"

"Roger that."

"You're shitting me?"

"One hundred thousand dollars worth."

Andrew looked at the bundle, then at Danny, then back at the bundle. He put it back on its stack.

"OK, man. Tell me why the fuck you have a hundred thousand dollars of weed in your barn."

Danny pulled the tarp back in place over the pallets. "Let's go get another beer and I'll tell you."

Andrew tried his hand at the barn door, pulling it along the track until it clanked into the latch on the jamb. "I can't imagine you want the sheriff snooping around in your barn with all that weed in there," he said, testing the latch with a shake.

"No fucking shit," Danny responded with another roll of his eyes. "But around here, nobody, not even the sheriff, snoops in anybody's barn. First, they'd need a warrant and second, they might get shot doing it. Farmers and ranchers are real funny about people being on their property without permission."

They pulled two rocking chairs into a sunny spot on the porch and put their feet up on the railing. The sun was warm on their faces and the breeze that had come and gone most of the day was not in evidence. Two miles to the south, the trickle of vehicles on I-70 was barely visible.

"I'll give you the short version of a long story," Danny said. "Everything about this is just between you and me, OK?"

"And Connie, I assume?"

"Sure. She's a major part of it. But, I mean don't say anything to Susan or any of your buds back in Denver."

"Not a word."

Danny extended his hand to Andrew. "Airborne?"

"All the way," Andrew responded, gripping the outstretched hand.

"Well, you'll love this," he began. "I'll start with how I met Connie."

Chapter 24
The Chevy

The whole county had turned out for the funeral. Ed Sevilla had been a well-liked and respected farmer for the twenty-three years he'd lived in the county. That he could always be counted on to help with harvests, machinery repair, volunteer fireman duty or a myriad of other circumstances had endeared him to the little community.

Many also remembered the skinny kid from Kentucky who came out each summer to stay with his father on the farm, and they were astounded to see the tall, handsome, Green Beret trooper who followed the casket and its VFW honor guard from the hearse to the graveside.

Danny had remained at the grave for nearly an hour after the service, greeting people and answering questions about Vietnam. Children took turns trying on his Beret and marveling at his brilliantly shined "jump" boots and the ribbons and badges on his formal "greens" uniform.

He knew the farmhouse would be full of people and he wanted to avoid that crowd as long as possible. The church ladies had taken over, preparing food and getting the house ready for the wake, and he knew it would progress with or without his presence.

As he was walking back to his father's ancient flatbed truck, a cute girl he'd not noticed before approached him shyly. She was tall for a girl, maybe five feet seven, and very slender. Long and straight brown hair grew to the middle of her back. The hair framed a narrow, dimpled face and she flashed a crooked smile at him when he noticed her. Small breasts rose behind the fabric of her dress.

Her name was Connie, and she expressed her sympathy at the death of Mr. Sevilla and admiration for Danny's military service. Danny was happy to talk to the pretty stranger and, for a few moments, push the funeral and his imminent return to Vietnam to the back of his mind. He asked how it was that he'd missed such a pretty girl during his many summer visits. She explained that she'd only lived in Flagstaff for three years, having moved up from Dallas with her mother following the breakup of her parent's marriage. Her aunt lived in town with her large family and insisted that her sister and children come to stay until deciding what to do next. So, dragging Connie along reluctantly, her mother packed the car and headed to Colorado. A brother, Aaron, remained with her father in Dallas. The situation proved so agreeable that her mother took a job at the grain co-op, rented a small house and began a new life. Connie's numerous and gregarious cousins allowed her an easy assimilation into the town's close-knit batch of teenagers.

Danny, being somewhat of a celebrity for the duration of his week-long leave, had intrigued her and she wanted badly to meet this mysterious soldier.

"Well," he said, after they'd been talking for ten minutes, "I guess I'd better be getting back to the house. Trust me. I'd rather stay here and talk to you."

"I know you need to go," she said sympathetically. "How 'bout a beer first?"

He looked at her quizzically. "How far away is this beer?"

"Trunk of my car," she said, nodding towards the parking lot.

She was wearing high heels that matched her frilly cotton dress, and she took his arm to steady herself as they walked across the uneven lawn of the Flagstaff cemetery. At her car, she took off the shoes and pitched them in the open window of her 1964 Chevy Impala. She opened the trunk and pulled a blanket off a metal cooler. Within the cooler, eight Coors bottles rested on their sides in two inches of water. Blades of straw and plains grass floated among the bottles.

"Well, crap. They were iced down last night," the girl remarked.

"They're cold enough," he said, lifting out a bottle. Reaching in his pocket, he produced a multi-bladed knife and pushed out its bottle opener. He popped the caps off two beers and handed one to her. She took it and held it up to him.

"To your dad," she said, clinking their bottles together.

"Airborne," he responded.

"Airborne?" she giggled, crinkling her nose. "What's 'Airborne'?"

"Oh...I guess that does sound strange to a 'Leg'."

"A...what's a...'Leg', did you say?"

He chuckled at his reflexive use of Army jargon. "A 'Leg' is someone who's not a paratrooper. I mean, you're a 'straight leg', not Airborne-qualified. You're a civilian."

She took a long draw on her Coors, regarding him coyly over the tilted bottle. She looked down at her bare feet and pulled her dress up several inches. "But I do have legs, don't I?"

Danny felt his face flush. He clinked her bottle again. "Indeed you do, young lady." Then he tilted the bottle to his mouth and emptied it in four satisfying swallows.

"You saving these for anybody?" he asked, surveying the remaining bottles.

"They're all yours, baby. But, we've got to sit down. My feet are killing me."

The two young people spent the rest of the afternoon on the Chevy's couch-like front seat, talking and laughing. Connie had one more beer. Danny drank the rest. By the third beer, they were holding hands. After the fourth, he pulled her to him on the passenger side. Half way through the fifth, they were embracing passionately, his uniform jacket and Green Beret having been pitched into the back seat with her shoes.

"Baby, we have to be careful," she breathed between long, penetrating kisses.

Danny was lost in his passion for the girl. Taking a quick look around at the empty parking area, and the even emptier grassy plains surrounding the lonely cemetery, he pulled her dress up over her head. It joined the other clothing items in the back seat.

They made love three times over the next hour, Danny cradling her in his arms as they recovered.

On his first climax, he withdrew and directed his ejaculation to the rubber floor mat. "Oh, baby!" she had exclaimed. "Oh, yuckers!" The next two times, he remained inside her.

He was in the hospital in Japan when her letter announcing the pregnancy finally reached him. An embarrassed Army nurse had been reading the letter to him since his eyes were bloodshot and painfully swollen.

"Uh, maybe you'd better read this on your own, Sergeant, when you can see better."

"No, ma'am. Go ahead, please."

The nurse read through three more pages of the pregnant girl's professions of love and fear. "Please write to me," she implored. "I haven't heard from you for so long."

"Now, Sergeant," said the female nurse, a tall, willowy Captain, with a Texas drawl, "you're going to answer that girl's letter right now. You talk, I'll write. That's an order." The officer wasn't kidding. She pulled a metal chair close to his bed and took a pad and pen from the bedside table. She needn't have been concerned.

Danny was far from despondent at this turn of events. He was badly injured but, barring infection, his survival was not in doubt. But, that was all he knew for sure. He had the farm but didn't want to be a farmer. He liked the Army, but stateside duty he could not tolerate. Besides, Special Forces was on the Army shit list. He could end up reassigned to a 'Leg' unit. *No fucking way,* he thought.

Now, he had a girl back home who was carrying his child.

Suddenly, his whole life had a focus and direction he'd not felt since his training days back at Ft. Bragg. Of course, he didn't love the girl; not yet anyway. But, this was "duty," and he understood duty. Duty was no fucking problem.

He turned his blast-reddened face to the nurse, and grinned sheepishly. "Guess I'd better get my ass out of here and go marry that girl."

"Well…God bless you, Sergeant."

"Dear Connie," he began. "Sorry I haven't written. I've been kind of busy." The nurse wrote the words, then put her hand to her nose and stifled a sob.

~ * ~

They were married in Denver by an Army chaplain while Danny convalesced at Fitzsimmons Hospital. Danny wouldn't hear of a ceremony that couldn't be attended by the other wounded men in his bay, so the ceremony was held in a tiny chapel on the first floor of the patients' wing. Afterwards, the boisterous wedding party of ambulatory buddies, Connie's high school friends and family members celebrated with cupcakes and a smuggled bottle of champagne in a kitchen off the patients' bay. Connie's mother was so delighted that her very pregnant daughter was marrying her baby's father that the grim and austere surroundings were the furthest thing from her mind.

Baby Janon was born in the same hospital in Limon where Danny had been delivered twenty-one years before. His medical discharge in hand, the little family moved into the farmhouse and began the process of getting to know each other.

~ * ~

"I'd just got discharged at Fitzsimmons and we moved out to the farm. A month later, Connie's brother, Aaron, shows up. He moved out on his dad back in Dallas, and he'd been living in Santa Fe. Guess he thought he was going to sell Turquoise jewelry or some shit," Danny shifted in his rocking chair to alleviate the pressure on his wounded side.

"That still hurt?" asked Andrew.

"Only when I laugh." Danny tried to do his demonic grin, but could only produce a toothy grimace. He found a comfortable position and continued.

"So, anyway, the boy visits a few times. Stays with his mom in town a couple times, stays here a couple times. One visit he asks if he can hang around for a few weeks. I'm thinking, 'Shit, a few weeks. Go stay with your mom in town.' But, Connie begs me and I say 'OK'. What's funny is, he wants to live out in the barn. Kind of like a clubhouse, I guess. So we fix him up a bunk room out there and he's happy as shit. So, Aaron hangs around, drinks beer with me, we have a great time. A few times he disappears for a couple days, then shows up again. I'm starting to like the kid. One day he takes me aside, you know, all 'Secret Squirrelly' and says he's got a business proposition for me."

The story Danny told astonished Andrew with its sheer criminal simplicity. Aaron had a "friend" in Santa Fe who made a lot of money bringing up marijuana from Mexico and selling it through a loose network of distributors in a few western states. Indeed, Aaron worked intermittently for him in Santa Fe, and found that activity thrilling and lucrative. The friend employed a few drivers to make the long delivery drives. The Denver-Boulder territory had proven particularly lucrative and eventually absorbed all the product he could import.

Transporting the contraband was risky, and repeated use of the speedy direct approach up I-25 had cost the loss of several shipments due to the effective "profiling" of drivers by the Colorado State Police.

Aaron's friend had become intrigued by his descriptions of the farm his sister lived on far out on the state's eastern plains.

"What's the chance we could run up there through Lamar, store product at her farm, break it down to smaller shipments and then come in from the east?" the friend inquired. "Set it up, Aaron, and I'll cut you in for a piece."

Aaron was thrilled at the thought of easy money. "I'll check it out and let you know. My sister would be for it, but her husband is a weird dude. Ex- Green Beret. Got shot up in Vietnam. Haven't figured him out yet."

For his part, Danny was incredulous that Connie's ne'er-do-well brother would be involved in such a shady endeavor.

Aaron explained, "Look, man. All we need is a dry, safe place to stack a few pallets. We'll deliver it in a one-ton van so it won't draw attention. Then, occasionally, someone will drop by in a normal passenger car, pick up a few bundles, and head out for Denver. You get paid just for storing it and keeping quiet."

"How much money we talking about?"

"I think I can get you a grand a month."

Danny told Aaron he'd think about it after talking to Connie. Connie would have provided the service free of charge just to do something for her brother, but Danny put a pencil to his current situation. He collected $400 per month disability from the VA. Another $250 monthly came from 'unemployment' insurance from the State of Colorado, but that would be running out soon. He would get a payment from the farmer who was renting his crop land, assuming a profitable yield, and, lastly, he received another $250 monthly from the Department of Agriculture for letting some of his acreage lie fallow.

Hmm... he thought. *Property taxes will take the crop share. Connie's Chevy needs tires and a battery. Dad's truck is just about dead. Unemployment is running out. Unless we move to Denver or the Springs, I'm not going to find a job worth shit money. Connie wouldn't move at gunpoint anyway.*

"OK," he said to Aaron the next morning, "tell your buddy I'll go for it. They have to keep it low profile. I don't want more than a few pallets on my property at one time. I want them to come and go quickly. Never ever call me. Never ever show up unless I'm here. We can set up a schedule. No fucking around. Don't get drunk in town. Real quiet."

"Great." Aaron was clearly delighted at his impending windfall. "That's great!"

"Hold on," Danny interjected. "I want $1,500 a month. First payment in cash when they show up with the first shipment."

"Uh…, I'll take care of it," Aaron answered, swallowing hard. He didn't like the thought of trying to negotiate with his 'friend'. "I'll, uh, take care of it."

The Santa Fe friend chuckled as he told Aaron of his acceptance of the $1,500 payment. The friend, an olive-skinned, dark-haired man with wire-rimmed glasses, held up a hand as Aaron pleaded with him to believe he wasn't shaking him down.

"Forget it," the man said. "Your friend's not stupid. Time will tell if he's too smart for his own good." He didn't tell Aaron he'd have paid $2,500, maybe more, had it been demanded. After all, one bundle divided into "baggies" brought $1,500 at retail. All told, he was netting three times that much per day in his growing Denver Boulder enterprise.

Chapter 25
The Business

Two weeks later, a nondescript Chevy van pulled up in front of the farm house. A large Native American man emerged from the van and extended his hand to a nervous Danny.

"I'm Hawk. You Sevilla?"

"Yo."

The big man looked Danny up and down. "Hear you got the Silver Wings. I was with the 82nd up in I Corps. Airborne, all the way."

In spite of himself, a smile spread across Danny's face. "Airborne," he responded. "Call me 'Danny'." He regarded the man for a few seconds. "You Crow or Arapahoe?" he asked.

It was the man's turn to smile, though a bit self-consciously. "Dad was Crow, Mother Arapahoe."

Danny directed Hawk to back the van into the barn, then helped him unload two pallets of tightly packed bundles of Mexican marijuana. In short order the shipment was stacked innocuously in a corner and covered with a canvas tarp. Back outside, Hawk walked to the side of the barn and motioned Danny over. Reaching in the pocket of his thread-bare, Army field jacket, Hawk pulled out a folded manila envelope.

"Count it," he said.

"You're Airborne, brother," Danny said. "I know it's there."

Hawk looked at the ground, amused by Danny's nonchalance. Other men he'd dealt with in this dangerous business seemed near to soiling themselves in similar circumstances.

"Damn right it's there. And it always will be."

The first transfer of product occurred a week later when a Ford sedan pulled up in front of the farm house. Hawk and another man got out and stretched. Danny heard the car and walked out of the barn. Connie, who'd been nursing baby Janon in a rocker on the front porch, retreated into the house as the car slowed to turn from the main road. She watched curiously through a curtained front window.

Hawk introduced his passenger, a slender, dapper, Latin-looking man with a narrow face partly hidden behind dark, wire-rimmed glasses. "Danny, this is Mr. Boulé." He pronounced it "Boo Lay". "He's the big chief. Wants to check out your location."

"Boo Lay?" Danny repeated, taking an instant subliminal dislike for the man. As he shook Boulé's limp hand he asked, "Isn't that 'Frog' for 'Bullshit'?"

Speechless momentarily at the pejorative reference to the French people, the man just looked at Danny.

"Frog?" he said finally. "No, asshole. It's not. And I won't bother you with the correct pronunciation." Boulé was not amused by Danny's attempt at humor, if that's what it was, and tried, unsuccessfully, to stare him down. Hawk wished he had admonished Danny in advance about the man's humorlessness. Mr. Boulé was thinking to himself, *This prick doesn't show respect. That's not good.*

"Oh, my mistake," Danny said, still looking at the man. Turning to Hawk, he said, "So, you drawing down the inventory?"

He had them back the sedan through the barn's large doorway, then helped them load eight bundles into the trunk.

"That easy enough for you, wise ass?" Mr. Boulé said as he slammed the trunk closed. "In and out in ten minutes."

"No complaint from me," Danny offered. "Just don't drive through town honking the horn."

Boulé shook his head at Danny's irreverent attitude. "You know," he said, irritation rising in his voice, "we've got a damn good business going here. You keep your end of the fucking bargain. We'll keep ours."

~ * ~

Over the next few months, a simple routine was followed. The van would arrive from Santa Fe with pallets of product, Danny would help Hawk unload, then the man would disappear. Days later, Hawk would return in a sedan to take some bundles away.

Van deliveries became bi-weekly events. The sedan would return twice or, sometimes, three times a week. Hawk was always at the wheel. With each arrival of van or sedan, a schedule would be set for the next event.

Since Danny's phone service was a "party line," it obviously could not be used for "business," and he eventually had the service disconnected. He told his fretful wife, "Connie, if you need to use a phone, go up to Susan's place. I don't want to risk having Hawk or one of those other shit birds calling here. The whole county would listen in."

One day, driving through town, Danny noticed Hawk's van parked in a vacant garage near the I-70 interchange. He knocked on the door of the house next to the building and feigned interest in buying the vehicle to the old man who answered.

"Yeah, that's my building. Don't think the truck's for sale, though," said the man, running an arthritic hand over his ancient, bald head.

Moreover, he said he was making $150 a month to let a "big Injun fellow" store it there. "Sometimes he parks a car in there and takes the van. Kind of funny, but none of my business."

The Indian had access via a huge padlock, and the property owner thought it was a great arrangement. "A couple more deals like that," he said, "and I could move to Flora-dee."

Heading back home, Danny thought, *Hawk drives the van up from New Mexico, unloads at my place, then parks the empty van here. Takes the car and drives back to Denver. A while later, he drives back to Flag, picks up some product and takes it back to Denver. Then drives back here, gets in the van and drives back down to New Mexico for another shipment. Bet that boy's got a royal case of the 'rhoids' from driving around that much.*

As the business relationship went on, Danny and Hawk, the unlikely business partners, became good friends. Though Hawk's schedule of deliveries kept him moving, he often lingered at the farm to chat with Danny and his pretty young wife. Though from vastly different backgrounds, the men had colorful stories to share of their childhoods and, of course, their time in the Army.

Danny had little contact with other men in the area, though there was a tiny VFW post that he visited on the occasional weeknight. Those members had performed the graveside service for his father, a Navy veteran of World War II. However, he was the only Vietnam guy, and the older men considered him a curiosity--if they paid any attention to him at all. He preferred instead to wander the fields and stream beds, work on the old flatbed, repair fences or other farm chores. So, Hawk's frequent visits became events he looked forward to.

Baby Janon was also a big fan of Hawk, spending many sunny afternoons perched on his lap, jabbering happily as he spoon-fed her from jars of minced fruit. Connie, sensing his innate affection for children, found she could leave Janon in the care of the two men and run into town for groceries and errands without concern. Had Hawk not been there, Danny would have insisted she take the baby along due to the constant attention her care required.

On one visit, after the pallets had been unloaded in their customary corner, Hawk pulled a long, blanket-wrapped object from behind the van's driver's seat.

Beaming, he handed it to his friend. "Careful. Don't hurt yourself," he said.

Danny took the item, eyes widening as he felt its weight and familiar shape. "A rifle?" he asked.

"Not just any rifle."

"Holy shit!" Danny exclaimed, a huge smile spreading across his face. "An M-14." He dropped the blanket on the barn floor and held the weapon up to inspect it. Instinctively, he removed the magazine, pulled back the bolt and locked it open. Then he swung it skyward, butt first, and looked down the muzzle.

"Wow, man. Clean as a whistle. Where'd you get this?"

"Happy Grass isn't all these white men deal in," Hawk answered, matter-of-factly. "Don't ask me more."

Unable to take his eyes from the rifle, Danny sited down the barrel and ran his hands over it again. "OK, I'll take it. How much you want for it?'

"It's yours. No wampum."

"Come on. Don't bullshit me, Crazy Horse. I'll pay you for it."

"Crazy Horse was Lakota. Don't insult me, fucking white man," Hawk said, trying to stifle a grin. He stepped to the truck and rooted behind the seat again, this time bringing out a box of 7.62 millimeter ammunition. "Let's load up and see if you can still remember how to fire one of these."

"No fucking problem," Danny said, as he began pushing the long brass cartridges into the magazine.

Hawk, rubbing his face with a large hand, chuckled audibly, drawing a glance from his friend. "What's so damn funny?" Danny asked.

"Just the irony of an Indian giving a firearm to a white man. Grandfather is turning over in his plot up at Lodge Grass."

Chapter 26
The Sideline

As the story became more involved, the beer flowed freely and Andrew had to excuse himself. The toilet flushed and he walked back into the living room. Danny had gone to the refrigerator for two more beers.

"Damn bladder's only good for two beers," Andrew said with irritation. "When I was up at IU, I could drink a six-pack before taking a leak."

"Getting old's a bitch, my man," Danny said, handing his friend another beer.

Andrew took it and, glassy-eyed, said, "This is the last one, buddy. I've got to get going soon. Can't drive back to Denver blasted out of my gourd."

"No sweat, man. That's most of the story anyway. Hawk is…"

"Wait a minute," Andrew exclaimed suddenly. "Hawk…shit, I think I met your buddy."

Danny's eyebrows arched. "Really? Where?"

Andrew scratched his head and took a drink from the fresh bottle. "Is he a big dude?"

"Yeah. Maybe six feet two, 200 pounds, shoulder-length black hair."

"Month or two ago…I was still living in my old place, a real shit hole over on Logan Street. I was sitting on the porch one Saturday night. Must have had five beers, I'm getting drunk. This big Indian guy comes up on the porch. Bunch of other guys with him. Looks me over, says they're looking for a place to crash for the night. I tell him to help himself, you know, the place has a common area plus the porch."

"Sounds like Hawk."

"Well, he's pretty friendly so we shoot the shit for a minute. His friends are pissed off that he's talking to me. So, I notice he's got on a pair of Corcorans and I ask if he's Airborne. It was kind of funny because he thought I had psychic powers or something. Looked at me real funny. Anyway, I tell him, '…the Corcorans'. He's all relieved and we have a good laugh."

"I can't believe this shit," Danny said, shaking his head in disbelief. "That's Hawk for sure."

"You know, when that van drove by when I was at Susan's, I thought the driver looked familiar. That was Hawk, right?"

"That was him. Holy shit."

Andrew thought for a moment, his beer buzz giving him a wave of euphoria. "I'm not sure I should tell you the rest," he said.

"So, have I been holding out on you, Lieutenant Ass Hole?" Danny said, with mock disgust.

"That's a negative, Drill Sergeant," Andrew responded. In his buzz he looked around as if to see if anyone could overhear, then spoke again.

"He had a huge wad of bills in his pocket. I was drunk enough to ask him where he got it. He says, I shit you not, 'selling happy grass to the Hippies.'"

Danny clapped his hand over his face in annoyance. "No God damn shit? That stupid son of a bitch."

"Hey, I hope I didn't get him in trouble. It's none of my business, but…"

"Nah, don't worry about it," Danny remarked, shaking his head again.

The men said nothing for a minute. Danny seemed to be pondering something. Andrew stood and went to the bookcase. Retrieving the CAR-15 magazine, he sat down again and examined the object closely.

"Amazing," he began, "how this thing doesn't have a mark on it, even though that AK round hit about an inch away…"

Danny nodded. "Not to mention those `yards that got greased right in front of us and we didn't get a scratch. You ever think about that?"

"Sometimes," Andrew responded, his beer buzz evaporating as quickly as it had come. "Sometimes, when I'm drunk. Then I just drink some more."

Danny chuckled at this. He slapped Andrew on the knee and began to laugh heartily. Andrew also began to laugh, and the mood of the men lightened again.

"Look," Danny said, becoming serious suddenly, "I'll tell you the rest, but you've really got to promise…"

"Airborne."

Danny held up a hand in acknowledgment. "Hawk and me," he said, then paused to take a drink, "Hawk and me are doing a little side business."

"What kind of side business?"

"Well, one day it occurred to us that we got beaucoup weed out there in the barn. So much of it comes and goes, it's hard to keep track of it. So, we decide, what the fuck, we can take a bundle every once in a while and, you know, sell it ourselves."

"Whoa."

"Yeah."

"OK, so…"

"So, we pilfer a little bit, not much you understand, just a little. We bag it up and sell it in Denver. You remember that night at Lucky's? I sold a half- dozen baggies in an hour. Made $150 before I saw you hanging out at the bar."

"Shit. What do you do, stand in the back of the pickup and yell, 'Weed for sale'?"

"No fucking way. It's a little more trouble, but not much. It's like this. Connie and me go to a dance club, you know, like the Lemon Tree, Lucky's, Aurora Lounge…there's a million of them. Connie hangs at the bar like she's alone. Guys ask her to dance. She only dances with dudes that have a certain 'look', like they're city studs, you know, gold chains, tight pants. She avoids cowboys. So, second or third dance she says something like, 'Baby, I am so buzzed. I just hit some really great grass'." Danny used his time-honored falsetto voice to mimic Connie. "Well, almost without fail, they go, 'Do you know where I can get some?' She goes, 'Well, maybe baby, but you're not a cop are you?' They shit all over themselves to prove they're not cops, you know, pulling out their driver's licenses, business cards, whatever."

Andrew is intrigued. "Holy shit."

"So, she walks back to the dude's table, takes his money, asks what kind of car he has and where it's parked. We wait for the next song, and I ask her to dance. While we're dancing she tells me how much he bought and where his car is. I drop her off at the table after the song, get the weed from my pickup, find the dude's car and stick the weed behind a tire. I come back in and walk by their table as a signal to Connie and she tells the dude to go get his weed. Off he goes to the parking lot. Sometimes they walk back in all happy and want to dance some more, you know, try to pick up Connie. Sometimes they just get the weed and take off."

"Wow. So, how much you make doing that?"

Danny gave a sly smile. "$500 a weekend, give or take."

Andrew whistled. "So, $2,000 a month, tax free…"

"Don't forget, I'm getting $1,500 for storing the weed in my barn."

Andrew was stunned. He gave his head a quick shake as if to clear his mind. "I guess that would cover the pickup payment."

"Shit. That's only $225."

"So, what happens if the big boys find out you're ripping them off?"

Danny seemed to dismiss that possibility. "I'll just tell them the same thing that black lady in Louisville said."

"Black lady?" Andrew was momentarily stumped. Then, "Oh, that one on the way to the whorehouse?"

"Yeah. Remember what she yelled when she walked out of that honky-tonk?"

"Y'ALL", Andrew bellowed, Danny joining in the refrain, "can just kiss my big fat BLACK ASS!"

Laughter of remembrance rolled from the two friends.

Collecting himself, Danny added, "Besides, they're a long way off in Santa Fe. There's this one guy, Mr. Boulé, comes by every once in a while to check things out. Rides around with Hawk. He's a pussy."

"You'd think guys in that business would be bad dudes."

"Oh, well…," Danny shrugged.

"So, how 'bout Hawk?"

"Works Capitol Hill," Danny replied. "Beaucoup fucking Hippies everywhere, as you well know. He humps Colfax between the Red Beret Tavern and the Trumpet Lounge. He also hangs around that laundromat across the street from the Fast Mart on Corona."

Andrew nodded. "Yeah. I put in phones for Hippies all day long. None of them seem to have jobs. Just wander around looking for parties."

"Great life, huh?" Danny chuckled. He tilted his beer and, noticing it was empty, began twisting the bottle in his hands. "Hawk makes more off those jerk-offs than I do at the clubs. Of course, he puts in more hours."

"Amazing. What about those guys he hangs with? Are they in on it?"

"Nah. They're just some of his buddies from the 'Res. Fuckers follow him around like baby ducks. They watch his back and he pays for their whiskey."

"They were sure shit-faced when I saw them," Andrew recalled. "Well, if I see him again, I won't say I know you."

"That's a good idea…"

"Man, forget it. I'm not saying a thing to anybody. This is your deal. I won't cause problems."

"Thanks." Danny shifted again to ease the strain on his wound. Fatigue was beginning to show in his face.

Andrew glanced at his Seiko. "I'd better get going."

"Yeah. Connie will be coming back soon. You'll never get out of here if she sees you. She'll want you to stay for dinner, play with Janon, you know, all that domestic bullshit."

Andrew finished his beer and the two men stood up.

"Another thing about Connie," Danny said as they walked to the LeMans. "God damn married girls, they hate to see a single man walking around. She'll try to fix you up with her cousin, Carol."

"Tell her I fell in love with Susan."

"That will work, for a while anyway."

Chapter 27
The Sunset

Andrew Starkey had another typical work week of ten-hour days, dozens of installations, many miles of city driving and many poles climbed. Given the continuing tenderness of the wounds on his chest and arms, he tried to avoid climbing with his "hooks" and, instead, used one of his ladders from the roof of his truck. But, the necessity to move around at the top of the poles eventually forced him to forego the safer alternative. After some initial anxiety, he strapped on his hooks, found his rhythm and soon put the painful fall in the back of his mind.

As the days went by, his excitement grew at the upcoming date with Susan. On Saturday morning, he caught Bob in the garage and asked a favor.

"Hey, Boss," he yelled over the noise of trucks and shouting men. "I got a hot date tonight. You OK with me clearing out at three-thirty?"

"You gonna get laid, Starkey?"

"Doubt it. This one's got some class. Got to move slow."

"Well, bullshit, boy. Promise me you'll try to fuck her and you can have off. Otherwise…"

"OK, boss," Andrew laughed. "I'll try real hard."

"Take flowers."

"Boss, where in hell am I going to get flowers?"

"King Soopers. Get it done, boy."

Oscar greeted him with the rope toy as he stepped from the car. He looked towards the house and, not seeing the woman, began playing with the dog. After a third toss and retrieval, Andrew heard the door open and turned to see Susan walk out on the porch.

Wow, he thought to himself. *What a tough babe.*

She smiled broadly and waved. "Hi there, cowboy. I see you're still getting a good character reference."

Andrew was puzzled, then remembered what she was referring to. "Oh, yeah. He won't take money, so I have to do the fetch routine."

She wore a tight denim skirt that was hemmed two inches above the knee. An off-center slit provided ease of movement for her long, tanned legs. A brown leather belt cinched a white blouse at her waist, accentuating her large breasts. Her blonde hair flowed to her shoulders, and braided strands on either side were pulled back and fastened together by a gold spring clip.

"You look fabulous," he said, almost reflexively.

Susan smiled at the compliment. "So do you."

"Yeah, right. Sorry I'm a little wrinkled, but I'm clean." At the garage, he'd changed into his best Levis and a dark-brown Izod sport shirt, the trademark alligator on the left breast.

"Did you have something to eat?"

"I was counting on some popcorn," he said.

"Come on in the house. We've got time for hors d'oeuvres. It's only ten minutes to town and there's never a line at the Plainsman."

"Oh, uh, just a minute." Andrew went back to the car and pulled the seat forward. From the rear he grabbed her novel and a bundle of newspaper-wrapped cut flowers. Walking towards her, he extended the flowers. "These are for you."

She was clearly touched by the gift. "My goodness. Thank you, Andrew. Why, they're beautiful." She lifted the bundle to her nose. "My goodness."

A tray of bacon-wrapped water chestnuts sat on the stove top. Wine glasses were arranged on the small table and a bottle of French Pinot Noir had been opened, the cork resting on a ceramic coaster.

"Do you drink wine?" she asked.

"Sure," he fibbed. "I'm a beer guy, but wine's OK every once in a while."

"I figured as much. These little things taste so good with a red wine." She poured them both a half glass, then pushed a few of the hors d'oeuvres on to each small plate with her finger.

"Try one," she said.

Andrew examined the morsels closely, having never before seen such an odd combination. He selected one and put it in his mouth, extracting the toothpick skewer as he did. They were still very warm from the oven, and he had to take a quick sip of wine to cool his mouth.

"Umm..." he uttered through closed lips. He chewed and swallowed. "Wow. Those things are great. Hot, but great."

"Knew you'd like them. They're my favorite."

He devoured two more quickly and drank the remainder of his wine.

Susan sipped her wine and watched her guest examine the morsels. He continued to hold the paperback.

"So, did you...," she said, reaching under the table and tapping the book as it rested on his leg.

Andrew swallowed again quickly, nodding his head. "Yes. I read your book," he said, laying it on the table. She poured him more wine and he took another sip.

"I really liked it. You're very talented."

"It's probably the only one I've done that a man could stand to read," she said with a dismissive wave of her hand. "I usually follow a formula, kind of like 'young woman lives with widowed father on small ranch, Native Americans resent their presence and try to drive them away, mysterious handsome cowboy appears from nowhere, father dies, handsome cowboy fills the paternal void, befriends the Native Americans and saves the day. Everyone lives happily ever after'."

He nodded. "Yeah, like Jimmy Stewart movies." Then, fearing he may have offended her, quickly added, "But I read a lot of western history while I was at IU. I don't think there are many girls that know about Cheyenne 'Dog Soldiers' and 'cartridge-converted 1860 Army Colts'. That kind of detail adds a lot."

"Indiana University?" she said, an eyebrow rising. "So, you have a degree?"

"Not yet. Still have a couple years to go. I, uh, dropped out and got drafted."

"Ahh," she said. "I bet there's quite a story there." As she watched him, a shadow of unease crossed his face.

"Oh," he replied, "an author like you would call it a short story."

"But you'll tell it to me, won't you?" The words were coy and flirty.

"Susan, I've got a feeling…"

The woman chuckled at his reluctance to discuss his youth and returned to the former topic.

"You've no idea how hard it was for a 'girl' (she made quote marks in the air with her fingers) to understand how one could convert a cap-and-ball pistol to use metal cartridges. I finally found this old jerk in Limon who knew all about such things. Unfortunately, he was a drunk as well as a jerk. Cost me a bottle of Wild Turkey to get him to talk." She smiled as she recalled the meeting. "That's the penance I pay to the gods of authenticity."

"Gods of authenticity," Andrew repeated the phrase. "Jeez…"

~ * ~

Flagstaff consisted of a town center formed by two intersecting thoroughfares; one coming north from the highway, lined with agricultural businesses and capped at the end by a grain elevator--and the other, Main Street, running east and west, lined with retail shops, a restaurant, a bar and the Plainsman Theatre. He parked the Pontiac on Main among battered pickup trucks. The theatre marquee read "EZ

Rider." As Susan predicted, there was no line and they walked directly to the window and bought tickets. An old man carefully counted two dollars change from the five-dollar bill. He drooled on one of the bills before sliding the money through the window slot. Andrew took the bills without comment and put them in his wallet.

Susan had her hand to her mouth as Andrew held the door for her. Inside, she stuck her tongue out and made a nauseated face.

"Yuckers," she exclaimed. "I'd have thrown that dollar away."

"Why?" he asked, smiling. "I'll just give it back to him when we buy popcorn."

"If he pops it, I won't eat it," she said.

"We're in luck," Andrew said, taking her arm and directing her towards the snack counter. "The snack bar kid is between drooling ages."

After purchasing popcorn, Andrew glanced down the aisle of the dark theater. There were dozens of empty seats. Several teen couples already occupied the back row.

"Let's stay out here until the previews start," he said. "Looks like we've got a few minutes. You can explain, 'Yuckers' to me."

They went back outside and stood together eating popcorn on the sidewalk. The summer sun was still well above the horizon, and a warm breeze blew from the west. A tumble weed rolled lazily down the center of the street, startling two magpies that were picking at a flattened prairie dog carcass.

"'Yuckers' is an odd little Flagstaff colloquialism. I picked it up from Connie."

"Gets the point across," he said.

A memory came to him. "You know, when I saw this movie in Sydney, I waited in line for forty-five minutes. Then it sold out, so I got a ticket for the next showing." He flashed a grin. "I went in this pub next door to wait. These Australian sailors were in there, just back from overseas. Started buying me beers. I was shit-faced when the movie started." He paused for a moment, and tilted his head, as if to recall something. Failing to gain the memory, he resumed eating popcorn.

Susan watched him with amusement for several seconds while he surveyed the dusty main street. A wind gust came up and Andrew turned his face into it, a barely discernible smile of contentment on his lips. Almost inaudibly, he whispered, "God, freedom."

She started to say something, decided against it, and continued to watch him a second longer.

"Hey," she said, finally. "Earth to Andrew."

He turned to her. "Was I gone that long?"

"Just a few moments. But I was afraid you wouldn't come back."

"Come back? From where?"

"From wherever that memory took you."

"Uh...,"

"Memories can be tricky things," she said, tugging idly at a button on his shirt. "They can move you from one life context to another completely different one."

"O...K," he said, with an inflection that he knew she would continue.

She gave him another coy smile. "I'm enjoying getting to know you, but I think there may be more than one Andrew. I want to get to know the Andrews one at a time."

He put a hand on her shoulder and turned her towards the door. "Come on, Susan. Show time."

~ * ~

"That was the ugliest man I've ever seen," Susan said as they walked back to the LeMans.

"You mean the guy with the shot gun?"

"Yes," she hissed. "It looked like he had a doorknob sown under the skin on his neck. Yuckers."

She directed him to drive a circuitous route through the countryside to the north of the small town. The county roads were on a precise north-south, east-west grid requiring many ninety-degree turns. Their route descended steeply into stream drainages, then climbed just as steeply up the far sides.

As they drove, she prodded him to talk about himself, his family, his home in Indiana. He talked easily through his early life in New Vernon, providing details about his parents, sister and friends. When he told her of the road trip to Colorado after high school, she perceived a warming in his recollections.

"Have you ever seen the Collegiate Peaks?" he asked. "I mean, can you imagine having lived where the tallest thing around is an oak tree, and then seeing those mountains."

"Yes, I've driven through the area a few times. Those are magnificent mountains," she agreed. "We stopped at a hot springs near there once. It was so much fun. I hated to leave."

Andrew gave a wistful nod. "I've been there," he said. "Would you believe...?"

He seemed reluctant to finish his thought.

"Would I believe...what?" she asked.

"That hot spring. It's like that was the first day of my life."

Suddenly, he braked the Pontiac to a sliding stop on the gravel road. Several antelope bolted across the road in front of them.

"Oh, aren't they gorgeous," Susan said. "I've always loved those critters."

Andrew watched the Pronghorns disappear into a grove of cottonwoods, then shifted into first gear and began climbing up a steep hill. The car's rear wheels spun in the loose gravel and he shifted quickly to second. A plume of dust spread out behind them as the wheels gained traction.

Susan shifted to face him. "Now, this is getting interesting, Andrew. I should warn you. I was Journalism major with a 'Psych' minor. Let's explore this 'first day of my life' theme. I suspect there's a Freudian sexual aspect to this story."

Andrew directed a crooked smile at her. "Don't I get to recline on a leather couch, doc?" he joked.

It was her turn to become distracted by another thought. "My ex-husband got his doctorate at IU," she said, flatly. "Political Science."

Andrew had noticed her earlier interest when he first mentioned IU and assumed it was due to her hope that he was well along in his education.

"A Ph.D.?" he responded. "Must be a smart guy."

She shook her head. "In some respects."

Andrew read the disappointment in her voice. "Not the first guy with a lot of diplomas and not a lick of common sense, huh?"

"Oh," she began, "it takes two to tango. He was this new hot-shot assistant professor at CU. I was a star-struck grad assistant. We were married way too soon."

"In Boulder?"

"Yes, 1967. It was quite a social event in the 'Movement'."

"Movement?"

"Anti-war," she answered. "Alan's friends from all over the country came. Several of the 'heavies', you know, Jerry, Tom and Jane, David and Joan, William. It was a 'who's who' of the anti-war crowd. I expected John Lennon to walk up any second."

"Wow. Glad I wasn't there."

She directed a surprised look at him. "Don't be like that, Andrew. Those people are very sincere. They want to end this stupid war."

Andrew didn't respond as the car slid to a stop at a 'T' intersection. He turned to her and smiled. "Which way, your highness?"

"Your highness?"

"You became a 'princess' in the 'Movement', right?"

"Well, I'm glad you know your place," she purred. "Left."

The road climbed steeply for a few hundred yards, then flattened abruptly offering an expansive view to the west.

"Turn here," she said. He steered the car between limestone fence posts. She pointed west towards a barbed-wire fence line. "Over there."

The LeMans rolled to a stop, the sun flooding through the windshield. "Oh, man," he whispered. The sun's disk was just touching the horizon. Almost immediately, a golden blush filled the sky. "Did you plan this?"

"I'm a princess, remember?"

"Can we walk?" he asked, innocently. "I mean, are we trespassing? I don't want us to get shot."

"Don't worry. Friends of my dad own it."

As Andrew stepped from the car, he was entranced by the vast expanse of prairie. Pike's Peak bulged to the southwest beyond the thread of I-70, barely discernible in the distance. Silent trucks and cars moved as if on a conveyor belt. The stillness of the place was palpable.

Susan walked to him and took his hand. "Not bad, huh?"

"Unbelievable," he answered, still taking in the view. He raised their entwined fingers to his lips and kissed the back of her hand.

Her mouth opened slightly but the tender gesture left her speechless.

Arriving at the fence, they stepped through an opening and sat down on a limestone post that lay discarded on the ground. Neither spoke until the sun's last orange sliver disappeared into the blue-tinged horizon.

"God, that was gorgeous," he sighed. "It just doesn't get any better than that."

Susan had carried her purse along and was now rummaging in it. She pulled out a plastic bag and a book of matches.

"This can make it even better," she said. "Do you mind?"

Andrew looked down at the bag, then at her. The bag contained joints. "Uh, no, of course not."

"Yes you do. I can see it in your face."

"No, really. You just surprised me." He put his arm around her and squeezed her shoulder gently. "Whatever you want…"

Susan seemed confused by his reaction. "You've smoked pot before, haven't you, Andrew?"

"Never have. Remember? I'm a beer guy."

She took a joint from the bag, lit it, and took a deep drag, holding the smoke in her lungs for several seconds. She exhaled and closed her eyes. Scooting next to him, she lifted the joint to his mouth. "Come on. This stuff is amazing."

He squeezed her shoulder again. "It's all yours."

She stared up at him quizzically for a moment, then looked back towards the orange afterglow. "Wow. Would you just look at that color?" She took another drag and rested her head against his arm. "Unreal."

They sat quietly for quite some time, each enjoying the view of the vast rolling prairie, the darkening hump of Pikes Peak and, soon enough, the distant, emerging head- and tail-light procession of vehicles on the highway. Stars were beginning to flood the sky and, behind them, the dusky face of a three-quarter moon had risen.

"Were you ever a flower child, a 'Hippy'?" he asked her.

"No, not really. I dressed up a bit when Alan and I were together. It seemed like I needed some tie dye and denim to fit in. He was always in jeans and a tweed jacket, of course. That's the standard uniform of the male left wing, academic elitist and those that emulate them. Add round, wire-rim glasses, blue work shirt, some beat-up Keds, and you're 'de rigueur'."

She sat up straight and looked up at him. "I know the pot hit a nerve with you. Is this going to ruin our chance to be friends?"

"Susan, I promise, I'm not mad." He sorted his thoughts. "Where I'm coming from, it won't make sense to you."

She smiled expectantly. "I want to know. Talk to me."

"You left out a critical item of that uniform."

"Uh, hmm. OK, I give up."

"The pot. Weed. Marijuana."

"How so?"

"What's more 'de rigueur' than a stoned Hippy at a peace rally?" he said. "Of course, they don't 'wear' it, but without it, most of the peace people wouldn't show up to protest. It's not a war protest. It's a fucking party using poor slob soldiers as an excuse."

"Andrew, didn't you and Danny smoke pot in Vietnam? Come on. All you Vietnam guys smoked pot, did drugs. I know you did."

He fought the impulse to laugh at her ignorance. "Susan, I never saw a joint during the year I was in Southeast Asia. Not one. No drugs. Never did any, never saw any, never saw anyone else smoking weed, taking pills, nothing." His voice had begun to rise, and he stopped talking to let the tension pass. In a moment, he said, "What other bull shit have you taken as gospel?"

In the growing darkness, he couldn't read her face, but knew he hurt her feelings.

Andrew glanced down at the glowing hands of his Seiko. "Hey," he whispered to the top of her head. "It's getting late. Oscar may be getting worried."

She didn't answer for a moment, then brushed ashes from her denim skirt. Raising her arms over her head, she stretched and yawned. "He knows I'm with you," she said.

She found his hand and pulled him up as she came to her feet.

"And I've got a chunk of I-70 to go yet," he said, doing his own brief stretch.

She suddenly pressed her body to him and draped her arms around his neck. Cocking her head, she said, "You mean you're not staying with me?"

He wrapped his arms around her and kissed her, gently at first, then hungrily as her passion for him became apparent. Many long kisses and embraces followed, both lost in discovery of the other person. At one point, he hugged her tightly and lifted her from the ground. When she wrapped her legs around his waist, he fought the urge to make love to her there on the prairie.

"Susan, Susan, hey…sweetie," he tried to stem her passion. "Let's go home."

"You bastard," she breathed as he held her. Kissing him one more time, she let her legs fall to the ground. "Yes, my dear. We do need to find a bed."

Back at her house, Oscar galloped to meet them from his doghouse at the end of the driveway. Susan opened the unlocked door to her kitchen and pulled Andrew into the darkness. Her passion returned, and she pulled his shirt tail out and ran her finger nails up his back. As her fingers moved to his chest, Andrew suddenly gasped in pain.

"Ahh, wait…Susan, honey, ow."

"Oh, I'm sorry, babe. I forgot you're hurt."

He took off the Izod carefully and threw it over a chair. Returning to her, she ran her nails lightly through the soft hair of his chest. A dozen red welts stood out against his pale skin.

"You poor baby," she cooed, and began kissing his chest between the punctures. "Is that better?"

"Much," he sighed, closing his eyes and running his hands through her long hair. "Much better…"

~ * ~

Oscar's bark awoke them the next morning. Andrew lifted the

curtain of the bedroom window and watched a white van disappear in a dust trail as it headed down the hill to Danny's place. He lay back on the warm bed and saw that Susan was awake and looking at him. A sheepish grin appeared on her face.

"Good morning," she murmured, licking her dry lips. "Water."

He leaned over and kissed her on the forehead. "Good morning, your highness."

A glass of water sat on her nightstand and he reached for it. "Want me to get you some fresh?"

"No, anything will do." She guzzled the water. "Oh, wonderful. Thank you." She lay back on the bed, still smiling at him.

Andrew caressed her face with his hand. Impulsively, he took the sheet and pulled it down.

"Holy shit," he said, almost reverently, taking in the view of her naked body. "You are one beautiful girl."

Large, well-formed breasts rested on her chest, still retaining their youthful density, and where her long legs came together, a neat patch of light-brown pubic hair confirmed the naturalness of the blonde tresses that cascaded around her face.

She let his eyes linger for a time, then pulled the sheet back in place. "Why, thank you. It's nice to be ogled from time to time." She tugged his arm and pulled him to her side.

"I've got goat breath," he said. "I'll be right back."

He rolled out of bed and walked to her tiny bathroom. Finding a tube of paste, he squeezed some on his finger and massaged it onto his teeth and tongue. After a minute, he cupped his hands and sipped warm water from the vessel they formed. He sloshed and spit several times then grinned into the mirror to confirm an adequate result. Crawling back into bed, he slid next to her and took her in his arms, hugging her lustily. He rolled on to his back, pulling her on top. As her hair fell over their faces she kissed him, then slid her lips to his neck. He was very erect now and moved his hand down to guide himself into her.

"My…God," he breathed.

Susan drew her knees up and pushed down on him. Putting her hands on his shoulders, she lowered her head to view the place where their bodies joined. Responding now to his movement, she looked back into his eyes, a glow of serene pleasure on her face. Reaching a hand down, she began touching herself. Moments later, she reached a moaning climax that spasmed through her body for nearly a minute. Halfway through, Andrew lost his own control and joined her in orgasm.

Another hour passed before they woke again. Andrew reached for his Seiko that lay on the floor near his jeans.

"Ten," he said, groggily. "What am I doing in bed at 10AM?"

"Fucking the brains out of a friend," Susan muttered, answering his rhetorical question.

He showered first and held the curtain for her as she next stepped into the hot water stream.

From the shower, she called, "Can you make coffee?"

"Yo."

A rich smell of brewed coffee greeted her in the kitchen. Andrew was outside on the porch reading the Sunday Denver Post, the paper having been delivered in the pre-dawn darkness to the box at the entry to the driveway. Oscar lay contentedly at his feet. She picked up the mug he'd poured for her, opened the kitchen door and felt the cool breeze on her face. Tightening the cloth belt of her robe, she walked out and joined him.

She draped her arm over his neck and kissed him on the cheek.

"So…" she said, rubbing her head against his shoulder. "So…"

He smiled at her. "So, what?"

"So, where did you learn that 'feet on the shoulders' thing you did to me last night?"

"Fort Benning."

She laughed out loud. "You didn't learn that in the Army," she said, watching his face. "Did you?"

He tried hard not to laugh himself. "Infantry School. When attacking a fortified position, it's important to bring pressure on the flanks first."

She hid her face in her hands. "Stop it!" she laughed.

~ * ~

Andrew stood and looked out towards Danny's farm. The white van was backed into the barn's open door.

Susan started flipping through the newspaper. "Do, uh…" she began. "Do you know about Danny's business?"

He turned to look at her, nervous surprise on his face. "No," he said. "I mean, wheat, his disability payments. He does OK, I guess."

"Connie told me that Danny told you everything."

Andrew became somewhat agitated. "Susan…"

"Now don't be mad, babe. I've known what's going on for a while. Connie and I are pretty close and, uh, she really wanted to tell someone she could trust about it."

"She shouldn't have."

"And then, last night, when you told me how you felt…" she hesitated. "Your friend is in 'that' business. How could I know you were so different?"

He shook his head. "Susan, Danny's no more a drug user than I am. He's got his reasons for doing what he's doing but, trust me, it's not because he wants it for himself."

She licked the rim of the mug to cool it, then took a sip of coffee. "He just gives me the little I use," she said. "On occasion, I've taken orders for friends in Denver. I tell them to meet him at such and such club."

Andrew shook his head again, this time in frustration. "You're all crazy."

Susan kept pushing. "He likes to get Connie stoned."

"I know," Andrew responded. "That drive between Aurora and Limon can be pretty boring." After a few moments of silence the two began to laugh hysterically.

She too knew the story. "I'm here taking care of little Janon, giving them a night out. Danny's driving along in his pickup, Connie's head… bobbing up and down…" she began to laugh again. "Oh, that poor woman."

In a moment he turned serious. "Uh, last night…I have to assume it was the weed that made you so passionate."

"It played a role last night. How was I this morning?"

"Wow."

"Babe, I don't need pot to respond to a good man."

A puff of breeze lifted a section of the newspaper and Andrew stomped his foot on it to keep it from blowing into the yard. He gathered up the loose paper and sat his heavy coffee mug atop the pile.

Sitting back beside her, he said, "Let's just keep this between you and me, OK? I really like you. You're something special. What Danny does is his problem, not yours or mine."

Oscar appeared with the rope toy and Andrew pitched it away for him.

"Susan, your dad is the sheriff, if I recall?"

"Yes, you know he is."

Chuckling, he began, "I met some CIA guys in…overseas. Crazy bastards, always wore civies, you know, civilian clothes. Carried sterile 1911 Colts. Anyway, they used to joke about (he did quote marks with his fingers), 'plausible deniability'." He took her chin in his fingers and turned her face towards him. "'Plausible deniability' is what you want to maintain."

Susan rubbed his arm and said nothing more about Danny. Taking another sip from her large mug, she said, "You know, another good character measure is how a man makes coffee. You passed again."

"Whew."

She rested her chin on his shoulder. "Andrew?"

"Hmm?"

"What on earth is a 'sterile 1911 Colt'?"

Chapter 28
The Movement

After throwing on jeans and a T-shirt, Susan took Andrew for a walk through the tall grass prairie east of her house, Oscar galloping happily around the two. On a hillside, a dilapidated windmill yet pulled a trickle of water from the aquifer hundreds of feet below, partially filling a stock tank.

"When I was little," she began, "I used to sneak up here and soak in this tank. Cows would stand off to the side waiting for me to leave."

Her remembrance was interrupted as they noticed the white van head back towards town.

"Like you were saying?" Andrew put his hands on her shoulders and turned her gently away from the distant, dusty road.

"Yuckers," she said, glancing into the tank. "The pump used to bring up a lot more water. This stuff is rancid."

Andrew took his own look. "Not rancid. Just a little accumulated Magpie shit."

He asked, "Which did you prefer? Flagstaff or California?"

She thought a moment before responding. "Well, it's great to be a child in a farm town. I mean, kids are treated like just another crop. Always watched, but never over tended. But," she continued, "as a teenager, it's a bit bleak. California was paradise by comparison."

They left the windmill and continued to stroll towards a rise. At the crest, Flagstaff could be seen in the distance as a dense cluster of trees and buildings between their viewpoint and I-70.

"But, after high school, I wanted so badly to come home to Colorado. CU was the only school I applied to." She spread her arms and tip-toed along a toppled limestone post. "Sold my first work in Boulder, while I was married."

"They actually allow people to earn paychecks there? I thought everyone was on a trust fund."

"Andrew…" she scolded, "so young and so cynical."

He gave her a sheepish grin. "Would you…Your husband…?"

She took his hand and reversed herself on the limestone beam. "Hmm…" she seemed to ponder a response. "First, let me ask you a very personal question. Was I…did you…like making love to me?"

Andrew looked at her with surprise. "Are you kidding?" he asked.

"No." She wanted a response.

"Susan, you are the loveliest, most passionate lady I've ever made love to. How's that?"

"Sorry to be so direct. But, my husband seemed to want to get laid everywhere but at home." She sat down on the post and pulled him to sit with her. "We married six months after I met him," she began. "I was a student, on top of the world that I'd snagged such a stud professor. Kept him entertained for about a year. Then, as he became somewhat of a local celebrity in the 'Movement', he started screwing all the anti-war groupies. God…It was like he'd give this impassioned speech down at the commons. Hundreds of people would be there with their signs, chanting slogans, campus police trying to control the crowd. And, after all that, his main focus seemed to be finding a cute groupie to fuck." She raised her face in parody. "He'd just project his earnest chin, bite his lower lip and you could just hear the panties going down all over Boulder."

"Yuckers," Andrew said. He waited for her reaction, delivered as an irritated sock to his arm by her fist. He began to laugh. "I'm sorry," he said, straightening his face. "I know it's not funny."

Susan gripped the arm she'd just socked with both hands and shook him gently. "Oh…maybe not funny. But, it was certainly pathetic." She looked at him with eyes that betrayed an ongoing sadness. "Even among our mutual friends, and I use the term 'mutual' lightly, it seemed to be an OK thing, you know, like, 'well, after all, Susan, he is Alan Rayle. He's such a superior human being. Of course, he has needs greater than normal men'." The contempt in her voice was visceral. "Oh, and he's doing so much for the 'Movement..'"

Andrew whistled softly and Oscar came to be petted.

"And," Susan paused, as if she couldn't bear to continue, but felt compelled to verbalize her pain, "I found out he'd slept with several of my girlfriends. It was this huge, private joke they all had. Some of us would go out for a drink, and he'd be screwing the one that, wink wink, couldn't make it for one reason or another."

Suddenly shaking his head in aggravation, Andrew exclaimed, "And you wonder why I'm so cynical about the sincerity of those people? There's not one of them, from dancing Hippy to a guy like your husband in the fucking 'Movement', that isn't having a great time."

To Susan's distress, Andrew hocked and spit off to the side. He wasn't done. "They don't want the war to end. If it does, 'Party's over'. No more excuse to drop out and go ape-shit." He paused a few seconds, then, "Fucking 'Moratorium Day' Washington DC, the day I got off the plane in…biggest fucking party, biggest one-day sale of weed in world history. Probably a hundred GIs, maybe more, got greased on fucking 'Moratorium Day'. But, man, 250,000 morons in DC got high and got laid."

The outburst ended as suddenly as it began. It was as if he'd never verbalized such sentiment before. In fact, she was sure of it as she looked over at him. The anger had visibly lined his face. Wetness showed at the corner of his eye.

She took a deep breath. "I…think…maybe this little talk has been cathartic. You and I have some suppressed anger and…"

A distant horn honked and distracted them. Susan stood and looked back towards her house, a half mile down the hillside.

"Well, now," a smile of relief brightening her face. "It's your lucky day, babe. You get to meet the sheriff." She took his hand and pulled him back towards the house.

"You'll like him," she said, as she saw a look of 'What next?' disquiet cross his face. "He's a great guy."

"Uh, Susan? There's something else I have to tell you." Andrew strained to keep a straight face. "I'm only fifteen."

~ * ~

Sheriff Jerry Casper picked up the lilt of his daughter's laughter on the light breeze and, looking east, saw the couple walking quickly back to the house.

Denver plates. Ft. Bragg officer's ID on the bumper. He ran his thumb over the sticker. *Benning sticker underneath the Bragg.* Rubbing his chin, he thought, *This boy's in way over his head.*

"Hi, Daddy!"

Andrew was surprised and oddly charmed by Susan's child-like greeting and embrace of her father. The man was large, white-haired, red-faced and stern, at least until his daughter threw her arms around him. He wore a khaki uniform adorned on the left breast by a six-point star badge. A minor pot-belly hung over a black leather gun belt. Black cowboy boots adorned his large feet, and a narrow-brimmed Stetson was clutched in his hand as he returned his daughter's hug.

"Sheriff Daddy, I want you to meet my good friend, Andrew Starkey."

Andrew stepped up to the man and shook his hand firmly. "Good to meet you, sir."

"Likewise," the man responded. "Starkey, is it?"

"Yes sir. I'm not famous like Susan. Just a telephone man from Denver."

Sheriff Casper turned to his daughter, a look of amusement on his face. "So, you're famous, now? What have you been up to, young lady?"

Susan chuckled. "Mr. Starkey thinks anyone who sells seedy romance novels in grocery stores must be famous."

As the threesome walked towards the front porch, Andrew noticed the Sheriff's side arm.

"Sheriff, that looks like a 1911 Colt. Is that normal for law enforcement work?"

The man reached for the ornate, nickel-plated weapon, unsnapped its tie-down and pulled it from the holster. "Good eye, boy," he said, releasing the pistol's magazine into his palm. He locked the bolt open, glanced into the chamber, then handed the weapon to Andrew.

"Beautiful," Andrew muttered, admiration in his voice. "The 45s we carried were pretty beat up." He handed it back butt-first. The sheriff reloaded and holstered the weapon and snapped its tie-down back in place, all in one fluid movement.

"Out here," the sheriff said, "there's not much that's normal, so to speak. I carried a Colt like this one plus an M-3 'Grease gun' during the war. Just got used to 45 caliber."

Andrew nodded. "I understand. Who were you with in the war?"

"The old 11th Airborne. Did some hard time in the Phillipines."

"Paratroopers?"

"Yep. One combat jump on Luzon, late in the campaign," the man said. To Susan, he offered, "I bet you didn't know that, Susie Q. Your old man was a paratrooper."

"Why no, Dad, I didn't. You jumped out of airplanes?"

Andrew noticed Susan's incredulity. She'd reached mature adulthood and had no idea of her father's wartime service.

The man smiled, then said to Andrew, "Noticed your Ft. Bragg sticker. You wear the wings?"

Andrew nodded. "Yes, sir. Jump School at Benning in '69. I've been out for a year now."

"Vietnam?"

"Yes, sir. 5th Special Forces."

The Sheriff turned to Susan. "Now, Susie Q, how's it feel to be surrounded by the nation's best, the Airborne?" He winked at Andrew and both laughed, knowing she could fathom none of their instant camaraderie.

"Uh, Dad, will you stay for some tea?"

Susan brought a tray with glasses and a large pitcher on to the porch. She served the two men and returned to sit between them at the rattan table.

Andrew waited a polite few minutes before excusing himself. "Susan, I'd better be getting back to Denver. I'm sure you and your dad have things to catch up on."

"Of course, Andrew. I'm so happy you could drop by."

Sheriff Casper spoke up. "Boy, you don't need to rush off. I'm just checking in on my girl. Hard to get through to her on that dang party line."

Oscar appeared and nearly toppled the table trying to reach the sheriff's outstretched hand for a scratch.

"Whoa, dog," the man laughed, grabbing the pitcher.

"Thank you, sheriff. Tomorrow's a work day and…"

Sheriff Casper raised a hand in acknowledgement. Susan stood and walked with Andrew towards the car.

"Say," the sheriff spoke after them, "Sevilla a friend of yours?"

"Yes, sir. One of my best."

"OK, then." He waved again.

At the car she whispered, "I can't kiss you in front of Dad. Am I going to see you again?"

"The second you'll let me," he said, shaking her hand as would an old friend.

"Saturday afternoon?"

"As soon as I can get here…"

Chapter 29
The Sheriff

Andew's car turned left onto the road, and he waved to them as the LeMans gathered traction on the loose road surface. In a second, the car was gone.

"Nice kid."

"Dad, he's twenty-three."

The big man nodded, scratching the dog's ear. "Like I said…"

It wasn't a show of disapproval exactly, but it was clear her father wanted her to be with someone closer to her own age of thirty-one.

"Oh, I guess there's always Deputy Dave," she remarked, waiting for his reaction. Her father's deputy was thirty-five, single and a hopeless bore.

"Honey, you could move back to the front range. It's too lonely for you here."

She squeezed his hand. "When I get my novel published, maybe I will move to Denver. Then you can come live with me in my luxury Cheesman Park condo. Until then, I need to stay here where I can focus and crank off the pages."

The man sighed softly. He held up his iced-tea glass to the sun and seemed pleased, somehow, at how the light played through the cool refreshment. Ice cubes tinkled as he finished the last of it.

"Well, Susie Q…At least this old place is good for something. It sure wasn't worth a shit for farming."

She'd heard him speak this way before over the years, echoes of his sadness at the farm's failure to provide their family a living and, eventually, its failure to hold the family together.

"Daddy," she said, sympathetically, "you always forget two very important items. First, you fought off the drought a lot longer than most of the other farmers. Second, Mom would have left anyway. She'd been dreaming of California and movie stars since the Plainsman opened in 1936. She let you down. You didn't fail her or me."

Her father stood up, stretched and adjusted his pistol belt. "And I've still got you, don't I?"

Susan came into the man's arms. "Yes. You're the Daddy, I'm Susie Q, and the rest of the world can go screw itself."

A deep laugh erupted from the big man. "You know, girly? After you were born, I thought to myself, 'God, what a perfect, beautiful, fragile little thing she is.'" He tossled her hair with a free hand. "Then I thought I needed a boy to kind of round things out."

She turned to walk with him as he headed towards his patrol car. "But, I swear, I got a perfect combination, a beautiful girl with a man's attitude towards life. It just doesn't get any better than that…"

The car's two-way radio crackled unintelligibly as he opened the door. Sheriff Casper cocked his head momentarily to listen, then unbuckled the pistol belt and threw it over to the passenger seat. With his back to the open car door, he raised a hand to shield his eyes from the sun and looked off in the direction of Danny Sevilla's farm. A quick shake of his head puzzled Susan.

"What is it, Daddy?"

"That dad gum 'party line' phone we've got out here. Guess there's some gossip about strange comings and goings out at Sevilla's."

"Oh…really? What are they saying?"

"Not much. Some mysterious van. Couple strangers in a sedan. You see anything funny?"

Susan tried to look thoughtful as she scratched Oscar's neck. "Well, I don't spend a lot of time at the window. But, I'll let you know if I see something odd."

"Actually, that's…" she tried to think quickly, "how I know Mr. Starkey. He and Danny are old Army friends. On his first visit last week, he got lost looking for the farm and asked for directions. Maybe he's a source of the gossip."

"Could be," the man responded. Smiling, he said, "Honey, nothing about either one of those boys could be considered old."

"Chronologically speaking, you're right. But Mr. Starkey…well, let's just say he's not like any twenty-three-year-olds you'll find around Flagstaff." Under her breath, she said, "Or Boulder thirty-five year olds, for that matter."

"Pull in those claws, girly," he chuckled. Starting the car, he had one more thought. "Do me a favor. For the next month or so, lock up your place when you leave. And, uh, does Sevilla still keep that cannon of his up here?"

"Yes…Leaning in the kitchen corner."

"Move it somewhere so it can't be seen from a window. Guns are what thieves want next, right after the cash."

"You think something's going on out here, don't you?"

He directed a nod off to the south. "That God damn I-70. It's just an open sewer of scum flowing across the country. You never know what it might flush out on us."

She bent over laughing at his metaphor. "Good grief, Daddy. What a description for a poor sterile strip of concrete."

"Sterile my ass."

Clearing her throat, she said, "Well now, Mr. Starkey thinks of I-70 as the carotid artery of his existence. It brought him from Indiana to his new life in Colorado." She folded her arms across her chest. "I'd love to watch the two of you over a few beers."

The sheriff shifted into reverse. "Sounds like you're getting to know the Mr. Starkey pretty well." He winked at her and backed the patrol car towards the road.

Chapter 30
The Ship

As he walked up to the doorway of the converted 1920s dwelling that included his first-floor apartment, Andrew glanced at his Seiko. "Shit. Seven o'clock already. Oh, well. Got the day off tomorrow." He twisted his key in the lock of the heavy door, pushed it open and flipped on the wall light. The main room was a combination living and dining nook, with a small kitchen set at a right angle from the nook. A doorway to the bedroom and its attached bath was at the opposite end from the kitchen. Low windows provided a view of the tidy front yard from the nook. Furnishings were old and threadbare, but spoke of solid middle-class origins from the 1930s.

Clayton Street had little traffic, thus providing the many apartment dwellers in the area a leafy, inter-urban ambiance. Though he'd initially balked at the $130 monthly rent, he reconsidered and wrote out a check for the eccentric landlady.

"Now, you'll be real quiet, won't you?" she'd admonished him.

"Yes, ma'am. All I do is work, eat and sleep. I'll go somewhere else to make noise."

He walked to the TV and pulled its "on" knob. A minute later, the color picture glowed to life, giving the room a reddish tinge. Pulling open the refrigerator door, he extracted a bowl of left-over Rice-A-Roni and a cooked hamburger patty. Retrieving a sauce pan from the drying rack next to the sink, he ran a half inch of water into it. Next, he dumped in the rice mixture and, on top of that, the patty. From the pantry, he found and opened a can of peas and spooned half the contents over the patty. Finally, he turned a burner on "low" and set the pan on to heat through. Suddenly, the red phone he'd brought along from his old Logan Street place began to ring.

He didn't answer, muttering instead, "Boss, you asshole." Doubtless, it was Foreman Bob calling to advise that the mid-week day off was, as usual, a luxury Ma Bell could not afford, regardless of the mandatory Saturday schedule.

"Shit." Resigned to his fate, he picked up the receiver. "Boss, one of these days..." he began.

"Boss?" the voice was female. "Andrew?"

"Uh, ha, I'm sorry. This is Andrew. Who's this?"

"'Boss' is OK, but I kind of liked 'your highness.'"

"Susan?" His heart jumped.

"Hi."

His faced burst into smile. "Hi, babe. It's great to hear your voice. Wow."

"That's better. Have you missed me?"

"What do you think?"

"Tell me."

"I'm in pain."

"Good," she said softly. "My hips are still sore."

"I'd never hurt you on purpose."

She began to giggle. "Oh, I'm glad I caught you at home. I'm in Denver, down at the Brown Palace. I'm so lonely."

"God, babe. Can I see you?"

"Will you come down? I bet you're exhausted."

"Give me 45 minutes. I just got home. Need to shower."

"I'll see you in the lobby. Eight-fifteen or so."

She embraced him warmly as they met in the old hotel's expansive public area. He had never before been in the Brown Palace, and was clearly impressed by the history and tradition that seemed to ooze from every corner.

"Come on. I'll buy you a beer in 'The Ship'."

The Ship Tavern had an entrance from the lobby. Inside, a rowdy, mostly male, clientele turned to watch as Susan strode in. She was dressed in a knee-length black skirt with matching sleeveless top. Four-inch red high heels and patterned-silk stockings gave unnecessary extra shape to her long legs. Loose blonde hair fell to her shoulders.

Andrew felt like a fish on a sidewalk. Wearing, himself, Levis, hiking boots and a flannel shirt, he was stunned at how fabulous Susan looked. He fixed his face to display, he hoped, a look of confident indifference to anyone sizing him up.

A thought crossed his mind…"Eat your hearts out men. I've seen her naked." He bit the inside of his cheek to keep from grinning foolishly.

"I'm out of my league in here," he said, under his breath as they took a small two-top table. He nodded discretely to his right. "That's Governor Love over there."

Susan smiled at his ill ease. Taking a casual survey of the various tables, she said, "He's with one of the Coors brothers."

"Oh, well," Andrew responded, flipping his hand dismissively, "he can stay then."

The smile expanded, lighting up her face. "You'll allow the

Governor of Colorado to remain in the Ship Tavern only because he's sitting with a beer baron?"

He let the grin he'd surpressed burst forth. "Just kidding, babe. I'm too new to Colorado to be ragging on the politicians yet."

A waiter brought Susan the martini she'd ordered and a bottle of Coors with frosted glass for Andrew.

"Will there be anything else, Ms. Casper?"

"Nothing for me, Jimmy. Andrew?"

"Wait about five minutes, then bring another Coors. Thanks, buddy. Oh, take this back."

He handed Jimmy the frosted glass.

"It's kind of like with you and me, Ms. Casper." he winked. "Being with a beautiful woman bestows a lot more dignity on me than I'm worthy of. I don't know anything about the Governor, but if he's with one of the Coors boys, he's got my vote."

Once again, she found herself giggling at this strangely irreverent young man. The smoky room contained any number of Denver power brokers and politicians in pinstripes and wing tips. Were she not escorted, she'd have been approached by a few familiar faces and invited to join a table. But, those men weren't fun, and seldom funny. They took themselves too seriously, and were consumed with business, politics and self-promotion. Yet, of those that she was acquainted with, none was hateful. Indeed, there were former lovers in the bar. Those two men retained deep affection and respect for her. Never was she looked upon as a trophy or adornment. They respected her privacy and took pride in her continuing friendship.

The roomful, even those who didn't know her, universally loathed her ex-husband and that man's world only twenty-five miles up Highway 36 in Boulder. Such knowledge helped her rebuild, albeit slowly, her self-respect. There was little doubt which environment had proved more fulfilling for a talented, assertive woman.

But, Andrew Starkey. Well, he had seemed to take very little, let alone himself, seriously. Then Sunday happened. He was much more complicated than she had at first imagined. Cynical, judgmental, angry, yet so affectionate and attentive that she felt utterly free and comfortable in his presence. He projected a sort of innocence, yet apparently had experience of something so unfathomable to average people that he'd speak of it only obliquely unless, as with her father, a man with similar experience, he connected with them on a subliminal level. As a defense, he projected inordinate interest in the cares that other, less deeply troubled people, like herself, faced.

Oh, Susan, she thought to herself, *you've known him a matter of days. Lighten up and enjoy the man. You're not getting any younger.*

~ * ~

A Monday morning call from her editor for an unscheduled contract review had provided an excuse for a quick trip to Denver.

"May I get you a room at the Brown?" asked Leandra, her editor's assistant.

"Yu....ess," she'd hesitated. "Hmm. Wonder if I could call Andrew and stay at his place?" She thought better of it. "If we get together and something happens, I can still work from the Brown."

"Sorry, yes, Leandra. Please get me a room for Tuesday evening. 202 if it's available."

~ * ~

"My life is picking up speed, babe" she said, excitement in her voice. "'Arapaho Trail' is going to print next week. It will be in Safeway in a month, Kings soon after."

Andrew nodded in admiration. "And I'm sitting with you in the power palace of Denver. Man, I must be living right."

Susan reached under the table to squeeze his hand knowing it rested on his nervously bouncing knee.

"Thank you, and stop that," she said. His leg movement stopped abruptly. Now aware of it, his nervous tick didn't return.

"There's more. They're letting me spend more time on my novel. Usually, editors won't advance money on a partial. But they're so confident in it they'll let me have an advance and let me spread out the romances. If I go non-stop I can finish 'Elements of Shame' in three months."

"And I can say, I knew you when..."

"Honeybun, it will take a year after that to get it on the shelves. That's if all goes smoothly. 'Til then, maybe we can still, you know, become even better friends."

"I'm putty in your hands."

Susan raised the martini to her lips and looked at him seductively over the tilted glass. "Maybe I'll have one more." She raised a manicured finger. "Jimmy?" The waiter headed to the bar with her order. A minute later, he arrived with her martini and Andrew's second beer.

In the corner of his eye, the glint of horn-rimmed glasses distracted Andrew and he glanced in that direction. The man Susan identified as a 'Coors' made eye contact with him and, now, held up his own bottle as if in tribute. Clearly tickled, Andrew raised half out of his seat, held up his bottle, and took a long satisfying swig. He held the bottle up once again to the grinning executive, then sat back down with Susan, his face flushed.

Susan cleared her throat softly. "And I thought you were just this sweet, unaffected Midwesterner with a mysterious past. I can see you've got the makings of a natural pin-stripe cowboy."

They enjoyed their drinks quietly for a few minutes, the interlude marked by occasional looks of luminous affection on both their faces.

Pushing her glass back and forth on its paper napkin, Susan started to speak. "Uh, babe, we need to talk."

Surprised at the shift in her mood, he said, "I scared you on Sunday. I'm sorry. It won't happen again."

"No, babe. Sunday was good for us. We needed it. Now it's behind us."

She took a breath and continued. "Daddy thinks something's going on at Danny's."

"Shit." Andrew's mind began to race. "What...did you tell him, anything?"

She spread her fingers and waved them as if dismissing such a notion. "Of course not."

"Keep talking."

"He said there'd been a buzz of rumor going around on our party line. You know, the old biddies saying things about vans and sedans and strange people in the area. I tried to infer that your visit last week might have stirred it up. He didn't think one man in a Pontiac could do that."

"Damn. Well, any idea what he'll do next?"

"No. Maybe nothing will come of it. But..."

"Honey, keep talking."

"It's like he knows more than he's saying. I really don't believe he knows what Danny has in his barn. But, you know he has information that other police agencies share with him. I'm wondering if he's been told something by some agency that knows about the people Danny's involved with."

Andrew rubbed a hand over his face, then stared at the bottle for a long moment.

"Well", he said, "I've got to warn him."

"How? You can't call him. His phone isn't hooked up."

"I know."

"And now we have to be careful, because anything he finds out will be a result of Dad talking with me."

"Susan, whatever I do, you'll not be involved. Believe me."

A moment later, resignation softened Andrew's face. "Am I still invited for Saturday?"

"Unless we kill each other tonight."

He looked at the table top. "I'll stop by his place first and talk to him. I'll think of something to tell him, so he'll watch his back. Maybe say something like, 'The guy at the gas station says you're a drug dealer'. I don't know. I'll think of something."

"OK, babe. Just please be careful...and discrete." Resignation marked her face as well.

She did a nonchalant perusal of the room. "I should leave alone. You sit still and finish your beer. Take your time. When you're done, leave through that door to Glenarm. Then come back around to the entrance. I'm in Room 202."

She put two fingers to her lips and blew him a kiss. "See ya soon." With that, she rose, shook his hand, and walked quickly from the room, heels clicking lightly on the polished hardwood floor.

Andrew moved to the bar to finish his beer. A moment later, a distinguished-looking man in his forties leaned on the bar next to Andrew's barstool. He wore an expensive blue suit and bright "regimental" tie. He turned a friendly face to Andrew.

"So, who's the lucky man who got to share a drink with Susan Casper?" His speech, though not slurred, betrayed the influence of alcohol.

Andrew looked at him impassively. "Nobody special. Who are you?"

The man chuckled. "Guess the Jack Daniels is eroding my manners. I'm Gil Schnell. Susan and I are old friends. I was her first literary agent. I moved on to insurance. Oil and gas."

Andrew extended his hand to the man. I'm Andrew Starkey."

Schnell shook hands, then jerked a thumb towards a table of men. "I would have invited you both over, but those boys got mouths like Drill Sergeants. Susan's too classy for that."

Andrew nodded in agreement. "Yes, she is indeed. I met her through a mutual friend. Sometimes, when she's in town, she'll let me be seen with her. Does my fragile ego a world of good."

The man laughed warmheartedly at the stranger's self-deprecation. "Buddy, that woman could make Robert fucking Redford look better."

Andrew killed his beer, then took the opportunity to explore this fragment of Susan's past.

"You're my hero," he said, "...if you and Susan had a serious relationship. She's way out of my league."

The man held up his left hand. A wedding band was prominent. "Buddy, that one won't let a married man buy her a donut."

He lowered his voice and continued, "And if my wife caught me trying to buy her a donut, well, that son of a bitch would end up shoved where the sun don't shine, if you know what I mean."

Andrew laughed out loud. "Roger that," he said.

Andrew stood and placed a five-dollar tip on the bar. "Well, that's the kind of wife to have, right?" He gave the grinning man a friendly pop on the shoulder and headed out the street entrance.

~ * ~

His anticipation rising, he knocked softly on #202.

"Yes?"

"It's Andrew, your highness."

She pulled the door open and stood aside to let him in. She took a quick glance left and right down the hallway and closed the heavy door. Coming to his arms, she kissed him and snuggled her face in his chest.

"Ooh," she said, pulling her head away. "Did that hurt?"

"Not enough to make me want you to stop."

She still wore her outfit, though the shoes lay in the closet. "Got stuck on the phone. Leandra loves to gossip."

"Wow. This is nice," he said, walking around the spacious hotel room. "Must be like this in London and Paris."

"I wouldn't know. When I visited those cities, I stayed at youth hostels." She walked to the window and pulled the heavy curtain closed. "Not much of a view."

She returned to his arms and Andrew held her tightly, stroking the back of her head. Susan leaned back and looked to find his eyes closed, contentment warming his face.

"Are we awake?" she asked.

"Yep. Uh, Susan, as nice as you look in that blouse and skirt, you'd look a lot better if they were hanging in the closet."

As she stepped from the closet in bra, garter belt and stockings, he whistled softly. Wrapping his arms around her yet again, he moved his lips to her neck and cupped her bare bottom.

"Any chance you'd put the heels back on?"

She slipped into the red heels and walked back to him, a seductive smile on her face.

"By the way," he said, nibbling her ear. "Do you like donuts?"

"Babe, do I look like I eat donuts?" She cocked her head, wondering what he'd say next.

"I didn't think so. You know, as nice as you look in that bra…"

Chapter 31
The Warning

He pondered what to say to Danny all the rest of the week. Saturday came and the demands of the installation schedule kept him working 'til five. Finally back to the garage, he jumped in the LeMans and peeled rubber down the industrial block towards the I-70 interchange. Ninety minutes later, he was racing down the gravel road. Passing Susan's place, he looked back to see the house brightly lit, Susan on the porch, reading at her rattan table. He honked but the dust behind the car was too thick to see her acknowledgement.

The LeMans slowed as it approached Danny's drive. Andrew looked to see if any vehicle was parked near the house or barn. None were, and he turned in. Stepping from the car, he massaged his stiff neck and looked to the house to see if anyone had noticed his arrival. Connie walked from the kitchen carrying Janon, and he heard her call to her husband. Danny was at the screen door an instant later.

"Yo," Andrew called out.

Danny opened the door and returned the greeting. "Yo, buddy. Susan's house is a click back that way. You lost?"

The friends shook hands warmly. Connie came on to the porch and put Janon down. The toddler immediately ran to the men and held her arms out to Andrew.

"Whoa," he said.

Danny needled him. "Come on, troop. Pick her up or she'll start bawling."

Andrew did as instructed, marveling at the child's weight as he lifted her. "Wow, you're a big girl," he said, and kissed her cheek. "Hi, Connie. Sorry to drop in on you. I need to talk to Mr. Businessman here. I'm taking Susan out later."

She came to him and kissed him affectionately on the lips. "Lucky girl," she said. Janon went to her arms, to Andrew's relief.

They watched as the females went back into the house. "Come on," said Danny and began walking towards the barn.

Pulling open the heavy door, he said, "So, what's up your ass, Lieutenant? You look just like the time those 'no shit' pills wore off. You were trying to get your pants down before that brown round cooked off in the tube."

Andrew laughed at the memory. "So, I really look that bad?"

Turning serious, Danny said, "Come on. What's up?"

Andrew had practiced what to say in his mind for several days. He stuttered slightly as the monologue began. "When I, uh, was leaving Susan's last weekend, I stopped for gas, you know, at the highway. This old dude was pumping gas and starts talking about bullshit going on in town, said there are rumors…"

Danny's demonic grin stopped Andrew's performance. "Give it up troop. I talked to Susan today. She filled me in. Said Connie had spilled her guts. I knew she didn't hear it from you. She was going to tell you not to come by, but since you weren't home all day and then roared right past her house, well you're the 10% that didn't get the word."

Danny had seen the sheriff's car parked in Susan's driveway next to Andrew's, the previous Sunday. Although it was not unusual for the sheriff to look in on his own daughter, Hawk's delivery the following morning had not been at all usual. The two events together spelled trouble.

The big Indian was grim as the two men unloaded the van. "Boulé caught me selling happy grass. Fucking white man set-up. One of his distributors had some Hippy cocksuckers find me and make a buy."

"Tell Boulé to kiss your big fat red ass."

Hawk knew the Louisville story, was not amused by its Indian version, and shook his head in irritation. "My friend, we're in deep Buffalo shit. Boulé said we set off a price war that got the Feds' attention. Too much cheap grass on the street in East Denver and Aurora. Boulé's distributors were getting priced out of the market. Now he knows he's been competing with his own weed and he's beaucoup pissed off."

Danny paced around the barn for a minute. "What do you want to do, Hawk?" he asked.

"He's coming with me on Sunday morning. Wants to pow wow with us. Could get ugly."

"What can the son of a bitch do? Send us back to Vietnam? Fuck him."

Hawk paused to collect his thoughts. "Look, Danny, I want to stay in his outfit. I'll figure a way to pay him back. Do whatever it takes. I can't go back to the 'Res and cut firewood."

~ * ~

Andrew was shocked as Danny finished his description of the turn of events. "So, what did Susan…?"

"She didn't. Soon as Hawk left, I went up to see her. I did all the talking. She just nodded or shook her head to the questions I asked.

Maybe five of those. To be honest, I don't think Sheriff Casper knows anything more than that there's some weed coming though the area. Maybe the Feds in New Mexico have asked the State and local cops to watch for suspicious traffic outside the normal north-south routes from Mexico."

"Shit, buddy."

"Hey, don't worry about it. That honcho Boulé will be here in the morning, we'll talk and I'll probably just tell him to deal me out. It's not a contract like my truck loan. He can write off the loss and move his shit to a barn in Julesburg."

"I hope you're right."

Danny chose his words carefully before continuing. "On the other hand, maybe he can see that I'm not as dumb as his distributors. Maybe he can move me up in the organization. Kind of like, 'Hey, motherfucker. I got your attention. Now, let's rock and roll'."

"Danny, don't do that."

"I'm only thinking out loud."

"You've got too much to lose. You could do time in Leavenworth fucking around in that business."

The barn door clunked to a close. Danny clapped a hand on his friend's shoulder. "No fucking way, buddy. Now, go see that hunk on the hill. She's probably giving a blow job to my M-14 'cause you're screwing around down here with me."

Connie was at the screen door as the men returned from the barn.

"See you, Connie. Bye, Janon."

"Bye...bye," the toddler said. Connie blew him a kiss.

At the car, he shook Danny's hand and placed the other hand behind his friend's neck, giving him an affectionate squeeze.

"God, doesn't it seem like just the other day I was loading your sorry, half-dead ass into that 'Dust Off'? I thought you were het roi for sure."

"Buddy, it was just the other day. And...it always will be."

Andrew looked at him. "Is that what's wrong with us?"

"Shit. Who says there's anything wrong with us? We're just fun-loving American boys, always looking for a better whorehouse."

The Pontiac's engine rumbled. Andrew pushed the stick shift into reverse and began to back away. Danny gave the car's hood a rap with his knuckle and the car stopped.

He leaned down at the window. "Oh, Susan did say one thing. Something she said you taught her."

"This ought to be good."

Danny's eyebrows raised as he spoke…"Plausible deniability."

His friend was embarrassed. "Yeah. I told her to keep her nose out of your business. Damn, Danny. Her dad's the fucking sheriff."

"Best advice you ever gave," Danny agreed. "You tell that chick, from now on, she's to remain in the womb of 'plausible deniability'."

Susan jumped up as the Pontiac turned into her driveway. She stepped quickly from the porch, a hand to her mouth.

"Hi babe. You were supposed to stop here first. I couldn't reach you."

Andrew smiled and threw his arms around her. "I know. It's OK. We had a talk. I'm glad you didn't stop me." He looked around. "Where's Oscar?"

A muffled bark told that the dog was stuck in the kitchen. "Oh, I've been so nervous. I didn't notice he was trapped."

A second later, Oscar bounded outside and ran for the rope toy.

"I think Danny's business energies will soon return to agriculture," Andrew offered. "He's, uh, well, anyway. This problem could work itself out sooner than you think."

Susan sighed. "My goodness, what a melodrama. I can't believe how simple my life was before Oscar dragged you into my world."

Andrew knew what she meant. He felt somewhat the same since the chance encounter at Lucky's.

"I'm not sorry," he said. "What doesn't kill us makes us stronger."

"Nietzsche," Susan noted. "And, no, I'm not sorry either."

"Well, let's go into town and have dinner at the Corral. If that doesn't kill us, we can go to the Round Up for a beer. If that doesn't…"

Susan leaned against him. "I want you tonight," she purred. "Are you sure you need the Corral and the Round Up?"

"Have I told you how much I love to talk to you?"

She was touched by his simple heartfelt statement. There was no need for him to patronize her for sex since she'd just offered herself. He obviously really cared for her and enjoyed her company.

"Sniff." She was crying.

"Oh, now what did I say? Honey, I'm sorry. We don't have to go to the Corral."

"Start the car you bum. I've got to blow my…nose. Yuckers."

Chapter 32
The Barn

Sunday morning came clear, breezy and warm. Andrew moved his arm from beneath Susan's neck as carefully as he could to avoid waking her. Her mustiness from their lovemaking seemed to cover his body. The aroma aroused him immediately, but to wake her for his own gratification seemed a childish excess. Instead, he pushed himself from the bed and went into the bathroom. Running the hot water quietly, he squatted in two inches of water and gave himself a quick but thorough wash. Naked still, he went to the kitchen and started a pot of coffee. Back in the bedroom, he dressed and headed for the paper box at the end of the driveway. It was quiet at Danny's. No van or car out front.

Leaving the paper on the rattan table, he decided to take Oscar up the hillside, maybe to the ridge, to see if the Sunday morning town of Flagstaff was stirring yet.

At the windmill, the water flow had increased mysteriously, and the tank was overflowing down a muddy gully.

"How'd that happen, Oscar?" he spoke to the puzzled dog.

"No sign of life there, boy," he said, surveying the still dormant town. Church bells would begin any minute, he figured. The town's trademark flagpole did not yet display its massive American Flag.

"Oscar, don't those boys know Reveille's at 0600? It's almost eight. Not a STRAC outfit. You think her highness is up yet? Should have brought some coffee along. Boy, you just never learn."

Oscar paid no attention to the odd mumblings of the man. A dog liked to play and to walk. The man liked to do those things, too. The woman who fed and cared for him seemed more attentive and affectionate when the man visited. How could it get any better than that?

She was in her robe on the porch when the two of them returned, a mug of coffee held in her lap. As they approached, she rose to greet them. "Kiss me, you animal. No, not you, Oscar. Him."

"Morning, sunshine."

"My bed is destroyed."

"You are a lively lady."

She put a hand to her forehead. "I'm hung over. I'm not sure from what."

"You had, what, two beers at the Corral, one more at the Round Up?"

"Wasn't that fun? I haven't danced like that in years."

Andrew smiled. "Not a bad three-piece combo. Guitar, accordion and drums. Played everything from 'Cotton Eyed Joe' to 'Wipe Out'. I think you educated people call that an eclectic mix."

"Pandemonium is what sane people would call it."

Andrew was in the kitchen refilling their cups when the sedan went by. He saw only the dust trail as the car descended the hill.

"Here you go," he said, handing her the mug.

"Did you see?" she said, looking up at him.

"Read your paper, young lady."

He rummaged through the Post for a section he'd not yet seen. There were several but he couldn't concentrate. His eyes returned again and again to the farm. A dark-colored sedan was now parked in front of the house.

"Show time," he said, under his breath.

~ * ~

Susan had stripped the bed and was washing her sheets in a recently purchased machine that filled most of a closet near the back door.

"Come help me turn the mattress," she asked him. "It's heavy. Don't hurt your back. Lift with your legs. There. Ugh. Thanks, babe."

"If you'll let me cook, I'll whip us up some breakfast."

"Well, if you do eggs as well as you do coffee, we'll be fine. Can you fry potatoes?"

In twenty minutes Andrew had prepared them piles of scrambled eggs, fried potatoes and sliced ham. A plate of buttered toast sat between their plates.

"Chow time," he announced. "Give me five little girls with pink panties…"

The way she looked at him, he knew he'd better explain quickly. "Basic Training. Danny and I had this mess sergeant…"

Eventually satisfied with his explanation, Susan looked around her kitchen suspiciously. Nearly all the utensils had been washed and stacked already, save the ones they'd soon eat from.

She tried the potatoes. "Excellent. This is great. Umm."

Soon their plates were clean, and third coffees were being sipped.

"Oh, guess where I'm going week after next?" he asked, swirling his coffee to cool it.

"No idea."

"New Vernon. They're doing an 'All School' reunion. My bunch was Class of '66."

Susan smiled but was, nevertheless, pained to have their age difference so innocently presented. "That should be fun," she said.

"This is the first one I've been able to go to. A bunch of my buddies went last year, and I've been threatened with bodily injury if I don't show up."

"So, we can still do next weekend?"

"Absolutely. I'm not leaving 'til a week from Tuesday. Uh, but...my apartment," he paused, "we have to be real quiet. My landlady would go nuts if we make noise."

"Sir, what sort of noise are you referring to?"

They agreed that Susan would come to his apartment Saturday evening. Sunday morning, they'd head to the mountains for a hike and picnic.

He put his arms around her from behind as she rinsed their dishes in the sink. "Babe," he said, "I know you need to get to work. I'll head out in a minute."

"You're a dear. You can tell I'm getting antsy to hit the typewriter, can't you?"

"I noticed a certain longing in your eyes as you walked past it. I'm jealous."

He avoided looking at the sedan as it sped by. Oscar bounded towards the road to investigate the approaching rumble but, as usual, stopped well short and merely roared a hollow bark at the car. A cloud of dust drifted towards the house.

Susan joined him at the Pontiac a moment later. He opened the car door and threw his dopp kit and yesterday's clothes onto the floor behind the driver's seat.

"They were really flying," she said, irritation in her voice. "Look at the dust, damn them." She ran to close the kitchen door to keep the uncharacteristic plume from entering the house.

"Probably PO'd at Danny," Andrew said, flatly.

He walked back to her to say goodbye. Susan stood on a porch step looking towards Danny's farmhouse.

"Babe," he said, "thanks for everything. I'll see you Saturday, huh?"

She looked down from the step and took his face in her hands. "Yes. I think I'm beginning to like you, Mr. Starkey." Still holding his face, she glanced up. A second later, she said, "Andrew, something's wrong down there."

He turned to look. Nothing seemed unusual. "What, babe?"

"Janon. Do you see her sitting there?"

Andrew shielded his eyes and looked harder. The toddler was

sitting on the ground between the house and barn.

"She's crying. She was walking along and just sat down. The way she flopped down, I can tell she's crying and upset."

They watched another few seconds and no one came to comfort the child.

"Andrew, we have to see what's going on."

A few minutes later, the Pontiac was nearing the farm's gate. Andrew turned in slowly and drove to within ten yards of the hysterical toddler. They got out and Susan ran to little Janon and picked her up.

"Oh, baby, baby, there, there. What's the matter with my baby girl?" Susan said trying to calm the child.

Janon couldn't express herself but pointed to the barn. Her cries were unabated. Andrew ran to the barn and, stepping inside, waited a second for his eyes to adjust to the dim light.

"Shit! Susan, hurry up!"

Danny was lying on his back, his head cradled in Connie's lap. His eyes were partially closed, and blood was pooling in the dirt under his body. Connie didn't notice Andrew as he arrived at her side. Her face was misshapen, and blood ran from her mouth. It appeared she had taken a terrible blow to the side of her face.

Susan screamed when she saw the scene. "Oh, my God! Oh, my God!"

"Danny!" Andrew yelled. "What happened?" He searched over his friend's body looking for injuries. Soon enough he found two bullet wounds, one in his abdomen and another in his right shoulder. He noticed Connie's diaper bag nearby. He scrambled to it and pulled several cloth diapers out and began using them to staunch the blood flow from the wounds. The shoulder wound had an exit hole in his upper back. It appeared that a bullet remained in Danny's abdomen.

"Susan! Call the…" suddenly remembering they had no phone, he grimaced and swore. "Shit. We've got to load him up and…"

"Hey, buddy." Danny's eyes were open, and he was looking at Andrew. "Is…Connie OK?"

"She's right here with you buddy. She's fine. Damn Danny, what happened? We've got to get you out of here."

Susan was crying and holding Janon. The child had begun to whimper and was reaching down towards her mother. Connie was glassy-eyed and clearly in shock. Her hand seemed frozen to the side of her husband's head.

Andrew's mind was frantically sorting options. The closest hospital was in Limon, thirty miles away. Loading Danny in the car and driving him into town to the fire station would be better. But he feared the blood loss on the drive would kill Danny. Summoning the firemen made the most sense and he turned to Susan.

"Honey, you need to drive up to your place and call your dad. Tell him Danny's been shot and we need a Dust Off, uh…an ambulance."

"Oh, my God," she cried again. She was shaking and trying to keep hold of the now-struggling child.

Andrew took Janon from Susan's arms and sat the toddler down next to her mother. For the moment this quieted her.

"Susan," Andrew put his arms on her shoulders, "Honey, I need you. Can you go?"

"OK, I'll go," she sobbed and turned towards the car.

Andrew closed his eyes in anger and frustration and knelt back down by Danny. "Buddy, Susan's going up to her place to call in a Dust Off. We can't move you. You lay still. You're going to make it."

Danny's eyes were no longer able to focus on Andrew's face. "Thanks…An…drew…," he whispered. "It…was Boulé. Wasn't Hawk. He's my…buddy."

"OK, Danny. I'll tell the sheriff. They'll get the son of a bitch."

"Wait." Danny was struggling to remain conscious. "They went…in town for…the van. They're…coming back."

Andrew jumped to his feet and ran to the car just as Susan was pulling away. He pounded the hood with his fist and she slid to a stop.

"I've got to do it," he yelled. "You wait here. Try to keep pressure on Danny's stomach wound. Do you understand?" Susan stepped from the car and nodded her head in acknowledgement. "I'll try. Please hurry."

Seconds later, the Pontiac was flying up the road, a trail of dust behind it. He turned into the drive and skidded to a stop inches from the Mercedes' bumper. Oscar sensed Andrew's panic and barked at him in confusion.

Tearing into the kitchen, Andrew reached for the phone, picked up the receiver and heard female voices. "Well I just said to her, I said, Amanda, you tell that man he's no good…"

"Break break!" he yelled at the voices. "Call the sheriff! Tell him we need a Dust Off at Sevilla's farm. Danny's been wounded. Hurry the fuck up! You got that?"

Silence greeted him. "Hey! Are you listening to me? At Sevilla's…"

He began clicking the phone cradle. "Hey!" No dial tone, nothing. "Shit!" He slammed the phone down and looked to the corner where the M-14 had leaned. It wasn't there. Frantically he ran to the living room. It was there by the typewriter. He grabbed the weapon and ran back to car.

Andrew threw the rifle in the back seat and roared backwards towards the road. Just then, the white van flew past. The Pontiac backed into the main road and was enveloped in the van's dust cloud. Andrew fishtailed through gears and soon was on the van's rear bumper. He whipped the car to the left and floored it, Hawk's shocked face turning to watch as he raced past.

The Pontiac flew through the farm gate and side-slipped to a stop in the barnyard. He reached for the M-14, slammed the car door and ran for the barn. The van was not yet in sight, but a plume of dust and the crunch of tires on the road left no doubt they were coming on.

Looking into the barn, he saw that the four people were clustered together on the bare floor. He was breathing heavily and sweat had begun to burn his eyes.

Andrew turned to face the road, then leaned back against the door frame, the rifle in the crook of his left arm, his right hand wiping sweat from his brow.

He called to Susan. "How's he doing?"

She had calmed down and walked towards him. "Andrew, Danny is dying. Oh, my God."

"Your dad's on the way with the Dustoff…with the ambulance. The firemen will be able to help Danny."

She began to walk in front of the large, open doorway. He held up his hand. "Susan, stay there. Stay out of sight."

"Wh…why? What's wrong?"

"The men that shot Danny have come back. They want the weed." He nodded towards the covered pallets in the corner.

Her face was red and contorted. "Well, give it to them!" she yelled. "Just tell them to take it and go. My God, what kind of people are they!" She began to cry again.

"Honey, I need you to stay with Connie and keep pressure on Danny's wound. I'll handle this. Go back over there."

He looked out to the road. The van was now slowly pulling into the barn yard. Andrew for the first time glanced down at the M-14. He extracted the magazine and looked to see how many rounds it held. With relief, he noted the same six that he found the first time he saw the weapon in Susan's kitchen. He reinserted the magazine with a hollow, metallic click, pulled the bolt back and released it chambering a round. Another metallic click was heard as he pushed the safety off with his trigger finger.

Both van doors opened at the same time. Boulé came around first, followed reluctantly by Hawk. The men conversed for a few seconds, then began walking towards the barn. Andrew watched them carefully, the majority of his attention on the slim, dapper man with dark, round glasses.

The two men walked quickly at first, then stopped abruptly as they noticed Andrew braced against the door frame, the rifle now pointed at them.

Startled by the weapon, Boulé spoke. "I don't know who you are, but we're here for our property. Move your junker out of the way so we can back in."

"I don't know you either, cocksucker, but you shot my friend, and you're not getting near him again. Now, back out of here. The sheriff's on the way."

Andrew noticed that Hawk was trying to edge away but Boulé grabbed his belt, holding him. Harsh words were exchanged between the two men and Hawk's face was twisted in rage.

The Indian looked at the ground, then at Andrew. "I didn't do it," he shouted. "You're Andrew, Danny's friend, aren't you?"

Andrew decided to further divide his enemy. "I know you, too, Hawk. Danny said you didn't shoot him. He said that little cocksucker shot him."

Boulé increased his grip on Hawk's belt and pulled a pistol from his own waist band. "Tell you what, asshole," he spat. "You let us back the van in, pick up our merchandise, and we'll be on our way. You refuse, and this dumb Indian and I are coming in after it. I'll give you about ten seconds to decide."

Andrew remained in plain sight, bracing himself against the jamb, the weapon now pointed at Boulé's belt buckle. The pistol the man held was nickel-plated and glinted brightly in the late-morning sun.

At that moment, he saw movement to his right. It was Susan, both hands to her face, sobbing.

"Danny's dead, Andrew!" she choked. "He just died. He's laying there in the dirt and he's dead." She had stopped at the edge of the doorway and leaned in exhaustion against the jamb on that side.

Andrew's heart sank. He looked back at the two men, a mixture of rage and sadness making the veins in his head feel as if they would burst.

Suddenly, Boulé brought up his pistol and sprayed four wild shots towards the barn. One hit the ground near Andrew's foot sending dirt into his face. Two others passed through the door into the barn's interior. The last hit the door frame where Susan was resting her head. The bullet didn't penetrate, but its impact caused the rough wood inside to bounce into the side of her face. She gasped and put a hand to her temple. Bringing the hand down, she saw blood on her fingers and felt more beginning to run down the side of her face. She looked at Andrew and began pleading with him.

"Please, Andrew!" she cried. "They're going to kill us. Let them have what they want!"

Andrew prepared to fire a warning shot over Boulé's head, but was startled to see that Susan was going to walk to him, across the open doorway. He whispered, hoarsely, "Susan, stay there!" She walked out into the light.

Boulé saw her and brought up the pistol again. Andrew took a step towards Susan, the rifle still leveled at the men. An odd grin broke Boulé's face and he aimed down his sights.

The M-14 boomed once. Susan screamed and recoiled in horror from the sound and flash. Boulé flew backwards, still holding onto Hawk's belt. As the man collapsed, Hawk yanked the hand out and pushed Boulé away, contempt on his large face.

Andrew threw an arm around Susan and tried to pull her back into the barn's shadow. Immobilized by shock, her feet wouldn't respond. She looked out to where Boulé writhed on the ground.

"Oh, no! No, Andrew! No!"

He released her and turned back towards Hawk and Boulé. Hawk was facing Andrew, hands at his side. No fear showed on his face; only bewilderment.

Incredibly, Boulé was gathering himself. The bullet had hit him low on the left side, at belt level. He came to his knees, then stood up, the pistol still in his hand. Blood was dripping from his pant leg and pooling in the dirt.

Andrew yelled out to him. "Hey! Give it up!"

Boulé, moving on pure adrenaline and rage, began to wave the pistol menacingly. Catching sight of Hawk standing there, he raised the gun towards him. Once more the M-14 boomed. Boulé's body shuddered and collapsed.

Andrew began walking quickly towards the fallen man, the rifle yet leveled at the motionless body. Raising the rifle to his shoulder, Andrew aimed down at Boulé's face and cautiously put his foot down on the Beretta. He poked the body with the muzzle of the M-14, watched for a moment, then kicked the pistol from the dead man's hand.

Hawk watched, almost impassively, as Andrew sought to remove completely any remaining threat to those in the barn. Neither man spoke for a time. Rather, they just stood ten feet apart and looked at each other. Instinctively, Andrew kept the rifle across his abdomen, ready in an instant to point and fire.

"God damn it, Hawk," he said flatly. "God damn it to hell."

Hawk shook his head slowly and looked at the ground as he spoke. "I remember you. That beer on Logan Street. My brother paratrooper. Danny talked about you, but I didn't remember."

"He's dead, Hawk."

The man winced and turned his head away, a large hand coming to his face. He was crying.

"I'm...damn sorry," Hawk said, choking on the words. "He was my friend, too. We were in deep. Boulé was teasing Danny, acting like he was going to make him a honcho. Then he started to laugh him down. Danny went for him and Boulé shot him twice. Connie grabbed his arm and he whacked her on the jaw with that Beretta."

Andrew stared at Hawk for several seconds. He held the rifle level with his right hand and rubbed the back of his neck with his left, grimacing from the strain of the last few minutes.

He took a deep breath and exhaled. "OK, Hawk," he said finally. "What do you want to do?"

Hawk looked puzzled.

"You'd better go. Get the fuck out." Andrew nodded towards the barn. "I got to take care of those people. The sheriff's on the way, as far as I know. But if he doesn't show up soon, I'll have to pile them in my car and drive into town." He couldn't imagine leaving the women with two dead bodies.

"You'll let me drive away, just like that?"

Andrew nodded. "Danny would want you to have a chance. I'll play dumb and say as little about you as possible. Connie might..."

"She won't," Hawk responded.

The big man assessed his options, his mind racing. "I'm gone," he said, finality in his voice. "If I can ever return the favor, come up to Lodge Grass on the Crow Res'. Tell any Indian you see you're a brother of Nathan Walking Hawk. They'll know where I am." He turned and began to jog towards the van. As he opened the door, he looked back at Andrew and raised his hand. Andrew cradled the rifle in his left arm and raised his right hand to acknowledge the gesture of gratitude and friendship. In a moment, Hawk was back on the road and heading north, away from town and into the rolling plains of Eastern Colorado.

~ * ~

The van had only been gone long enough for its dust trail to lay back down before the sound of sirens could be heard in the distance.

Shortly, Sheriff Casper's car and a volunteer firemen's truck turned through the gate.

Andrew had his arm around Susan's shoulder when the men came into the barn, the M-14 remaining cradled in his left arm. Connie still sat with Danny's head in her lap, Janon at her side drawing in the dirt with a stick.

Sheriff Casper watched Andrew closely as he pulled the 1911 Colt from its holster. Pointing it at the ground, he approached cautiously.

"Boy, talk to me."

"Dad!" Susan cried. She left Andrew and ran to her father. Sheriff Casper hugged her with his free arm but kept his eye on Andrew.

"Son, I want you to put down that rifle. Real slow."

"Yes, sir," Andrew said reflexively, and laid it carefully on the barn floor.

The sheriff motioned with the pistol…"Let's go outside and talk about this."

Two firemen remained in the barn bandaging Connie's face and pleading with her to stand up and come out with them. Danny's body had been covered with a tarp dragged over from the marijuana pallets. Outside, two more firemen were standing over Boulé's body.

"Sheriff, this boy is door-nail dead. Two gut shots," said a fireman. "There's a handgun over there." He pointed at the Beretta.

"Susan, honey," the sheriff began, "who's the bad guy here? Talk to me."

She struggled to speak and took several deep breaths. "That man," she said, but could not look at the body nor even point. "Before he died, Danny said that man shot him." She paused and put her hand to her temple where the blood had dried. "Andrew wouldn't let him come in." She lifted her eyes now, and looked at Andrew. "Andrew…killed him."

Hours went by at the sheriff's office before Andrew was allowed to leave. The investigation was methodical and was just beginning…

"One more time, Mr. Starkey. Why did you let the other man go?" Deputy Dave Graham asked.

"Danny told me Boulé shot him. He said the other guy was his buddy. When they came back for the marijuana, I could tell that guy was being forced to participate and he wasn't armed. When I…shot the second time, it was because…it, I thought Boulé was going to waste him."

"Waste"? asked the deputy.

Exasperated, Andrew said, "Grease, zap, kill."

Andrew paused and took a sip from a Pepsi bottle. "I'm sorry I snapped at you. The guy was clearly, to me, an innocent party. I couldn't just stand by and let Boulé shoot him. As to why I let him go, there were three people in the barn to think about. I just wanted the guy gone so I didn't have to worry about what he might do."

~ * ~

In a separate office, Sheriff Casper took his daughter's chin in his hand and turned her head. He ran a finger gently along her temple, examining once again the bruise and laceration caused by the bullet's impact with the door frame.

"Honey, now once more. You came to tell Mr. Starkey that Mr. Sevilla had expired. You were leaning on the door frame. The suspect fired his gun several times."

"Yes. I don't know for sure. Four or five times."

"Is that when Mr. Starkey fired the rifle?"

"No. Like I told you before…" she was also becoming exasperated from the repeated questions, "I was pleading with Andrew to let them have their stuff. He wouldn't even look at me. He kept watching those men. I walked towards him and…"

"You stepped out in the open?"

"I don't know," she whined. "I guess I did. I just wanted him to listen."

"What did Mr. Starkey do?"

"He told me to stop, to go back. Then he came towards me, but he wasn't looking at me. He wouldn't listen."

"And that's when he fired the first time, when you walked out in the open?"

"Yes. That's when he shot that man."

Susan put her head down on the desk. "I wish…" she said softly as her father watched her, "I wish Andrew had let them take what they wanted. Danny was already dead. They just wanted their…stuff."

Sheriff Casper made some notes on his pad. "Now, once again, Mr. Starkey drove up to your house to use the phone…"

~ * ~

After numerous recounts, there'd been no inconsistency in Andrew's version of the events. The same was true of Susan Casper's version, though she seemed especially traumatized by the stand Andrew made at the barn.

"Morally conflicted," he said to his deputy as they consulted in private.

"Better than dead," responded the deputy.

Walking Andrew to his car, Sheriff Casper pointed to a park bench and asked him to sit for a minute.

"Boy, you'll need to stick around Denver where we can reach you for the next few weeks. Any problem with that?"

Andrew, groggy from his ordeal, said, "No, sir. Uh, wait, I was going back to Indiana for a week. Not this week, the next one. My high school reunion."

The sheriff rubbed his chin. "OK. I think we can handle that." He took out a pad. "What's a number where you can be reached back there?"

Andrew repeated his parent's phone number. "You won't call them, you won't tell them anything?"

"No. Just make sure to get back to me immediately if I leave a message. I'll say I'm your old drinking buddy and I need bail money." Andrew forced a smile as the sheriff chuckled.

"Then you stop by here on the way back, got that?"

"Got it, sheriff. You've got my word I'll come in."

The sheriff ran a beefy hand through his white hair. "You know, this is about the damnedest pile of shit I've seen in a long time. Poor kid survives Vietnam then gets killed over a pallet of souped-up prairie grass."

"Yeah." Andrew took a breath. "Will, uh, Susan be OK? I'm worried about her."

"Oh, I'll take care of her, son. It's going to take some time. Her world's been split between two-bit Boulder flag burners and those cowboy heroes she conjures up for her novels. First time she's privy to some honest-to-God heroism, she can't deal with it. That's you I'm talking about."

Andrew shrugged uncomfortably. "Well," he said, "if it's OK with you, I'll head down the road. Got to work tomorrow." The two men stood together.

"One more thing," the Sheriff said, a crooked smile on his face. "Next time you need an ambulance, don't call it a 'Dust Off'. You scared hell out of those old broads on the party line. If you hadn't said 'Sevilla's', I'm not sure whether they would have contacted us." He put an arm around Andrew's shoulder. "And, uh, 'Hurry the fuck up'? Well, let's say your phone manners need some work."

Chapter 33
New Vernon

Sunday morning, Andrew Starkey joined his classmates in cleaning up the broken glass and other debris from their party scene of the previous night. Before the group broke up, they took turns riding Fat Chuck's old Harley around the 440-yard track. Luckily, the engine had a cracked head and couldn't manage rapid acceleration. Otherwise, someone surely would have run into the oak tree trying to manage the tight turn.

Vowing to meet again the following year, they went their various ways. Jack walked to the LeMans with Andrew.

"Shit, buddy. You've got some days left. Why are you blowing us off early and going back?"

"Like I told you last night, I'm in some deep shit back in Colorado. It's going to work out, but I can't…I'd just rather get back and see what's up."

"The Sheriff said he'd call you, right? He hasn't, so stick around here."

Andrew grabbed Jack affectionately by the neck. "You guys don't want me moping around here. Let me get this monkey off my back. Next visit, I'll be a new man."

"And all these assholes will be married. No fun then."

"One gets married, another one gets divorced. It balances out."

Jack reached in his shirt pocket. "Here you go. I showed this to my folks last night, once I sobered up." He chuckled. "Mom's calling your mom later today. Now they can worry about your sorry ass again, like when we were overseas."

Andrew held up his hand. "Keep it. I've got another copy. That's how I broke it to mom and dad this morning. Just pulled out that article and let them read it. That way all I had to do was answer questions instead of telling the whole story."

"I thought you looked better this morning. Spilling your guts to your folks must have taken some of the weight off your shoulders."

"Yes, it did. I…uh…didn't know what they'd say. But I sure didn't want them to find out from someone else. Mom's pretty upset, but, man, Dad just took it, no sweat."

"I would think so," Jack said, unfolding the wrinkled newspaper clipping. "Uh, hum," he cleared his throat and began to read:

AP. Tuesday August 17, 1971
Denver Man in Flagstaff Drug Shootout
A Denver man, Andrew Starkey, 23, of Clayton Street, found
himself between drug dealers and their contraband, Sunday, in rural
Black Kettle County. Dropping by to visit a friend, Mr. Starkey found
that friend, Daniel R. Sevilla, 23, Flagstaff, to have been shot and
wounded by partners in a drug deal gone sour.

Sevilla was able to warn Starkey that the shooters had gone for
a truck and would be returning for a stash of marijuana stored in
Sevilla's barn. Arriving back at the Sevilla farm, they encountered
Starkey, who was now armed with a rifle obtained from a neighbor's
home. The wounded Sevilla was, by that time, being attended to by his
wife and the neighbor.

Responding to a barrage of pistol shots directed at him by the
perpetrators, Starkey shot dead one Etienne Boulé, 32, Santa Fe, New
Mexico. An accomplice, name unknown, fled and remains at large.

Witnesses at the scene include Ms. Susan Casper, 31, daughter of
Black Kettle County Sheriff Jerry Casper. Her account confirmed the
heroics of Starkey in the defense of herself, Mrs. Connie Sevilla, 22,
wife of Danny Sevilla, and their daughter, Janon, age 14 months. Mr.
Sevilla later died at the scene. A full investigation of the incident is
underway by the Black Kettle County Sherriff's office and the Colorado
State Patrol.

Jack refolded the clipping. "And I knew you when you were a beer-puking low life, flunking out of IU. Now, you're…"

"Shove it up your ass, Jack. I need to get going."

"OK if I show this to the guys?" Jack asked sheepishly.

"Sure, as soon as I'm out of the city limits. Give me an hour."

Chuckling together, they shook hands. Andrew opened the car door.

"You know, buddy," he said, "I-70's still there. You can come out and visit me. Maybe this winter. We could go up to Breckenridge and teach ourselves to ski."

Jack thought for several seconds. "Maybe Christmas Break." The wheels in his head began to turn in earnest. "I'm going full-time at ISU this fall. That's what students are supposed to do on their breaks, right? Go on road trips and get shit faced."

Andrew smiled at his friend's growing excitement. To cement Jack's commitment, he offered, "That Jean Claude Killy dude is hanging around. Ski Bunnies all over the place."

"Fuckin' A, I'm coming…"

He sat in the LeMans as Jack drove away. Then he got back out of the car and surveyed the old high school building again. He leaned against the car, folded his arms across his chest, and closed his eyes. No thoughts dominated…just fleeting images of the faces of his friends, football games, Sally, the warehouse dock and the Cubans, his mother in the kitchen, his father in the driveway as he asked for the car.

He turned and looked towards the corn field. Drawn to it, he walked deep in among the rows and stood silently for a time. He inhaled the fragrance of the field. Harvest was still a month, maybe two away. Nothing in his memory smelled better than a corn field, or maybe fresh cut hay…or, a woman. Each fragrance was unique, but they were all of the earth. It just didn't get any better than that. It was time to head west.

Chapter 34
The Cemetery

He drove straight through, missing Kansas altogether in the darkness. The first rays of sunrise caught the "Welcome to Colorful Colorado" sign and, despite his continued malaise, cheered him nearly as much as the first time he saw it.

Another hour passed before he took the exit to Flagstaff. Glancing at his gas gauge, he thought, "Better fill up when I leave."

The one station was not yet open. Driving down Main Street, he parked in front of the Corral. Pushing coins into a Denver Post box, he pulled out one of the papers left by the delivery man an hour before. The familiar headings and font were pleasing to his eyes and he smiled down at it.

"I love this paper," he said audibly to no one. "I don't care what the news is."

Though the events at Danny's farm were still big news in town, no one knew his face. As he walked into the restaurant and took a seat at the counter, farmers glanced up at the stranger, then went back to their conversations of wheat prices and weather. KOA Radio was playing behind the counter, and a familiar baritone voice spoke of "barrows and gilts" and "feeder cattle auctions."

A pleasant, matronly waitress came to fill his coffee cup. "Hi, honey. What will you have?"

"Will you throw me out if I order biscuits and gravy?"

"I sure won't. If anyone else does, sweetheart, I'll just take you home with me."

That old discussion with Danny about hookers and waitresses came to mind. The waitress giggled as he blushed.

Now, filled with a heavy breakfast and several refills of strong coffee, he left the paper on the counter and walked down the block to the Sheriff's Office. Glancing at his Seiko, he thought, "It's early but not for cops."

Sure enough, Sheriff Casper was sitting at his desk, a report of some kind in his hand. He noticed Andrew as he walked in. Watching the young man for a second, he saw Andrew begin to take deep breaths as if he was struggling with his emotions.

"Hey, boy. Come on in," the sheriff yelled. "Hey, Francine. Get this boy some coffee."

"Thanks, Sheriff Casper. I'm coffee'd out." He smiled at Francine and she went back to her seat at the two-way radio.

"How'd the funeral go, Sheriff?"

The big man shrugged and shifted in his chair. "Not too bad. Short. Started raining, so that helped move it along. VFW did a nice job with the flag folding and rifle salute."

Andrew shook his head at the thought of the dreary ceremony. "Must have been awful."

"Yep," Sheriff Casper said softly. Then he brightened and asked about Andrew's trip to Indiana. The two men exchanged pleasantries for several minutes and, as they talked, Andrew perceived, rightly or wrongly, that the Sheriff had no residual concerns about what took place at Danny's. *Maybe,* Andrew thought, *He's trying to get me to relax.* His guard remained up, but he did his best to appear calm.

Sheriff Casper directed a smile at the young man in front of him as the conversation slowed. *This kid is still scared to death,* he thought. *I've got to ease his mind.*

He reached to his right and picked up a brown, hard-sided folder. Opening it, he lifted a plastic sheet that protected a large photo of someone. Reversing the folder, he slid it towards Andrew.

"Here's our boy," he said.

It was a mug shot of Etienne Boulé. A date stamp on the upper-left corner read, "Montreal, Quebec. 11Jul68 Prefect du Police".

Andrew looked at the young face of the man he had killed. He felt a wave of nausea, and closed his eyes to fight it off.

He took a breath and blew it out slowly. "OK if I flip through some of this?"

"Sure. Just keep it to yourself. The investigation is still going on, but I think our little piece of it is petering out."

Boulé was the scion of the Canadian arm of a French crime syndicate. That he was operating at such a low level of return on criminal investment pointed to the fact that he had become impatient with his slow rise in the parent organization. Instead, he tried to build his own drug empire from a base in Santa Fe. "Hands on" management had been his downfall. He was frenetically trying to build and maintain a distribution system without first developing a loyal cadre to keep the system's machinery moving. In essence, he was a well-financed, though inexperienced, CEO trying to do everything himself. "Everything" came to include the proverbial arm-twisting and leg-breaking normally done by the "wise guys" of American crime families. That Boulé was pathological was only an advantage in the short run. He never envisioned running into an angry man with an M-14.

"If you like irony," said the sheriff, "Sevilla's M-14 was one of several dozen stolen from the arms room of a Basic Training Company down at Ft. Leonard Wood, Missouri. Boulé met his end by a weapon his organization had sought to make a profit from by selling to whoever had the money to pay."

"Wow," Andrew responded. "So, Danny got it from Boulé somehow? He told me he got it from a buddy, end of discussion."

The sheriff nodded. "Yep. Maybe it was a gift or a bonus for services rendered. We'll probably never know for sure. What I do know is that if you hadn't had that rifle, well, our little local tragedy might have had more victims. Even if you and Susan hadn't come by, Boulé's MO would have been to finish off the witnesses, meaning Connie for sure, maybe the child. I hate to think..." he paused and cleared his throat, "I hate to think what would have happened when he came back for his contraband and found you and Susan in the barn with Sevilla."

Once again walking with Andrew Starkey to his car, the Sheriff was affable.

"Boy," he said, "you're free and clear. There's a chance the Feds might like to ask you some questions, but it's unlikely. This is an open-and-shut case to them. It dead-ended here in Flagstaff. The only loose end is that boy you turned loose. I'm positive he was a small-time runner trying to make a fast buck, just like your friend, Sevilla."

The relief Andrew felt was viseral. The last few years of his life had been tough enough, but then this event happened. Maybe he could move on now. Maybe things could return to normal. He thought, *I wonder what 'normal' is?*

"Sheriff, how's Connie doing?"

"Not great. Broken jaw. But she's got lots of family around. She's young, and she's got little Janon. In time, not much I'd wager, she'll be back at 85%, maybe 90%. You never get over your husband dying in your lap."

"Damn," Andrew sighed. "Uh, so..."

Sheriff Casper selected his words. "Susan? Well, she's another story." He pointed at a bench. "Sit down, boy. My ass is dragging. Out most of the night at a train derailment down at Hugo." Lifting his Stetson, he shaded his face with it and watched the firemen raise the American flag across the street in the park. "Don't those boys know reveille was two hours ago?" he said.

Andrew smiled and waited for the man to continue.

"I think you feel some affection for Susan." It was a statement.

Andrew nodded.

"She's, uh, let's say she's going to need some time, maybe a lot, to get over what happened. Like I told you before, she's got some strange ideas about life. Suffice it to say, you may not get a warm welcome when you drop by. I assume that's your next stop, right?"

"Yes, sir. I was really looking forward to seeing her."

"Well, get going then. I've taken enough of your time."

The two men stood, and Sheriff Casper shook Andrew's hand, clasping it firmly with his left hand as well.

"Let me leave you with this thought, son," the sheriff began, then glanced around and lowered his voice. "I've been around this world a long time. Two things I know for sure. Number one, some people need killing." He paused as if to give those words a moment to sink in. "Number two, you probably saved my daughter's life, not to mention Connie and little Janon. I won't forget that. Now, you ever need anything from me, and I mean anything legal (he winked), you let me know."

~ * ~

The rumble of the dirt road as he left the black top flooded his mind with the pleasure of the few but intense visits he'd made to see the woman… the sweeping curve of the road as it passed beneath the rise, behind which her small house sat, the cement steps, the battered mailbox, the fierce-looking lovable dog and, finally, Susan's open, hungry arms.

"God, don't let it be over," he pleaded. "I need her. I may be in love with her."

She was on the porch, typewriter on the rattan table, iced-tea glass catching the morning rays and looking like it was electrically powered. Her eyes widened as he pulled in and parked behind the Mercedes. She didn't rise to greet him and looked back down at the typewriter.

"Well, I guess that's that," he mumbled to himself, her body language saying it all. Yet he had to at least see if there was anything he could do or say to…*To what?* he thought.

"Hi."

She looked at him with an expression that spoke of controlled anger and irritation. "I guess you've come from seeing Dad."

"Yeah. He gave me $200 for passing 'Go'. No jail time."

She was in no mood for humor.

"I tried to call a few times," he offered. "Couldn't get through on the party line. I was worried."

She looked down at the typewriter.

"How's 'Elements of Shame' coming?" he asked with a resigned sigh.

"Well. It's coming along well," she responded, chin to her chest.

"Uh, can we talk for a minute? I've missed you. You've no idea…"

Without looking up, she pulled a rattan chair over to the table. "Sit down." As she raised the tea glass to take a sip, he could see her hand was shaking.

"Susan, I'm sorry…"

"Andrew," she snapped, "…just a minute." She took a breath. "Look, Andrew…I'm…older than you."

It was obvious to Andrew that she'd been preparing a speech for his eventual visit.

"You are young and you weren't allowed to grow up normally. It's not your fault. You've been…"

"Wha…what are you talking about? I'm me. Grow up normally? Where's that coming from?"

She looked away, waiting for him to finish. Beginning anew, she said, "You're something…you've been turned into something…a person I can't fathom nor relate to."

His confused anger was building but he kept his voice low. "Bullshit, Susan. I thought we related real well. What happened was terrible. It couldn't be helped. I didn't…"

"Andrew," she glared at him now, her voice harsh, "do you know that when we've talked you never say the word, 'Vietnam'? You stutter and you stammer and then you say 'Overseas' or 'Southeast Asia'. Why can't you say, 'Vietnam'? I know where you were, and what you and Danny did. You killed people, didn't you? You went over there a fine young man and then you killed people. That's why you shot that man. It was easy for you. It's how you people…" she paused in her tirade and took a breath, "You people…"

He closed his eyes. The chair was jarred suddenly. He looked down at Oscar, the omnipresent rope toy hanging from his mouth. Andrew took the opportunity to stand and turn away from the woman. He threw the toy well out into the yard and watched the dog gallop after it.

"You people?" he repeated, taking his seat again. "Now, I get it."

She raised an eyebrow. "Get what?"

"Your cowboy heroes. At least the one in 'Cheyenne Crossing', Jason Heaton. He never fired his 'cartridge-converted Army Colt'. All he did was talk to the evil doers. He talked his way out of everything."

"Andrew, there are no 'evil doers' in my romances. People are forced into situations, cultural conflicts, racial conflicts. There's a way to settle everything if only people can talk and work through their differences. Unless…"

"I'm listening."

"Unless there's a pathology that prevents it."

"Pathology?" he repeated. "What's that supposed to mean? That I'm crazy? You think…" He paused to get control of himself. "May I…" he began again, carefully watching his tone. "May I please ask you a question? I'll go then. Please?"

For the moment she seemed resigned to humor him. "Yes, you may."

"Your dad, you didn't know your dad fought in World War Two, did you?"

She shifted in her chair. "I…of course I did…he never talked about it. It was…"

"You didn't know your own father fought the Japanese in the Philippines."

"I told you he wouldn't talk about it."

"What did you ask him that he wouldn't talk about?"

"I never…nothing. I didn't know, so I never asked."

"If you asked him if he killed any Japs, what would he say?"

"Please, Andrew…"

"If he said, 'yes', would you think he was crazy? Would you hate him, then? Would he be one of those 'people' you're so contemptuous of?"

"No, of course not. He's my father. I would understand. He did what he had to do to survive. Andrew, my father was defending his country. You were a tool of American imperialism. A tool…"

"Susan," Andrew interrupted in controlled exasperation, "America took colonial control of the Philippines at the end of the Spanish American War. It was an American colonial possession from 1898 until we granted them independence after the war ended. Was your father an imperialist tool fighting the Japs to see which country got to keep the Philippines?"

She was stunned, unable to respond. Hands limp in her lap, she just looked down at the typewriter.

As he watched her discomfiture, his eyes softened and the anger subsided. He thought, *You're not so smart, babe.*

There was no point to further discussion. She was who and what she was, but she could not shame him.

"Well," he stood slowly, concerned she might be afraid of him, "Good luck with the novel." Mustering as much good cheer as he could, he offered, "I'll look for it at the Tattered Cover."

He walked casually to the car and gave the rope toy a final toss. As the Pontiac's engine started, she rose and walked slowly to the edge of the porch. Oscar returned to nuzzle her leg and she scratched his head absentmindedly. Andrew backed down the driveway and onto the road, shifted to first gear and drove away.

~ * ~

The Flagstaff Cemetery was a flat, grassy expanse bordered by a white-washed, wrought-iron fence. Scores of stones, many dating back to the previous century, were arranged in carefully manicured rows. It was no more sad or lonely than other cemeteries, with a person's individual comfort with eventual death making it a place of dread, hope or indifference.

The town was a mile away, and passing vehicles were rare at this or any other time of day. He walked straight to the grave as the dirt was freshly turned and the flowers still bright.

Incredibly, as the event was barely more than two weeks past, an engraved VA grave marker was already in place. It read:

Daniel E. Sevilla
January 21, 1949 - August 15, 1971
Sergeant US Army
Vietnam

"Man, the local VFW must have some juice to get you that stone so quick," he said out loud, surveying the tidy grave. He walked to the stone and knocked on it like a door, recalling instantly the afternoon near the river when Danny had similarly rapped on the hollow trunk of a cottonwood tree.

"Looks like you didn't get your wish for that grave in the river channel," he said, "but at least Connie and Janon can visit you here." He picked up some dried flower petals and pitched them away. "Sorry I didn't make the funeral. Sheriff thought it best if I didn't come."

Next to Danny's grave was that of his father:

Edward M. Sevilla
March 8, 1914 - May 15, 1970
BM2 US Navy
World War II

"So, I see you're not alone here. Hi, Mr. Sevilla. I'm Andrew Starkey. Danny and I are...old buddies..." Tears welled in his eyes as he choked on his sentiment. Suddenly he broke down completely, sobs racking his throat, his eyes flooding and burning.

"Damn it!" he swore, embarrassed at his breakdown. He began

rubbing his face feverishly and turned to see if anyone had seen or heard him. He was utterly alone on the breezy flat. Sniffing hard, he looked for a place to spit that would not be disrespectful to any of the surrounding graves. Finding it behind a wooden box that held metal flower stands, he spit and blew his nose, a finger-closing one nostril at a time.

After strolling the yard for a while, he walked slowly back to the grave. Kneeling, he ran his fingers along the newly etched letters in the marble.

"You know," he spoke conversationally, "everything's turned to shit, buddy. Susan hates my guts. Thinks I'm crazy. Can you...believe... that?" Tears started again, but he breathed deeply to forestall the flow.

"God, uh...God really threw us in the shit this time. What the fuck was He thinking?"

He recalled the first time they'd encountered each other. It had been in the chow line at Ft. Knox with Danny's wise-cracking insults directed at a moronic mess sergeant. Shortly after, Danny had saved Andrew from pushups by whispering a name the Drill Sergeant demanded that he know. Andrew thanked him later.

"No problemo," Danny had responded with a friendly grin. "Your turn next time."

"I'm sorry...Danny, I'm so God damn sorry."

A car door slammed. Andrew turned and was relieved to see a man and woman walking towards the other side of the fenced yard. He decided it was time to get back on the highway.

"OK, buddy." He tapped the stone again. "I'm out of here. I'll stop by from time to time. And, uh, I promise to look in on Connie and Janon real soon."

A few steps from the grave he stopped and turned back to face the headstone. Coming to attention, he saluted. "Airborne!" he said, and walked away.

~ * ~

An old man in overalls was sitting on a dilapidated bench outside the office of the Texaco station as the blue Pontiac rolled up to the pump. Intending to get out of the car, Andrew nevertheless continued to sit behind the wheel, staring off into the distance.

"Fill 'er up?" the man asked, unscrewing the gas cap. He watched Andrew out of the corner of his eye wondering if he might be ill.

Startled momentarily, Andrew answered, "Uh, yes sir. Regular."

Andrew reached under the dash, released the hood latch and climbed out. He pulled a rag from the top of the gas pump and walked around to the front of the car to raise the hood. Checking the oil, he asked the man to add a quart of 10W30.

"Look tired, son. Come a long way, have ye?" asked the man, as he limped from the office with a quart of oil.

Andrew didn't feel like talking, but the friendly old timer deserved simple courtesy. "Yeah, Indiana. You pick up I-70, keep rolling steady and it's only a long day to Denver."

The old timer's eyebrows raised. "Indianer. First wife come from Princeton, Lord rest her soul. Good corn country." He twitched suddenly and, finding a lady bug on the side of his face, carried it to a tuft of prairie grass and set it down carefully, then walked back to the car. He shoved a metal nozzle into the oil can and tilted it into the fill hole.

"So," he continued, "that home for ye?"

Back into thoughts of his difficult morning, Andrew stuttered, "Hmm? Home? Ah, Indiana. Used to be. Living in Denver now."

The man nodded, then leaned into the engine well. "She's topped off," he said, wiping the dipstick with a rag he'd pulled from the back pocket of his overalls.

As Andrew handed over his payment, the old timer took a quick glance up into his eyes, then looked back down and counted out the change from the ten-dollar bill.

"Son," he said, "you got a look that says you need a change in your luck. Stick around Denver and you'll get lucky."

Embarrassed and not knowing quite how to respond to such an intimate comment, Andrew said nothing and folded the bills into his wallet. He got in the car, sat for a moment, then looked up at the old timer.

"You know," he said, a sheepish smile coming to his face, "I can feel my luck changing right now." He extended his hand to the man and they shook warmly.

"Now," he continued, "you ever find yourself in trouble with Sheriff Casper, you tell him Andrew Starkey said to give you a break."

The man's eyebrows arched again. "Well now, you're him, ain't you? The boy done saved those gals down at Sevilla's?"

The Pontiac's engine sprang to life, its low rumble, a full tank of gas, and the sound of wheels speeding by on I-70 contributing to Andrew's lifting spirits.

"Danny Sevilla was a good man," he said, "and he was my friend."

Chapter 35
Friends

The apartment was musty and stale when he opened the door. Though he'd been gone barely a week, the old furniture gave the room its aroma quickly without the regular introduction of fresh air. He threw his bag onto the bed, and went to the bathroom sink for a glass of water. He gulped two of those, surprised at how dry he'd become. The water felt and tasted wonderful, and he closed his eyes in relief as the cool liquid settled in his stomach.

Glancing at himself in the mirror, he said, "You don't look too bad. Tired maybe. You look tired, boy."

Returning a day early, he would have all of Wednesday to relax and get himself together before facing Bob and the crew again. Their delight in being friends with a guy whose name had appeared in the newspaper had become an ordeal of ribbing and banter. "Hey Wyatt Earp!" they'd yell in the garage. "Yo, Tombstone Starkey!" He knew it would pass, but not soon enough.

He went to an overstuffed chair and sat down, kicking off his shoes as he did so. In minutes, he was asleep.

The phone rang, jarring him from a deep slumber. He sat stunned for several seconds, then glanced at his Seiko. He'd been asleep for two hours. It was late afternoon.

He picked up the receiver.

"Hello?"

"Hey, Airborne asshole." It was Ron Spinelli. "You're home. Couldn't remember when you said you'd get back. Thought I'd check in with you, see if you wanted to have a beer."

"Yeah…" Andrew put his hand over the mouth piece and took a deep breath, "came back a day early."

Ron's voice was sympathetic. "Like the man said, you can't go home again, or some bullshit like that."

"Actually, I had a good time with my old buddies. You won't believe this military ritual they came up with, busting full beer bottles against a wall. I'll tell you about it later."

"Full beers against a wall? That's about as unpatriotic as anything I've heard lately. So, how about the College Inn, six or so? Nurses from CU come in around seven. We'll have an hour to get charming."

"Sure. Beer and pizza. I'll even buy."

"Hey, I'm loaded. GI Bill check came today. I've got $175 burning a hole in my pocket."

Andrew laughed. "OK, buddy. Cash that bad boy and I'll see you at six."

He hung up the phone and blinked his eyes repeatedly, trying to clear his head. "Shower," he muttered, but continued to sit a while longer.

After a long soak, he emerged and toweled himself off. He walked with the towel around his waist to the front windows and looked out at the leafy afternoon street. It was quiet with only a new Volkswagen cruising by, the driver looking for a place to park. He glanced toward the refrigerator and recalled there was nothing much in it.

"Better hit King Soopers in the morning."

Returning to the bathroom, he began brushing his teeth. A knock at the door barely caught his attention. He listened for a second and hearing nothing, returned to his brushing. A louder knock came and hearing this one, he tried to respond through the foam.

"Yusst a mimutt!" he called out.

He rinsed his mouth, then quickly pulled on the same jeans and T-shirt he'd worn since leaving Indiana the day before. Opening the door, he expected it to be his landlady, no doubt irritated at his cavalier use of hot water. Instead, he saw the back of a woman who was looking at old photos on the opposite side of the hallway. At the sound of the door, she seemed to freeze momentarily. Then she turned around.

The face was oval, with high cheekbones and a narrow, classic nose. Her eyes were bright and expectant, dark brows arching above them. Shining dark hair swept back from her face in a stylish cut. Her hands were folded together at her waist.

He didn't know her but smiled and said, "May I help you?" He sure hoped so, because she was very pretty.

The woman smiled back with a disarming pleasantness that put him oddly at ease with a complete stranger.

"Hi, Hoosier," the woman said, very softly. The smile turned shy as she tried to control it.

A flash of memory hit him; the sound of the voice, the arch of brows over her dark eyes.

"Nancy?" he said, the name coming to his lips almost painfully. "Nancy," he said it again, stronger this time.

She walked to him and held out her arms. "Hi, Andrew. You didn't recognize me, did you?"

He was staggered by the rush of feeling as he felt his arms close around her.

"Oh, my God," he whispered, as the touch and fragrance of her overwhelmed him. "I…it's you. My God."

She leaned back. "Well, Mr. Starkey. Let's have a look at you. It's been a while."

"Five years and a couple life times," he said. "Yes, it's been a while."

"You're taller," she observed, a feigned critical eye looking him up and down. "Hair's a little longer and blonder. You've filled out. Still too skinny, though." She rubbed his abdomen with her fist. "More pizzas with Ronnie should take care of that."

For several moments, they just beamed at each other. Her hands slid down his arms and she took his hands.

"Well…" she said.

"Uh, would you like to come in?" he said, awkwardly. "I'm sorry, Nancy. Please come in."

She giggled, "Why, yes, thank you."

Closing the door behind them, he said, "I, uh, just got off the phone with your brother. We were going to meet…"

"That was a set up. He called for me to see if you were home and up for a visitor."

Andrew laughed with her. "So, he didn't really want to try and meet some nurses at the College Inn?" he said.

He was able to find soft drinks for them in the refrigerator. His eye caught the dog-eared, faded photo of the two of them taped to the refrigerator. He snatched it off and put it in a drawer.

She wore a dark-blue, silk blouse and a matching blazer. A pleated, grey skirt graced her slim hips.

"You look like a school teacher," he said, handing her the Coke. "You look fabulous."

They sipped their drinks awkwardly a moment, then she put hers on a coaster and took his hand.

"Andrew," she said, "I want something from you."

"Anything…absolutely anything."

She looked down shyly. "I want, first, for us to be friends again." She lifted her eyes and there were tears in them.

Andrew stood and pulled her up with him. He put his arms around her.

"What could possibly be wrong with that? You know I want that. Why would it make you sad?"

She began to cry in earnest now. Andrew was bewildered, and didn't know whether to hug her harder or release her. Nancy pushed him away gently and reached down to her purse for a tissue. The simple act of watching her blow her nose melted his heart.

He thought to himself, *I'm losing my mind. Am I dead? Can this be real?*

"And," she sniffed, "I want you to forgive me, Andrew. I failed you. I was young, impatient, immature, all those words that apply to stupid, selfish people. I…"

"Nancy, please. Enough. What's going on with you?"

She took several deep breaths and sat back down.

"Ronnie and I…" she began, "are very close. He's my brother and I love him. Sometimes I want to kill him, but…" she searched for words, "I've been hearing about you from Ronnie ever since you first wrote to him after you got drafted. You wrote to me for a while but…so, anyway, Ronnie's letters from you were completely different. He knows you very well, Andrew."

"Of course he does. We're brother paratroopers." He puffed out his chest comically. "Airborne, all the way."

She looked at him with sad eyes. "Well, he's your biggest fan. When your letters trickled away, I was so hurt. I had no idea what you felt about me, after how I treated you…And yet, Ronnie could read between the lines of your letters, that you…" She began to cry yet again.

"Sweetie, you're breaking my heart. I don't understand what you're trying to say."

Her fist clutched the tissues against her eyes. "Andrew, he told me that you thought you were going to die."

"Grrrr," she said suddenly, trying to calm herself. "I've got to get through this." She rested a minute and regained her voice. "He had you figured out, but he wouldn't tell me…not as long as I was with Mark. It wasn't 'til you were safe, and you moved to Denver. Then he told me. He said you thought you were going to…die over there, and you were trying to push me away so I wouldn't be hurt so badly when it happened."

Andrew massaged the back of his neck with his hand and tried to reconcile what she said with his own thoughts.

"Maybe…" he replied, hesitating as the morning's encounter with Susan came back to him. Smiling weakly, he said, "Nancy, I had someone else trying to psychoanalyze me recently. It didn't work out so well."

A bemused look came to her face. "Well, I'm sorry about that. I hope you didn't pay too much."

"Oh, it was free and unsolicited," he replied flatly.

Nancy cocked her head and looked into his eyes. "Andrew, would you believe Ron hates Mark, just despises him, and yet by keeping what he knew about you to himself, he let our engagement happen. He wouldn't risk interfering in my life to that degree."

"That's the kind of brother to have."

She dabbed at her eyes once again, then put the tissue back in her purse. "May I use your bathroom. My face is a disaster."

When she returned, Andrew stood, put his arms around her and kissed her lightly on the forehead.

"Say," he said, "do you have time...could we go for a walk? Cheesman Park's just a few blocks away."

~ * ~

It was a beautiful late summer afternoon and the park was filled with frisbee throwers, sun bathers and strolling young adults. Since it was a weekday, families with small children were not as well represented as would be the case on a weekend. To the west, Mt. Evans and the Front Range were shadowed by their typical seasonal crest of thunder heads.

Strolling the vast grassy expanse, they caught up on family and friends back in New Vernon and Buena Vista. He told her of his job with Ma Bell, the long hours, the good friends he'd made, how it felt to "burn" a pole. She had another year to go in graduate school and then would teach grade school children in reading and math.

"I'm really getting excited," she gushed. "All those little faces just beaming up at you. It's the most wonderful thing in the world."

"You'll be great at that. All those little boys will be falling in love with you, too."

She smiled up at him innocently. "Too?" she said. Andrew's face reddened and he looked off towards the mountains.

Angry with herself for the coy insensitivity, she quickly continued. "Third-grade boys don't fall in love with their teachers."

"Oh, yes they do," he said, still gazing at the Front Range. "Heck, I fell in love with Miss Coleman and that was second grade."

"My goodness," she muttered. "None of my professors covered that."

As they walked along he sensed she was preparing him for something. He didn't know what, but looking up an old boyfriend when you're already engaged, well...then it dawned on him. She was going to announce her marriage plans and she wanted his blessing. He'd give it gladly, having already invested far too much of his emotional energy in this one person. And he was almost, but not quite, amused.

Two women blowing me off on the same day, he thought. *I am one snake-bit son of a bitch.*

But seeing and touching her again, hearing her voice, gave him strength to accept the news. At least now he could see her on the street, or in a social setting, at Ron's place, wherever, and know he'd be at peace. What they'd had for those few days those years ago had been worth it, and he imagined he'd be yet thinking of her on his deathbed. Anyway, it had already been one hell of a long day, and whatever else this day brought, he would deal with it.

His mind continued to drift as he watched a rain squall far off against the foothills. *I need to move on, go back to IU...hey, wait a minute... maybe CU...GI Bill... Yeah, CU! Tomorrow, I'm going up to Boulder.* Suddenly the value of that extra day off had increased exponentially. *Wow,* he thought, *what am I fucking waiting for?*

Nancy cleared her throat. "Andrew?"

"Hmm? Yes, Your Loveliness?"

"Your what?" she giggled. Socking his arm playfully, she did her quiet "Grrrr" again and became serious. A bench was nearby and she pulled him to it and they sat down.

"Andrew...Mark and I," she began, "umm, Mark...it's, um, not working out. I'm giving him his ring back." She held up her left hand. "I took it off this morning. I'll tell him this weekend. Actually, I think he knows how I feel."

Andrew was speechless. "Wha...? uh, what?" he stuttered. Then he burst into an almost painful grin. "Great!" he exclaimed, and was immediately sorry. "I didn't mean it that way, Nancy. I'm sure this is painful for both of you."

She tried to give him a hurt look, but lost her composure and began to laugh. "Oh, you...But, what could I expect from a man?"

Continuing, she hunched her shoulders and gave out a sigh. "Uh, so Mr. Starkey, I know you're a very eligible, handsome and prosperous telephone man, but, um...could we...could I maybe see you occasionally? I mean do you still have some feelings for me after all this time?"

Now his mind was on overdrive and he wondered if she could fathom that there had never really been anyone else, not since she squeezed the ketchup packet all over the two of them at the A&W.

"Nancy...feelings for you?" he began. "Look, Sweetheart, you're the only girl I've ever said, 'I love you' to. Now you're telling me you're free again. I've got five years of feelings for you all saved up."

She was crying again but was beyond caring about her makeup.

Andrew used his thumb to wipe a rivulet of mascara from her cheek. Taking her in his arms he kissed her like he had the first time in the hot spring on Chalk Creek; not with passion but only his purest expression of affection. As then, he had to resist hugging her too hard, though the slender girl he'd held those years ago now had a woman's body.

As they sat together in a warm glow of romantic rediscovery, intuition told Nancy that the sweet midwestern boy was still there behind the fatigued face. He needed time, and he needed her. That same intuition convinced her that Andrew's character was not only well formed, it was actually honed.

And she had not gotten over him anymore than he had her. Had he not moved to Denver, she would have dumped Mark anyway. The relationship might have dragged on a bit longer, but with Andrew so close (and Ron so disappointed in her), that accelerated her decision. Having reached her own threshold of self-supporting adulthood, she'd quite suddenly seen Mark as the phony that Ron had seen immediately. It unsettled her to say the least, but had made the breakup far from traumatic; rather, it was merely a chore to get through and nothing more.

"Andrew," she said, smiling up at him, "you know, Ronnie really is planning on meeting you at six. He said I could come along if 'we' (she did her finger quotes) worked things out."

Worked things out? he chuckled to himself. *She just jump-started my life. Things are working out just fine..."*

"Sure, Sweetie," he said. "Somebody's got to protect him from those student nurses."

"Protect him?" she said.

They left the bench and walked in silence for a few minutes. She decided it was time.

"Andrew?" she began, praying she wouldn't spoil their reunion. "Ronnie showed me the article in the Post, about what happened in Flagstaff. Are you...OK?"

He hadn't expected the topic to come up and was unprepared for it. After an awkward silence he began, "It was bad. I...uh...lost a good friend. Do you...I had to..."

She squeezed his hand, hoping he'd say more, not sure what she'd do if he didn't. She was relieved when he began again.

"Nancy, what happened, what I did...there's nothing wrong with me. I had to...I had to shoot this guy. It wasn't what I wanted...He was going to fire again..."

She stopped and turned to him. "Andrew, I know there was nothing else you could do. My God, sweetheart..."

He felt a twinge of anger coming back from his encounter with Susan and fought to remember where he was. "Someone I was close to, uh...said there's something wrong with me. The war..."

She gripped his arm with her two hands. "Andrew, don't worry about what people might say." She squeezed his arm for emphasis. "Feel pity for them if you want, but don't let them define right or wrong. They weren't there...they can't know..."

To himself, *Susan was there. She's convinced I'm a cold-blooded killer.* To Nancy he said, "Yes, Miss Spinelli. I promise to behave from now on."

"Don't make fun of me, Mr. Starkey," she scolded. "You've been through awful things. This time I want to be here for you, OK?" Her eyes were sad as she looked up at him.

He took her hand and began walking back towards Clayton Street. "Pizza time," he said with a smile.

Ron was waiting with a booth table in the smoky neighborhood bar and waved them over. He was already well into a pitcher of Coors, and extra beer mugs had been delivered in anticipation of their arrival.

Four young nursing students had the adjoining booth, and Ron had, apparently, been doing an excellent job of entertaining them. The arrival of Ron's guests, especially the cute brunette, made them fear losing his attentions.

"A sucking chest wound," he said, stopping mid-sentence as Nancy and Andrew scooted into the booth. Nancy threw her arms around her brother and kissed him on the cheek. "Andrew invited me along. Hope you don't mind," she said out loud, then leaned up to his ear and whispered, "Thank you, Ronnie."

Blushing, he turned to the students. "My sister," he said. "In-breeding is rampant in Bueny." Nancy buried her face in her hands while Andrew laughed heartily. "You should know better than to give him any material," he said.

One of the students, a pixie-faced red head with designs on Ron, wasn't buying it. "Yeah, sure. That's the story of my life," she pouted.

"He's not kidding," said Nancy, lifting her head, still embarrassed. "I'm with this callow fellow." She tosseled Andrew's hair for effect.

Ron winked at Andrew, then continued his discussion with the students. "So, no shit, you can use pizza as a 'field expedient' bandage for a sucking chest wound. Thin crust is best. 'Chicago-style' would suck too much hot tomato sauce into the lung. You ladies need to know these things."

The aspiring RNs gave a collective groan. "You are deranged!" said the red head. Then, "I know she's your girlfriend. You're just stringing me along."

Ron turned back towards Nancy and Andrew and found them snuggled nose to nose, oblivious to the others. He gave a nod to the red head and jerked his thumb towards the couple. "Would I ask you for your phone number if she was…"

The young woman grabbed a cocktail napkin, wrote her number down and stuffed it into his shirt pocket. Her friends gave her a chorus of wolf whistles.

"We're causing a scene," Nancy whispered, and kissed Andrew's cheek. "Let's re-join the group."

Andrew sat up and pulled the beer pitcher towards them. He poured two mugs full of Coors, handed one to Nancy and clinked them together.

"To you and me, and Ron…and Danny."

Nancy sipped her beer and looked at him over the tilted mug. She pulled a coaster over and set her mug down. "I wish I could have met him," she said. "He must have been quite a guy. Friends like that don't come along very often."

Andrew shrugged and stared down at his beer. "No, they sure don't."

He killed his beer and poured more for himself, leaned over and refilled Ron's empty mug.

Ron turned, flashed a smile and held up his beer to toast. "Airborne," he said, clinking their mugs. He put down the mug, took the nurse's napkin out of his pocket, folded it neatly and put it in his wallet.

"Damn, Andrew," he said, "can you believe we're here together? I mean, you and me, alive, drinking beer in this fine tavern, pretty girls to left and right. Wow." At that, he laughed and turned back to the red head.

"A large pepperoni and three side salads," Nancy said as the waitress jotted on her order pad. "Oh, and it looks like we'll need another pitcher. No hurry. Thank you."

Andrew put his arm around her again and gave her shoulder an affectionate squeeze. He looked around the crowded bar, filled with young professionals and students. *Bet Ron and I are the only military guys in the whole place,* he thought. *GIs dying by the score every week and back here in the 'World' it's…nothing. Yo, Danny…, they think…nothing…* Closing his eyes, his thoughts leaped to images of muddy jungle trails, leeches, Danny's bloody, limp body being loaded on the 'Dust Off',

Boulé's grinning face. That final image caused him to shudder and he shook his head to clear it.

Suddenly, he remembered laying in his hammock in the sodden jungle blackness, hoping merely to dream of the girl now at his side. It was so vivid in his mind that it unsettled him.

This…may be a dream, he imagined. *If it is, God, thank you. Thank you for this dream.* Then he felt a tear running down his cheek. Before he could wipe it away, Nancy raised a napkin to his face and dabbed the drop and the wet path it left from the corner of his eye.

"You're home, Hoosier," she said, emotion cracking her voice. "You're home."

Embarrassed, he turned away from her and rubbed the back of his hand across the offending eye. Collecting himself, he reached under the table for her hand and squeezed it softly.

"Yes, I am," he said, his spirits rising again. "I'm not dreaming, and you're really here." Then he leaned close to her ear. "And you know what, Nancy Spinelli? It just doesn't get any better than this…"

The End

ACKNOWLEDGMENTS

I want to thank my fellow Vietnam veterans Dennis Reynolds, Kit Brazier and Randy Nevils Ph.D for their encouragement and feedback during this project.

Wayne Muehlenbein provided my earliest editing assistance and critical review of the story. Only such an old friend could get me to slow down and pay proper attention to the basics.

Lastly, I want to again thank Randy Nevils Ph.D, my cousin/brother, for his exhaustive final proof-read which provides the reader a far more polished manuscript.

ABOUT THE AUTHOR

William (Bill) Gritzbaugh grew up in the midwest, served in Vietnam with the 5th Special Forces Group, and is a graduate of Indiana University. Recently retired from a 36-year insurance industry career, he and wife Deb reside in Oregon.

Bill is an avid hiker and Harley rider and volunteers with the Disabled American Veterans, the Red Cross and the Patriot Guard Riders.

This is his first novel.

www.alongdaytodenver.com

Made in the USA
Charleston, SC
24 March 2015